'One of the most masterful crime fiction writers in the country, Bailey has done it again. Timely, absorbing and full of suspense, you will not be able to put this book down. While utterly readable, Bailey seamlessly imbues every page with depth, insight and stark observation. This is a story that haunts women all over the world, and Bailey dared to go there.'

Jessie Stephens, author of *Something Bad is Going to Happen*

'Sarah Bailey's *Click* is a masterful crime thriller. A complex police procedural that takes a deep dive into the darker side of our digital lives. A gripping, propulsive story told with an eye for the real pressures of modern policing and the challenges of a relentless news cycle.'

Michael Brissenden, author of *Smoke* and *Dust*

PRAISE FOR

BODY OF LIES

'Bailey writes utterly riveting crime novels like no one else. *Body of Lies* is her best yet.'

Mark Brandi, author of *Eden*

'Whether you read as part of the Gemma Woodstock series or as a standalone novel, this exceptional police procedural from one of Australia's finest crime writers is not to be missed. Intensely twisty, gripping and emotionally charged, *Body of Lies* is Bailey at her page-turning, razor sharp best. I could not put it down.'

Anna Downes, author of *Red River Road*

'Gemma is back, baby! With *Body of Lies*, Sarah Bailey proves she is the master of the relatable protagonist and the queen of dramatic tension. I defy readers not to root for Gemma Woodstock, and I'd love to see them try to put down this book once they start.'

Hayley Scrivenor, author of *Girl Falling*

PRAISE FOR

THE HOUSEMATE

'With *The Housemate*, Sarah Bailey expertly plays with memory, guilt and grief to build a tension-filled, vivid world, where there are many ways to be haunted by the ghosts of our past. You'll be right there with the fascinating, flawed Oli Groves as her professional investigation of the Housemate Homicide increasingly veers toward personal obsession. Each new twist in the story skilfully balances bombshell revelations and believability, in a crime that feels achingly familiar, yet shocking at the same time. Much like Oli, I couldn't stop until I knew the truth, too.'

Jacqueline Bublitz, author of *Leave the Girls Behind*

'The plot is brilliant, the pace is relentless . . . Oli Groves is a brilliant protagonist: brave and fragile, kick-arse and compassionate—and so very human. *The Housemate* is a book of great emotional power and depth—Bailey's best yet.'

Chris Hammer, author of *Legacy*

'An enormously immersive story with Bailey's trademark gordian knot plotting, true to life characters and twists galore. This is Australian crime at its best and *The Housemate* is destined to summit the bestseller charts.'

J.P. Pomare, author of *17 Years Later*

'I'm as obsessed with Bailey's protagonist, Oli Groves, as Groves is with the story she is chasing. Clever, ambitious, prickly: she's the perfect journo to lead us through this clever and ambitious thriller. Loved the deep dive into the rotten underworld of secrets and corruption, and Bailey's wry take on the changing face of journalism. *The Housemate* is addictive reading in the very best of ways. Sarah Bailey knows her stuff.'

Kate Mildenhall, author of *The Hummingbird Effect*

PRAISE FOR

WHERE THE DEAD GO

'Sarah Bailey has excelled herself . . . a well-written and exciting crime novel that builds to a taut and bloody conclusion.'

Canberra Weekly

'As riveting as the previous two, with a multilayered plot, compelling characters and vivid atmosphere . . . another addictive read from Bailey.'

Good Reading

'A tense, gripping end to a highly praised trilogy.'

Who

'Bailey always writes a killer thriller, and this is gritty and real.'

Readings

'[Gemma] is a well-rounded character, relatable in her frustrations and insecurities at work and at home but also an exemplar of the type of kickass female detective that Australian crime fiction writers are adept at creating.'

The Age

'A must-read for crime lovers.'

Better Homes and Gardens

'Next level crime fiction . . . police procedural at its finest . . . *Where the Dead Go* is compelling reading. Gritty, realistic, atmospheric and chilling. An absolute cracker of a read that I can't even begin to recommend highly enough.'

Theresa Smith Writes

'Sarah Bailey's writing is both keenly insightful and wholly engrossing, weaving intriguing and multi-layered plots combined with complicated and compelling characters.'

The Booktopian

PRAISE FOR

INTO THE NIGHT

'Melbourne's wintry streets come alive on the pages, keeping the dramatic tension high . . . Bailey's writing has grown stronger and more assured in this novel.'

Good Reading

'With its deft exploration of the intersection of public and private lives and a chance to peer more deeply into the mind and heart set of an engagingly flawed heroine, *Into the Night* seems set to be just as successful as *The Dark Lake*.'

Sydney Morning Herald

'*Into the Night* is a solid procedural, full of constant twists and reveals that keep the investigation fresh . . . with this expansion of her world, it feels like Gemma Woodstock might be with us for a while.'

Australian Crime Fiction

'Bailey's writing is stronger than ever, and the prickliness of her characters is a natural fit for the jarring confines of Melbourne's central business district . . . a bristling police procedural for fans of Emma Viskic and J.M. Green.'

Books + Publishing

'Every bit as addictive and suspenseful as *The Dark Lake*.'

The Booktopian

'Bailey's writing is sharp, her sense of place harrowing, and her mystery intriguing. A great read for anyone who likes complex characters and gritty crime.'

Glam Adelaide

PRAISE FOR

THE DARK LAKE

'*The Dark Lake* is a thrilling psychological police procedural as well as a leap into the mind of a woman engulfed with guilt.'

New York Journal of Books

'*The Dark Lake* hooked me from page one! Sarah Bailey combines the very best elements in this stunning debut thriller—a troubled detective still trying to find her way as a female investigator, a small town haunted by secrets both past and present, and a beautiful victim whose unsettling allure appears to be her biggest asset and largest downfall. With clever twists and all-too-human characters, this book will keep you racing toward the end.'

Lisa Gardner, #1 *New York Times* bestselling author of *Kiss Her Goodbye* and *Find Her*

'This polished debut is a winner from the first page.'

Daily Telegraph

'I read *The Dark Lake* in one sitting, it's that good. A crime thriller that seizes you from the first page and slowly draws you into a web of deception and long buried secrets. Beautifully written, compulsively readable, and highly recommended.'

Douglas Preston, #1 *New York Times* bestselling author of *The Lost City of the Monkey God* and co-author of the bestselling Pendergast series

'Debut author Sarah Bailey depicts both the landscape and Gemma's state of mind vividly, bringing into focus the intensity of Gemma's physical and emotional pain and her increasing discontent. *The Dark Lake* adds to the trend of haunting, rural Australian crime fiction, and provides a welcome addition to the genre for those left bereft after finishing Jane Harper's *The Dry*.'

Books + Publishing

Sarah Bailey is a Melbourne-based writer with a background in advertising and communications. She has three sons and is currently the Managing Director of the Melbourne and Sydney offices of advertising agency VML and the founder of social media brand and podcast, *He Read, She Read*. Her internationally award-winning Gemma Woodstock series includes *The Dark Lake*, published in 2017 and winner of the Ned Kelly Award for Best First Fiction and the Davitt Award for Best Debut, followed by *Into the Night* in 2018, *Where the Dead Go* in 2019, and *Body of Lies* in 2024. Sarah has also published the bestselling *The Housemate* and Audible original *Final Act* in 2021. *Click* is the second book featuring journalist Oli Groves.

SARAH
BAILEY

CLICK

ALLEN&UNWIN
SYDNEY • MELBOURNE • AUCKLAND • LONDON

This is a work of fiction. Names, characters, places and incidents are products of the author's imagination or are used fictitiously. Any resemblance to actual events, locales or persons, living or dead, is entirely coincidental.

First published in 2026

Allen & Unwin
Cammeraygal Country
83 Alexander Street
Crows Nest NSW 2065
Australia
Phone: (61 2) 8425 0100
Email: info@allenandunwin.com
Web: www.allenandunwin.com

Allen & Unwin acknowledges the Traditional Owners of the Country on which we live and work. We pay our respects to all Aboriginal and Torres Strait Islander Elders, past and present.

NATIONAL LIBRARY OF AUSTRALIA
A catalogue record for this book is available from the National Library of Australia

ISBN 978 1 76106 918 5

Cover design by Luke Causby/Blue Cork
Cover images by Adobe Stock
Typeset in 13.1/18.3 pt Garamond Premier Pro by Bookhouse, Sydney
Printed and bound in Australia by the Opus Group

10 9 8 7 6 5 4 3 2 1

FSC www.fsc.org MIX Paper | Supporting responsible forestry FSC® C001695

The paper in this book is FSC® certified. FSC® promotes environmentally responsible, socially beneficial and economically viable management of the world's forests.

FOR RIPLEY. MY LITTLEST LOVE.

2020

MONDAY, 20 JANUARY

Text from Yvonne Gilchrist to Lyra Makris, 9.02 am
Hey L, I tried to call you but it went straight to vm. Just wanted to make sure everything is okay because you weren't at brekky. No big deal, we can reschedule. Speak soon xx

Text from Yvonne Gilchrist to Lyra Makris, 1.17 pm
Heya. Where are you? I'm getting worried. Let me know you're okay x

Voice message from Lyra's mother 6.56 pm
Lyra, honey? Are you all right? I got a text from your friend at work saying you're not there. Are you sick? I can pop over later and bring some food if you like. Call me when you get this. Love Mum

Text from Yvonne Gilchrist to James Delway, 7.34 pm
Hi James, it's Yvonne. Long time no speak. Hope ur good. I know this is weird but I'm trying to get on to Lyra and I just want to check she's not with you? Long shot I know but I'm getting worried.

Reply from James Delway to Yvonne Gilchrist, 10.05 pm

Hey Vonnie. All good with me. Sorry I haven't seen her since my xmas party at the bar. Maybe she lost her phone, she's pretty good at doing that. be good to catch up sometime x

CHAPTER ONE

TUESDAY, 21 JANUARY, 5.48 AM

The photo is sent via a bogus Instagram profile while the city sleeps, save for some enthusiastic joggers, exhausted shiftworkers, and early-bird media types fuelled by caffeine and the slim possibility that today might be the day they catch the worm. The message lands in the Instagram inbox of Melbourne's largest newspaper, *Melbourne Today*, where it sits unread for over ninety minutes.

Brian Pocock arrives at the office, hungover and rumpled, having stayed at his mate's house after an unexpectedly long session at a Fitzroy pub the previous evening. Brian didn't wake early enough to go home and get either his literal or figurative shit sorted, and now he perches at his desk with remnants of beer and the coffee he just drank churning ominously in his stomach.

Swallowing down the threat of vomit, he scans the subject lines of the emails that landed in the 'hot tips' inbox overnight. His bleary eyes catch on the occasional word or phrase. *Suspicious. Probably nothing. My neighbour. Promised I wouldn't say anything.*

Brian lifts his hands high above his head, attempting to stretch the god-awful feeling out of his body.

'Good morning.' The new cadet sashays past, her eyes glowing with amusement.

'Hi,' Brian mumbles, a beat too late.

She and her hips disappear into the kitchen, and Brian drags his eyes back to the screen. He reads an email about a dangerous dog that Jan from Melton believes is a threat to society and another about a neighbour who might be growing 'illegal smoking plants'. He checks the *Melbourne Today* Instagram profile, pleased to see the followers have gone up by over one hundred since yesterday. Then his eyes lock on a message from an account called 'Click_Click' with three followers. The preview of the message shows the first three words: *Photo of #2.*

Brian yawns, laces his fingers together and cracks his knuckles. 'Here we go.' Before he took this job, he was vaguely aware there were a lot of nutty people in the world, but he didn't realise how much weird shit actually happened or how many people were hell-bent on sharing it with the media.

Rubbing his eyes, he opens the message.

Good morning. Please find attached a photo of victim #2 just after her death at 9.40 pm yesterday. Regards, The Photographer.

Brian huffs out a nervous laugh. He shouldn't open the attachment; he should wait until his boss gets in. It could be a virus or a scam, like the ones the IT team are always warning everyone about.

He glances at his watch. His colleagues are starting to trickle in, but his boss won't arrive for at least an hour, and what if he makes a big fuss and it turns out to be some dickhead sending a nude?

Fuck it. Brian wants to know what this weirdo is on about. He squares his shoulders and summons bravado; nevertheless, he experiences a sharp flare of apprehension as he opens the attachment.

It's a close-up of a young woman's face. Strands of long dark hair. Vacant, made-up eyes and puffy, mottled skin, wet with tears. An ugly gash at her throat, so deep it almost separates her head from her décolletage. Blood.

In his peripheral vision, Brian registers that the cadet and her hips are on their way back from the kitchen. He glances at her, desperately hoping that when he looks back at his screen the awful image will be gone. But it's still there—and somehow, it's even more obscene than before. Vomit surges in his throat, and this time there's no stopping it.

CHAPTER TWO

TUESDAY, 21 JANUARY, 8.03 AM

The muted blare of the buzzer echoes above them for the second time. Detective Constable Penelope Kibbs double-checks the address and presses the buzzer again. Still no answer. She shrugs and looks at her partner, Detective Inspector Mike Barnes.

'Try the other apartments,' he suggests. 'See if we can find someone who will let us in.'

Pen nods. She likes working with Barnes. He has confidence without ego, not like some of the other male detectives, who make every shift feel like a test. Barnes actively shies away from drama, a trait that Pen particularly appreciates at times like this. She's had a bad feeling ever since she spoke to the missing girl's mother earlier this morning.

Barnes ambles off to answer his mobile, and Pen tries the other buzzers, starting at number one. Most of the occupants aren't home, but a reedy voice comes through the speaker after she rings the buzzer for number six. Pen explains who she is and holds her badge up to the scratched camera lens. She's rewarded with the click of the door opening and gestures at Barnes, who ends his call and strides over to her.

'Boss wants us back asap,' he says, looking energised. 'Wants us to follow up a lead on Douglas Jackson.'

Pen scowls. 'Do you have any details?'

'Frost wasn't specific. Just said he'd brief us when we get back.'

Rusty Frost is their new supervisor, and so far she likes him a lot more than Superintendent Clive Sanders, whom she reported to for the past two years. Frost is a workaholic and has incredibly high standards, but like Barnes, he seems to have a handle on his ego. He always makes a point to not only seek out her opinions but also take them seriously. And he's kind. He was especially supportive when Barnes's sister was killed at the beginning of last year.

But Pen has noticed that Frost has been short-tempered over the past few days, and she can tell he's desperate for a break in the Mackenzie Jackson case. The Camberwell mother left her house after an argument with her husband ten days ago and is widely presumed dead. The case has consumed Pen and Barnes for nine days, and it's Frost's first major case since his promotion to superintendent, so the pressure is on.

Frost isn't married and doesn't have children. Everyone knows he was in a long-term relationship with a journalist, Olive Groves, several years ago. She broke his heart. Late last year, Pen sensed there was still a spark between them when Groves turned up at a crime scene and started asking Frost questions, but he quickly became dismissive toward her, probably wanting to ensure he remains above reproach, considering his new title. Regardless of how Frost feels about Groves, Pen figures Groves regrets dumping him back in the day—he's a total catch. Not that Groves isn't, of course.

All Pen says to Barnes is, 'Hopefully we won't be here too long.'

Apartment eight is on the second floor. There's no lift, so they make their way up the narrow staircase to the door.

Barnes stands to the side, and Pen raps her knuckles against the smooth grey surface. 'Lyra? Lyra Makris? Are you in there? It's the police.'

No sound comes from the apartment. Pen exchanges a glance with Barnes and recalls the smiling face of the missing girl from the photo her mother gave them.

'Could be a medical emergency?' Barnes offers. 'She might have slipped in the shower.'

'Maybe she met someone,' Pen says, although from the conversation she had with Lyra's mother, this seems unlikely.

Lyra broke up with her long-term boyfriend just over a month ago, and it sounds like she's been apprehensive about throwing herself back into the dating scene. Her ex, James Delway, an arrogant bolshy type who runs a bar in Flemington, claims he hasn't spoken to her since she turned up uninvited to his work Christmas party in mid-December. Delway alleges he politely but firmly informed Lyra there was no chance of a reunion. Reading between the lines, Pen suspects that he enjoyed conveying this sentiment to her in front of his colleagues. Regardless of how it played out, Lyra's mother believes her daughter has been very upset.

Barnes says the unthinkable but statistically possible. 'Suicide?'

God, please not that, thinks Pen. 'Maybe she's just sick. Or she's gone away somewhere last minute.'

Barnes's voice remains even. 'We need to get inside. I'll call the body corporate—the number's on the letterboxes downstairs.'

After knocking one more time, Pen checks her phone while she waits, trying to ignore the fluttery feeling in her chest. It's been a rough few months. A tough year. In March she attended the scene of a tragic murder-suicide of a toddler and his drug-addicted mother, then in July she was assigned the case of a drunk teenager who had accidentally killed his mother when he pushed her during a heated argument, causing her to hit her head against her newly installed designer kitchen bench.

And then on Christmas Eve, there was the backpacker murder. Marta Holm, a young Swedish woman, was stabbed several times, her body left under a tree in the Treasury Gardens for a drunk couple to stumble upon the following morning. Under her body was a Polaroid photo of her wearing the same outfit she'd been killed in, smiling and posing with a glass of champagne in her hand. Someone had written *#1* beneath the photo, and a handwriting expert dismissed the possibility it was written by Marta. Speculation has been rife within the case team that the picture and number are a warning, an evil taunt, but so far there are no further clues to lend credence to this theory—and, thankfully, no similar murders. The DNA and prints found on Marta's body and at the scene haven't produced a match. To date the Polaroid detail has been contained to the case team but that hasn't stopped a general sense of unease settling over the entire force.

Since these events, gruesome images have hijacked Pen's thoughts at random moments, disrupting mundane tasks. Often her first thought on waking is Marta Holm's pretty smile from the Polaroid morphing into the horrible expression on her lifeless face in the postmortem photos. Pen is finding it increasingly difficult to banish gory scenes from her mind, and her faith in humanity is waning. None of the cognitive behavioural techniques her counsellor has suggested are working, and she's questioning her relentless pursuit of a detective role. Maybe she needs a holiday—or a career change. Her anxiety is taking on a life of its own.

Barnes returns up the stairs. 'The property manager will be here in thirty minutes.'

Pen tries to quell her racing heart as they lean against the banister, making small talk. Barnes tells her anecdotes about his teenage kids. He doesn't mention his recent separation, which Pen only knows about because Frost asked her if she thought Barnes was okay in the wake of his relationship breakdown. Pen had been a little stung that her colleague hadn't confided in her, but she understood he might want to keep his personal life separate to his work. She doesn't like to discuss her personal life either—not that there's much to discuss. The only relationship she's been in lately is with her slobbery bulldog, Elliot.

Barnes is recounting a story about being mistaken for a popular reality star while on a holiday in the United Kingdom, when the property manager arrives. A slight woman in a boxy cream suit, with frizzy brown hair, excess jewellery and palpable nervous energy, she studies their identification. With a sharp nod, she jerks a bejewelled finger toward the lock, the keys in her hand jangling. 'I'll just open the door for you then?'

'Yes, please,' Pen says. 'Thank you.' Despite the apprehension she feels about what they might find, it's a relief to be moving. The stagnant air in the stairwell is warm and cloying.

'If you can just wait here,' Barnes instructs the woman, as they enter the apartment. Once they are inside, he closes and locks the door behind them.

The lounge room is neat and odourless. Nothing seems out of place in the adjoining galley kitchen either. Pen registers dried flowers in a vase, a trio of vitamin bottles on the bench and two wedding invites anchored by magnets on the fridge. There's a weekly planner on the bench that she reads aloud from: 'Ned's party Saturday night, kickboxing on Sunday night, breakfast with Yvonne on Monday morning. Pilates this morning.' The bad feeling is back, an uncomfortable fizzing in her stomach. She clears her throat and points beyond the kitchen. 'How about you check through there? I'll go this way.'

In Lyra's bedroom, forest-green sheets are pulled tight across the mattress, the pillows fluffed and propped neatly at the bedhead. Near the window, a round mirror hangs above a small wooden desk that doubles as a dresser. Pen stares at her own worried-looking face, noticing that the humidity has curled the ends of her brown shoulder-length bob.

The dresser boasts an impressive collection of make-up as well as a MacBook Air, a keyboard, a large screen, and a ring lamp with a smartphone holder attachment. A retro hatstand in the corner is heavy with colourful scarves, coats and bags. Dozens of photos jostle for position on a pinboard, and Pen recognises Lyra's smiling face in several shots. Her father is Greek, her mother Irish, and her features showcase a glorious mix of these lineages. She's perfected a flattering pose: in most of the photos she stares directly into the lens as if challenging the photographer to take a bad shot.

'A storage cupboard and the smallest laundry I've ever seen,' Barnes calls out. 'Both clear.' His voice fades. 'Hang on, there's another room.'

Pen checks the cupboards and under the bed.

'Spare room is clear,' he calls again. 'You have anything?'

'Bedroom's clear, just checking the bathroom.' She shuts her eyes briefly, inhaling as she nudges open the door.

A dark green towel hangs on a metal hook. On the vanity a pink toothbrush and a tube of toothpaste sit in a square perspex container that could do with a wash. A puddle of lilac wax fills a shallow china plate on the floor, the black wick drowned in the centre. Mirrored cabinets reflect Pen's solemn face. Behind the navy shower curtain, a tap drips.

Aware of Barnes in the bedroom behind her, aware of her heart beating wildly, aware that her day might be about to go to absolute shit, she draws another deep breath and tugs the cheap plastic to the right.

The hooks rattle against the metal rod. There's nothing in there.

Just as her phone rings, Barnes enters the room with a flushed face. 'All clear?'

Her insides are still tight with latent dread, but she nods at him, answering the call with a crisp, 'Kibbs.'

'I need you and Barnes back here.' Frost's voice is strained. 'We think your missing woman has been murdered.'

CHAPTER THREE

TUESDAY, 21 JANUARY, 8.32 AM

Oli Groves holds the plastic sheet and stares at the blurry grey shapes. The room tilts, and she grips the sheet, contorting it between her fingers. *Breathe.* The fingers on her right hand drift to the groove on the underside of her left wrist, and press gently until she feels the pulse of her heartbeat. A childhood habit she has never outgrown.

Oli hasn't felt this overwhelmed since the aftermath of her colleague Cooper Ng's murder. That was such an intense, confusing time, with her guilt about Cooper exacerbated by public commentary regarding her failed engagement and her decision to start a news business. But that was half a decade ago, and she's in a good place now. Broadly speaking, so is her business. How can this innocuous blurry image of her insides be threatening to ruin everything?

Her fingers press on her wrist again. *One, two, three. Breathe.*

She blinks and forces herself to refocus on what Dr Fraser is saying. 'The tumour is quite small, which is good news.' Her

French-manicured finger points at the fuzzy circle near the centre of the scan. 'It means we've caught it early, but we do need to get right onto it.'

Good news, Oli thinks, fighting the urge to laugh. Her breast cancer is *good news*.

To the doctor, she simply says, 'Okay.'

Dr Fraser's eyes are full of concern, but Oli notices them slide to her rose-gold watch. News, whether good or bad, must be delivered with efficiency. Oli knows this all too well. As a journalist, she frequently writes about life and death to the tick-tock of the clock.

'What happens now?' she asks.

Dr Fraser indicates that Oli should put the scan down on the table and shifts her body so they're facing each other. She drops her chin, pale blue eyes determinedly fixed on Oli's, and reels off a list of next steps, using her fingers to count each item. The language is both familiar and alien. Oli has picked up the words from movies and news stories, from friends of friends, from vague knowledge she absorbed but didn't retain because it wasn't relevant to her. And now suddenly it is. Tumour, surgery, chemo, radiotherapy, review, assess, repeat. Side effects, tired, energy, options. 'Then we'll see.' The doctor uses up all her fingers and starts again with her left thumb.

What Oli feels isn't shock exactly, more like a sense that something inevitable has finally happened. One in two people get cancer, don't they? That's fifty per cent of people. Half. It's an unpleasant but well-worn path. Oli tries to recall any movies or books where the main character gets cancer while being single and childless but can't think of any.

'Everyone's different,' Dr Fraser says, though Oli suspects the woman never deviates from the little speech she's just delivered.

'I'm a swimmer,' Oli blurts. 'I swim at least four times a week. It's very important to me.'

Dr Fraser smiles but narrows her eyes as if Oli has asked a complicated question. 'Swimming will mainly be fine.' She nods slowly as if to confirm the statement to herself. 'Assuming you have surgery, you won't be able to swim for a while, and I doubt you'll feel like it during your treatment, but you can certainly keep swimming around that. I suggest you discuss it with Dr Brooks, the surgeon I'm referring you to, once he's confirmed the plan.'

Oli studies a framed photo on the desk: Dr Fraser standing next to a tall handsome man, her hands on the shoulders of a teenage girl. The teenager wears a floral dress and light make-up. Grade six graduation, Oli guesses. Dr Fraser has her brown hair loose in the photo, and Oli thinks it looks a lot better than the way she has styled it now, parted down the middle and scraped away from her face.

'Do you have people you can lean on, Oli? You'll need people to help you through this.'

'I have a sister,' Oli murmurs, although it was her ex-boyfriend Rusty's face that flashed up in her mind.

Dr Fraser looks pleased. 'Sisters are a wonderful support.'

Lily is many things, but the only time she tends to be supportive is when Oli agrees to another wine.

The doctor busies herself with pulling together the surgeon referral along with a bundle of printouts and brochures. Oli returns to the waiting room clutching a thick wad of papers and the oversized envelope containing the evidence that a deadly disease has set up camp in her right breast.

She settles her account with the cheerful secretary and rushes to her car, praying she has been spared a parking fine. Tendrils of sun reach her face, signalling another hot day ahead. Bike bells bleat gentle warnings to distracted drivers and phone-addicted pedestrians. Oli smiles at a black dog with white eyebrows that is tied to a pole outside a cafe. Encouraged by the attention, it strains against its lead and wags its tail.

There's no ticket on the windscreen of her white Toyota, and she breathes a sigh of relief before remembering she has cancer. She studies herself in the rear-view mirror when she gets in the car. Her thick blonde hair is still a little damp from her early-morning swim, her pale skin is clear, her green eyes bright. Around six weeks ago she asked her hairdresser to cut her a fringe, and it already needs a trim. She smiles, sending creases from her eyes into her hairline. She looks a little tired, perhaps, but certainly not ill.

Retrieving her phone from her handbag, she connects it to the charger. Twelve missed calls, which is a lot after forty minutes, even for her. Four are from her business partner at *Newsday*, Timothy 'TJ' Jack. There's also a news alert from the *Washington Post*: a coronavirus case has been confirmed in Washington, DC. That must be what he's calling about. They debated doing a deep dive on the SARS-like virus but decided against it, seeing as it hadn't spread beyond China. Now it looks like they might need to interview an infectious diseases specialist after all.

She throws the car into reverse. 'Siri, call TJ.' Her trademark husky voice sounds deeper than usual at the tail end of the sinus infection that prompted her visit to the doctor the week before last, when she casually mentioned the small lump she'd found when shopping for bathers. Her relationship with her voice is complicated. It's distinctive and a huge part of why her podcasts are so popular, but she finds the public discourse about it uncomfortable and for this reason tends to avoid talking about it.

TJ's rich baritone rolls through the car. His voice is also popular with their audience, but unlike Oli, he doesn't shy away from the praise. She doesn't begrudge him for being so self-assured; his confidence has always been at odds with her modesty, and she's convinced it's why their business partnership has been so successful.

'Oli! Where the hell have you been? I've been calling you.'

'You do remember I have the day off?' she replies drily, steering the car into the flow of traffic. 'Is this about the Wuhan virus spreading to the United States?'

'What? No. I haven't even looked at that yet.'

Oli brings the car to a stop behind a 4WD and waves at an elderly lady to cross the road in front of her. 'What's up then? It's not Mackenzie Jackson, is it?' Her insides coil nastily as she braces herself for bad news about the missing woman.

'No, there's still nothing on Jackson. I'm sorry to hassle you—I know you wanted to have a day off, but I'm hearing there's been a murder. A twenty-three-year-old woman from Melbourne went missing on the weekend. She worked in media, some kind of community management gig for an online magazine.' His words tumble over each other as though in a rush to get out of his mouth.

Oli grimaces. 'Domestic violence?'

It's a topic that has demanded a lot of her attention lately. She's spent the past few months developing a six-part investigative series on the issue that will combine audio episodes and online content. It's the most ambitious project she's tackled since they started *Newsday*, and something she's been wanting to do for a long time. Despite the grim content, she's enjoyed working on the series immensely, and after a recent spate of senseless deaths, the project feels increasingly urgent. She's still working out how to conclude the series; she doesn't want a clichéd rallying cry, but it needs a crescendo and resolution. Hopefully this poor woman, Mackenzie, isn't the answer.

'It's not clear yet,' says TJ. 'But I don't think so.'

'Why? Where was she found?'

'That's the thing, Ol. She wasn't found. It's all online.'

'Online?' Oli shakes her head, trying to understand. 'How do you mean?'

'Someone sent a photo to *Melbourne Today*.'

'A photo of what?'

'Of *her*, Oli. Of her body.' TJ pauses. 'This could be it, Ol. What we've been speculating about. Maybe Holm wasn't a one-off.'

His tone is cautious, and Oli knows why. Her hands curl tightly around the steering wheel as emotions ricochet through her system. They've been chasing a lead for over a fortnight, based on information that came from her source at the morgue—apparently a printed photo carrying some kind of threat was found with the body of murdered Swedish backpacker Marta Holm. The police have remained particularly cagey about the case, and neither Oli nor TJ has been able to verify the existence of the photo or the message, but they've discussed at length the potential of further violence.

Trying to stay calm, Oli says slowly, 'You're saying that someone sent a photo of a dead body to *Melbourne Today*?'

'That's what I'm hearing. And from what I can gather, we're talking super graphic stuff.'

'Jesus Christ.'

'I know,' he says. 'It's crazy.'

Images flash through Oli's mind: crime scene photos and the occasional autopsy photo she's secured during investigations. But those pictures are clinical, presented as information without any sense of emotion. Puzzle pieces to help establish what happened. They are controlled and never appear out of context. Most of the bodies she's seen are part of cold-case investigations, and although it shouldn't make a difference, she finds death easier to deal with when the shock and pain occurred in the past.

Oli's seen death in real life too. Not often, but enough to know there's a sacredness to it, a horrible intimacy in witnessing someone transition from this world into whatever comes next. Killers insert themselves into the final moments of a person's existence, further torturing loved ones left to deal with knowing that a monster bore witness to such an intimate moment.

'But why would someone do that?' Oli asks TJ. 'Normally a photo is sent as part of a ransom demand, but that doesn't make sense if this girl is dead. What does the sender want? Do they want it published?'

'Who knows? But it's certainly causing lots of drama. I've had three ex-colleagues reach out in the past hour, and I've been added to four WhatsApp groups. It's total chaos.'

Oli's phone is buzzing, no doubt receiving similar messages. TJ sounds hyped, and she feels ashamed of the anticipatory beat of her own heart. 'Any mention of a link to Marta Holm?'

'The cops aren't saying anything yet—and bear in mind this is coming from a mate of mine who's freelancing at *Melbourne Today*. Apparently, the kid who received the message this morning totally flipped out in the middle of the newsroom, so a few people saw the image on his screen and a few took photos of it, probably thinking it was a hoax. The paper hasn't published it, of course, but a bunch of tweets have popped up with people detailing what happened and mentioning they've seen the image.'

'Maybe it *is* a hoax . . . ?'

'The cops don't think so. Not with this woman missing since Sunday. They obviously believe it's her.'

'Right,' Oli whispers, as the gravity of the situation continues to set in.

'The cops will have to make a statement soon, or they'll be spending all their time putting out media fires. The pressure is going to be on, especially if they thought something like this was a possibility. Them being so cagey doesn't make sense unless they're sitting on a clue they can't risk getting out. You know as well as I do that we can normally get *something*, even if it's just an admission they are keeping things tight for some reason—but no one is saying a thing.'

He's right. Each time Oli has tried to push the query about Holm via her usual avenues, she's been met with a dismissiveness she hasn't encountered since she was a cadet. And her ex, Rusty, a newly minted superintendent, has been uncharacteristically unresponsive. It's hard to know if that is strictly work-related or a result of the ongoing tension between them. She's not sure what their relationship status is following her admission of having feelings for him again, and she senses he isn't sure either.

'Rusty hasn't returned my calls from last week,' she admits. 'But I think that's because he's sensitive about being squeaky clean in the wake of his promotion.' She recalls the way he snubbed her in front of a junior colleague at a crime scene recently. Keeping a professional distance in public is something she respects and understands, but she finds it hard not to take it personally when he's overtly cool toward her—especially after she spilled her guts to him.

'Something is definitely going on,' TJ declares, with his trademark conviction. 'If your source is right and a threatening message *was* found with Marta's body, then the cops must think her murderer might strike again.'

Oli bites her lip slowly. And if it turns out the cops suspect there's a potential serial killer on the loose, then that will be a story in its own right. Despite what Hollywood would have everyone believe, serial killers are extremely rare.

'I guess they've had the Mackenzie Jackson case to deal with,' she says.

'Sure. But that seems to be cut-and-dried DV. This is totally different.'

As Oli edges her car along Victoria Street, she sighs loudly and massages her temples. 'Did you hear back from Marta's friend about anyone she was dating? Once we confirm the new victim's ID, we should try to work out if the women are linked, perhaps by a boyfriend.'

In the hours after news of her murder broke, they found Marta Holm's Instagram page and her popular travel blog. It was clear she was very social—there were dozens of friends referenced in both platforms—but it wasn't clear whether she was in a relationship.

'Good idea,' TJ says. 'Hang on, Ol. I've got another call coming in.'

He puts her on hold, and she exhales, headlines and copy appearing in her mind's eye as if she's typing them. *Increasingly, we live our lives online, and now it seems we die online too.*

She lets a merging car slip in front of her and receives a grateful thumbs-up from the driver. The flailing arms of an agitated toddler are visible in the back seat.

TJ returns to their call. 'The police commissioner and the premier are holding a press conference about the incident later today.'

'Shit. They're really bringing out the big guns.'

'This is going to be massive, Ol. No one will know how to report on it. *We're* going to need to work out how we handle it. It's going to take up a lot of oxygen.'

The comment follows from a clumsy argument they had yesterday about how best to manage their growing business. Neither of them enjoys confrontation, but they need to have a serious conversation about it. The business isn't going to scale itself, and they can't keep hiding behind the news cycle where they're most comfortable.

Oli pictures TJ in the *Newsday* offices. He'll be on his feet—he never takes a phone call sitting down—and his skin will be glowing from the daily run he does with his wife, Carol. He will be combing his fingers through his blond hair as he leans over the oversized white dining table they share as a desk, refreshing Twitter on his laptop. They'd argued about the table. Oli thought it was an extravagance they couldn't afford; TJ insisted it made a statement. He is big on making statements.

Before they started *Newsday*, they were colleagues for several years at *Melbourne Today*, both covering crime. TJ's profile was bigger than Oli's; he was always more extroverted. And while they were competitive, they had a lot of respect for each other. This respect has served them well as business partners, but the journey hasn't been easy.

'I'm about to break the story on the site and our socials,' says TJ. 'I've kept it brief, just verifying what we're hearing and clarifying that it's speculation. No names yet, obviously, just the victim's stats. There's a chance the cops will be pissed. Are you cool if I go live?'

Oli slows the car at the lights. 'Your call is my call.' They used to say this to each other all the time, but the phrase has fallen out of their dialogue in recent months.

'Okay, great.' She can hear his fingers tapping and clicking on his keyboard.

A group of tourists cross the road in front of her car, talking excitedly, arms around each other as they take selfies.

Oli pulls the plastic sheet partway from the envelope and stares at the grey circle. She traces it with her index finger and then moves her finger to the soft skin at the base of her breast. The lump is so small she can barely feel it, but she could swear it starts to burn hot. Tears prick her eyes, and her jaw and mouth tense as she fights to keep her composure. Heat from her chest radiates across her body, reddening her cheeks and dampening her underarms.

The driver behind her toots their horn. She jumps, and the car bunny hops as she double taps the brake before gently pressing the accelerator and moving forward.

'Done,' TJ says. 'If you're out of action today, Oli, I can just—'

'See you in ten.'

CHAPTER FOUR

TUESDAY, 21 JANUARY, 9.46 AM

Pen sits on a closed toilet bowl in the level three bathroom and takes another deep, steadying breath before lifting her head and getting slowly to her feet. The photo of Lyra Makris's lifeless, bloodied face on the presentation screen in the case room sent her nerves into overdrive, and she needed to get out of the stuffy space. She faked an incoming phone call and slipped out quietly before bolting to the toilets.

While the panic has subsided, she now feels hollowed out. There's a low-level ringing in her ears that she can't seem to get rid of. And the intrusive thoughts are back, flickering in and out of her mind like bats. She can't stop thinking about the anguish of the victim's mother when she and Superintendent Frost spoke to the woman earlier, or of her friend Yvonne's primal wails when they told her, or of Lyra Makris herself.

She was a community manager at an online publication and fluent in all things internet. Her Instagram and Facebook profiles are full of videos and photos, and for almost two years she has posted long-form vlogs to YouTube every Monday night as part of her *Quick Cooks with Mak* series. The fun, helpful cooking videos have garnered her a following of almost twenty thousand, as well as a few low-level sponsorship deals. She even amassed a healthy following on the new app TikTok, with over seven thousand followers in just three months.

Pen focuses her thoughts on Elliot, her loyal bulldog, and feels a little better. She washes and dries her hands, emerges from the bathroom and makes her way back across the office to the case room, soundlessly opening the door and sealing it shut behind her.

It takes a moment for her eyes to adjust to the dim light. There aren't usually this many people at a briefing. Yet her boss, Superintendent Rusty Frost, is nowhere to be seen—she assumes he's still leading the Mackenzie Jackson case. He'll be annoyed to lose members of his team, but it's unavoidable. The Makris case takes priority over the missing mother, and they are stretched thin as it is. Pen counts at least twenty uniforms and six detectives, along with a media officer and four people she doesn't recognise, likely from specialist divisions, perhaps psych or forensics. And cyber, of course.

Deputy Commissioner Faye Cloak opened the meeting this morning with confirmation that the image sent to *Melbourne Today* is real. Adam Farina, one of the few cybercrime detectives in the unit, briefly explained that while it looks like a filter has been applied, their initial analysis indicates it's a real photo taken of the missing woman. Cloak informed the room that Farina and his team are attempting to trace the sender—the person who calls themselves The Photographer—but that the Instagram account has already been removed and was linked to a bogus email address.

It will take some time to see if Instagram can assist with providing backup information.

This is the problem with online crime, Pen thinks. Not only does it have more dead ends than in the real world, but the bad guys seem to be several steps ahead as well.

Pen has returned to find all eyes still fixed on Cloak, who has finished recounting the small amount of information available and is answering questions. Pen suddenly realises that the older woman is looking directly at her, so she trains her eyes on the presentation screen, pretending not to notice. Luckily, the photo of Lyra Makris has been replaced with a blown-up image of the Instagram message that accompanied it. Pen reads the words over and over.

She won't be the last.

Fuck you, Pen thinks. The killer's words are so cocky, so casual and so dismissive of this woman's death. There will be no more *Quick Cooks with Mak* videos on Monday nights, and this alone feels like a tragedy. How dare he rob a young woman of her future and then boast about it.

There isn't any doubt: this monster is a man. Women might be holding more leadership roles, the gender pay gap might be slowly closing, and some men are even taking time off work to raise their kids, but male representation in the world of crime remains stubbornly high. Men continue to kill women *and* men. Men rape and beat. Men commit acts of terror. Not all men, but enough for most women to feel a constant thrum of low-level vigilance. Now a man has stolen the life of this vibrant young woman—and apparently he isn't done. He's made a threat, but there are no conditions, no instructions about how to prevent further horror. The only possible response to his message is fear and panic.

Pen's fingernails start to cut into her palms, and she releases her balled fists. She notices that Cloak's hands are curled into fists too, and the veins in her neck are straining against her pale tissue-paper skin. The deputy commissioner's delicate appearance belies her legendary toughness, and while the authors of several long-form articles have tried to understand what makes the petite high-profile career woman and grandmother tick, she remains an enigma. Pen wonders how she copes with the devastation and gore she continually bears witness to.

'I want to make it clear that no one should have any kind of dialogue with the media about this incident. We will establish a process for information-sharing, and this will be detailed at a press conference later today.' Cloak surveys the room, grey eyes flashing a warning. 'It is critical that this order is adhered to, and I'd like to reiterate that the consequences of any deviation will be swift and extremely serious.'

No one replies, but one of the young constables in the front row raises her hand.

Cloak takes a greedy swig of water from her stainless-steel drink bottle and tilts her head, inviting the question.

'Ma'am, is it still assumed that Ms Makris encountered her killer late Saturday night or early Sunday morning?'

'Yes, she didn't use her phone after 2 am on Sunday and failed to attend her exercise class that evening, so we believe it's most likely she was abducted and killed sometime in the early hours of Sunday morning.' Cloak looks at the presentation screen. Grimaces. 'Without a body, it's obviously impossible to say for sure, and whether her murderer was known to her or not is unclear. She lived alone, and she wasn't in a relationship. There's nothing to suggest there was any kind of incident at the party she attended—but the host, Ned Higgins, is known to us. He was accused of rape just over twelve months ago by his then girlfriend. Shortly after filing the report, she retracted it and moved interstate. I've been informed that he often hosts wild parties and has been issued with several warnings about underage guests being supplied alcohol. Obviously he is person of interest.' Cloak glances at her phone. 'And he's the grandson of a former judge.' The unspoken instruction to tread carefully is clear. 'We are yet to determine whether Makris returned to her apartment after the party, but hopefully her phone and bank records will confirm this and help us to create a timeline. Ms Makris didn't have a car—she didn't even have a driver's licence—and the only security cameras at her apartment block are in the car park. We're hoping there are working cameras at a nearby shopping strip. As usual, we'll need to source as much CCTV from the area as we can, as well as footage from Ned Higgins's house and the surrounding neighbourhood.'

Pen feels a pang of irritation. Most cases these days hinge on abbreviations like CCTV, DNA, AVO. Codes for various types of crimes, procedures and evidence. Proof that rules people in or out, that narrows everything down until the speculation fades away and only facts remain. Seconds of footage buried in hours of video files and microscopic remnants of skin cells can be like tiny keys that unlock a case, forming the critical information required to determine what happened in the last moments of someone's life.

Before Pen joined the force, she had no idea how many cameras exist all over the city, nor how many are faulty or disconnected, or blocked by overgrown trees and newly erected signage, or fail to save their recordings to a central database. Like insurance, the cameras are only useful after the fact. Ensuring their functionality is rarely proactive, despite passionate lobbying from victim advocacy groups every time a brutal attack takes place.

Pen prays there is footage identifying Makris's killer and providing her family with much-needed clarity—and possibly even some kind of justice. Pen's dealt with enough homicides to understand that knowing is awful but not knowing is worse. It casts a long, bleak shadow, and she shudders at the thought of Makris's loved ones having the 'what' without the 'why' for the rest of their lives.

Pen glances at the wall clock. Almost five hours have passed since the Instagram message was sent to the newspaper. For six hours, Makris's killer has been out there somewhere, planning his next move. Pen wonders what he really wants. From what she understands, crimes like this can almost always be tracked back to power and control. These types of individuals get intense satisfaction from overpowering another human. But the note to *Melbourne Today* is unusual. Clearly the perpetrator desires notoriety and gets a sick kick from taunting the cops and having the media on the hook.

A detective near the front of the room asks whether the victim had any exes, and Cloak confirms that Makris was seeing James Delway, a thirty-year-old North Melbourne man, until December last year. 'He claims he was with his new girlfriend on Saturday night, but we'll need to verify this,' Cloak adds. 'We're obviously keen to rule him out as quickly as possible to avoid wasting time.'

'Does he have a history?' the detective asks.

'No record. We've been told that his ten-month relationship with Ms Makris didn't end well, but it seems he was the one who initiated the break-up.'

A few cops look disappointed. Most intimate partner homicides are triggered by a female-initiated break-up, so Delway instigating their split makes him less suspicious.

Cloak responds to a few more questions about the origin of the Instagram message and fields a query regarding the possible link between this murder and that of Swedish backpacker Marta Holm. 'We have no choice but to consider that the two incidents might be linked,' she admits, jaw clenching. 'The timeline, the victims, and the communication we have received all point in this direction. But this does not change the way we investigate. Whether the deaths of these young women are related or not, we proceed with professionalism, empathy and determination to deliver answers to their loved ones, to find whoever is responsible and to ensure all Victorians are safe.'

Ignoring two other raised hands, Cloak continues to detail her expectations around case management and immediate tasks, reading from a list of items. Pen and another detective are to speak with people who attended the party, starting with the host, Ned Higgins. She tunes out after that and doesn't hear what task Barnes is assigned.

Cloak says that all questions are to be directed to Pen and Barnes's former superintendent, Clive Sanders, who will lead the investigation. She requests that everyone regroups in the case room at 6 pm for a debrief, then she ends the meeting, exiting the room stony-faced. Everyone gets to their feet, squaring their shoulders and arching their backs, fire in their eyes.

Pen remains where she is and thinks about the Mackenzie Jackson case leads she was planning to follow up. Douglas Jackson claims his wife had been acting increasingly erratically for weeks before she picked a fight with him a fortnight ago and stormed out of their St Kilda apartment with only her phone and keys. He says he didn't go after her because it was clear she needed to cool off, a decision he deeply regrets now. Mackenzie's bank accounts remain untouched, and there have been no sightings of her. The last call she made was to Douglas earlier that day, during which he says they discussed what they were going to have for dinner. Her mobile was switched off around midnight, and the last location it can be traced to is the St Kilda precinct.

The Jacksons live next door to another family whose security camera points directly at their driveway, helpfully capturing the Jacksons' front gate as well. Mackenzie can be seen rushing out of her house just before 10 pm, but there is no evidence that Douglas left the property until the following morning. Their backyard is secure with a high fence, so unless he climbed onto the roof from the back porch and managed to avoid the neighbour's camera, it seems he's telling the truth about his whereabouts that night.

But then one of Mackenzie's colleagues at a market research firm came forward. She revealed that the missing woman had recently confided that her IVF treatment wasn't working and that she was scared of what her husband would do if she couldn't have another baby with him. The focus of the investigation returned to Douglas.

Pen thinks of his earnest public statements about his wife's disappearance, and her gut clenches in anger. Barnes is convinced he's involved, and so is she.

Now Barnes sidles up to her and cuffs her gently on the arm. 'You okay, Pen?' he asks, his chubby face concerned.

She ducks her head and avoids his gaze. 'Just tired.' She smiles ironically. 'And that was before I knew about this.'

He rocks on his heels and nods hello to a passing constable. 'Your bad feeling was right. That poor girl.'

'I know.' Pen recalls Lyra Makris's lighthearted jokes in one of her cooking videos and pictures her neatly made bed with the green sheets, the remnants of the lilac candle puddled in her bathroom. 'It's awful. And the message sent to *Melbourne Today* is bizarre, like this guy wants to be caught. I just don't get it. Is it an attention thing?'

'I'm no profiler, but I'm guessing whoever did this wants to create chaos. They know this will have all of us running around like chickens with our heads cut off.'

It's a poor choice of words, but Pen pretends not to clock it. 'Based on what Cloak said, it sounds likely it's linked to the Holm murder.'

Barnes shrugs, pragmatic as always. 'She has to say that so there's not a question we didn't consider it down the track, but it's too early to be sure. It could just be an opportunistic nutter. Hopefully the tech team can work some magic, and we can shut this whole thing down before the newsrooms have a chance to work up their inevitable serial-killer graphics.'

'Fingers crossed,' Pen replies feebly.

In late December, before Mackenzie Jackson disappeared, she'd followed up several leads on Marta Holm's murder, but they had amounted to nothing. A cash-in-hand job at a busy city pub had gifted the bubbly, fun-loving backpacker an instant friendship group and active social life, and her new-found friendship circle insisted she was a charming and reliable worker with a penchant for adventure. She received a lot of male attention during her shifts, but by all accounts she handled it well, managing to politely reject unwelcome advances while making it clear she wasn't interested. Holm's boss at the pub, a cheerful curly-haired Irishman named Simon—whom Pen suspected had been keen on Holm—explained that she was a wonderful employee, always on time and offering to pick up shifts. She was passionate about her travel blog and offered to take photos of the food for the pub's Instagram page.

'She was really good at photography,' a wistful Simon told Pen. 'She even came up with little captions to go with the photos. We barely changed a thing. She was too smart to work in hospo, but she loved people. She wanted to study design when she went back home.'

No one Pen has spoken to recalls that Holm had any notable interactions at the pub or when she was out socially, and while her summery dress and full make-up the night she died indicate she had plans, her phone records haven't provided any clues. Several comments on her social media pages carry a mildly sinister tone—men asking her on dates and inviting her to do private tours of various tourism destinations with them—but nothing that stands out from the typical cesspit of anonymous interactions online.

'Frost's not getting a look-in on this case?' she asks Barnes.

'Depends what happens with the Jackson case, but my bet is he'll get pulled in on this soon. The top dogs love him, and we all know he's very media friendly.'

Pen isn't sure if Barnes is being genuine or making a subtle dig about Rusty's history with Olive Groves. 'I better get moving,' she says.

'You'll be fine, Pen.' Barnes looks her in the eye. He knows how she feels about Sanders.

She nods, appreciating his solidarity.

He checks his phone. 'Jeez, they're talking about restricting Chinese flights into the United States because of that new SARS virus. Seems like it's getting serious.'

'Yeah, I saw that,' Pen murmurs. Her forehead and top lip bead with perspiration, and she lifts her hair away her neck.

Barnes gestures for her to walk in front of him. 'Look after yourself, Pen,' he says as they reach the door.

She glances at the photos of the two dead women pinned to case boards positioned along the rear of the room. 'You too.' She's aware of the second hand of the wall clock above them, ticking its way through another rotation.

CHAPTER FIVE

TUESDAY, 21 JANUARY, 9.54 AM

Oli parks behind TJ's BMW in the narrow laneway adjacent to the Fitzroy warehouse they lease for office space. She takes the stairs two at a time, impatiently keying in her security code and pushing the heavy door open. The small reception area boasts two imitation Danish chairs, a transparent coffee table with some artfully positioned magazines, and three oversized indoor plants. It's just enough for them to be taken seriously when they need to host a meeting, and it leaves no doubt they prioritise substance over style.

When they first left *Melbourne Today*, Oli and TJ spent weeks debating what they should call their fledgling business before finally settling on *Newsday*. They still love the name, but it has painted them into a corner somewhat, setting an expectation that they deliver news every day. The past five years have been relentless and, at times, extremely stressful. Establishing a credible news platform and creating quality content without the engine of an established newsroom has been hard enough; growing and nurturing a brand

and a burgeoning product portfolio while navigating the required technology and ecommerce is a lot more difficult than they anticipated. They started making a profit after eighteen months, and three years later they continue to grow.

Now they desperately need to make some decisions about the next phase of *Newsday*. She remembers her sister Lily's husband, Shaun, a successful entrepreneur, explaining in his insufferable tone that establishing a roadmap to scaling the business should be their number one priority when they first started *Newsday*. Unsurprisingly, amid the madness of the daily news cycle, they never got around to it. It's now clear they need to scale the business, but first they must agree on how far their brand can stretch, along with how to map out more clearly who does what. Although they have strong and varied views on these issues, they agree that their current pace of operation isn't sustainable. The demands of running the business mean that going on holiday is near impossible, and neither of them has taken more than a long weekend in the past twelve months.

Oli thinks about the sick leave she'll need to take soon. How on earth will TJ manage without her?

She steps past reception to find him standing in the middle of their open-plan office, clicking his left fingers while scrolling on his phone with his right thumb, AirPods in his ears. He glances up at her, and they lock eyes, the intensity of the story burning between them before he shakes his head and returns his attention to his phone. She wonders if perhaps what he heard about the photo is incorrect or exaggerated. From experience, she knows how easy it is for a spark of apparent truth to set a fire that blazes across the industry before everyone realises it's not what it seems.

'Yep, hang on, mate,' TJ is saying. 'I'm trying to get it up on my screen.'

He hasn't changed in the fifteen years she's known him. He's still lean, with a thick crop of blond hair, and he embraces all aspects of his life with the youthful energy and assuredness of someone used to things working in their favour. Oli disliked him when they first met, but that was mainly due to how intimidated she was by his confidence. While she'd never admit it to him, his ambition and drive kept her on her toes during their time at *Melbourne Today* and still does.

Their partnership is the main reason why the unexpected job offer Oli received from Marion Disney last week has thrown her into a spin. The role is to anchor the drive show at a popular radio station, Air 24/7. Marion is a powerhouse in the industry, and the thought of working with her and anchoring a show is something Oli has started to fantasise about—even though she can't imagine leaving TJ and everything they've built together. She's aware that the confusion she feels about Marion's proposition was one of the reasons she picked a fight about the business with him yesterday.

'Ol, hey. Are you okay?'

Lost in thought, she didn't realise TJ is off the phone.

He cocks his head. There's a hint of sheepishness in his expression, and she realises that he thinks she wanted the day off because she's mad at him. She hooks stray hairs behind her ears, smoothing them unnecessarily but feeling an urge to keep her hands busy as he scrutinises her.

She and TJ are close in a very specific way. Their relationship is built on history, knowledge and respect, not intimacy. She can reel off his resumé, can name his favourite foods, knows exactly how he likes his coffee and could probably pick out every item of his wardrobe in a line-up. She knows his moods, but only in relation to work. His innermost thoughts are a mystery—she's not even certain how he votes. And while she's friendly with his wife, Carol, she and TJ rarely discuss their personal lives. Their bond is built on a passion for the news, their innate competitiveness and a shared ambition for their business.

After spending years in the cut-throat and dying world of print media, they had a lot to prove when they launched *Newsday.* Oli can't imagine being in business with anyone else. She trusts him as a professional and knows that he feels the same way, but they've never confided in each other.

She decides then and there that she doesn't want to tell him about her cancer diagnosis yet. She doesn't really want to tell anyone. Keeping it to herself makes it feel manageable. Like an exam she can study for in secret, then sit without the pressure of anyone's expectations.

'Everything's fine,' she says. 'I have some life admin to catch up on, but this trumps that.'

TJ looks unconvinced but bobs his head. 'Right, good. That's good. And honestly, thank god you're here. This story is huge.'

'Tell me everything.'

His mobile rings, and he almost drops it in the process of answering. 'Hey, mate. Do you have it?' He presses mute and says to Oli, 'Do you want to check the website content? Change anything you're not sure about.' She nods, and he returns to his call, his thumb scrolling his screen. 'I can't see anything on TikTok,' he says to the caller, his blue eyes flashing with irritation. 'Maybe it's been taken down . . . ?'

Oli hides a smile. TJ hates TikTok as much as she does. Their office Christmas drinks had seen the two of them passionately trying to convince their Gen Z staff that the last thing the world needed was another social media platform.

She takes a seat at her desk, connects her laptop to the monitor and enters her password, glancing around the office. All eight TVs mounted on the back wall are showing different news broadcasts. The TVs were one of their first investments; Oli wanted to emulate the vibe of a serious media organisation and ensure they were always plugged in to the news cycle. Now, she quickly scans each screen. *Missing Melbourne woman feared dead* appears in the breaking news ticker of the Australian news channels, and even the BBC references the story.

Chelsea's computer monitor is on, and her desk is covered with Post-its, notebooks and pens, but she and her laptop are nowhere to be seen. Yael isn't in either, and Oli remembers that she is pitching advertising and sponsorship packages to prospective clients today.

Loading the *Newsday* home page, Oli scans the breaking news piece TJ uploaded. It reads well and feels appropriate, considering how little they know. In lieu of a photo, TJ has used the generic Victoria Police logo with their custom 'suspected homicide' ribbon graphic—neutral and appropriate.

A guiding principle is that she and TJ report news the way they'd want it reported if it were about one of their own loved ones. This is a surprisingly helpful north star that ensures their written and audio content is always calm, clear and as objective as possible.

She plucks a pen from the *COFFEE IS A CONSPIRACY* mug on her desk, finding comfort in the feeling of it between her fingers, overwhelmed by the notion of a killer communicating so blatantly with the press. It's reminiscent of the infamous American serial-killer cases in the seventies and eighties; those murderers became household names by flaunting their horrific crimes and goading the authorities. Oli has always assumed that technology has rendered that impossible. Surely by sending a photo, this guy has laid down a yellow brick road directly to his front door.

She draws a breath as the *Melbourne Today* website loads. The home page features a dramatic stock image: crime scene tape positioned across a shadowy alleyway. The word 'exclusive' is housed in a red box. MISSING GIRL FEARED MURDERED, screams the headline. Oli bristles at 'girl' used to describe a woman in her early twenties.

She scans the copy. There's no by-line. The article is vague, mentioning only that *Melbourne Today* was sent information about a missing woman that implied she had met with foul play. There's no mention of a link to the Marta Holm murder, and there's nothing that hints at the identity of the woman or alludes to a graphic photo. They are being careful too. Clearly, it's going to be a game of chess until someone decides to flip the board.

The doctor's appointment already feels surreal, as if it happened weeks ago or perhaps to someone else. Her fingers hover over the keyboard, but she refrains from googling about her cancer diagnosis. For someone pathologically obsessed with facts, there is an illogical pleasure to be had in delaying knowing everything she can about her illness.

Her phone pings with an ABC news alert about the suspected murder just as she receives a message from her sister, Lily, inviting her to lunch at their mother's on the weekend. Another text follows: *Mum says she hasn't seen you for ages.* Oli sighs, the weight of family obligation even heavier than usual as she dreads the thought of telling them she has cancer. Lily will no doubt find a way to make it about herself, and their mother's anxiety, suffocating at the best of times, will intensify.

Ignoring Lily's message, Oli stares impatiently at TJ, willing him to end his call.

'Yep, okay.' He spins on his leather heel and walks around to her side of the desk. 'I'm not sure yet, she's only just got in. Yep, okay, mate. Talk later.'

Oli looks at him expectantly as he ends the call.

'Twitter has exploded with this.' He holds up his phone as if to show her. 'And it's trending on TikTok—a bunch of teenagers with huge followings have recorded videos of themselves speculating about a police cover-up.'

TJ's pupils are dilated, his eyes huge. His hair, usually styled in a thick wave, is ruffled from his manic finger-combing, and his normally calm demeanour has morphed into a palpable energy that feels dangerous and contagious. Over the course of their careers, they have been summoned in the middle of the night to attend crime scenes, have pulled all-nighters to file stories, and have physically chased down soundbites and photos, but Oli doesn't think she's ever seen TJ look so wired.

'Where's Chelsea?' Oli asks.

'I sent her to the *Melbourne Today* offices. She went to uni with the community manager who opened the message, so she's trying to get a grab. I'm pretty sure their management will shut it all down, which means we'll need to be ready to go live with a couple of versions.'

'Trust Chelsea to know the guy.'

They exchange a brief smile.

Chelsea Waters is their junior reporter, digital-marketing expert and social media adviser. She knows her way around every social media platform, unsurprising seeing as she spends most of her waking hours in cyberspace. Lily described her as 'zany' when she met her, and it's a good word for her. Chelsea is full of contradictions. She changes the colour of her naturally dark hair on a weekly basis, and her personal style is impossible to pinpoint, ranging from metallic space alien to *Little House on the Prairie*. She abhors fast fashion, spends more on skincare products than Oli spends on rent, and has an uncanny knack of being connected in some tenuous way to newsworthy people. At twenty-three, she is wise beyond her years, with good storytelling instincts and an admirable work ethic, but she requires a lot of what TJ calls 'reining in', something Oli softens to 'a bit of polish'.

Chelsea suffers from extreme anxiety, and this, alongside her deep-seated moral compass and passion for justice, occasionally leads to poorly timed outbursts and misguided opinions on how they should cover the news. She and Oli have had several conversations about the importance of separating personal viewpoints and political activism from reporting, something that Oli senses Chelsea will always struggle with. An upside to this is that she is a good barometer for their Gen Z audience, and TJ and Oli joke that she's the best investment they've made, worth more than all their expensive subscriptions and indoor plants. They are fiercely protective of her, and Oli lives in fear that she'll be poached to work for a trendy not-for-profit or convinced to move overseas by some hotshot news editor.

TJ asks, 'Did you look at the site?'

'Yep. It's good.' Oli pauses. 'Maybe we need to consider running a live blog on this. We can pull grabs from our socials so there's not too much extra work, but I feel like we should be providing as many updates on the main site as we can. And it's obviously good for traffic. I guess it depends on where we land in terms of how much we lean into this.'

'Do you mean whether or not we even try to cover this properly?' TJ's voice is stiff, and Oli knows how much he hates the thought of having to compromise—or lose.

They try to supplement their curated news offering with local reporting and Oli's deeper investigations, but the reality is they are a small team.

She gathers her hair into a low ponytail. 'We should do as much original reporting on it as we can,' she says firmly, before TJ has a chance to speak again. 'It's a Melbourne story and something that people will expect us to cover.' She lifts her navy jacket off the back of her chair and pulls it on, smoothing the lapels and tucking her faded V-neck T-shirt into her jeans.

TJ gives her an intense look. He's perceptive, and she wonders if he'll somehow sense her illness or that she's been offered the Air 24/7 job.

She raises her eyebrows expectantly, summoning a confidence she doesn't feel as she hopes to distract him from any sixth-sense suspicions. 'We need more reasons for people to come to the site, so let's lean into this. Depending on how it evolves, I might be able to work it into my family violence series so we have more opportunities to link the stories and cross-promote the podcast to the paper, seeing we know that tends to work so well.'

This approach should make him happy. He's obsessed with their audience numbers, and it seems like he's constantly talking about clicks and dwell time.

Oli glances again at the bank of television screens and sees the news ticker along the bottom of Channel 9: *Victorian Premier to hold press conference on the suspected murder of missing Carlton woman.* Another frisson of adrenaline charges through her, underpinned by something she can't quite identify. Fear? Overwhelm? Anger? Her cheeks flush, and she has an urge to rip her jacket off again.

'What more have you learned from your sources about the woman in the photo?' she asks TJ.

'Just the basics.' He flicks open his notebook. 'I'm ninety-five per cent sure her name is Lyra Makris. Twenty-three years old and missing since Sunday. If I've got the right person, she posted a photo on Instagram on Saturday night at a party.'

'Show me.'

He loads the screen and passes her his phone.

'Lyra,' Oli murmurs.

She studies the smiling young woman, her arms around a friend. It's a candid shot, and there's at least a dozen people in the background, talking and drinking. It looks like they're at a house rather than a bar—there's a mantelpiece cluttered with photos and a mirror reflecting a room full of people.

'We should record a news drop,' says Oli. 'It will be a good way to launch the investigation and tie it to the deeper report we're doing.'

One of the TVs is now showing a Channel Seven reporter standing outside the *Melbourne Today* offices, her face solemn as the hot northerly wind attempts to shift her lacquered hair.

'And people will want to hear us talk about this,' Oli adds. 'It's that kind of story.'

Chelsea has been doing the majority of the daily news podcasts since October. When they first made the switch, they received over fifty email complaints and several comments on social media demanding TJ and Oli return to hosting. Several hundred people unsubscribed in protest. But after that initial wobble, the numbers have grown and held, and Chelsea has been building her own dedicated fan base. Oli is still struggling to get her head around the apathy and outrage their audience seems to oscillate between daily.

TJ nods. 'Agreed. Okay, let me just dash to the bathroom. I'll meet you in the studio.'

She fetches a glass of water and steps into the pokey room at the rear of the office. Her eyes sting from the biodegradable pine-scented fragrance sachets Chelsea insists on hanging on the door handle.

Taking a seat at her preferred side of the table, Oli places the headphones over her ears and feels her body relax. This is where she feels the most comfortable, the most capable. There's an intimacy to audio that she likes, a sense she is sating her curiosity in real time and bringing the audience along with her. Podcasting reignited her journalistic passion and reset her interest in the media industry more broadly.

She looks around the small space: the microphones they spent a fortune on, the mugs full of branded pencils she ordered last year for an industry event, Chelsea's bloody sachets, and the photo of their former colleague Cooper on the wooden stool in the corner. He would have loved *Newsday* and would be excited about taking it to the next level.

TJ pushes into the room. He takes a seat and puts on his headphones. 'Want me to drive?'

'Sure.'

As is so often the case, he reminds her of a little boy. He has the same naive confidence, the proud jut of his chin making it easy for her to picture him as a child being told to share his toys or wait his turn. She reminds herself that it's not his fault he was born with good looks, a quick brain and an easy manner, and that life has rolled out the red carpet for him. At least he has the decency to be grateful.

He flicks on the sound equipment, and the fuzzy white noise fills her ears. They nod at each other, and he presses record.

I would miss this if I died. The intrusive thought is shocking, and she grimaces, prompting a questioning look from TJ. She smiles reassuringly and adjusts her headphones, pushing the thought away.

Staring at the red light, she waits a beat then speaks, her deep voice catching on the words. 'We've jumped in to the *Newsday* podcast studio to record a quick news drop in light of a major story breaking in Melbourne.'

'We don't have many details at this stage,' TJ chimes in, 'but we're bringing you what we've heard from our sources. Please note, some listeners might find this information distressing.'

Oli calmly relays the key points, stressing that the information is unverified. She doesn't reveal Makris's name, and she's careful to avoid sensationalising the alleged correspondence with *Melbourne Today*. 'This news follows that of the brutal murder of Swedish backpacker Marta Holm on Christmas Eve. Ms Holm's body was discovered in the Treasury Gardens, and her case remains unsolved. Whether or not these cases are linked, Victoria Police will be under a lot of pressure to identify those responsible. These incidents fuel the ongoing discussion about the increased levels of violence toward women across Australia.' She promotes her upcoming domestic violence series, records an outro and signs off.

TJ does the same, and they remove their headphones and quickly plan out the rest of the day as best they can.

'I'll edit this now and send it to you to check,' says TJ, already scrolling through his emails.

'I'll start a deep dive on Lyra Makris,' Oli says. 'But I think we should both go to the press conference.'

'I agree.'

She senses he's thinking what she is, that going together presents a united front in the face of industry chatter that there's bad blood between them. They're convinced the speculation can be traced back to the freelancer they hired before Christmas, whom they let go early due to poor performance. This is another reason why Oli is so cautious about letting people into the tent.

TJ has started making notes, his handwriting impossible to decipher as it fills a page of his small notebook. 'I'll brief Chelsea to pull together some points on similar stories to reference. No doubt the other pubs will.'

'You mean stories where a killer has interacted with the authorities?'

'Yep. There are some obvious ones—the Zodiac Killer, Dennis Rader, David Berkowitz. Plus those recent cases in the US where the killers sent photos of their dead wives to the media.'

'That criminal psychologist I've used in the past might be worth talking to. I'll flick you and Chels her details.'

He makes a thumbs-up with his left hand as he keeps scrawling. 'Can you think of anything else like this ever happening in Australia?'

'Only that man in Western Australia who tried to livestream his suicide on YouTube last year. He told a friend about it, and the police made it to his place just in time to get him to hospital.'

'Jesus,' TJ mutters, adding it to his list.

They lock eyes, not needing to articulate the complex feelings that come with a story like this. They share a primal impulse to dive in, to forensically examine every awful detail they can get their hands on. And there's the undeniable excitement of the arrival of such a big news story, the camaraderie it creates across the journalism community, the reinforcement of the critical role they play. This sense of responsibility paired with adrenaline enables them to evade sleep and run on coffee fumes for days. But there's also intense guilt. The awareness that someone's worst day might be one of their most exhilarating.

'I'll update the site with the info about the press conference.' She stands up. 'Let me know when the episode is live, and I'll pop a link at the top and tail of the piece.'

'Perfect.' TJ folds his lips together and nods, but she notices his hands are shaking.

Returning to her desk, Oli logs on to the system and writes website copy to accompany the audio drop. She proofs it twice before pushing it live, then creates a social tile and links it to the piece, checking the posts Chelsea has done on the morning headlines: a mysterious virus, a mystery killer, world leaders on trial for a raft of crimes. Oli feels as though the already mad world has finally jumped the shark.

TJ emerges from the studio and returns to his desk. 'I've done the edit. I didn't change anything, just cleaned it up a bit.'

Oli clicks on their shared file server and drags his nine-minute edit onto her desktop, then puts in an AirPod and presses play as she preps the links. Her own voice fills her ears.

TJ glances at the wall clock. 'Shit, we need to get our skates on.'

'Give me five minutes,' she murmurs. They always listen to their audio recordings in full before they publish. Their reputation is too important to risk errors or sound-quality issues.

The audio keeps playing as her phone buzzes with a text from an unknown number. She opens the message and gasps, pushing away from the desk.

TJ springs to his feet. 'Ol, what is it?'

She points to her phone, and they stare in horror at Lyra Makris's lifeless face. She's lying in a pool of blood.

CHAPTER SIX

TUESDAY, 21 JANUARY, 11.03 AM

Pen flashes a polite smile at Goldie Silverman, the detective constable she's been partnered with, and presses the doorbell of Ned Higgins's impressive East Melbourne home. Not for the first time Pen wonders what Silverman's parents were thinking. Ridiculous name aside, she seems solid, grounded and intensely focused on the task at hand, which is more than Pen can say for herself these days.

The front door is open, and thanks to the wide light-infused hallway, Pen can see out to the backyard, where three forensic techs are standing on the lawn. Impatient, she presses the buzzer again. She wants to get this done in time to watch Premier Dunkley's press conference. It's making her nervous, possibly because she knows that as soon as certain details are stated out loud, the public scrutiny will come, and it will remain until they have answers.

A text from Barnes flashes up on her phone as they wait, and she quickly reads it. *Someone is texting random journos the photo of the dead girl. Total nightmare.*

Unnerved, Pen tries not to react, but her heart rate quickens.

'Hello, hi. Sorry to keep you waiting.'

Pen looks up to see a tall man in his early twenties holding out his hand to her. She shoves her phone in her pocket and shakes his hand.

'Ned Higgins.' He turns to Silverman and they shake hands too. 'Please come in. Apparently, your boys are done with the kitchen, so I reckon we'll chat in there.'

They follow him down the hallway. Even without shoes, Ned is at least a foot taller than Pen. He gestures to a large wooden table and tells them to sit, busying himself with fetching three glasses of chilled water.

Once he's seated, Pen nods at Silverman and fixes her gaze on Ned, watching him as Silverman explains that they want to ask him some questions about the party he threw on Saturday night.

Ned is good-looking and radiates a masculine energy that Pen finds tedious. Not only is he tall, but he also has a thick shock of dark hair, sculpted brows and clear olive skin. Faded jeans paired with a worn white T-shirt accentuate his athletic frame, and his eyes are an unusual colour, a light hazel that makes them appear backlit. Pen imagines there's a globe inside his head where a brain would normally be, and the more she speaks with him the more it seems like her theory has legs. Ned talks in circles, jumping from one train of thought to another. No matter the questions they ask, he uses them as a segue to his views on modern society, gender dynamics and the climate.

He's devastated about what's happened to Lyra Makris, and Pen knows this because he tells her several times. 'This is so sad,' he says for the third time, looking anguished. 'I'm utterly devastated. It's such a tragedy. Do you know when the funeral will be? Or will there be a delay because of the forensics? I know it's not like on TV, those tests can take ages, right?'

Pen pushes away an intrusive mental image of Lyra's slashed neck. 'Her family isn't able to plan a funeral right now. There's no body.'

Ned looks flustered. 'Well, no. I guess I wasn't thinking—'

'Tell us a bit about yourself, Ned.' Pen forces a smile.

'What do you want to know? I'm keen to help.'

'School. Work. Siblings. Relationship status.'

He takes a sip of water and nods earnestly, clearly trying to remember each part of the question. 'I'm at uni, I don't work, I'm an only child and I'm single.'

'Where do you go to uni?'

'I'm enrolled at Melbourne, but honestly, I'm not sure the course is for me. I want to be really careful about what I spend my time doing, you know? The older I get, the more I realise it needs to be meaningful, and I'm starting to think I'm too young to be locked into anything.'

'Right,' says Pen. 'And what is it you're studying? Or supposed to be studying.'

'IT. Computer science stuff.' Ned waves his hand. 'It's pretty boring.'

Out of the corner of her eye, Pen sees Silverman write in her notebook.

'Tell us about the party, Ned.' Pen makes a mental note to investigate his uni attendance and grades.

He waves his hand. 'I have a lot of parties. This one wasn't particularly special. It was low key, like really chill. The one I threw at New Year's was much bigger.'

'How many people were here?' Pen asks.

'One hundred, maybe one twenty. I wasn't counting, obviously, but I can generally tell when we've hit a hundred because people move into the yard.' He points to his left. 'It's 'cause the introverts start to find the house a little claustrophobic, and they need some space. I always make sure there's some chill areas for those personality types.'

Pen notices Silverman's eyes bulging as she takes notes.

'That's a big turnout,' Pen says evenly. 'Anyone underage?'

Ned shrugs. 'Not that I know of. My circle is just a great crew of people who want to do good things in the world. I have get-togethers here every few months—my parents are away a lot, and they don't mind. Sometimes I theme them, like a few months ago we raised money for this climate charity. I asked everyone to bring their best idea for a clean energy start-up. I had a mate in town, an international DJ. It was wild, but we raised, like, twenty grand. I like to party with purpose as much as possible.'

Although Pen is only six years older than Ned, the gap feels like a chasm. He's an overgrown child, his earnestness long past being endearing. 'I understand that police have attended your get-togethers in the past, is that right?' she says frostily.

'There's been some misunderstandings with the neighbours, but it's not a big deal. A guy across the road always complains—he has beef with my dad, so I don't let it get to me.'

'Do you often have misunderstandings, Ned?' Pen asks. 'Misread situations?'

'No.' He blinks and looks back and forth between them, his eyes wide. 'Or if I do, I apologise. It's important to own your errors.'

Despite the aircon, Pen's neck becomes hot. He must know that she's referring to the allegations against him—but he seems unfazed, and she starts to wonder how much of his laidback naivety is an act.

'How do you know Lyra Makris?'

Ned deflates melodramatically in his chair. 'God, yeah, Lyra. I allowed myself to forget about what happened for a moment. She's such a cool chick. I can't believe someone would hurt her. It's so sad, just tragic.' He runs his hands through his hair and inhales deeply, shaking his head. 'We have a real problem, us men. A real problem.' He shifts his golden gaze back and forth between Pen and Silverman. 'Women should be able to move around the world without having to fear for their lives. They should be able to walk home or go for a run or whatever. Some of my chick friends, they pretend to be on the phone when they go out at night just so they feel safe. It's bullshit.' He looks outraged at the thought of all the women walking around taking fake phone calls.

'Lyra Makris,' Pen repeats. 'How do you know her?'

Ned pouts slightly. 'She went out with a mate of mine in high school for a few months, and we stayed friends after they split.'

'So, you'd known each other for a while?'

'Almost eight years, I guess.' He flashes his dimples at them. 'We're getting old.' His face falls. 'Of course, I know ageing is a privilege.'

Pen ignores this last comment. 'You saw her often?'

'Just around the traps, you know. Parties and stuff.'

'Did she come to your party on her own?'

He squeezes his eyes shut in an exaggerated attempt to remember. 'I think so.' He drops his head to the left and fixes his gaze up at the ceiling. 'I didn't see her arrive or anything, but I think she was just there with mates. She's got a solid crew.' He looks stricken. 'They are all going to be so devastated. What's happened to her is going to mess up the whole gang.'

'Was anyone at the party acting oddly toward her?'

'No. I didn't see anything bad the whole night. Like I said, it was a super chill vibe. The weather was great—heaps of people were in the pool.' He points at the window on the north side of the kitchen. 'It's just through there. Things were good. Makes it even harder to believe something like this happened.'

'Was anyone paying her particular attention?' Pen presses.

Ned looks bewildered. 'Like, everyone was chatting and vibing. She was cool. There was no hassle.'

Pen pictures Lyra's photo board in her empty apartment, the appointments she will never attend, and has an impulse to lean across the table and grab Ned by the scruff of his faded T-shirt and scream at him to stop being so infuriatingly obtuse.

'Did you speak with Lyra on Saturday night?'

He makes a figure eight with his head. 'Like, yeah? I mean sort of. I said hi and stuff, but you know how it is when you're the host. It's all a bit of a blur.'

'How convenient,' Pen says, and Ned shrugs good-naturedly. 'Did you see her leave?'

'I wish I had, but I was, you know, playing host.'

'How did you invite everyone? Over text?'

'Just, like, on Snapchat and texts and whatever. Like I said, people bring people. My motto is the more the merrier. I never restrict the numbers—everyone is welcome. I'm lucky I don't seem to attract dickheads. Never have.'

Silverman seems to sense that Pen is losing her patience and asks, 'Do you have a guest list you can provide to us?'

He looks puzzled. 'Sort of? I can give you access to my messages, but I didn't keep an actual list. And I invited some people when I saw them out and about at other parties. I don't really do admin. It's kind of a rule I have.'

Pen's insides are curdling. 'Please give us whatever you have—messages, photos, security footage, everything.'

'Too easy.' Ned brightens. 'I had a digital photo booth set up in the lounge.' He points to a huge room that intersects with the kitchen; it has three large couches, a billiards table and a piano. 'You can have all the files from that too. It was super popular, so Lyra probably used it. Not that I *witnessed* her using it.'

Pen sighs. 'Great. We'll arrange for our team to collect all the information.'

Ned continues to look pleased, and Pen wonders if there is social currency in providing content to the police.

'James Delway,' she says. 'Know him?'

'James.' Ned's gaze is suddenly on the table. 'I know him, and I told him about the party, but we're not really mates.'

'Was he here on Saturday?' Silverman asks.

Ned fingers the band of his complicated-looking watch. 'I don't *think* so. I didn't see him, but that doesn't mean he wasn't there.'

'Doesn't it?' says Pen.

'He might not have come inside,' explains Ned. 'There were a lot of people hanging out the front, and I wasn't, like, keeping track.'

'Do you know if Lyra saw him?' says Pen.

Now Ned looks her straight in the eye. All traces of his naivety have disappeared. 'Like I said, I didn't see him so I can't say. I'm just acknowledging he may have been there at some point.'

Pen locks her gaze on Ned's and sees a spark of defiance in the golden flecks. 'And why aren't you mates?'

'I only met him a couple of times when he was with Lyra, but he doesn't give good vibes.'

'What does that mean?'

'You know they broke up recently.' Ned again stares at the table between them. 'He was the one who ended it, and she was pretty devo, or at least that's what one of her friends told me. He wasn't aware of her needs. Seems like a selfish dude.' Ned scowls then rearranges his mouth into a smile. 'But he's moved on, and Lyra was obviously ready to move on too.'

'How do you mean?'

'Just the way she was dressed and how she was acting—you know, checking her phone and taking lots of photos.' Ned laces his long fingers together and leans his forearms against the table, looking back and forth between Pen and Silverman. 'I'm good with people, always have been. It's sort of like a sixth sense I have. Plus, I've done a bunch of online psychology courses, and it was like, *really* obvious she was trying to impress someone on Saturday night.'

CHAPTER SEVEN

TUESDAY, 21 JANUARY, 1.04 PM

Oli is pushed into the back of TJ's charcoal suit by an enthusiastic Channel Nine reporter with blinding white teeth as they wait for the press conference to begin. He throws her an apologetic expression then strains forward again, eyes fixed to the front of the room as he whispers loudly into his phone. He's familiar, but she can't recall his name. He's been on air for a year or so and has a wooden style, a bit like a ventriloquist puppet that comes to life. Into his phone, he says, 'I'm, like, about ten metres from the front, slightly left of centre.'

Oli allows herself a little smirk. More like five metres from the front, ten o'clock if you're standing on the stage. How is it that even basic facts are lost in translation these days?

She sneaks another look at him. His teeth are so white they are almost blue, and she imagines the nerves withering inside their porcelain prisons. Surely that amount of bleach can't be healthy. Not for the first time she considers how unsuited she is for a visual medium like TV. She dislikes any form of public speaking, and the relentless scrutiny regarding her appearance would cripple her.

It's bad enough now with the modest profile she has through *Newsday*, but the invisible wall that exists between her and the audience allows her to put her energy into storytelling, rather than having to worry about *being* the story. Again she thinks about Marion Disney's job offer. The lines are blurring across the board: radio personalities are popping up on television segments, and print journalists are under pressure to promote their work on social media. The audience flip-flops between wanting their news sources to be neutral and railing against journos who refuse to be activists, demanding they disclose their opinion. And all the paid media data suggests that everyone wants everything to be in video format, even radio and podcasts, something Oli has resisted.

'Can't hear you, mate,' White Teeth snaps. 'Just get whatever shots you can.' He ends his call and steps heavily on Oli's right foot.

She stumbles forward, her nose pressing into TJ's suit again and she holds out her hands to steady herself, shooting daggers at the reporter, who is already on another call. TJ turns around and smiles at her distractedly.

Oli hasn't seen so many journalists in one place for a long time, and the Spring Street press room doesn't have the ventilation required to accommodate such a large group of people on a thirty-five-degree day. Everyone is wiping their brows and pulling their tailored shirts away from their chests, trying to force in some air. A few of the female journalists peer into mirrored compacts and dab at their noses and foreheads with matte powder. TJ, however, seems unbothered by the heat. He returns his eyes to the stage.

At the front, a door swings open. The premier sweeps in with her communications adviser and two other staffers. Clarissa Dunkley makes her way to the stage and takes position behind the lectern. She adjusts the microphone so it's poised a few centimetres from her freshly lipsticked mouth and gazes out at the crowd. Her glossy brown hair has been styled into a no-nonsense boyish crop, with a few thick strands resting on her forehead and accentuating her lively brown eyes. After a moment, the rumble of chatter settles into silence.

Dunkley will turn fifty-five on 7 April. She lives in Balaclava, the suburb she was born in, the middle child of three. Her parents were teachers, and her brothers are in construction. She has a serious peanut allergy and has been hospitalised twice since she took office because of accidental consumption.

Oli knows more about the premier than she does about her own mother, partly thanks to a podcast episode she put together last year, but also because of the premier's willingness to share information about her life on social media in lieu of granting interviews. This non-traditional approach has worked for Dunkley; she has almost half a million Instagram and Twitter followers, more than double the amount of any other Australian politician, and she often posts livestreams, talking candidly about the highs and lows of political life.

The Chief Commissioner of Police, Maurice Lew, strides into the room. Upon realising the premier is already on stage, he doubles back to stand against the door. His meaty hands hold his police hat at his waist, the fluorescent lights causing a glare to bounce off his bald head.

Dunkley speaks. 'Thank you all for being here, and apologies about the temperature. We are trying to rectify that.' She looks pointedly at her staffers, and a woman in a garish floral dress nods nervously, her mobile glued to her ear. 'I wish we were here for a progress announcement about our world-class transport infrastructure projects, or so that I could share an update on our ambitious renewable energy initiatives, but unfortunately we are here for a far more sombre reason.' She pauses, her face serious as she scans the room. 'It's only the third week of the year, and at least three Victorian women have lost their lives because of domestic violence. Last year across Australia, that number was over thirty-five.' She fixes her gaze on a Channel Seven reporter in the front row, then shifts it to the white-toothed man in front of Oli. 'Over. Thirty. Five. Women,' she repeats. 'Of course, any death is tragic, but these women didn't die in accidents or from illness. No. They died because someone decided to cut their lives short. And I don't know about you, but I'm getting pretty fed up with these statistics. I'm getting pretty fed up with the *murder* of innocent, vibrant women. As you know, domestic violence is an issue close to my heart, and I'm pledging to do more to put a stop to it.'

There's a smattering of applause from the rear of the room.

'We don't know that this woman is a victim of domestic violence, though, do we?' Oli whispers to TJ. 'Unless the cops already know who did it . . .'

'She doesn't miss the opportunity for a campaign speech,' TJ whispers back.

It's no secret that domestic violence is an issue Clarissa Dunkley's known to be passionate about. Before she switched to politics, Dunkley was the CEO of Women's Inc, an advocacy group focused on improving the lives of marginalised women and widely credited for weeding out problematic managers across a range of industries in the wake of the global #MeToo movement. Her extensive experience in community and stakeholder engagement, plus her popularity with Gen Z voters, made her an obvious choice for Labor preselection. She was briefly named opposition health minister before becoming opposition leader when the former premier resigned due to an unexpected illness. Twelve months later, she was elected premier. It was a swift ascent by any measure and came with a whirl of positive feminist PR.

Dunkley and her husband Shane Willoughby—a former high-profile swimming coach who trained four Olympians before he moved into commentating and sports management—are known for their ambition, philanthropy and activism. They met during their first year at the University of Melbourne, and the rumour goes that Willoughby proposed within weeks and that Dunkley turned him down, but they stayed together; he proposed another three times before she finally agreed to marry him two decades later, on the condition that he organise the whole thing. His impressive event-planning skills are documented on his Mr_Dunkley Instagram page. Oli suspects that the story has been embellished by the Labor PR machine, their hearts set on connecting with young woke women; Chelsea has pointed out that this is exactly what a cynical elder Millennial woman would think.

What isn't ambiguous is that Dunkley's post-election glow has started to fade. Her party has compromised on key environmental issues, has admitted to budget blowouts on major infrastructure projects, and has been accused of branch stacking and illegal donations. All of this has fostered a general sense that Dunkley is struggling to control the more traditional members of her party; it's widely speculated they're envious of her immense popularity. She's taken a hit in the polls, and the weekly column inches dedicated to questioning her leadership are stacking up.

TJ moves his head to mutter into Oli's ear: 'I guess she knows Bryson is nowhere on this issue, whereas it's her bread and butter.'

Dunkley reads out a brief biography of a woman from regional Victoria who was killed on 5 January, beaten to death by her husband following an argument.

TJ's jaw tenses, but Oli isn't sure if it's in response to Dunkley or the plight of the murdered woman. He's not a fan of Dunkley. Oli suspects the premier's socialist agenda clashes with his views on business—and he thinks she has an intense personality and her husband is a sap.

'It will be interesting to see how Bryson responds to this,' TJ murmurs. 'He'll need to tread very carefully.'

The leader of the opposition, Victor Bryson, has little in common with Clarissa Dunkley. Born into wealth, he turned to politics after a successful corporate career, most notably as Qantas CEO during its most profitable three years of operations in the early 2000s. He's married to a woman who has never worked outside the home, and they have four sons, all of whom married in their twenties and work in finance and law. The family home has been featured in style magazines, with his wife pictured cooking in her breathtaking kitchen or picking herbs from her chef's garden. Bryson isn't shy about enjoying the finer things in life, having recently celebrated his sixtieth birthday with a small gathering on his luxury yacht. A self-declared family man, he has happily deemed himself enemy number one of the woke left.

Dunkley frequently dismisses Bryson and his views as out of date and out of touch, but her party's recent mismanagement of budgets and the public disquiet about her senior team have seen her opponent land some heavy blows. The *Victoria needs Victor* campaign line the Liberal party soft-launched at the end of last year is picking up momentum.

Dunkley concludes her speech with some words from the murdered woman's sister and father, pausing to look around the room, her dark eyes gleaming. 'These family members and friends are living with impossible grief, and now another woman has lost her life. Her name is Lyra Makris.'

The journalists in the room who weren't aware of the name scramble to type it into Google and various social media platforms.

'Or Lyra Mak as she was known to her family and friends.' Dunkley coughs softly and runs a finger under each eye. 'Another woman robbed of her future, and another family broken in half. She leaves behind a community that will never recover from the shock.'

An air conditioner rumbles to life at the rear of the room, and there's a collective sigh of relief from those in its proximity.

Dunkley's hands are curled around the sides of the lectern. 'The horrible news about Lyra's murder hits especially hard because she was known to my family.'

Murmurs move like a Mexican wave through the room.

Oli and TJ exchange a puzzled glance. Dunkley's three children, a son and two daughters, are in their late teens and early twenties—perhaps they knew Lyra.

'Lyra was a wonderful young woman with everything to experience, her whole life still to live. And I am so, so sorry that we let her down. Of course, every woman impacted by domestic violence has loved ones, hopes and dreams. None of them deserve to have their dreams cut short. None of them want their legacy to be their tragic demise.'

Oli looks across at the police commissioner, whose round face is hard to read. Behind him, Rusty is standing with a group of his peers, his hands laced together, a solemn expression on his face. He's had a haircut, and she's pretty sure he's wearing a new suit.

She knows how happy he is with his recent promotion to superintendent, how seriously he takes the job. When they were together their drive was common ground, their intrinsic sense of purpose something they didn't need to explain to each other. At the time, she found their similarities concerning. The easiness felt too bland compared to the mesmerising thrum of excitement that she felt every time she interacted with Dean Yardley. She and Rusty weren't right for each other back then, not exactly, but she regrets breaking up with him to be with Dean. Somehow Rusty is exactly the same as he was back then but also totally different.

Oli tries to catch his eye, but his attention is fixed on Dunkley. She feels a familiar pulse of uncertainty as she observes him. She wishes she knew what was going to happen between them and whether or not to be optimistic about a shared future. Should she move on?

'I want a safe world for my children and their friends,' Dunkley is saying. 'I want all young women to be ambitious and active in our community, to take up space, to have opinions, to stand up for what they believe in, without fear.' She swallows, her jaw clicking noisily into the microphone. 'I don't think this is too much to ask. It also isn't too much to ask that we report on this issue in an appropriate way—that we think about the language we use and the words we choose. It starts and stops with us, and I implore you all to help me stop it.' She virtually whispers this last line, and her delivery has the desired effect.

It seems like everyone in the room is holding their breath.

Oli notices a tall young woman standing with Dunkley's staffers: Wendy Willoughby, the eldest daughter, a model turned social media influencer. Both Willoughby girls have been blessed with wholesome good looks, a blend of their parents' best features, tanned limbs and long, sun-kissed blonde hair. Wendy's younger sister Bronte is an aspiring musician. Both have large social media profiles and appear to have embraced having famous parents.

The son, Cole, a former professional athlete turned high-school teacher, has a less public profile but made headlines several years ago when he started a relationship with Ms Melbourne—real name Michelle Glass—a woman from the western suburbs who built a large following in the early Instagram days based on daily posts on things to see, hear, do or eat in Melbourne. Along with almost half a million other people, Oli follows her and enjoys her quirky and authentic reviews.

Dunkley lifts her chin and makes her petite frame seem as authoritative as possible. 'Let me be clear: this issue *is* my priority. I know the opposition and some corners of the media have a lot to say about what I should and shouldn't be doing, and what I should and shouldn't be drawing attention to, but nothing is more important than women feeling safe and valued. There's nothing more important than protecting women from being *murdered.* Make no mistake, domestic violence is terrifying, and it's not acceptable. *None* of us should accept it.'

There's a loud whoop, before murmurs rumble across the room again.

Oli finds herself unexpectedly emotional at the premier's words. Violence against women has underpinned most of her podcast investigations over the past few years, and the more stories she has covered, the more hopeless the situation has felt. For a leader to stand up and publicly declare it to be so important means something.

'Thank you for your attention. Commissioner Lew will now provide a briefing regarding the circumstances of Ms Makris's homicide. Before he does, I'd like to take a minute to honour her memory and send love and support to loved ones experiencing the most unthinkable pain. Thank you.' Dunkley's dark eyes execute a swift sweep of the room as if daring anyone not to participate, before she bows her head.

A phone rings, there are shushing sounds, then everyone is quiet with their heads tilted forward.

White Teeth steps on Oli's foot again, and she scowls and shifts it out of the way.

Her mind's eye keeps serving up the horrible image that was sent to her phone. When she tried to call the number there was no answer and no voicemail. She was about to call the cops, but TJ suggested she talk to Rusty first.

She looks back to where Rusty was standing, but he isn't there, and she can't see him with the cops on the other side of the lectern. She sends a quick message to his personal phone. *I need your advice.* In a separate text, she adds, *Off the record*, not wanting him to think she's mining him for information.

At the podium, Dunkley lifts her head and blinks several times, giving the impression she's woken from a deep sleep. A big part of her personal brand is her seemingly endless energy reserves, but today Oli thinks she looks tired.

She trades places with Lew. While not known for his youthful exuberance, he looks particularly weary as he shoves his hands in his pockets and rocks back on his heels. 'We're dealing with a highly sensitive scenario.' His voice booms across the room, so different from Dunkley's melodic tone. 'Like the premier said, we need to work together, especially as we are dealing with someone who has reached out directly to the media.' He pauses as chatter flares up again. 'Come on now. Quiet please.' He holds up a hand, which has the desired effect. 'In addition to some correspondence sent to a news organisation early this morning, alerting us to Ms Makris's death, we believe several people in the media have been targeted in the hours since. They have been sent a graphic image of a deceased woman.'

TJ and Oli exchange another glance, and Oli's heart rate surges.

Lew pinches the bridge of his nose then resets his gaze on the crowd. 'We are not yet in a position to confirm whether the same person is responsible, but it seems likely. Based on the extent to which this person concealed their identity, we can conclude we are dealing with someone—or someones—with considerable technical skill.' Lew gives the impression of being in control, despite the information he is delivering making it clear this is not the case. 'If you have received correspondence of this nature, we want to hear from you and will provide information on a number to call momentarily.' He leans forward and hugs the lectern with his forearms, his hands gripping the corners. 'I am aware the image is already in circulation, which is causing her family a great deal of distress. We are working with various publications to have it removed. If you have received this message, you are not to share it. This is a serious police matter, and I will remind you that a family is suffering and needs answers. I want our resources focused on the right things, not slapping criminal charges on members of the media.'

White Teeth lets out a low whistle and raises his eyebrows. 'We're not the enemy, mate,' he mutters, and the woman next to him bobs her head in agreement.

Lew recounts the scant details the police have determined the media can make public as a large photo of Lyra Makris is shared on the screen behind him. Despite the heat, a shiver runs up the length of Oli's spine.

CHAPTER EIGHT

TUESDAY, 21 JANUARY, 1.41 PM

Pen watches the press conference online at her desk, taking small bites of her salad roll in between replying to emails and making phone calls. She likes Premier Dunkley and found her appointment refreshing after the procession of self-important middle-aged men being in the driver's seat, but she's finding the tone of this press conference a little odd. Plus, the premier alluded to a personal connection with Lyra Makris, a detail that wasn't mentioned in the briefing earlier. Understandably, this is bound to make Dunkley more emotional. Although her contained rage is appropriate for the circumstances, it's unusual for a leader to express such raw emotion. Still, Pen supposes anything that might help stop the onslaught of violence is worth a try. She really doesn't want to keep looking at photos of dead women.

Calling Makris's friends is depressing work too. They're all keen to help despite their overwhelming shock. They repeat the same things over and over—*I can't believe this, I don't understand, this is a nightmare*—clearly wanting Pen to say something that will help. Their grief bites at her, and her left foot has started to twitch involuntarily. If only Lyra Makris hadn't gone to the party. If only some psycho hadn't decided he had the right to end her life. If only the police could do what they are supposed to do and keep people safe.

She and Silverman have agreed that Ned Higgins needs more follow-up, especially seeing as one of the friends said he asked Makris out over Christmas. It's also unclear how close Higgins is to her ex-boyfriend, James Delway, despite what he said in the interview. Pen's quick internet search unearthed photos featuring the two men on a bachelor party weekend in Sydney last year and on a beach trip in November. She's also uneasy about the industrial cleaning Higgins arranged at the house on Monday and the way he looked at her when she asked him about Delway, the strange challenge that had entered his gaze.

She drops her unfinished salad roll in the bin and turns her attention back to the press conference. Commissioner Lew is explaining that police believe Lyra went missing in the early hours of Sunday morning.

A text comes through from Barnes. *I might need some help looking into possible leads. Check out the comments.*

Pen clicks on the YouTube link in his message. It's one of Makris's cooking videos, dated just over a month ago. She's in her kitchen, wearing a navy pyjama shirt and matching silk shorts. She leans forward and speaks conspiratorially into the camera. 'Today I'm going to show you how to make one of my favourite brekky meals in less than five minutes.' Smiling, she cracks an egg into a bowl then shakes in some herbs and spices, her easy narration complementing the upbeat music that plays softly in the background.

As Makris explains how she likes to grate some chorizo into the egg mixture for an extra kick, Pen scrolls through the six hundred comments.

I love you.

You're so beautiful.

You have no idea what I would do to you irl.

Your face is okay but your body is average

Lyra please cook for me!

All the messages are accompanied by love heart emojis in various colours, or music notes, or the yellow kiss face, or flames. Some of the messages are in other languages: French, Spanish and a few Pen doesn't recognise. She's never understood the desire to interact with strangers like this. The outpouring of emotion seems pointless—an unnecessary endorsement of whatever mundane thing a stranger is doing online. It's all so fake.

She keeps scrolling through emojis, until her eyes snag on the word 'bitch'.

I hate you you stupid bitch.

The username is Davey_David411. She clicks on the hyperlink, and a dummy account loads with no image and no followers. She returns to the comments, scrolling past a few more hearts before she sees a message from Good_one##.

I love watching you, Lyra. You're so hot. Next time I say hi maybe stop and talk to me and don't be such a rude bitch.

The hair on the back of Pen's neck prickles, and her face flushes. Who are these creeps? What kind of person spends time writing messages like this, setting up fake accounts. But of course, she knows what kind. It's young guys, old guys. Married guys and single guys. These messages aren't even too bad considering the swill of shit that exists online, but the last one implies a physical interaction. Did Lyra have a stalker?

Clicking on the username, Pen is taken to a profile with a picture of a dog, some kind of husky. This user has just over five hundred followers and engages with a bunch of rock band and film profiles.

She calls Barnes. 'See it?' he asks.

'The guy saying hi and then calling her a bitch . . . ?'

'Yep. The same username left her Facebook messages as well—all about how hot he thinks she looks and always including abusive language. The IT team traced him using his email address to a Hamish Atwell, a physiotherapist from Richmond with three kids. He doesn't have a record. As far as I can tell, she never responded.'

'A lot of people receive abusive messages,' Pen points out. 'I'm not sure it means anything.'

'The internet is the fiery bowels of hell,' Barnes agrees matter-of-factly. 'But this guy seems persistent, and he lives pretty close to her apartment. I'll follow him up after I'm done here.'

Pen wonders how Makris felt receiving such a strange catalogue of unsolicited comments. She interacted with a lot of her followers, often liking their messages and replying to their questions, so she must have noticed abusive ones. Did she ever feel scared or overwhelmed? She would have had to compartmentalise it somehow.

'Where are you?' Pen asks Barnes.

'At Lyra Makris's office in the city, about to interview the next bunch of her co-workers. I spoke to her boss, and I can tell being here is a total waste of time. She only started working here a few months ago after a friend got her the gig, and she barely knew anyone else.'

Pen empathises. Grunt work is unavoidable but frustrating when an officer's time could perhaps be better spent elsewhere. On the off chance even the smallest speck of gold will turn up, they will keep panning through the detritus of this dead woman's life. Pen thinks about Makris's poor mother and clenches her jaw, turning it into a dam against the emotion that threatens to spill out of her.

'Did you see any of the presser?' she says quickly.

'The campaign launch, you mean?'

'It was a bit like that, wasn't it?'

'Look, whatever's going to poll well, I guess,' he says. 'Clarissa Dunkley is always—' There's a muffled sound. 'I've got to go, Pen. Buzz you later.'

She takes a sip of water and rubs her eyes, turning down the volume on the livestream of the press conference, which has descended into a long-winded Q&A session about police funding and a lack of resources. The premier and the commissioner look like tired boxers determined to go another round.

Turning to her list of Makris's friends, Pen picks up her phone—but before she can input the next number, a WhatsApp message from Mia, one of her old schoolfriends, appears on her personal mobile. It's an invite to birthday drinks in early February. Another message follows. *Hope you can come. Are you good? Free for a drink this Saturday night? I'm not seeing that weird accountant guy anymore—but have been seeing W again. Lots to tell you! x*

Mia is a teacher who seems to believe that because they're both public servants, their jobs are similar. Pen replies that she'll call Mia later.

Next, Pen calls Makris's uni friend Brittney, who also attended Higgins's party on Saturday. There's no answer. Frustrated, Pen leaves a message asking Brittney to call her back.

The press conference is still going, and she turns up the volume in time to hear an ABC reporter ask if the police have any suspects yet. She turns it down again.

Rolling her shoulders to release tension, she enters the number of Yvonne Gilchrist, who initially raised the alarm to Makris's mother about her being missing. Yvonne answers, sounding closer to five rather than her real age, which is twenty-three.

Pen quickly identifies herself. 'How are you holding up?'

Yvonne sniffs and murmurs, 'I'm okay.'

'I'm putting together a timeline of the weekend Lyra went missing. I believe she called you on Saturday. From her phone records, it looks like you spoke for several minutes.'

'I *saw* her on Saturday.'

Pen's spine contracts into a straight line. Timelines are so often the key to making progress on a case and this hadn't come up in the initial interview with Yvonne, although she had been so distraught that it had been abandoned after only a few minutes. 'You saw her?'

'Yes.'

'I don't believe we knew about this,' Pen says.

'I told the officer I first spoke to after Lyra's mum reported her missing,' Yvonne says, sniffing.

Pen silently curses their internal processes. 'What time did you see her?'

Yvonne starts to cry. 'Around one o'clock.'

Pen steels herself against Yvonne's sadness. 'Where did you meet?'

'At my apartment. I live in the city, near the market.' Yvonne attempts to control her emotions by taking a deep breath. 'Lyra called me. She—' Her voice cracks painfully before she murmurs, 'She wanted to borrow a dress.'

Pen recalls the stylish black dress Lyra was wearing in the social media posts. 'To wear on Saturday night?'

When Yvonne loses the battle against a tidal wave of sobs, Pen winces. After a few moments, the young woman continues speaking, now in a detached monotone. 'She wanted to borrow a dress of mine that she's always liked. It cost a fortune, and she never spent a lot of money on clothes. Her passions were cooking and travel. She bought herself a four-hundred-dollar saucepan for her birthday last year, which I thought was totally insane.' Yvonne gives an odd little laugh that sounds like a dog whimpering.

'So, Lyra called you to see if she could come over to borrow your dress. And she came to your apartment at around 1 pm?' Pen wants to get the details straight; she needs to nail down as many minutes as she can of Lyra Makris's final hours.

'Yes.' Yvonne's voice rises as she wails again. 'And now I can't stop thinking about her wearing my stupid dress when she died.'

Murmuring words of comfort, Pen knows there's nothing she can say to make Yvonne's grief go away.

After a minute or so, Yvonne's sobs subside once more, and Pen gently asks her about Makris's visit to her apartment.

'She was only at my place for about half an hour.' Yvonne's voice shakes ominously. 'She wanted to find a hairdresser who would squeeze her in later that afternoon. She told me she wanted to look good for some new guy she'd met. But I'm pretty sure it was because she'd heard her ex, James, was going to the party—and she was still obsessed with him, even though he's an arsehole.'

'How is he an arsehole?' Pen presses.

'He's very manipulative.'

'If you know something about James Delway you need to tell me. We can—'

'Do you know he hit on me before he started seeing Lyra? He was full on,' Yvonne chokes out. 'And then, when they were a couple, he would always say dodgy stuff to me behind her back. He was so outrageous, like he thought he could get away with anything.'

Pen's heart thuds loudly in her chest. Was Yvonne jealous? Making excuses? Was there something between her and Delway, or is she simply standing up for her friend posthumously?

'Did you ever see anything that made you worry for her safety?'

'All I know is that he didn't deserve her,' Yvonne replies vehemently. 'And she didn't deserve this.'

CHAPTER NINE

TUESDAY, 21 JANUARY, 2.04 PM

Oli and TJ move with the throng, shuffling out of the stuffy room, along the corridor and through the Parliament House security doors, making their way down the concrete stairs onto Spring Street.

Oli listens to the frenzied speculation about Lyra Makris's murder. Her peers are vampiric, eyes glowing and teeth bared, saliva dripping from their mouths as they feast on the juicy story. Their anticipation will be shared by their audiences, who—while genuinely distressed by the violence inflicted on a young woman and the threat her attacker presents to the community—will inhale every detail they can find, then wait for new information to drop so they can analyse and debate it. Everyone will bemoan the capacity men have to kill, while scrutinising what Lyra did, or didn't do, to wind up dead.

The words 'serial killer' swish past Oli's ears like wind in tall grass.

Women in tailored dresses take up position at the bottom of the stairs and blot their faces with tissues, quickly applying lipstick and smoothing their hair before summoning solemn smiles. On the nod of their camera operators, they launch into a breathless summary of the press conference. A couple of photographers head further along the street to the concrete nook at the side of the building to smoke and scroll, and a few print journos Oli recognises talk into their phones, promising copy within the hour. Gone are the days when a piece could be drafted and rested, then reviewed a few hours later over a glass of wine before being sent off to an editor. Speed is its own currency. The future is fast, and accuracy is increasingly becoming an optional extra.

Oli watches a young woman talking quietly into her iPhone, staring at the other journos with disgust. She's dressed in a crumpled white T-shirt with *STOP THE PRESS* printed on the front. 'It's not ethical,' she says, her voice rising. 'A woman has been *murdered*. There's no way I'm writing something like that. It's gross.' She stamps her booted foot.

A few metres away from the stairs, a man with thick black-rimmed glasses and a mustard satchel walks backwards as he films himself with his phone, AirPods wedged in his ears. 'It was here, at Parliament House in Melbourne, that Premier Dunkley confirmed a serial killer is on the loose and targeting young women. I've already shared some videos to my page of the woman who went missing on the weekend for you all to check out, and now I'm going to see if I can find a cop who will talk to me. But even if I can't, don't worry, this is an evolving story and I'll be posting all night.' He embarks on an awkward backward ascent of the concrete stairs, still filming.

Oli has an impulse to shout at them all to stop, to tell everyone just to sit and think for a moment. There's no denying she's part of this world, but it often infuriates her, and at times like this she feels deeply ashamed. Not least because of the burning desire coursing through her body to shape her own version of the story and to find out everything she can about Lyra Makris, whose gruesome death is forever frozen in time for the world to see.

An attractive woman in a designer shirtdress is doing a live cross back to a news desk. She adjusts her earpiece and makes a listening face, her shiny dark hair falling theatrically over her left eye. She straightens and nods grimly at the camera. 'That's correct, Ed. The police have no suspects at this time but seem very worried that the killer will strike again.'

Oli and TJ don't speak until they're a safe distance from the crowd. He indicates that they should cross the street, and as they walk in time to the electronic pulse of the green man, she wonders what he's thinking. She doubts he despairs at the state of their profession the way she does, but she knows he worries whether they have a strong future in it. Confidence is TJ's secret weapon, and for as long as Oli has known him, it has manifested success. But she senses he's starting to acknowledge that when it comes to the success of their business, there are forces outside of his control. He can't make people value the kind of news they offer; he can't make people subscribe to their podcast or e-blasts. He can't predict whether all their hard work will be worth it in the long run.

They reach the footpath and walk a few more steps, sidling up against the wall of a hotel. 'Let's get a drink.' TJ gestures to the European, one of Oli's favourite restaurants.

She looks at him, surprised. 'What, now?'

'We can log the main points from the press conference, then get Chels to edit and upload it. Come on, Ol. We're always chained to our desks.'

She knows he didn't mean it as a dig at her but she feels defensive.

He must sense her mood dip. 'All I mean is that we're either in the office or out working on a story. After this morning, we've earned a nice glass of something and a meal that doesn't come out of a packet. And it was supposed to be your day off. So come on, my treat. We're as on top of things as we can be, and the cops aren't going to give us anything else today.'

Feeling disorientated, Oli steps past him as he holds the door open. She breathes in, enjoying the pleasant musky scent of the restaurant. A compact waiter expertly steers them to a table near the window. Oli's stomach signals its hunger with a soft gurgle, and she feels relieved to be sitting down after standing for so long at the press conference.

Vignettes from her doctor's appointment swirl in her mind alongside grabs from Dunkley's impassioned speech. The whole presser was surreal but also validating. Just as she's putting the finishing touches on her DV investigation, the issue has been propelled into the spotlight.

'We should try to interview Dunkley,' Oli says to TJ.

He opens his laptop and types in his password. 'About Lyra Makris?'

'Yes. But also about the broader issue of DV. She could be my guest for the final podcast episode—the missing ingredient.'

TJ's eyes glow approvingly. 'Good idea. There's a lot you can grill her on, based on that performance today.'

He types copy about the presser, and Oli texts a freelance photographer they often use to see if they can purchase some shots of Dunkley and Lew speaking. This is how they've learned to do news. She laughs when she thinks about how they used to complain about the resources at *Melbourne Today*; in hindsight, they had an embarrassment of riches. But the content they create from scratch is some of the highest-quality journalism out there. As Oli watches TJ type, she feels the same fire she felt when they first set out on their own.

Her phone lights up with a reply from the freelancer. 'Micky is sending you a couple of pics to use,' she tells TJ.

He nods but doesn't miss a beat, his fingers as fast as those of a concert pianist.

Oli calls the police hotline to report the text she received, then contacts Chelsea to let her know a piece is incoming for review.

Putting her phone down, she attempts to relax. She looks around at the other tables. Couples. A handful of colleagues. An elderly woman and a young man who is most likely her son. They all laugh and talk, oblivious to the horror that TJ is writing about mere metres away.

Oli wonders if any of them have an invisible illness.

She and TJ order—a prosecco for him and a G&T for her. Dr Fraser didn't say anything about not drinking alcohol, but maybe she didn't feel she needed too. Oli feels a rush of irritation. Surely one drink won't make a difference. She's not even a big drinker—not compared to her sister, Lily, and most of her friends. Even TJ and his wife, Carol, the fittest people she knows, drink more than she does. She used to smoke—is that why she's ended up with cancer? She supposes it might be genetic. She barely knows anything about her father's family, and up until now she's wanted to keep it that way. He already robbed her of a happy childhood; perhaps he's not yet done causing her pain.

A robust woman wearing a stylish vest over a crisp white shirt places their drinks in front of them, just as TJ announces his piece is done. Oli quickly reads it over and makes two minor corrections before they send it to Chelsea. The waitress returns with complimentary servings of crusty bread and olive oil mixed with a dash of balsamic. Oli rips the dense bread in half and pushes one piece into the shallow dish, watching the little black beads merge with the yellow oil before taking shape again.

As TJ chews, Oli senses him transition from frenzied bloodthirst to business mode. Cool energy radiates from him as he sips his prosecco and gets out his notepad and expensive pen. Carol gives him two pens with his name etched on their sides every year, one for Christmas and one for his June birthday. Oli notices that his white shirt has tiny blue noughts and crosses embroidered on the collar. He flashes her a smile as he checks his phone, then twirls his pen between his fingers. She and TJ shouldn't make a good team, and yet they do.

Oli thinks of the call with Marion Disney. What had surprised her the most wasn't just the call itself, although it was out of the blue, but her reaction to Marion's offer. She was flattered and tempted. Two radio gigs had been presented to her over the past few years, but never anything like this: the lead anchor of such a high-profile show.

Her eyes meet TJ's, and she senses he's about to bring up their argument. She feels an intense desire to fold her arms and refuse to engage. She doesn't want to talk about this again, not today. She's not sure she's feeling strong enough to say what she needs to say.

'What?' she says, looking up at him from under her lashes, a challenge.

He leans forward. 'We need to make a big splash with this story.'

She pushes the ice blocks around her G & T with the straw, thinking about the microplastics that are probably penetrating her bloodstream. 'What do you mean exactly?'

His eyes glow with intensity. 'We need to take some risks. We need to *break* the news, not just report it. I know it's not our style, but the slow and steady approach isn't working hard enough, and I think being bold is our best chance at getting our numbers up.' He holds up his hands defensively. 'To grow the business and put on more staff, we need more clicks and a shitload more subscribers—and you know it. This isn't me being difficult or a sellout, this is just the facts.'

'I know,' she murmurs.

She hates that the commercials matter so much, but she'd be a fool to pretend they don't. The news isn't their own private art project, and they're not writing stories and recording podcasts for personal fulfilment. They are in the business of engagement. They are in *business* full stop. They have staff and invoices to pay. They need ears and eyeballs, and they need them coming back for more every single day.

She has realised that there's no finishing line in business. It's a beast that needs to be fed, day in, day out. If she's honest with herself, she's tired of the self-editing. Her brain now automatically considers how a story will play with the audience, whether a headline will make someone click, whether one of her podcast episodes will convince someone to fork over ten dollars a month to access their bonus content. The pride she has about what they've built is marred by the obligation she feels to feed it, a constant pressure on her chest. It reminds her of the way some of her friends speak about motherhood: the exquisite pain of being needed.

Some of Marion Disney's words replay in her mind: 'I know what it's like to run a business but still be on the tools. You could just jump ship and leave all the hustle behind. If you take the job at Air 24/7, you can be in control without having to do all the legwork.'

It's an undeniably appealing proposition, but the thought of pulling the pin on her dream and of abandoning TJ and the team is still unfathomable.

She tries to keep her voice neutral: 'You obviously have a plan already.'

He pushes his drink to the side and tips his head forward. 'We need another *Housemate Homicide*.' His voice is strong and clear as he refers to one of their most popular series, the one that started her career in podcasting.

'You mean . . .'

'We need to do frequent podcast drops on this, and we need you to front it. We need you on your own, talking to Victorians about what Makris's murder means, especially considering Dunkley's presser.'

He's right. Their listeners will want her take on the investigation, and they'll want her voice. It will drive incremental subscriptions and give Yael something meaty to sell.

Nothing about it is a bad idea, but Oli feels a rising tide of dread. She's not sure she can do the investigation justice. She's not sure she's the same person she was before she found out she has cancer.

'But we can't afford for me to be taken out of daily news right now. We're struggling with the amount of content as it is, and Chelsea's good, but she's not particularly fast . . .' For some reason Oli wants to push him on this. Maybe it's a test; maybe it's because she's not sure what she wants. 'Okay, so say I'm out of action for the next three weeks while this story plays out. How are you going to handle the daily articles and the podcast drops?'

'I want to hire Spencer McIntyre,' says TJ calmly.

'The ABC guy?' She hears the scepticism in her voice and says more evenly, 'Surely he's not going to leave a steady job for a role with us.'

'He's good, Oli, and he's keen. We've been chatting a bit, and he's ready for a change. He really likes what we're doing at *Newsday*.'

'I don't know him.'

'But I do. You'll like him. He's smart. Diligent. Would make a good buffer between us and Chelsea.'

'Hang on, you want him to be a part of the team? A permanent hire?'

TJ fills his tanned cheeks with air before he exhales. 'Yes. I want someone who knows what they're doing to come in and report the news. Someone who can write stories and lead investigations and proof Chelsea's work.' He grimaces and holds up his hand to get the attention of the waitstaff. 'I thought this is what we've been arguing about . . . ? You said we can't keep doing it all.'

'I can't—I'm drowning in work, and I'm struggling to get to these deep dives that drive subscriptions. It's not sustainable.'

'But?'

She's worried she's going to yell at him—she imagines herself doing it—but manages to say, 'No buts. I'm just nervous about making changes. I'm not sure if Spencer is the right solution.'

TJ's intense gaze is fixed on her. 'How about I ask Spencer to come in for a few days next week?' he says finally. 'Between you and me, he's resigned from the ABC and is considering his next move, but I think he'd take a fixed-term contract or even just freelance with us for a bit.'

'Sounds like you have this all figured out.' Her tone is sulkier than she intended.

'Oli, this isn't an ambush. We need another grown-up in the mix, and Spencer is a grown-up who also happens to be a well-respected and versatile reporter.'

'Even if I was all in with your plan, we can't get an episode out tomorrow. We barely got any info from the presser.' Her phone rings, and she looks down at the screen. 'It's Rusty.'

TJ's eyes bulge with excitement, and he works his jaw at double speed to swallow a polenta chip. 'Answer it!'

Her phone to her ear, Oli turns to the window. 'Hi, Rusty.'

'I got your message. Everything all right?'

His voice weakens her already compromised resolve, and she tips her head against the wall, feigning concentration as she fights the prickling of tears in her eyes. Rusty was one of the only people she wanted to talk to after the appointment this morning, but it would be unfair to burden him with her bad news when things are up in the air between them.

'I'm fine. Turns out I'm one of the journos who was sent the photo of Lyra Makris. Don't worry, I've called the number from the press conference and will follow it up later.'

'Make sure you do.' Rusty's voice is strained. 'We need every piece of evidence we can get on this guy.'

'Of course. How are you holding up? This is so intense.'

'Yes.' He offers nothing else, and Oli feels a stab of loneliness.

'Anything you can tell me?' she asks just as something to say, without genuinely expecting information.

'No, Ol. This is being tightly held, as you can imagine. Honestly, it's like nothing I've ever seen.'

TJ gestures for her to ask him a hard-hitting question.

She shakes her head at him but asks Rusty, 'Did Lyra Makris have a boyfriend? Or an ex?'

'Ol, come on. This is all still being worked through.'

She barrels on. 'The killer obviously has tech skills. Maybe it's someone who works in IT. Are you looking at someone with a criminal record?'

'Oli!' Rusty sounds pissed.

She shifts her gaze back to the window and watches a male pigeon puff out his feathers and strut in a circle to impress his bored-looking mate.

'I called to check you were okay, *off* the record,' Rusty snaps. 'Today's been a lot.'

A siren whoops in the background, and she hears the chatter of a police radio before he mutes the phone. The voice sounded urgent.

'Rusty, what is it? What's going on?'

There's silence for a few seconds, then his voice returns alongside a wailing siren. 'I've got to go. You'll understand shortly. I'll call you later.'

He hangs up, and the waiter returns to clear their plates.

TJ's phone flashes. He scans it then waves his hand to get her attention, holding out his phone to show her a message from Spencer McIntyre, their potential new hire.

Her heart beats like mad as she reads. *Mate, we're hearing a body's turned up at Fishermans Bend. We think it's the woman from the photo.*

CHAPTER TEN

TUESDAY, 21 JANUARY, 3.42 PM

Overhead, the trucks on the West Gate Bridge sigh and groan like old men. The afternoon sun struggles to penetrate the air, thick with smoke from the raging bushfires in New South Wales, and the resulting muted light gives the scene a dystopian feel. *The end is nigh*, Pen thinks grimly, wiping perspiration from her brow as another bead of sweat snakes down her spine to join the wet patch above her belt line.

An amateur birdwatcher called triple zero just before 2 pm, worried that something caught in the reeds looked like a human foot. He was right.

Before long, a crime scene was established. A rescue unit extracted the body of a female from the water, and a flimsy white tent has been erected to shield the corpse from view. Another white tent has been set up next to it, enabling evidence to be photographed, bagged and tagged away from the greedy eyes of the swarming media and a growing number of curious onlookers. There are at least twenty cops on-site already, along with forensics and a pair of divers.

Pen continues her solo line search, pausing as she uses tongs to collect and bag fresh-looking cigarette butts and a broken silver necklace. She feels uneasy, distressed on behalf of the dead woman in the tent and the unavoidable scrutiny her remains are being subjected to.

After speaking to Yvonne, she and Silverman hauled James Delway into the station and interviewed him. Makris's former boyfriend is arrogant, that much is clear, but he's also smart, refusing to talk without a lawyer and implying that they were wasting their time, seeing as he had an airtight alibi.

Pen sighs. The apartment Pen and Barnes searched this morning speaks of a perfectly normal life, a life of small things and big things, friends and family. Hopes, dreams and admin. Presumably, the young woman had no idea that her life was about to be cut short and that everything she'd ever worried about, worked toward and planned for was suddenly irrelevant. Pen wants to grab the throat of the person who did this and squeeze until they know what it's like to feel the fear that only comes when death is inevitable.

She takes another step, and the anger morphs into a despair that causes her knees to buckle. It's been happening with increasing frequency: an intensity grips her body before being abruptly replaced by an overwhelming sense of pointlessness. She's gone from having an almost evangelical sense of pride about her work to something akin to shame at the lack of impact it has.

She feels embarrassed when her mother talks about her job at family functions. During her brother Walter's birthday dinner last week, Pen snapped at Marnie to shut up, mumbling that her job really isn't that important, causing everyone present to avert their gaze and comment brightly on the deliciousness of the food. Walter tried to talk to her afterwards, but she brushed him off, not knowing how to explain what was wrong. She's aware her self-loathing isn't particularly constructive, but she can't seem to stop herself.

Maybe she should talk to Barnes about it. He's a good listener and tends to have good advice. Plus, he's clearly worked out a way to reconcile the limitations of the job with the good that can be achieved.

After reaching the cyclone fence, Pen walks back along the same strip of ground, making sure she hasn't missed anything. Rejoining her colleagues near the water, she watches as two cadaver dogs are released from the back of a car. Leashes are swiftly clipped onto their collars as they bounce around, eager to do their important work.

A text arrives: Silverman informing her that a witness from the party claims he saw James Delway out the front in a car around midnight. Pen tells Silverman to let her know when they can schedule an interview with Delway and his lawyer, then shoves her phone back in her pocket.

Barnes trots toward her from the forensic tents, where he was just talking to Sanders. He's subtly shaking his head. It's not Lyra Makris.

Pen feels relief, then guilt, followed by a frisson of fear. Silly to think this nightmare could conclude so quickly.

'Are they sure?'

'Yep. This one is white and blonde.' Barnes pauses and looks out to the horizon. 'There's a tattoo on her foot, and she's wearing a wedding ring.'

Pen inhales sharply. 'Mackenzie Jackson?'

'Yeah.' His expression is hard to read, but Pen knows he is thinking about his sister. She was killed by her husband just over a year ago.

Out of desperation to find someone to blame, Barnes's parents focused their rage on him. He was the experienced cop who should have, could have, saved his sister. Over a few too many beers one night, he admitted to Pen that he had suspected his brother-in-law of being violent, that he knew things were bad for his sister and had even spoken to his wife about it. He'd started stage-managing family gatherings, doing everything he could to reinforce what a great life his brother-in-law had, trying to ensure he didn't leave an event too boozed up or in a bad mood. He tried to talk to his sister about it too, but they weren't particularly close, and she deflected his loaded questions, making it clear her marriage wasn't up for discussion. He hadn't pushed it. Pen assured him that it wasn't his fault, but she can tell that he wears his sister's death like a heavy chain around his neck, one that tightens just a little more every time he's confronted with another woman murdered like she was. Pen wonders if this is what caused his separation; on some level, maybe he wants to punish himself.

Her thoughts shift focus from the tragic demise of one woman to that of another. They're different yet somehow the same. 'Does Douglas Jackson know?' she asks Barnes.

'Not yet. Although everyone is desperate for a formal ID because of the Makris case.'

Looking over at the white tent that conceals Mackenzie Jackson's body, Pen experiences an alarming rush of surreality. Her brain seems to be struggling to reconcile that the woman whose image has been splashed all over the news for two weeks is lying there dead.

In that time, Mackenzie Jackson has taken on a mythical quality, etching out a place in the folklore of the city, her name familiar, her pretty face as recognisable as that of a celebrity. Lyra Makris is on the same trajectory: her horrific death will undoubtedly be more memorable than her life.

Pen turns her head to the rabble of reporters who have appeared behind the police tape on the thin wedge of dirt to the side of the river. Two camera operators have removed their boots and stand in the water, getting shots of the bridge. She trails her gaze up one of the support columns to the elevated road and the impenetrable fence that runs along the side. Years ago, a man threw his four-year-old daughter from the bridge, his response to a custody battle with his wife. The state government soon erected fencing along both sides of the bridge, making it near impossible for anyone to jump or be thrown off. The family violence statistics since that incident have skyrocketed, but no one seems to know quite what to do about that. Only so many fences can be built.

'There's no way Jackson fell,' Pen says to Barnes. It's not a question.

'No,' he says, also looking up at the bridge. 'And there's no way she strangled herself.'

Pen clears her throat and surveys the media throng. At least twenty journos are present, all clamouring for something they can take back to their editors, a mouse to deposit at the feet of their insatiable audience. Pen pictures the little ticker that runs along the bottom of the TV news reports, a case summarised in a few words. *Woman found dead, suspected murder, police investigation continues.*

Pen once considered a career in journalism. She used to be good with words, but an ill-fated overseas holiday after high school—which saw her unceremoniously dumped in the middle of Paris by her much older boyfriend—meant she returned to Australia wanting, no *needing*, to do something more physical. She still religiously follows the news and takes an interest in the different mastheads, the new formats the networks are trialling, and the different industry personalities. She recognises several faces now. Glamorous women from TV, men with suspiciously taut skin and slicked-back hair. All wearing their crime scene outfits: cropped jackets and boots rather than dresses and heels.

She spies Olive Groves the podcaster, Frost's ex. Like a lot of people, Pen loves the woman's distinctive voice. Pen listens to her *Newsday* podcast most days, often at the end of a shift when she's in her bath, the water as hot as fire, scented candle burning, glass of wine in hand. 'Self-care,' she tells her bulldog, Elliot, who watches her intently as she ignores the mould on the ceiling and the relentless dripping of the kitchen tap that the landlord seems determined to avoid fixing. She lies in the scalding water, willing herself to relax, hoping the bath will counteract whatever horror she has been exposed to that day. She also enthusiastically consumes every deep-dive investigation Groves does, no matter the topic. There's something inclusive about her investigative style; it feels like Pen is right there with her, rolling up her sleeves, gently but firmly examining the facts of a story.

As Pen watches Groves now, she thinks how strange it is that she's heard hours and hours of her talking yet they've barely met. She supposes it's no different to the parasocial relationship she has with a lot of the journalists at press conferences and crime scenes, but the familiarity feels more pronounced with Groves. Presumably it's because of her connection to Frost. Taller than most of her peers, the podcaster keeps to the back of the media pack as she talks on the phone. Her hand is held to her throat, the tendons of her fingers flexed.

Barnes sidles up to Pen again. 'I'm heading back soon,' he says. 'The boss wants me ready to interview Douglas Jackson. They're pulling him in now.'

'Sorry. Who asked you to head back?'

'Frost. I think he wants some continuity now this has flared up again.'

Pen is annoyed that Frost hasn't asked her to return to the Jackson case. 'But what about the Makris case?'

'I think they're just having to make calls as they go, Pen. I'm an obedient pawn in the great game of policing.'

She feels torn. What he's saying makes sense but she wants to be there when they confront Douglas Jackson about finding his wife's body. Being in his house and listening to him talk about his missing wife was one of the most infuriating experiences of her career. Everything was telling her that this man was dangerous, yet so far they haven't been able to pin anything on him.

'Will Douglas ID her?' she asks.

'They'll get the brother or sister to do it. Anyway, I'll let you know what happens.'

She nods, not wanting him to see how disappointed she is. Perhaps Frost wants to keep an eye on Barnes, if he's still worried about him. Or more likely he prefers Barnes over her. Barnes is obviously more experienced, but Pen had made it clear to Frost how much she wants to work on the Jackson case, so it does feel like a snub. She chastises herself mid-thought: she and her feelings of inadequacy must be the last things on Frost's mind.

A shout erupts from behind the media pack, and she and Barnes strain to see what's going on. A camera operator has inched past the police tape and is being reprimanded by one of the detectives. Metres away, shadows move inside the white tent, the forensic team hoping to find clues on Mackenzie Jackson's corpse.

Pen watches as Olive Groves stares at the tent. She looks sad, anguished almost, before she tosses her head and turns toward the bridge, her jaw set. Last week Pen heard Groves advertise an upcoming special investigation series on domestic violence on her podcast, and she wonders if Mackenzie Jackson will feature.

Beside her, Barnes shoves his phone into his pocket, muttering under his breath.

'What?'

'I've got to go.'

She's startled at the urgency in his voice. Before she can say anything more, he rushes off toward the car park.

Perplexed, Pen walks back toward her colleagues. Frost has arrived and is talking to the coroner. The older woman's dark face is grim as she follows the line of his finger, confirming where the body was found.

Pen considers speaking to Frost about staying on the Jackson case, but she imagines how silly this would sound. She doesn't want to irritate him or come across as difficult.

Her phone vibrates with messages and emails, and she figures she should head back to the office and continue to unpick the final hours of Lyra Makris's life. She and Silverman need to follow up the alleged sighting of James Delway at the party and they need to review whether anything useful has turned up from Ned Higgins's security footage.

She wonders whose job it will be to tell Lyra Makris's mother that the body found dumped in muddy, rubbish-clogged water is not her daughter's—and Pen shudders at the thought of the poor woman's impossible reaction.

'Hey! Stop!'

Pen spins around. A tall man with a shaved head, dressed in black, has got past the security tape and is sprinting toward the white tents. '*Lyra*!' he yells.

On autopilot, Pen runs over.

The man can't get to the tents. He mustn't.

Hoping to stop him, she propels herself forward, aims her body like an arrow and leaps into the air.

The assembled camera operators lift their equipment and start shooting like crazy.

CHAPTER ELEVEN

TUESDAY, 21 JANUARY, 4.07 PM

A seagull is held in place by the strong breeze until it flaps its wings and lands on a wiry shrub. Safely moored, the bird cocks its head as if trying to make sense of the crowd. Stepping away from the group, Oli makes a few voice notes on her phone to capture the scene as best she can, hoping the recording will be audible over the sound of the wind. These days, she finds she can remember details better with audio references, and she likes to play back her recordings as she writes late into the night. Sometimes she uses her raw grabs in her podcasts, and listeners seem to appreciate her descriptions of scenes and her unedited thoughts.

Oli squints into the sun and takes in the city skyline, the light bouncing off its mirrored windows. Now the distraught man has been escorted away, the scene has returned to its previous calm state. No one seems to know who he is, but he clearly has a connection with Lyra Makris: he screamed her name repeatedly as he pushed the crowd of journalists out of the way and broke through the crime barrier, fighting off several cops attempting to restrain him before they wrestled him to the ground just outside one of the white tents.

Oli recognised one of the detectives who tackled him: the petite young woman who reports to Rusty. Kibbs. She came out of nowhere, and despite her small stature, seemingly had no qualms about leaping onto the man's back.

When Rusty and Oli had dinner in mid-December, he told Oli he was finding Kibbs difficult to manage and hard to read. Oli suggested that perhaps Kibbs was trying to prove herself and that she felt intimidated about reporting in to him, a notion that Rusty promptly dismissed.

It was this conversation that led to Oli telling Rusty that she thought they should give their relationship another try. 'Why do you think it's so unlikely she finds you intimidating?' Oli said. 'You're tall, you're handsome, you're empathetic, you're an incredible detective. It makes sense that she thinks you're . . .' She wasn't sure how to continue.

'What?' he asked, blue eyes blazing.

'Impressive,' she murmured, unable to look at him.

Oli shakes the memory from her mind. She said her piece; it's up to Rusty now.

She returns to the crowd of journalists standing near the fresh police tape. She nods politely at the familiar faces, but no one initiates conversation. The mood is sombre, more so than usual, but there's something else too: competitiveness. This is the kind of story that can make or break a career. Put one foot wrong, and you might be cancelled; be the first with a lead, and you'll be a hero.

That's why no one's talking, Oli thinks. *No one wants to share anything*. She avoids eye contact with the two journos in front of her and watches the cops instead.

The forensic team move between the two tents, holding cameras and various tools of death. Detectives talk to each other in small groups, their expressions grim.

Oli wonders if they will confirm the ID soon. They'll need to advise the family first, but with a case like this they're better off sharing information quickly or the news will be filled with speculation. She assumes the police want to avoid the public being whipped into even more of a frenzy.

Her phone vibrates in her pocket, and she steps away from the crowd, keeping her eyes trained on the detectives. Once she's out of earshot, she says, 'Chels, what have you got?'

'You're at the crime scene, right?'

'Yes.'

'Have the cops made a statement yet?'

'Not yet. Why?'

'It isn't the woman from the photo this morning.'

Oli's eyes widen. 'How do you know?'

'From Facebook. I tracked down the birdwatcher who found her. Before the cops got there today, he posted a video showing where he was and the birds he was looking at, so I figured it was him. He was the only person that posted anything relevant to the area, so I took a chance and called him.'

'You called him,' Oli repeats.

'Yep.' A hint of pride comes through in Chelsea's voice. 'His number was on his profile page. He said he thinks the body he saw is the missing mother.'

Oli's eyes dart around before she hisses into the phone, 'You mean Mackenzie Jackson?'

'Yes. He said he got a good look at her before the cops arrived.'

'Holy shit, Chels. Jesus.'

'I know.' Chelsea manages to sound devastated and excited at once. 'Is Rusty there? Could you get him to verify it?'

Oli holds a hand up to her head trying to think. 'Absolutely not.'

'Oli, you should be milking that coconut and making fancy cocktails.'

'I'm not asking Rusty about this,' Oli says firmly. 'Did the birdwatcher say anything else?'

'No. He was still at the scene when I called, and the cops got to him and made him hang up on me.'

Oli walks further away from her peers and spies a lean, elderly man in a navy shirt, tan shorts and hiking boots, sitting on a camping chair next to a stationary ambulance. His grey hair is arranged around his head like a scraggly doughnut, and the perfectly round bald patch in the centre glows red. Birdwatching paraphernalia circles his neck: a whistle, binoculars, a camera and, puzzlingly, a large torch. His left knee is jiggling uncontrollably.

'He's still here. Good work, Chels.' Oli knows praise is Chelsea's favourite love language.

'I've got more,' she says eagerly.

'I'm listening.'

Chelsea gives a dramatic sigh. 'I've got some photos and videos from the party Lyra Makris went to on Saturday night. It looks wild.'

'How did you get those?'

'I know a girl who was at the party.'

'Of course you do.'

'A couple we can't use—they'd make her look bad—but there are some good ones. I think you'll be okay to publish them.'

Oli allows a smile. Just over a year ago, they had a huge disagreement about a photo Chelsea wanted to use to support a story she wrote. Oli deemed its use unethical because of the way it portrayed a victim of sexual abuse.

'Send them to me, and I'll take a look.' She holds her phone out and goes to the photo app. 'And I'll send you some images of the scene here. Can you get them up on the site with a few lines of copy? I want to get this live asap.'

'Can do.'

Oli sends Chelsea the best of the photos she's taken since she arrived. 'Get TJ to help you. Just make sure he knows nothing has been confirmed yet.'

'Can I mention my witness source?'

Oli pauses. 'You'll need to get the man's consent.'

'He told me he's happy to be quoted.'

'Text him, get him to confirm. And please make sure it's clear we're not claiming anything. This is going to get very political, so be extra careful.'

'Will you cover this in your podcast series? Mackenzie Jackson, I mean.'

Oli closes her eyes. 'I'm not sure. I need to think about it. She might just be the full stop in the final episode.'

'There's been another DV case this afternoon,' Chelsea says. 'A murder-suicide.'

'I shouldn't have said "full stop".'

'It's okay,' says Chelsea. 'I know what you meant.'

'What happened?'

'An elderly couple in Donvale. That's all we've heard so far.'

'Keep me posted,' Oli says feebly. Her energy is fading fast.

'These photos you've just sent are depressing, Oli.'

She looks back to the white tents, which have a steady stream of uniformed people coming and going. 'The whole scene is pretty depressing.'

'I'm glad I'm not there.' There's a shudder in Chelsea's voice. As cool and tough as she is, she can't handle anything gory or gross. She refused to come into the office for almost a week after they discovered a family of mice living in the stationery cupboard.

Oli ends the call just as Rusty emerges from one of the white tents. His auburn hair catches the sun and glows like fire before he steps into the shade. He looks worn out, but she supposes it's been a long year for him already. He's only two months into his new role, and three women have been killed since the calendar flipped over, four if she counts Marta Holm on Christmas Eve. Five if she counts the victim Chelsea just told her about.

The woman Oli saw at the press conference wearing the *STOP THE PRESS* T-shirt arrives, walking self-importantly over to the throng. 'What's the latest?' she barks at no one in particular, before elbowing her way to the front of the group and squinting at the nearest white tents.

Oli sidles up to a nearby tree and leans against it, relieved to have offloaded some of the pressure on her body. Her head pounds with the threat of a migraine. What is wrong with her? Surely the cancer isn't suddenly making her feel like this. Maybe it's psychological; she's heard about the mind creating physical impediments.

She quickly types an email to Chelsea. *Check this copy with TJ and get it ready to publish once you hear back from the birdwatcher. I'll head back to the office soon.*

Pressing send, Oli pushes away from the tree just as a loud voice says, 'Right, everyone, listen up.'

Rusty is herding everyone away from the police tape, clearly trying to put some distance between them and the body lying in the white tent. He interrupts himself to take a phone call, tilting his head the way he always does when he's concentrating. When they were together, Oli used to tease him about that face; she would say, 'I can literally see you thinking.'

He ends the call and squares his shoulders. 'We're asking everyone to move on now.'

A groan rises from the group, and one of the camera operators swears as he adjusts his equipment and almost trips on a tuft of grass. A few reporters start yelling out questions.

'We appreciate your interest, but we won't be making any formal announcements about the body discovered here at this time. We have family to consider and a scene to process.'

The woman in the T-shirt cries out, 'This is bullshit! Women are *dying*, and we need answers!'

Oli stumbles slightly at the rear of the group, her hand over her eyes to block the glare of the sun, which appears to be strobing, casting beams of white-hot light onto the city.

'When we are in a position to share more, we will.' Rusty holds out a hand apologetically and takes a step back, almost as if he thinks that will be the end of it.

The crowd surges forward and shouts questions at him in an uneven chorus.

'What did Lyra Makris's family say when you told them about finding her body?' yells a journalist from Channel Nine who used to habitually ask out Oli by firing details at her.

Rusty ignores him, but the questions keep coming.

'Do you have any suspects?' 'Is there anything significant about this location?' 'Is there evidence of sexual assault?' 'Did Lyra know Marta Holm?'

Oli realises that thanks to Chelsea, she's the only journo here who knows the body of Lyra Makris isn't in that tent. The assumption is unsurprising considering the recency of Lyra's disappearance, but this means Oli and TJ really do have an exclusive on their hands. *Familiarity breeds context.* Oli frowns and squeezes her eyes shut. *No, that's not it. Familiarity breeds . . .*

The ground lurches beneath her as the world turns white. Staggering forward, she scrambles to stay on her feet. 'No!' she cries out. Or maybe the word was just in her head.

Oli collapses to the ground, shielding her head from a sharp rock with her arm.

Everything keeps spinning, even after she's certain she's stopped moving. For a horrifying moment, she's not sure which way is up—but then someone gently tilts her head and lifts her chin, efficiently arranging her into a sideways position.

I'm being given first aid, Oli thinks, recognising the movements. She blinks and focuses her eyes on Detective Kibbs's worried face. Her lips are moving but no sound is coming out. Oli notices she has a slightly swollen lip from tackling the intruder. 'Hi . . . Olive? Olive?'

Her short light brown hair is pulled back from her face, and her skin is pale and unblemished. Oli wonders when all the grown-ups started to look so young.

'Olive?' Kibbs's voice is sharper now.

Oli swallows and nods. 'Oli.'

'Do you remember me? We've met before. Can you please tell me your full name?' She's speaking very slowly, and Oli understands she's trying to make sure she hasn't had a stroke or some kind of episode.

'I'm sorry, I think I fainted.'

'Yes, I think you did.' Kibbs lifts Oli's head and slides something soft underneath it. Her movements are understated but confident, and despite the circumstances, Oli feels safe. 'It's probably heat stroke.' Quietly, Kibbs adds, 'Unless you have any pre-existing conditions?'

Oli shakes her head.

'I'm going to get an ambulance officer to check you over.' Kibbs rocks onto her heels and pushes herself to her feet, gesturing at the semicircle that has formed around them. 'Please, give us some space.'

There's a blur of faces above Oli, and she feels embarrassed to be lying on the ground in front of her peers. Her competitors. She vaguely wonders if Chelsea has published her copy yet. Her phone buzzes in her pocket as if to answer her question.

'I'm fine.' She arranges her hands on either side of her head and pushes herself up, but her elbows feel weak. She concedes, dropping her head back against the soft jacket.

Kibbs doesn't comment on her failed attempt to sit upright, but she gestures for an ambulance officer to come over.

From her spot on the ground, Oli can hear Rusty wrapping up his impromptu press briefing, explaining that there will be a formal update as soon as they have undergone due process. Part of her wants him to come over; the other part of her hates the idea of him seeing her so vulnerable.

Before she can wonder any more about Rusty, an ambulance officer introduces himself and presses an open water bottle into her hand. Once she's had several sips, he takes her blood pressure and asks her a few easy questions. Oli answers them and, after a few moments, allows herself to be helped to her feet and onto a nearby chair.

TJ calls her mobile, and she hopes like hell he hasn't seen her on the news passed out on the ground.

'Keep up your fluids and take it easy.' The ambulance officer clips his heels together, swings his bag over his shoulder and heads off.

'Your colour has improved.' Kibbs is still standing beside her. She doesn't make eye contact when she talks. Then she tips her head to the side with a questioning look.

Oli shakes her head. 'Sorry, what did you say?'

'I asked you if you drove here . . . ?'

'I got a taxi. I'll be fine.' Oli waves unconvincingly toward the remaining journalists who are recording soundbites or talking into their phones.

Kibbs nods and smiles tightly, signalling the end of their interaction.

'It's not Lyra Makris over there, is it? It's Mackenzie Jackson?' Oli speaks quickly, wanting to get a reaction, knowing this might be the only chance she gets to verify the identity of the body before the official press conference.

Kibbs moves her head back sharply and purses her lips. 'I'm sorry, I can't discuss that with you.' Pink colours her pearly-white cheeks.

'Are you going to charge the husband?' Oli presses. 'Is this the evidence you need?'

'I can't tell you anything, you know that.' The tendon in her neck pulses, but her voice remains even.

'I know you're investigating rumours that he abused her. I've spoken to a family member who told me about an incident in a shopping-centre car park before Christmas, and I have another source who claims he locked her out of the house overnight a few years ago. Has there been any further evidence to confirm Douglas Jackson's whereabouts the night his wife went missing? Are you concerned about the safety of their children?' Oli sweeps her hand toward the white tents, her voice charged with emotion. She feels the opposite of faint now; blood pulses through her limbs, and she navigates the incongruent push-pull of seeing the story as a tangible thing she can grab and hold in her hands, kneading the mess of it into shape.

Kibbs's jaw jerks a few times before it hardens. 'Our investigation is ongoing, and the press conferences will include all relevant information. I think you should go.'

Rusty strides over, covering the short distance in just a few steps. 'Is everything all right here?' His tone is businesslike, but he can't hide his concern.

'Totally fine,' Oli says, giving him a professional nod.

'I'm heading back to the station, sir,' Kibbs announces. To Oli, she says stiffly, 'I'm glad you're okay.'

'What happened?' Rusty asks, after Kibbs leaves. 'Someone said you collapsed . . . ?'

'I had low blood pressure or something.' She waves off his concern. 'How are you? I'm hearing that—'

His expression darkens, and he snaps, 'Not with this one, Oli. I came to check that you were okay. Just back off for once in your life.'

'Rusty, I—'

He leans toward her and hisses, 'This is my job, Oli. It's not just about what you want.'

He leaves her staring after him, mouth open in surprise.

CHAPTER TWELVE

TUESDAY, 21 JANUARY, 6.56 PM

Pen remembers her mother saying you should never meet your heroes because they'll only disappoint you. She declared this at the dinner table one evening, after pestering her favourite Aussie soap actress for her signature in the waiting room of a physiotherapist. The actress had politely declined, citing a sore arm, and Marnie had huffily shuffled away to sit in the opposite corner of the waiting room, no doubt glaring daggers at the injured soap star.

'She's so much nicer in the show,' Marnie told her family snootily later that evening.

'She's *acting* on the show, Mum,' Walter replied, rolling his eyes.

Marnie chewed angrily on her steak. 'Well, she could have bloody acted when she met me today and not been such a bitch! I'm not going to watch her scenes anymore.'

Pen and Walter exchanged glances, trying not to laugh. But now Pen experiences a rare stab of empathy for her mother. Driving back to the station, Pen decides to cancel her *Newsday* subscription.

It will serve Olive Groves right. Just as Pen was helping her, she went straight into journalist mode, grilling her without even saying thank you.

Pen isn't sure why she feels so affronted by this interaction. Rationally, she knows it's Groves's job to ask questions. Maybe it's the way Superintendent Frost rushed over to check if the woman was okay that annoys Pen. Or maybe she's annoyed at herself. The answers to Groves's questions were written all over her face.

Pen steps into the Makris case room, looking for Silverman. The case meeting is about to start, an hour later than originally planned, and she figured Silverman might be here, but the room is empty. After Hamish Atwell was restrained, Pen remembered his name: the man who was leaving comments on Makris's social media profiles. She called Silverman from the car, suggesting they arrange an interview with Atwell's wife, but now she can't find her.

After leaving her a message, Pen closes her eyes, frustrated. She rubs her aching shoulder, bruised from tackling Atwell to the ground. He was injured during the incident and is in hospital under police guard with suspected concussion, refusing to say a word.

Pen realises she hasn't seen Barnes since she got back either and texts him just as Frost and Sanders enter the room, followed by several detectives and uniformed officers. Frost gestures for them to take a seat as he faces the group. The events of the day have aged him, and there's a slump to his shoulders that wasn't apparent at the crime scene.

He tells the room what they already know: Mackenzie Jackson's body was discovered in the swampy water earlier today, and the circumstances suggest she was killed at the time of or just after her disappearance two weeks ago. Douglas Jackson remains a person of interest due to the alleged abuse that occurred during their decade-long relationship, but there is still no evidence to indicate he killed his wife.

'I know there will be speculation about this, so I want to be clear. There are no known links between the disappearance of Lyra Makris and the murder of Mackenzie Jackson. We are treating them as separate cases.'

Barnes texts her back. *Caught up with something. Will see you tomorrow.*

Pen frowns. He's not usually so obtuse. She wonders where he is.

She's still staring at his text when Frost says, 'I wanted to give you this update directly, as I know a lot of you put in the hard yards on the Mackenzie case before you were moved off. Those remaining on the case will pick it up from here, and we'll do our best to get a result. I know there's circumstantial evidence to suggest Douglas Jackson is responsible for his wife's death, but we need to keep an open mind. He has an alibi for the night his wife went missing, and while his movements over the subsequent days are still being investigated, we need to explore other options.'

Pen feels a primal need to continue working on Mackenzie Jackson's case, especially now her body has been found. Barnes said from the start that her husband must have killed her in the days after she stormed out of the house; that she fled somewhere known to him, and he went there and killed her, away from their family home and security cameras. And increasingly, Pen is inclined to agree.

'Mackenzie Jackson's autopsy will be conducted tomorrow afternoon,' Frost continues. 'We're planning a morning press conference, and I do not want this information leaking prior.'

Pen grimaces, thinking again of Groves. She wonders if she should tell Frost that his ex-girlfriend has already worked it out.

Exhaustion envelopes Pen, and she feels desperate to be home with Elliot. She wishes she could teleport herself to her apartment.

'I'll leave you in the capable hands of Sanders,' Frost says. 'We appreciate your flexibility as we navigate these cases. We'll continually be reviewing how resources are allocated as things evolve.' Frost nods at Sanders and makes his way to the back. He spots Pen and pauses.

'Grab a water or a coffee, everyone,' booms Sanders, parading across the front of the room like a sports coach. 'We've got a ton to cover off.'

'Good work today,' says Frost, dropping into the empty seat next to Pen as most of the room's occupants get to their feet to seek out caffeine. 'I mean, both chasing down Atwell and helping Oli.'

'Oh.' Pen hates that she's flustered. 'No worries on both fronts.'

'And you did solid work on the Jackson case. We'll get there on that one, don't worry.'

'Thank you, sir. I'm glad she's been found.' It's on the tip of her tongue to ask him why he doesn't want her to keep working on the case.

'Hopefully we'll find Lyra Makris soon. Give her family some reprieve.' Frost grimaces, then he smiles at Pen, looking her straight in the eye. 'I know you'll do solid work on her case too.'

She nods and repeats, 'Thank you, sir.' She can't ask him about working the Jackson case now, and she wonders if that was his intention all along. Instead, she says, 'Olive Groves was asking a lot of questions today. I think she already knew it isn't Makris's body.'

Frost looks at the case boards along the side of the room, chewing his lip as he considers this information. 'She does ask a lot of questions,' he says finally. 'She's a good journalist.'

'Are you all set, Kibbs?' Sanders re-enters the room, holding a large bottle of water. He takes an obnoxiously large swig and gestures for her to move to the front. 'Lots to do.'

'I'll leave you to it,' Frost says vaguely. He nods at Sanders and exits the room, passing Silverman on her way in.

'Atwell's wife is here,' she announces. 'Interview room three.'

'We'll be back,' Pen says, walking out before Sanders has a chance to reply.

A tall woman with cropped blonde hair smiles nervously at them as they enter the room. Her nursing scrubs feature a colourful blue-and-green pattern.

'Is this about Hamish?' Briony Atwell's voice is high-pitched and doesn't suit her size. 'The girls are at swimming training. I just checked to make sure, but I can't get on to Hamish.'

Pen introduces herself and Silverman. 'Your husband is fine,' Pen assures the woman, 'but I do need to give you some information that might be upsetting.' She explains what happened at the crime scene earlier and that they suspect Hamish contacted Makris online.

Briony doesn't move, just shifts her eyes from Pen to Silverman in disbelief.

'Ms Atwell?' Pen prompts.

'Hamish is in hospital?'

'Yes.'

'Can I see him?'

'Yes. You will be able to see him. But, Mrs Atwell, I need to ensure you understand that it's likely your husband will be charged with several offences based on what occurred today. Do you understand?'

Briony drops her head so dramatically into her hands that Pen worries she might hit it on the table. After a few moments, she stammers, 'I . . . This doesn't make sense.'

'We know this is difficult. Has your husband ever mentioned the name Lyra Makris?'

Briony lifts her head, eyes brimming with tears. 'No. Never. I have no idea who she is.'

'Were you aware that he was behaving like this online?'

'I didn't, I just—' Briony draws a sudden breath through her nose and tries to compose herself. 'I had no idea.'

Pen pounces on the thread that the woman has inadvertently exposed. 'Briony, this is incredibly serious. Your husband is going to be investigated—every detail of his life, and yours, will be turned upside down—so if you know anything, it's best you tell us now.'

Tears glitter in Briony's eyes. 'I don't know the woman you're talking about, but there was another woman a few years ago.' She leans forward, her expression pleading. 'It was a big misunderstanding, but she thought Hamish was stalking her. And he wasn't! He was a physio at the gym she went to, and he was just being friendly. It got sorted, but I don't want it to cause any issues now.' A tear escapes her eye and jags down her cheek. 'Sometimes Hamish is taken out of context. He would never hurt anyone.'

CHAPTER THIRTEEN

TUESDAY, 21 JANUARY, 7.12 PM

Oli is too hyped to go home. She parks her car in the basement of her apartment building and takes the lift to the foyer to collect her mail from the letterbox. Shoving three bills into her handbag, she exits through the main doors and walks the short distance to Oxford Street, where there is a vibrant strip of shops and eateries. The air has cooled only slightly, and a hot wind ruffles the trees.

Up ahead, soft yellow light radiates from the windows of her favourite restaurant, highlighting groups of diners seated at tables covered with red-and-white chequered cloths. Oli enters Tomato Tomato and immediately feels better. It's run by thirty-year-old male twins, Luca and George.

Luca accosts her and holds out his arms for a hug. 'Big day out there?'

'Big day out there,' she confirms, hugging him back. Her eyes fill with tears when she thinks about everything that has happened since this morning.

'You sit. I get you some bread.' He points to one of the tables in the corner that he knows Oli prefers. 'A drink also?'

'Just a soda water please.'

He catches his brother's eye and snaps his fingers good-naturedly, gesturing at Oli. 'Sparkling water for our special lady.'

George nods and flashes a smile at Oli, who can't help but grin back. She's sure the twins have their problems like everyone else, but they hide them well. They are relentlessly positive and perpetually tease each other with little digs that only serve to demonstrate the genuine appreciation and respect they have for one another.

George brings her the water and a menu, even though she knows it by heart. For a few moments she sips her drink and takes in the scene. She assumes most people here saw the news today and felt shocked and sad about Lyra Makris, but right now they're enjoying dinner with their friends and choosing not to think about the darkness that runs in alarming proximity to the light.

Thoughts of her cancer creep in. She pushes them away, telling herself there's nothing she can do until she meets with the surgeon.

Luca returns with her drink and two slices of their signature tomato garlic bread, and he takes her order for the Napoli pasta.

In anticipation of the cops making a formal announcement about Mackenzie Jackson's murder, Oli starts to draft a piece for the site using the shared Google drive she has with TJ so he can see what she's writing. She devours the bread in between paragraphs, weaving in all the details they've accumulated over the past fortnight. It will be both a tribute and a summary of the investigation, and as soon as the police confirm the ID, it will be sent as a special subscriber email blast with a teaser published on the main site.

Oli toggles to the screen featuring the photo of Mackenzie Jackson that her husband released to the press when her disappearance was made public. She's smiling, Douglas's arms are around her, and there's a cute dog at their feet. She looks happy, and she and her husband make an attractive couple. Oli stares into Douglas's face until the image becomes grainy. Is his expression perhaps a little smug? His hand a little too possessive around her shoulder?

The police have made no comment about Douglas being a suspect since the initial press conferences. With no arrest made, she can only assume they have either discounted him as a suspect or are biding their time until they have enough evidence to pin on him.

She looks at her phone. She wants to call Rusty.

As if on cue, her phone vibrates across the table. But it's her ex-fiancé, Dean, FaceTiming her. It's been years since they broke up, and they haven't spoken in months. At the sight of his handsome face on her phone screen, she is gripped so forcefully by nostalgia that her breath catches in her throat. She considers not answering but quickly decides it's better to find out what he wants. No point adding to the reasons she won't be able to sleep tonight.

Slipping her AirPods into her ears, she props her phone against the water jug and accepts the call. 'Dean, hey. What's up?' Oli focuses her gaze slightly above the screen but makes out his dark hair and tanned face in her peripheral vision. She knows he uses video calls because he thinks that if she sees his face she will find it harder to be dismissive. Dean works in PR and is good at getting what he wants. For a long time, it seemed like he wanted Oli, but she knows now it was always ultimately about Dean wanting control. She resists the temptation to look into his eyes now, not interested in testing her ability to resist his charms.

'Oli, hi. Jesus, how are you? I thought of you today. God, what a mess it is out there.'

Irritation courses through her. Trust Dean to open the conversation with that, he obviously wants something and is trying to get her onside. He was never particularly supportive of her journalism career when they were together.

'I'm fine, thanks. Busy, obviously.'

He ignores her subtle hint to get on with it. 'That poor Jackson woman.'

'The cops haven't confirmed it's her yet,' Oli says automatically.

'Sure. But it is, right? I saw your article. You've got a source, and I can read between your careful writing. You would never publish something if you weren't sure. Too much integrity.' He manages to make this sound like a character flaw. 'And that other story? The one with the dead influencer girl. Fuck, it sounds insane. I'm guessing there'll be some late nights ahead for you. And TJ, of course.'

Oli refuses to react. He always hated her having male friends and was intimidated by TJ, no matter how many times she made it clear their relationship was purely professional. Dean's paranoia is especially laughable considering that he started seeing their neighbour Toni less than a month after they split, a woman whose unashamed flirting Oli had been forced to tolerate throughout the duration of their relationship.

'What do you want, Dean?' she says pointedly.

He pauses, and she finally allows herself a proper look at his face. He bites his lower lip and casts his eyes down. If she didn't know him better, she would think he's nervous.

'Dean?' she presses.

He shifts his gaze so that his blue eyes bore into hers. 'Oli, I need your help.'

She looks over at the kitchen and catches Luca placing a sticker from a pasta packet on the back of his brother's shirt. 'Why, what's happened?'

'It's about the girls. It's about Amy.'

Oli is caught off guard by the emotion that seizes her entire body. 'Is she all right?'

'Physically she's fine. But fuck, Ol. She's done something really stupid.'

Amy and her twin sister Kate were almost Oli's stepdaughters. They were never close, though, and she's unsure if that was because her relationship with Dean was so fraught or because they resented her for not being their dead mother. Or maybe they were just too different from Oli to click with her. Whatever the reason, she found them hard to win over, and she hasn't made much of an effort to stay in touch. The girls must be almost thirteen now.

'Tell me.' She's apprehensive about inviting Dean to confide in her, but her curiosity is sparked. There's also a tiny part of her that is pleased he has come to her for help.

Dean has always been attracted to ambitious, assertive women; once he's in a relationship with them, he resents their autonomy and rails against the very characteristics he was drawn to in the first place. When they were together, her career became the enemy; he didn't like the way she prioritised journalism over family life. She supposes none of that matters now.

'She, well, she . . . Oh god, I honestly still can't believe it, Ol. A boy from her school filmed her.'

'Filmed her as in . . .'

'Yes. He took photos and videos of her naked. Topless, to be specific.'

Oli is finding it hard to reconcile the picture she has in her head of Amy with this type of sexually charged scene. Dean must be beside himself. He is ferociously proud of his daughters, but he's very strict, carefully managing their extracurricular activities and making it clear that he expects them to be above average in everything they do. Oli suspects he's never cautioned them about sexting or creating sexual content because it never would have occurred to him that he needed to.

She keeps her voice calm. 'That's not good.'

'It's a bloody nightmare!'

Dean has never been good at regulating his emotions, and he doesn't cope well when things don't go his way. Oli thanks the universe she doesn't have to navigate parenting two teenage girls with him. She would have been lumped with the bulk of the responsibility and blamed for any issues.

Taking a sip of water, she's careful not to react to his outburst. She only lived with him and the twins for less than a year but recalling that time of her life stirs up a lot of anxiety. The girls were emotionally distant, and Dean was controlling, wanting someone to pander to him rather than partner with him. Despite their undeniable passion, Oli is a lot happier now than when she was trying to second-guess his emotions, and she knows that any prolonged interaction with him is not wise.

'I could kill this kid, Oli. Honestly, I could.'

'What do you want from me, Dean?'

He drops his face into his hands before righting it and taking a few deep breaths. 'Sorry, Ol. This has been very hard. I've tried to talk to her—I have!' he adds defensively, even though she hasn't suggested otherwise. 'Clearly this kid coerced her, pressured her to let him film her, but she's refusing to talk to me. Kate's fobbing me off as well. Anyway, the parents of one of Amy's friends, Priscila, are threatening to go to the press.'

'Why?'

'Because Priscila found out about the video and told them. They complained to the school, which is how I was alerted, but they don't want to know about it. All the footage has been deleted, thank god, so as far as they are concerned, it's an unfortunate incident that everyone should move on from. I mean, I get it, the reputational damage will be huge, but the Mastersons—Priscila's family—they're determined that the school be held accountable. They're worried that since it went co-ed, the standards have dropped. Georgia, the mother, she's set up a parent group. It's active online, and they are campaigning for the school to revert to single sex and for several of the teachers they deem inappropriate to be moved on. Clearly, they've pounced on this to prove a point.'

'Makes sense,' Oli murmurs. She's still trying to work out what he wants.

'According to Georgia, this is not the only content that's been made.'

'Of Amy?'

'I don't think there were more videos of Amy,' Dean says stiffly. 'But there's definitely footage being circulated of other girls from the school and other schools in the area.'

'Where is it?'

'I don't know! On the phones of these sick little turds? On the dark web for paedos to find? I have no idea, but you need to find out.'

'*Me?*'

'It needs to be investigated. Properly investigated. Not flogged off to some tabloid for a hit piece that embarrasses everyone but goes nowhere. This whole thing is a ticking time bomb. It has the potential to ruin lives—it's bloody near ruined mine. People need to know, parents of daughters need to know what these boys are doing. It needs to be in the news.'

Dean works in PR, so he knows that once a story hits the media it can't be ignored. He's not a physical fighter; he prefers to attack with words, insinuation and the full force of public opinion. He knows the power of shame and embarrassment, and he wants to ensure these emotions are pointed away from his girls and firmly toward the boys who filmed the videos, their parents or, at the very least, the fancy school he is shelling out the best part of eighty grand a year for the twins to attend.

'This kind of thing is rife, Oli. Not just at St Mary's, but everywhere. I'm sure it's worse at the public schools. And there's no protection for the kids. It's the Wild West when it comes to the law on this stuff—no one knows how to deal with it so it just keeps happening. Amy is twelve years old, for fuck's sake. *Twelve.* And she's been forced to act like a *stripper.*' Emotion breaks his voice. He drops his head, pushing his fingers through his thick dark hair before he looks up, eyes pleading. 'It would make a great story, Ol. It's perfect for one of your deep-dive podcast investigations. I think you'd be able to make people realise how serious it is, maybe even drive some policy change. The tech companies need to take some responsibility too. This stuff is being shared on their platforms, and they do nothing.'

Oli pushes her lips together, thinking. She's annoyed but must admit her interest has been piqued. Damn Dean for knowing how to get to her. Issue-based topics are her weakness, and he's right: it would make an interesting investigation—extremely current, complex, and with real-world implications. But of course, he doesn't really care about any of that; all he cares about is getting in front of the story, of putting himself and his girls in the best position.

She sighs. 'Dean, I'm not sure that—'

'Please, Oli. At least think about it. Priscila's mum is open to talking to you, and she's great talent. I'm happy to talk to you as well, as long as I'm anonymous. And you'd obviously be able to find a bunch of experts and victims, and your cop mates. I reckon this could be massive for you and your business. People will be interested—*parents* will be interested.'

A little roll of excitement tumbles through Oli. She can feel the story start to come together in her mind. The good ones always start with a strong premise and have a mix of facts, opinion and real experiences from different perspectives.

'I'll need to speak to TJ,' she says.

'Sure, speak to him.' Dean is all confidence again.

'But even if he's on board, you know the story will go wherever it needs to go, Dean. There are no promises that it will turn out how you want it to. I have to be objective. It won't just be me either—I'll need to get a researcher. I'm too stacked with editorial and daily news.'

'Really?' Dean tips his head to the side. 'I know how much you love investigations, Ol.'

She shrugs. 'Can't do everything.'

'The perils of being a business owner.' He smiles, flashing his straight white teeth. 'Seriously, Ol, it sounds like the business is doing well. Your advertising packages have gone up, so your numbers must be growing.'

'You've been looking at our advertising rates?'

'Of course. I check in on your business all the time.'

Pride forces her shoulder blades apart. Despite everything, and notwithstanding she recently heard he was dating a thirty-three-year-old socialite, Dean's approval still matters.

'I have to go, Dean,' she lies.

He nods briskly. 'Yes, of course, I can tell you're out and about. I appreciate you taking my call. Let me know what you need from me to get this all happening.'

'No guarantees, but I'll let you know once I've spoken to TJ.'

'Great. And hey, it was nice talking to you, Oli. I do miss it, you know.'

He ends the call before she can respond. She knows this was intentional, a ploy to leave her without a right of reply, his compliment lingering for her to replay in her mind.

When Luca approaches the table, she remove her AirPods and smiles at him, but it turns into a yawn. He places the steaming pasta in front of her and refills her water. 'Everything is okay, here?'

'Everything is okay.'

He cocks his head. 'You are tired.'

'Very.'

He tuts under his breath but nods. 'You have a holiday planned?'

'No.'

'You must make a plan,' he scolds lightly. 'Good for the soul to have some time out.'

She murmurs her agreement as he heads back to the kitchen. Her cancer diagnosis means there's unlikely to be a holiday in her near future. She thinks about some of the elaborate holiday plans she and Rusty made when they were a couple and wonders if there's a chance they will get to go on them. Dean enters her mind again—trust him to contact her today of all days. She swears the man was put on this planet to mess with her.

Forcing herself to focus, she finds the voice notes she recorded earlier and plays them through her earbuds. She can smell the rotting rubbish at the edge of the water, the birds cawing ominously as they flew against the warm wind. She weaves these details through the article about Mackenzie Jackson and quickly proofreads it as she eats the rest of her food.

The second-last table of guests gets up to leave, and the staff start wiping tables and sweeping. Another yawn tears through her. She needs to try getting some sleep. She gathers her things, pays, and hugs Luca and George goodbye.

The night air is hot and still carries a hint of smoke from the interstate bushfires as she walks the short distance to her apartment. Seeing Dean has made her feel strange, like the past few years have been a hallucination. She remembers back to when they broke up and she decided to start the business with TJ, how it felt like jumping off a cliff without a parachute. This feeling lasted for at least a year, but somewhere along the way it shifted into something more akin to climbing a mountain. She's not the same person she was back then. She's stronger. Harder. She's trained herself to accept setbacks without fuss, to shake off nasty comments and mourn failures in private. She feels like a robot half the time, approaching decisions with a coolness that seems essential to doing her job. Then again, robots don't get sick. Nor do they have complicated thoughts about exes.

'Hey!' She cries out as a man speeds around the corner and slams into her.

He grabs her by the shoulders and mutters something, saliva flying from his mouth onto her cheek, before pushing her aside and running off.

Shaking, Oli wipes her face with a tissue from her bag as she watches him disappear down the street.

Once he's out of sight, she resumes the short walk home. She walks quickly to the entrance of her apartment block, forcing herself to keep her hands steady as she lets herself in. Her heart is still racing as she closes her blinds and puts away the plates she left to dry on the rack. She changes, washes her face and brushes her teeth. Setting her alarm for 4.45 am, she snaps off the light in her room and reads a few articles from US publications on her phone. The man on the street scared her, and anxiety flits around her ribcage the way it used to do when she was a child and she dreaded her father appearing in her doorway.

Oli experiences an impulse to call her mother and tell her that she's sick. Oli's surprised—she has never turned to her mother in a crisis, and she knows speaking to Sally won't provide her with the comfort she craves. Her mother is a clinically depressed, chronic hypochondriac who is increasingly agoraphobic. When she discovered the extent of the abuse her husband perpetrated against her youngest daughter, it triggered a suicide attempt. Oli discovered her mother just in time to save her life, and while she physically recovered, Sally never regained her confidence. Her guilt over what her husband did is so crippling, and their trauma so entangled, that a normal parent–child relationship will never be possible. Regardless, as Oli sits in the dark, cancer growing in her body, she wants her mother.

Rusty muscles into her thoughts, gently nudging Sally out of the way. Perhaps Oli can call him. She can apologise for their exchange earlier today, tell him that she understands he's just doing his job.

She picks up her phone but loses her nerve, deciding to text him instead. *Hey. Huge day. Hope you're going okay. I'm sorry I upset you. Drink soon?*

His reply is quick. *Thanks. Yep it's been massive. Sure. Take care.*

It's not the response Oli wanted. Frustrated, she tosses her phone to the other side of the bed and rolls onto her back. Her fingers find the small lump on her breast, and she traces it gently, watching the strange shadows of a tree dance across her bedroom ceiling.

CHAPTER FOURTEEN

TUESDAY, 21 JANUARY, 10.19 PM

Pen can hear Elliot's pitiful whines the moment she steps onto the landing. She fishes around in her bag for her keys and unlocks the door to her apartment, bending down to rub the bulldog's sagging jowls. 'Hello, beautiful boy.' She plants a kiss on his head and stares into his liquid brown eyes before retrieving his expensive dog food from the fridge.

Her mother is always bemoaning the money she spends on Elliot. In fact, Marnie is broadly negative about most of her lifestyle choices and is forever promoting the benefits of saving for a house deposit. 'A man is not a financial plan, Penny,' she's fond of saying, even though as far as Pen and Walter can tell, securing a wealthy male partner was the only financial strategy Marnie Kibbs ever pursued. 'Women today need to stand up for themselves,' is another of her favourite mantras, often followed up with, 'You need to be more independent, Penny.'

'She's a bloody cop, Mum,' Walter always replies.

Pen is only thirteen months older than Walter, but it may as well have been ten years, so different was their mother's attitude toward them. She had zero patience with Pen as a teenager and even less now that she is an adult. Walter, on the other hand, was given all the grace in the world and could do no wrong. Even now that he's in his late twenties, Marnie simply tuts when he arrives at family events late and hungover, beaming as she recounts his latest escapades at the cafe where he works as a trainee chef.

Pen knows Walter feels guilty about the favouritism. As a result he always sticks up for her, telling her family how brave she is and how amazing she is at her job—it's like having a personal PR rep. But despite his best efforts, their mother doesn't believe her profession makes her either independent or assertive.

Lately she's worried that Marnie might be right. Pen's uniform and badge used to make her feel confident and gave her a sense of purpose, and when she was first promoted to detective she felt proud and accomplished. But for the past few months she has sensed that her peers—and even members of the public—can see through her new corporate wardrobe to her festering doubt and uncertainty.

Elliot joyfully attacks his meal as Pen runs a bath. She makes a token attempt to tidy her small apartment as the water fills the tub before pouring a large glass of red and grabbing a box of crackers and a tub of hummus, placing both items on the edge of the bath. She fetches her laptop and rests it on the wooden bath tray before she dims the light and strips off her clothes, stepping into the foamy water. She inhales sharply when it hits her torso, her pale skin reddening. Breathing through the burn, she slides her legs out in front of her and leans back until she is submerged to her neck.

Her shoulder is still sore, the area already sporting a bluish hue, but mostly she's tired, the kind of tired that comes from being in proximity to tragedy. The inevitability of Mackenzie Jackson's battered body being found dumped like discarded rubbish is beyond depressing. From the moment Pen was briefed on her disappearance, she knew that the middle-aged woman was dead. She doesn't know how Douglas Jackson managed it—Frost is right, his alibi is watertight—but like Barnes, she's certain he did it.

The familiar build-up of male aggression is like a weather pattern. *Controlling tendencies with a hint of jealously are likely to lead to violent outbursts and possible broken bones this week. An intense drinking session means you should be on the lookout for bruises.* She wonders if Mackenzie Jackson had worried her life might end this way, whether she considered that her face might be splashed across newspapers and websites, her name uttered grimly by strangers as they bemoan the state of the world.

Pen polishes off the crackers and eats the remaining hommus with her index finger. Sipping wine, she checks Facebook, Instagram and Twitter. All her accounts are private, and she rarely posts anything, but she studiously keeps tabs on old schoolfriends and people from the part-time jobs she had before she joined the force, poring over their photos and reading their status updates, marvelling at the amount of information they share. A guy she dated briefly after high school has just had twins with his wife and has created the hashtag #mytwinswin. Many of her old friends have children already, chubby creatures dressed in stripey jumpsuits, with wispy hair and toothless grins. Pen just can't picture having her own child. She's not sure it's something she's going to grow into either, no matter what her mother says.

Resting her phone on the edge of the bath, she nudges the tap with her foot, closing her eyes as more hot water swirls around her body. She tries to relax. It doesn't work, and she picks up her phone and reads through her WhatsApp messages. Her mother has sent a long, convoluted message to the family group chat about plans for Easter. Pen is pleased to see that the only person who has replied so far is her cousin, Mischa, whom her mother dislikes with a passion. She screenshots Mischa's passive-aggressive reply and sends it to Walter with a laughing emoji. She replies to a thread about contributing $50 toward someone's birthday gift, then likes a few photos her friends have posted of fancy dinners and holidays.

After scanning the banter in her other group chats, she sends an apology for not being able to make drinks again the following week. She could probably get there if she really tried, but the last time she met her friends straight after work, she felt irritated for days afterwards. She can't pinpoint exactly why; it might have been the way they so easily seemed to transition from work to play, or perhaps it was the reality of how little they have in common these days. Their stories of drunken nights out and office gossip seemed so trivial. Almost offensive. When Pen tried to relay some anecdotes about her work they fell flat, viscerally pulling the mood to the floor. She quickly exits the app and puts down her phone after she sends the message, anticipating negative replies about the unreasonable demands of her job.

Pen allows her upper body to sink into the water until her ears go under. She stares at the ceiling, listening to her heartbeat. She's young. She should be out with friends or on a date.

After a few moments she pushes her feet against the end of the bath, manoeuvring her body upright, causing water to splash against the wall. She slowly and carefully shaves her legs, an activity she has found satisfying since she was a teenager. Even though she's short, she has nice, shapely legs, and she admires them stretched out in front of her.

Feeling determined, she opens Tinder, then Hinge, then Bumble. The familiar mix of dopamine and apathy surges through her body as she swipes through the photos. She's recognising some of the faces. She goes to her Tinder profile, which is the same across all the platforms. It's intentionally vague, and she only uses two photos: one of just her, backlit by the sun on a holiday in Fiji two years ago, and one of her with Elliot, his head obscuring most of her face. They provide a general sense of her features without making her recognisable. She calls herself Nel, a token nod to her full name, Penelope.

Squinting at her page, she tries to assess it objectively. It's not a very compelling sales pitch. She can't even kid herself that it's a case of quality over quantity; it simply screams that she can't be bothered, which is mostly true. Almost against her will she crafts half-hearted replies to a few of the messages she's received and deflects an offer to meet for a drink, citing a busy time at work. She deletes a message from a man threatening to hurt her if she doesn't reply. Such messages used to make her angry; now they just make her feel even more tired.

She thinks about Hamish Atwell and the abuse he unleashed on Lyra Makris. How will he explain it when they interview him tomorrow? Will he deny it and claim someone accessed his accounts, or will he try to justify his inexcusable behaviour? Based on Atwell's presumption that it was Lyra Makris's body discovered in Port Melbourne today, Pen assumes he isn't her killer . . . unless the whole spectacle was an elaborate performance. He certainly shares some exhibitionist tendencies with the killer, and Briony, his wife, admitted she was away with the kids on the weekend—so Atwell has no alibi.

Exiting Tinder, Pen refills the bath with hot water. She shuts it off and has more wine, avoiding the temptation to pick up her phone again. Of the four men she has dated after matching with them online, two were nice but not her type, one was an arsehole who fortunately ghosted her before it became a problem, and the other one broke her in every way it is possible to be broken.

Even now she recoils when she thinks about how she let him past her carefully constructed emotional security system. How she let him manipulate her and break her down until she felt like she was going crazy. And that was before he choked her. It's been almost a year, but she can still feel his fingers around her neck and recall his beery breath on her face. She thought she was going to die. She should have reported it, she should have done all the things she tells every woman she encounters in her line of work to do, but she couldn't. She didn't want to. She'd been very drunk, and the whole ordeal was hazy and confusing. Plus, she knew how it would go if she took it further, the intricacies of their relationship on display like dirty laundry, the stains exposed for everyone to examine. And she was a detective! What would it say about her instincts? All she knew was that she never wanted to see him again.

Yet he was the one who introduced her to the online portals that she now disappears into most nights. They used to spend hours interacting with strangers, and he would present Pen like a possession, asking strangers to describe what they wanted to do to her while he became increasingly aroused.

With a sense of inevitability, Pen pulls the tray closer and opens her laptop, making sure her breasts are covered by bubbles, and logs in to Chatroulette. She desperately wants to meet someone in real life and have the kind of relationship most people seem to stumble into without even trying, but the thought of going on a date is terrifying.

The green dot of the camera light comes on, and her pulse quickens, a surge of anticipation like a lightning rod through her core. She can't explain this desire to connect with strangers, but she can't deny it either. She clicks on the shuffle button, and a face appears on the dimly lit screen. A man. Dark hair, dark eyes and a two-day-old growth on the lower half of his doughy but attractive face. He looks a bit like a young Bruce Willis. He stares at her, and she stares back, an exquisite roar filling her ears. Neither of them moves for several seconds.

She has no idea who he is or where he is, and it doesn't matter: she is safe here in her home.

'Hi,' she says eventually.

'Tell me about yourself,' he says, barely moving his mouth. She thinks she can see a bookshelf in the background, the faint outline of a lamp.

'I'm Polly,' she says.

'Pol-ly.' He says the name in two beats and swallows hard, dipping his head nervously. 'And what does Polly like to do?'

She tosses her head and looks him directly in the eye, empowered by knowing she can say whatever she wants and leave whenever she wants. 'Polly works in law enforcement. What about you?'

'Well, I'm not called Polly, and I don't work in law enforcement.' He laughs loudly and takes a swig out of a bottle.

She feels nothing except the tiniest pulse of pity. If this were a date, she would be trying to work out how to leave early without being rude or awkward.

'Do you have a name?' she asks.

'No name,' he barks, his gaze hard. Another swig.

'Okay.' She shrugs, shifts her body up a little and reaches for the wine bottle, filling up her glass.

'Are you naked?'

'Sure am,' she drawls, taking a sip of wine.

The man makes a noise, something between a yelp and a sigh. Pen sips more wine. Hate bubbles up inside her, and she glares at him. Suddenly his broad cheeks make him look childish, and she notices his hair is wispy, arranged to conceal a receding hairline.

'Talk to me, Polly.' Urgency has crept into his voice, and she can tell he's aroused.

'What do you want to talk about?'

'I want to know what you like.'

From the side of the bath, her phone rings.

She almost slips under the water in her haste to snap the laptop shut and make the man disappear. Her breaths come out in abrupt huffs as she straightens and checks the screen. The call is diverted from her work phone. It's Barnes. At this hour there's no way this is going to be anything but bad news.

She dries her hand on a towel hanging behind her head and answers, hoping the acoustics don't make it obvious she's in the bath. 'Barnes?'

'Sorry, Pen. I know it's late, but Sanders just called. A body's been phoned in.'

She pushes the tray away and stands, water streaming from her and dripping noisily into the bath—but she no longer cares. 'Where?'

'Hampton. On the beach.'

Pen inhales, feeling the air go straight to her heart. 'Lyra Makris?'

'No,' says Barnes. 'But Sanders thinks it's the same killer.'

CHAPTER FIFTEEN

WEDNESDAY, 22 JANUARY, 6.03 AM

The cool water is like a balm for Oli's nervous system. For the first few laps she doesn't think, she just puts one arm in front of another, kicks her legs and follows the black line on the tiles below. She woke before her alarm went off and made a coffee as she scoured the online news and made notes to send Chelsea for the morning bulletin. As she drank her coffee, she searched up stories on revenge porn and other cyber-based sex crimes. She came across a recent *New York Times* article detailing the concerning lack of regulation in this space. She realised that various strands of Dean's proposed investigation have already started to braid together in her mind.

Ducking her head underwater, she curls her body into a somersault before pushing her legs against the tiled wall, guiding her body through the water like an arrow, holding her breath for as long as she can bear. Mouth to the side, she gulps air and torpedoes forward, her body on autopilot and her mind clear. But after several laps even the meditative effects of the water can't suspend reality for long, her mental to-do list expanding as she tires.

She needs to read the information Dr Fraser gave her and confirm the appointment with the surgeon, but an uncharacteristic childishness is causing her to push thoughts of the cancer from her mind. It feels too big, too serious, to fully immerse herself in. As she kicks off the wall to commence her final few laps, her shoulder starts to ache and the muscles around her armpits tighten.

The cancer, Oli thinks automatically, even though she knows it makes no sense.

Suddenly the possibility she might die is so intense that her entire body spasms, and she breathes in a mouthful of water, stopping in the middle of the swimming lane. She holds on to the lane rope, gulping for air as she coughs and splutters. Her tears mingle with the pool water, and she raises a hand to reassure an elderly woman in the adjacent lane that she's okay.

She swims for another few minutes, but she's lost her momentum. Strands of her long hair tangle in the rubber strap, and as she plunges the goggles back into the water to loosen them, she tries not to think about what chemotherapy might do to her hair.

Oli enters the change room and notices a sign on the door advising patrons that they are forbidden from using their phones inside and to report any concerning behaviour they witness to staff. As she showers, she thinks about what Dean told her. She knows teenagers sext, of course she does. She's covered several stories involving revenge porn and cyber abuse, and she has investigated paedophile rings and the prolific circulation of child pornography online—but she finds it hard to believe that quiet, shy Amy has been caught up in something like this. Her mind wanders to her own early teenage years, but that's not a good reference: Oli was too busy dreading her father's abuse and worrying about her chronically melancholy mother to be interacting with boys.

Still drying her long hair with a towel, she gets into her car, which despite the early hour is already an oven. She scrolls Twitter as she waits for the aircon to work its magic.

A tweet from Channel Nine: James Delway has done an exclusive interview with *60 Minutes* that will air tonight.

'God,' Oli murmurs, reading the promo grabs. *Missing girl had secret sex fetishes. Wild behaviour had me worried about her, says ex. 'Choke me' missing girl begged.* Oli feels a wave of shame on behalf of her profession. Delway sounds like an absolute creep, and he shouldn't be given a platform, especially when Lyra Makris has no right of reply. Oli feels physically repelled by this man—there's something all too familiar about his contrived concern. She assumes he's not a suspect, or the cops would have arrested him by now, but she makes a mental note to do some digging on him, to find out what their relationship was really like.

She's about to turn out of the car park when her phone beeps with an alert from the police media team. The body discovered yesterday has been formally identified as Mackenzie Jackson, although the police have made it clear that no arrests have been made in relation to her death. Oli lets out a breath she didn't realise she was holding. *Newsday* was the first publication to break the correct story.

She texts Chelsea to congratulate her and tell her to publish their confirmation piece. As she does, her phone beeps with another news alert.

A female body has been discovered on Hampton Beach overnight.

Heart pounding, Oli pulls up TJ's number, but he calls her first.

'I've seen it,' she answers. 'Lyra Makris this time?'

'Must be. I'm hearing a note was found with the body, like the one sent to *Melbourne Today*.'

Oli can hear TJ's wife, Carol, in the background, yelling for him to come look at the news.

'Channel Seven just used the words "serial killer", Ol.'

Throwing her phone into the console, she turns out of the car park. 'I'll meet you at the office. We can go to the crime scene together.'

CHAPTER SIXTEEN

WEDNESDAY, 22 JANUARY, 8.03 AM

Pen's eyeballs ache, and her tongue is like a slug in her mouth. The words on her computer screen blur. She clears her throat, attempting to dislodge the fog that has settled over her body.

Barnes's head appears above his monitor. 'Coffee? A proper one?'

Keen to get away from her desk, she says, 'I'll come with you.'

The sun hits their faces as they exit the station, the crisp white light jarring against the dark images that have rolled through Pen's mind since the early hours of the morning. Her imagination has created a nasty match-cut sequence of the mystery woman who was sexually assaulted and stabbed before being dumped at Hampton Beach, with Mackenzie Jackson's bloated face. The woman on the beach this morning was only the fourteenth dead body Pen has seen firsthand, and that includes her uncle's open-casket funeral when she was twelve.

They reach the cafe, and Barnes waves away her offer to pay. 'Pretty depressing morning, huh?' he says, driving his hands deep into his pockets as they move to the other side of the counter to wait.

'Yeah,' she says. 'I wonder who she is.'

He removes his glasses to rub his eyes. 'We'll find out soon enough.'

Pen watches people order their coffees, listens as they complain about the humidity and speculate about the virus from China. It's back in the news after reportedly being responsible for several deaths in the United States. Pen wonders if it's possible she has the virus. She feels awfully strange.

The scene at the beach last night was surreal. All the major players were there—Lew, Sanders and Frost—but it was Commissioner Cloak who called the shots. She stood cross-armed in the moonlight, the twinkling sea lapping rhythmically behind her as she barked orders. Detectives, emergency service crews and forensic techs crowded the space around the body and worked quietly through the night. It was an isolated spot, and they avoided drawing a crowd. One eager content creator climbed a tree to try to get a shot of the body before being ordered down by the commissioner herself and served a curt warning.

The dead woman was wearing a pair of Nike runners that Pen had tried on just before Christmas during a rare afternoon of shopping at Chadstone.

Usually, the discovery of a body in such circumstances generated a solemn sense of responsibility, a heaviness. This was different. The Polaroid found under the woman's body changed everything. The *#3* scrawled along the bottom linked her death to Marta Holm and Lyra Makris, and in the macabre way that these things tend to gain momentum, Pen sensed most of her colleagues felt energised by this development.

The Polaroid was a close-up of the same woman's face, lifeless, causing speculation about whether the Polaroid had been taken at the beach or whether they should be looking for a secondary crime scene.

Pen had dutifully recorded the details of the four cars in the parking lot and assisted with the line search before returning to where Barnes had stood metres away from the woman's body, which by then had been shielded by a temporary screen. The sporadic flashes of the camera made Pen jump as she stood in the dark, trying to avoid looking at those pristine shoes, feeling the rage that had seized her body when she'd interviewed Douglas Jackson.

Cloak sent everyone home at 3.30 am with strict instructions to get some sleep before an emergency briefing at 8 am. Curled in a ball in her bed, Pen was too wired to close her eyes and too scared to take a sleeping tablet in case she slept through her alarm. She finally dozed off at around five only to be woken by her alarm just before seven.

Barnes jumps now as the barista calls his name and tries to cover it up with an enthusiastic, 'That's me!'

They collect their coffees and head back to the station in silence. Pen wonders if Barnes keeps picturing the bloodied mess of the woman's chest and those bright white Nikes, or if he's picturing her delicate profile in the moonlight, her expression peaceful despite the violence so recently inflicted on her. Suddenly it seems important to know if Barnes struggles to turn off the avalanche of horrible thoughts.

But before she has the chance to work out how to ask such a question, he takes a swig of coffee and says, 'We're dealing with a sick arsehole.'

She nods, assuming it's a rhetorical statement.

'Smart move to switch back to analogue too. Hard to trace a Polaroid.'

'It doesn't sound like the techs are having much luck tracking the sender of the digital photo either.' Pen struggles to keep up with Barnes's long strides. 'I spoke to Farina before I left last night, and he said his team have hit a wall trying to trace the sender of the *Melbourne Today* message.'

'This guy clearly revels in the attention,' Barnes continues as if Pen hasn't spoken. 'Thinks he's some kind of criminal mastermind.'

She isn't sure how to respond. 'Are there any developments on the Jackson case since Douglas found out about Mackenzie's body being found?' she asks, as they reach their desks.

'Not yet,' Barnes murmurs, eyes glued to his phone. He appears deep in thought.

'Where did you head off to yesterday?'

He looks at her, brow furrowed.

'From the Jackson crime scene,' she clarifies.

'Right.' He nods. 'I had a lead to chase up. Turned out to be nothing.'

'Care to share?' It's a phrase she's heard him say to other detectives, but as soon as the words leave her mouth she feels like an idiot.

'Nah. Not worth your while.' He clears his throat. 'Douglas Jackson's not stupid. He's started to broadcast his wife's mental health issues at every opportunity he gets. Frost told me he's suddenly claiming he thinks she was sleeping around, which will muddy the waters in terms of suspects and just generally make her look less like the perfect victim.'

Pen grimaces as Barnes's words tug at a memory.

'He's got timing, I'll give him that,' Barnes is saying. The shadows under his eyes are more pronounced than usual.

She sips her coffee and squints, trying to follow. 'Who?'

'Douglas Jackson. This photograph thing is really going to pull all our resources now. You watch—every man and his blog will be jumping all over it. By this evening, Mackenzie Jackson won't even be second-page news.'

'I don't know . . . A white, middle-class, attractive mother of two disappears and turns up dead. It's a pretty big story.'

With a soft snort, Barnes returns to his typing.

Pen holds her gaze on him for a few moments but decides to leave him alone. He must be thinking about his sister. Her case was complicated by the fact she'd started using heroin in the year before she died, a detail the media seemed to suggest made her violent death less of a tragedy and more of an inevitability.

Pushing Mackenzie Jackson from her mind, Pen returns her attention to Lyra Makris. In around ninety minutes she and Silverman are due to interview Hamish Atwell.

Pen leaves another voice message for James Delway; he must be too busy doing insensitive TV interviews to answer. She sighs. They're going to have to go to his apartment and force him to engage.

She calls Silverman's extension. 'Have you read all the info the tech team sent about Atwell?'

'Sure have,' Silverman says. 'And I just had an illuminating conversation with the woman his wife mentioned yesterday—you know, the one he was hassling at the gym. Friendly indeed. What a creep,' she adds cheerfully. 'I can't wait to spend time with this hero.'

'Is there any evidence to suggest he was harassing other women online?'

'So far we can only pin him on Makris. But the team will keep digging.'

'Sounds good,' says Pen. Silverman's positivity is a nice contrast to Barnes's morose vibe. 'I'm waiting on his phone and bank records to see if there's anything to suggest he wasn't at home on Saturday night.'

'Fingers crossed,' says Silverman.

'Talking of creeps, I just tried to call James Delway, but he's still not answering.'

Silverman snorts. 'Speaking of Delway, I stumbled across something else interesting.'

'What?'

'Apparently, he went out with Dunkley's daughter several years ago. One of the women I spoke to earlier mentioned it but said it was extremely short-lived because Wendy ditched him for a TV presenter.'

'I vaguely remember her being involved with the guy on that property show.'

'I don't watch TV, so I have no idea, but she said Delway was not impressed. She also told me that Wendy was briefly at the party on Saturday. Said she turned up late and left fifteen minutes later.'

'Dunkley's team have done well to keep that out of the press,' says Pen.

'I know. Anyway, I'll see you at the case meeting, then we can go to the hospital to speak to Atwell.'

'He can't be our guy,' Barnes says when she hangs up. 'Atwell. He was at the hospital last night when the woman from the beach was killed.'

Pen feels defensive even though she'd come to the same conclusion. 'We don't know when she died yet. He could have dumped her there yesterday before he was arrested.'

Barnes looks sceptical. 'Maybe. But if he did, I think someone would have found her earlier. Half of Melbourne was at the beach yesterday.'

Pen shrugs, ending their conversation, and joins the uniforms and detectives filing into the Makris case room. It smells unpleasant: sweat, coffee, deodorant and something else, like someone has forgotten to change a vase of flowers. She smiles wanly at a few colleagues and receives tight smiles in return. Most of the group were at the scene last night, and it shows on their faces.

Sanders jogs in, clapping his hands self-importantly. 'Right, everyone. We have an unofficial ID for the woman found at Hampton Beach last night. Her name was Erica Pawley, a thirty-two-year-old woman originally from Sydney who now resides in Epping.'

Several photos appear on the screen featuring a South-East Asian woman in various poses: standing in a backyard holding a beer; sitting in the front seat of a car with the seatbelt cutting across her chest; smiling as she sits between two young children, one of them leaning forward to blow out candles on a cake.

'We'll know more once the autopsy is completed later today, but I can tell you she was sexually assaulted and stabbed multiple times,' Sanders says. 'Her body was doused with bleach after she was killed, which is going to make detecting any DNA extremely difficult. We have informed her ex-husband, who is on his way to Melbourne now to do the ID. He lives interstate and has been in New Zealand with their children since mid-January, so he's not a suspect. And while their relationship was fraught, they were in frequent civil contact. Pawley's mother and siblings live in Vietnam, and they have been contacted as well and may travel here over the coming days.'

Erica, thinks Pen. Erica with the new sneakers.

Sanders pauses. 'I don't need to tell you that this is a highly unusual situation. The note found with the body directly links the murder of this woman with the disappearance and suspected murder of Lyra Makris and the murder of Marta Holm. I've just had the premier on the phone demanding hourly updates, and the public scrutiny is only going to intensify.'

Pen suppresses the urge to roll her eyes. It's extremely unlikely that the premier spoke directly to Sanders, but she takes his point.

Despite the tiredness, there's a charge in the room, an invisible current keeping everyone tense and wide-eyed.

Sanders continues, 'We all have a responsibility to deliver justice for these women and their families, and I want to remind you that we also have a role to play in how their deaths are reported. Language is important, so just be mindful of this as you go about making your inquiries, please. This applies to the use of the term "serial killer", which from today we will be using in our statements.' He scans the room. 'I want to be very clear. The evidence we have to date suggests we are dealing with someone who has committed multiple murders, so we are using the term in a factual manner. What we don't want is to imply that we are dealing with a psychotic genius. The truth is likely to be far more mundane.'

Timelines are shared, and tasks are allocated

Pen is vaguely aware of Silverman taking a call and leaving the room.

Sanders doesn't mention Mackenzie Jackson, and before Pen can stop to think, she raises her hand.

'Yes, Kibbs?' His tone is pre-emptively dismissive.

'Is it worth us investigating a possible link between these murders and Mackenzie Jackson?' She falters, swallowing to moisten her dry mouth. 'Based on the timing and proximity to the other victims . . . I mean, it just feels like . . .'

'No.' Sanders shakes his head vigorously. 'At this stage there is nothing to link the two incidents. There was no note found with Jackson's body. It's a different situation, and we don't want to indicate they are part of the same case.'

'Does Douglas Jackson have an alibi for yesterday?' Pen presses, praying no one can hear the wild beating of her heart. 'Is it possible he could be involved somehow?'

'He's accounted for, seeing as he spent the afternoon and evening with yours truly.' There's a hint of a snicker from the front of the room. 'I want everyone here to focus their attention on this case, please.' Sanders looks pointedly at Pen and calls an end to the meeting.

She stands, rubbing her aching shoulder.

Silverman re-enters the room, and Pen is glad she didn't witness Sanders's public rebuke.

Pen joins her and forces a bright tone. 'Hey. Are you ready to go?'

Silverman shakes her head, her expression hard to read. 'Pen, I just got a call from the hospital.'

A rush of loud white noise fills Pen's ears. 'Atwell?'

'Yes.' Silverman's eyes become shiny. 'He's killed himself.'

CHAPTER SEVENTEEN

WEDNESDAY, 22 JANUARY, 8.13 AM

The Hampton Beach car park is full, so TJ parks on the road, expertly reversing his BMW into a spot next to a battered-looking Kombi van. He buys a parking ticket, and they walk in silence toward the large group of people gathered along the stretch of blue and white police tape. Oli wrestles her damp hair into a low ponytail, watching as a uniformed officer guides two sniffer dogs through the grassy banks, their paws sending sand flying as they move, noses to the ground, eyes darting back and forth. It's undeniably a nicer location than the swampy, rubbish-laden spot under the West Gate Bridge where Mackenzie Jackson's body was found, but there is a similar heaviness in the warm air.

Oli shades her eyes with her hand and scans the crowd. Women in activewear berate their impatient dogs; middle-aged men in lycra straddle expensive-looking bicycles as they sip from takeaway coffee cups; a tween boy takes in the scene with great curiosity, one foot on the path, the other on his scooter. A group of young women stand together, their arms crossed protectively at their chests, faces drawn.

Oli and TJ walk the perimeter of the cordoned-off area and look along the stretch of beach. The pale yellow sand looks clean; the water is an inviting blue. The trees block the road, and there are no streetlights or security cameras. Oli wonders if the woman came here willingly, on a date that went wrong, or whether she was killed somewhere else, her body brought here afterwards.

Luke Flatt, a Channel Ten reporter Oli is friendly with, spots her and ambles over.

'Hey, Flatty.'

'Ol.' He gives her a quick hug. 'Not the nicest circumstances for a catch-up. How are you?'

'I'm fine.' She introduces him to TJ.

'Hey, man.' Flatty reaches out to shake TJ's hand. 'I was thinking of giving you a buzz last week, Ol. I love what you guys are doing with the site and the podcasts. You hiring . . . ?'

'Oh.' Oli is surprised. She presumed Flatty was happy at the network. 'We—'

'We might be,' TJ interrupts. 'We've got some exciting things planned. Especially with video.'

'Cool.' Flatty smiles. He does a quick head check for eavesdroppers. 'I'd love to chat sometime. Confidentially, of course.'

'Sure, man,' TJ replies. 'Come past the office sometime.'

'Is there any word on an ID?' Oli asks, figuring she may as well take advantage of Flatty's keenness for a job.

He leans forward conspiratorially. 'It's not Lyra Makris. We got confirmation earlier that it's another woman. We think she's Asian, and apparently there's an ex-husband or boyfriend, but he lives in

Sydney. With their two kids. That's all I've got. Plus, you've heard the cops found a message, which is why everyone's getting their Zodiac knickers in a twist.'

'Do you have any details about what was found?'

'Nothing. But you can tell the cops are spooked so there must have been something.' He glances over at his colleague. 'I better go. We'll chat soon, yeah?'

Flatty heads off to talk to his camera operator.

'Is there anyone you don't want to offer a job to?' Oli says, keeping her tone light.

'He does good work. And he's your mate.' TJ sounds defensive. 'We should meet with lots of people and work out what feels right if we do decide to put on more staff.'

'I'm just winding you up,' she says, although she does feel uncomfortable at how willing TJ is to open up the business to new people.

He squints into the sun. 'I wonder if it really was the same guy who killed these women.'

There's a grotesque currency in the notion of a dangerous killer on the loose. Oli knows it's primal, a deeply ingrained instinct to seek information about danger, but it's difficult to navigate in their reporting. It's hard not to be alarmist when the circumstances are legitimately alarming, but Oli and TJ never want *Newsday* adding to public panic.

'It's just as likely to be domestic violence,' Oli says. 'We need to be really careful.'

'Of course,' TJ murmurs, distracted by Commissioner Lew arriving on the scene. His bald head glints in the sun, his expression unreadable behind his sunglasses.

They watch as he pauses to talk briefly to a woman in a tailored suit before ducking under the police tape. He raises a hand in greeting to the nearby group of uniformed officers as he approaches and settles into deep conversation with them.

TJ raises his eyebrows at Oli. 'Do you think Dunkley will make an appearance?'

'It would certainly play well into her narrative. And it makes Bryson seem even more out of touch.'

'There's always a silver lining,' TJ remarks wryly. 'Speak of the devil.'

Oli follows his gaze to where Dunkley and her husband Shane Willoughby are walking hand in hand toward the crime scene, flanked by two security guards. Dunkley's in a tailored navy suit and wears dark glasses. She breaks away from her husband and strides purposefully toward Commissioner Lew. As they talk, Oli notices the premier surreptitiously bend down to flick sand out of her shoes.

Willoughby approaches some officers, shaking their hands, his face arranged in a strained smile. In contrast to his wife, he's wearing tan chinos and a pale blue T-shirt, his tall athletic frame at home on the beach.

'Come on, let's get some photos,' Oli says. 'See if we can find out anything else and then work out what we go live with.'

TJ snaps some pictures of the scene on his phone, while Oli thinks about what Flatty said. On the surface, the three women didn't have much in common until their lives dovetailed in the most horrific way. Did they know their killer, or was their final encounter on earth with a stranger?

She checks social media and finds Instagram already filled with tributes to the unidentified woman. Ms Melbourne has uploaded a video of herself walking her dog with Premier Dunkley's daughter, Wendy Willoughby. Both young women look impeccably groomed as they express how devastated they were to wake up to the news of another senseless murder.

'Did Chelsea tell you her friend saw Wendy Willoughby at that party on the weekend?' Oli says to TJ.

He shrugs. 'Dunkley didn't mention that in her press conference.'

Nearby a young woman calls out Oli's name, and she makes eye contact and smiles but doesn't stop walking. She feels the discomfort that always comes with being recognised in public, something that's been happening with increased regularity.

'You're so popular,' TJ teases.

'Don't be silly. Don't you notice people staring at you?'

He rolls his eyes. 'You do know the Facebook group about your voice has over six thousand members now.'

She shrugs his comment away. She never knows what to do with praise, and TJ's compliment makes her think of Marion's job offer. The woman had made a big fuss of Oli's voice when they spoke.

Oli and TJ pause as he takes a few more photos. She attempts to talk to a cop guarding the crime scene but has no luck. She talks to a journalist she knew several years ago, but the woman seems to know less than they do.

They return to the car and pull the doors shut.

'Let's do a quick recording here.'

They occasionally do news drops while on the road, and she knows people love them. She also likes the intimacy of these impromptu records, the way little sounds work their way into their dialogue. Before Cooper introduced her to podcasting, she'd never given much thought to sound in news stories; now she incorporates it all the time, understanding the power it has.

TJ positions his phone on the dashboard between them and gives her a quick nod. She takes a deep breath and nods back. He presses record.

'Good morning. It's 9.15 am on Wednesday, 22 January 2020. I'm Oli Groves, here with my colleague Timothy Jack, and you're listening to a *Newsday* report from the road. We're sitting in TJ's car on Beach Road next to Hampton Beach, where the body of a woman was discovered earlier this morning. This grim discovery comes less than twenty-four hours after the body of missing Camberwell woman Mackenzie Jackson was discovered in Port Melbourne, and the suspected death of another woman, Lyra Makris, who has been missing since Sunday morning, was confirmed by Victoria Police. To say it's been a violent start to the year would be an understatement.'

TJ jumps in and details the scene, including the premier liaising with the police, then he steps out what they know. He pauses when an ambulance races by, siren blaring.

When they're done, the recording is about twelve minutes. 'Bite-sized' is how they have started referring to these mini-episodes, like a news snack people can consume on the way to work. TJ saves the file and sends it to Chelsea so she can edit and publish. Oli knows it will be gobbled up the moment it appears on their feed, so desperate people will be for their take on the unfolding events.

Oli reads out tweets as TJ drives, including one from Dunkley declaring this latest death a tragedy and vowing to provide the police with everything they need to keep the community safe.

'The hashtag #MelbourneSerialKiller is trending,' Oli says, hearing her voice shake.

TJ puffs out his cheeks and releases the air slowly.

Remembering Lily's text from yesterday, Oli vows to call her mother this afternoon and confirm she will be at lunch on the weekend. Sally Groves will not cope well with headlines like this and, as always, will think that Oli's job means she's in proximity to danger. Her mother thinks this even when the headlines are referring to international wars or a deadly disease in a foreign country.

Another alert pops up about James Delway's exclusive *A Current Affair* interview.

'I think we should interview one of Lyra Makris's friends,' Oli says. 'Go head-to-head with her stain of an ex.'

'I'm happy with that,' TJ says. 'He's clearly making the most of his fifteen minutes of fame.'

'He's the worst kind of human. Imagine making something like this about yourself.'

They arrive at the office, and Oli receives a notification that their podcast episode has gone live. She feels a wave of appreciation for Chelsea's efficiency as she follows TJ up the stairs.

'We're on track to have our biggest day of traffic ever,' Chelsea announces when they walk in. She looks beyond chic in a pale cream satin blouse with an oversized pussy bow at her throat, her asymmetrical haircut coerced into shape with god knows how much hairspray. Her tattooed hands fly across her keyboard as she talks, and Oli notices tiny silver stars have been adhered to her black fingernails.

TJ's phone rings, and he disappears into the empty meeting room they generously refer to as 'the boardroom'.

Oli turns to Chelsea. 'I want to interview one of Lyra Makris's friends for a feature. Someone who knew her well. Can you start to sus out who might be best?'

'Can do. I'll pull a list and contact a few people asap.'

'Thank you. And let's see if we can get her ex to talk to us. The one doing all the interviews.'

Chelsea sucks on the nozzle of her pouch yoghurt and steers her computer mouse with her right hand. 'One arsehole coming right up.'

Oli sinks into her chair and opens her laptop. She has dozens of emails to respond to, but it's impossible to concentrate with so much going on.

'This is shaping up to be our biggest engagement day as well, even bigger than when Trump became president,' says Chelsea. 'Seriously, these stats are ridiculous. There must be like, zero work being done out there today. Everyone in Melbourne is just online throwing around theories and talking about who the killer might be. You'd think every second person is a criminal profiler.' She takes a large swig from her army green water bottle, then returns her attention to scraping the last remnants of yoghurt from the pouch.

'I guess people don't know what else to do.'

'They need to change the laws. I bet anything it's some prick out on parole.' Chelsea crosses her arms and glares at her screen.

'We don't know the details yet,' Oli reminds her gently, despite thinking that Chelsea is probably right.

The young woman sighs. 'At least that arsehole Douglas Jackson might actually get done for murdering his wife now her body has been found.'

'Maybe,' Oli mutters, unconvinced. 'Maybe someone else killed her.'

'Statistically unlikely.' Chelsea shakes her head emphatically. 'Plus, he's a walking red flag. He's just smarter than some of the other losers out there.'

Oli watches as helicopter footage of the Hampton Beach crime scene appears on the Channel Nine news, followed by some crude mock-ups of the correspondence that *Melbourne Today* received from the killer about Lyra Makris. Then the footage cuts to the news desk with the breaking news graphic visible in the background.

'Hang on,' Oli says. 'Guys, something's happening.'

They all gather around the TV and watch the Nine news anchor explain that forty-five-year-old Hamish Atwell, arrested yesterday in relation to an incident at Mackenzie Jackson's crime scene, has died in hospital.

'There are no suspicious circumstances,' the anchor says, 'and a report will be prepared for the coroner.'

'Do you think there's any chance he was the killer?' says Chelsea in a small voice.

'I don't know,' murmurs Oli. 'Let's get something up about this on the site asap.'

For the next ten minutes they focus on drafting copy and working out the headline and imagery.

'I'll put your recording from this morning up the top of the article,' says Chelsea. 'We'll get more downloads that way.'

They publish the article, and Oli experiences the slight dip in energy that comes after a burst of productivity. She trains her eyes to the news coverage again, a loop of the Hampton Beach shots and the piles of flowers outside Lyra Makris's apartment interspersed with photos of her cooking videos. Added to the medley is a photo of Marta Holm lifted from her travel blog. The scrolling ticker reads: *Multiple killings have city on edge.*

'It's like a real-life reality show,' Oli muses, struck again by how much this story seems to be blurring the lines between news and a form of grim entertainment. 'Or maybe a thriller.'

'That's a good idea for one of your deep dives,' Chelsea says. 'The idea we're all finding it harder to know where the real world starts and stops.'

'She's right.' TJ reappears and strides to his desk. He plonks down on his chair and swivels it around to face the others. 'What do we do when murder becomes a game?'

'Do we really think that's what this is?' asks Oli.

His eyebrows dip, creasing his forehead. 'It certainly feels like this guy is taking inspiration from figures like the Zodiac Killer. Or that show *Black Mirror*.' He counts the similarities on his fingers. 'Communicating with the press and the cops, brazenly taunting the community, seemingly targeting victims at random—it's the same MO. And he clearly hates women.'

'I hate *Black Mirror*,' Chelsea says, shuddering.

Oli raises her eyebrows, surprised. 'I thought it would be right up your alley.'

'Nah, I hate all that existential shit that Millennials get off on. I'm strictly rom-coms or self-help disguised as disillusioned-woman-going-on-personal-journey-to-find-herself.'

'Is that a genre?' Oli wonders.

Chelsea snaps her gum. 'My Netflix algorithm certainly seems to think so.'

Something that TJ said jarred, and Oli's thoughts circle back to it. 'You know what isn't the same about these deaths,' she says slowly. 'The method.'

TJ's eyes lock on hers. 'You're right. We know Marta Holm was strangled, but it sounds like the woman on the beach was stabbed. And from what we can tell, he slit Lyra Makris's throat.' TJ taps his pen on the desk, his stare becoming glassy as he descends into deep thought. He doesn't seem to notice Chelsea shudder again. After a few moments, he refocuses his gaze on Oli. 'What if Atwell did kill Holm and Makris? Perhaps this latest murder could be a copycat.'

'It's very unlikely.'

'But possible,' he counters.

'At this point, anything is possible. But it's more likely we're talking about someone very sick and unpredictable. Atwell thought the body at Port Melbourne yesterday was Lyra Makris, so I don't think he's involved.'

'The killer is a chaos agent,' Chelsea adds, typing furiously. 'Someone with no pattern. Whatever this sicko's vibe is, we don't really know enough to put anything in print, do we?'

Oli smiles at her. 'No, but I'm guessing the cops are considering the differences between each murder, so we should try to find out what they think this means. I'll do some digging.'

Chelsea dabs pink gloss on her lips. 'Hey, is it cool if I use a cab charge to get home later? I'm sensing it might be a late one.'

'Where from?' TJ looks confused.

'From here.'

'Of course,' Oli interjects. 'That's fine.'

Chelsea gives her a grateful smile. 'Thanks.'

TJ sends a quizzical look her way, and she shakes her head slightly, indicating they'll discuss it later. She can tell Chelsea is apprehensive about catching public transport home, and she can't blame her. Channel Nine is right: the whole city is on edge.

Feeling wired, Oli listens to the edited version of the second-last episode in her domestic violence podcast series. Chelsea's done a great job on the edit. Oli's narration is interspersed with the interviews and quotes from various experts, while a solemn but propulsive tune underpins her words so perfectly that she can't imagine an alternative track.

She checks her email again, but there's still nothing from Dunkley's people about the interview. If she doesn't hear back soon, she'll need to work out another way to end the series.

She resends the request and instantly feels impatient. 'I actually think I might have the idea for the next deep-dive series,' she announces, pulling off her headphones.

Chelsea stops typing and looks at her expectantly.

TJ doesn't move his eyes from his monitor as he asks, 'What is it?'

'Cybersex crimes. With a focus on underage kids.'

'What's the angle?' he asks.

'I've only just started digging, but there's a lot of material. Images taken and shared without consent, fake images, blackmail. The platforms don't seem able to control people sharing content, or maybe they don't want to—either way, it's something parents are going to want to hear about.'

'We need more parents,' says Chelsea. 'Parents have money to spend on news subscriptions.'

Oli smiles gratefully at her. 'It's a topic that hasn't had much airtime in Australia yet. Would be good to be ahead of the pack. *The New York Times* recently ran a feature investigation on it.'

TJ finally looks up. He loves *The New York Times*. 'Sounds like it's worth a look. What's your personal angle? Think you'll find enough people willing to talk to you on the record?'

'Well, Dean's daughter is involved in a situation at the moment. She's twelve, almost thirteen. Sounds like the school hasn't handled it well, so I can start with that.'

TJ's head jerks to the right. 'Dean? *Your* Dean?'

'He's not *my* Dean,' she says. 'But yes, that Dean.'

'What kind of situation?' TJ can't keep the suspicion out of his voice—he dislikes Dean as much as Dean dislikes him.

Oli draws a deep breath. 'Apparently one of her classmates has shared inappropriate content of her with other students.'

TJ looks gobsmacked. 'Jesus. She's just a kid.'

Oli doesn't say anything, just watches him think. She knows he needs to get his head around pitches on his own, find his own angle rather than have it rammed down his throat.

'We're not talking about sex tapes or anything, are we?'

'I haven't seen the files, but no, I don't think so. Dean said topless photos and videos.'

'I've got nieces that age,' TJ mutters.

Oli adds, 'From my research at the crack of dawn this morning, it seems Amy's situation is not uncommon.'

'Humiliation and power fuelled by technology. It's the Paris Hilton sex-tape story on steroids.' TJ's getting excited the way he does when a story takes shape in his mind. 'You can interview the tech platforms too, assuming they'll talk to you. Maybe a cybercrime cop. And teachers—they'll have a lot to say on this.'

'Some will,' says Oli, 'and some won't. That's okay. I reckon including anonymous interviews will work well.'

TJ brings his hands together. 'It's good. And you never know, it might even prompt some policy reform.'

Chelsea looks between the two of them as if she's watching a tennis match.

'I'm glad you like it,' says Oli.

He bites his lip, still thinking. 'Yeah, it's got a lot in it. But we'll need to be super buttoned-up, Ol. Especially if we're dealing with minors.'

'If we go ahead with it, I'll work with the lawyers and make sure I get their input on what I need to avoid. I do want to interview some kids. Their perspective is going to be critical if we want to achieve something beyond the standard investigation.'

'Do you think you can give it enough love with everything else we have going on? If this Photographer story keeps going, you might be recording daily podcasts for weeks.'

'I know. But I'd love to try to fit it in. It's not like we need to work to a particular deadline.'

She's more worried about her cancer treatment and how she will manage taking on an investigation like this if she's recovering from surgery or having chemo. If she's going to talk to victims of abuse, she needs to treat them carefully and be available. She might need to bring Chelsea in from the start or consider hiring a producer to support her. Oli isn't used to tempering her ambition; for the past few years her work has been on her terms, and she has fit in whatever has been physically possible, but she's aware this might need to change.

To TJ, she says, 'I'm sure we can work it out. Maybe Spencer can help.'

'It's a great idea, Ol.' His expression is one she remembers from when they worked together at *Melbourne Today*, back when they were colleagues and competed for the best stories. It's part-admiration, part-envy, and she likes that she can still make him feel like that.

'If only we didn't have Dean to thank.' She laughs.

TJ glances at Chelsea. 'When did you see him?' he asks Oli in a casual tone, but the question is loaded. After she broke up with Dean, TJ confessed how worried he'd been about their relationship.

'I didn't,' she says. 'He called me. He's upset about his daughter and wants this issue to get more airplay. I said I'd think about it, and now I've done a bit of research, I do think—'

Chelsea's mobile rings, and she takes the call, listening for a few moments before saying, 'Okay, sure. That would be good.' She puts the call on mute and looks up at Oli, her beautifully made-up eyes shining. 'It's one of Lyra's friends I contacted for you to talk to. She's willing to chat with you about Lyra. And she's convinced James Delway had something to do with what happened to her.'

CHAPTER EIGHTEEN

THURSDAY, 23 JANUARY, 5.46 AM

Pen wakes with a start, scrambling out of her sheets as if they're on fire. She stands next to her bed, panting, as Elliot watches her from the second-hand armchair in the corner. Her laptop is propped open on the spare pillow, the screen timed out. She'd been talking to a guy on Chatroulette who said he was from Belgium. He told her he was a cabinetmaker who was obsessed with Beyoncé. He seemed nice enough—he didn't ask her to remove her clothes or say anything inappropriate—but she must have fallen asleep not long after they started talking. She hasn't shared a bed with someone since that horrible night with her ex. As she wonders if this man watched her sleep, she feels an odd rush of pleasure mixed with shame.

Still feeling wired, she lowers herself down to sit on the edge of the bed. What woke her so abruptly? The faces of the dead women loom in her mind's eye, but it's Hamish Atwell's suicide that has lodged in her consciousness. Recalling his wife's desperate insistence that her husband was just friendly, Pen feels deeply sad for the woman and her children.

She glances at her work phone on the bedside table with trepidation before she picks it up and checks her messages. Nothing. No new horror. Relief courses through her like an adrenaline rush.

Pen showers, downs an instant coffee and chews on some buttered toast. Still eating, she takes Elliot down to the courtyard in the centre of the building, tugging gently on his leash until he finds the right patch of grass upon which to defecate. Pen looks up at the dozens of apartment windows, feeling exposed. Back upstairs she fills Elliot's food and water bowls and then dries her hair, securing the mousey strands into a twist.

Planting a kiss on top of Elliot's head, Pen grabs her things and heads back downstairs, walking the hundred metres to the tram stop. On her personal phone she checks various apps as she waits, the air already warm. She has seven new matches on Tinder but ignores them. She opens Bumble and swipes through a few profiles before pausing on one. Billy. Thirty years old. Works in IT. He looks a bit like the guy she was talking to on Chatroulette last night. On a whim, she sends him a message. Then she exits the app and locks her phone. Her heart is beating wildly again, but she can't spend the rest of her life hiding away from the world and talking to strangers online.

The tram arrives. Pen helps an elderly man disembark before she steps on and performs the awkward dance of finding her Myki in her bag while she holds on to a pole as the tram rattles through the streets of North Melbourne.

There are plenty of spare seats, and she sinks into one gratefully, mentally mapping out everything she needs to do this morning.

Distracted as she is by The Photographer murders, she still can't stop thinking about Mackenzie Jackson.

Pen stares out at the dark Melbourne streets, recalling the night she attended the Jackson residence with Barnes. They must have missed something.

Phone records revealed that Douglas Jackson made six phone calls the night his wife disappeared and received one. Two of the calls he made were to Mackenzie, one was to his mother, one to his brother, and the remaining two calls were to Mackenzie's closest friends. Or whom he thought were her closest friends—Mackenzie barely spoke to those women anymore, probably aware anything she said to them would make its way back to Douglas via their husbands. He spoke to his mother and Mackenzie's former friends for a few minutes but didn't get through to his wife or his brother.

The incoming call is more mysterious. Logged around half an hour after Mackenzie left the house, it lasted for just over thirty seconds. Douglas claims he doesn't remember who the caller was, and the number is unlisted and untraceable. Could it be relevant to Mackenzie's murder? Douglas couldn't have known that she was going to storm out that night, so how could he have planned to hurt her? Could the mystery caller have told Douglas where his wife was? Pen isn't sure what her brain is trying to grip on to, but the mystery of the incoming call feels like it needs to be resolved.

She becomes aware of the man in the seat diagonally opposite; he's staring at her. She stares back for a few moments, then looks away. When she flicks her gaze to him again, he's still staring, seemingly unperturbed that she's noticed. She uncrosses her legs and points her knees toward the window, angling her body away from him. She only has three stops to go, but she's tempted to get off now. Either that or whip out her badge and ask to see his ID.

In the end she does neither and stares out the window until she reaches the stop near the station, averting her eyes as she passes him. She buys a coffee from the cafe at the bottom of the building and stands against the wall, facing the street.

As she makes her way up the concrete stairs of the station, she can feel eyes boring into the back of her head. But when she turns around, no one's there.

She's relieved to step into the artificial light of her office and be surrounded by the sounds of her colleagues arriving and starting their day. But when she reaches her desk, she's still thinking about Mackenzie Jackson.

Something Barnes said yesterday is bouncing around in her mind: that Douglas Jackson has suggested his wife was cheating on him. In the days after Mackenzie's disappearance, Pen spoke to several of her friends and neighbours, trying to determine if she'd run away or met with foul play. One neighbour, Annie Soto, told Pen that Mackenzie had seemed much happier in recent months. Now Pen wonders if Annie knows more than she let on at the time. Could she have been alluding to a new relationship?

Pen logs in to her computer. While she waits for it to connect to the network, she takes out her phone and continues to scroll through Lyra Makris's YouTube page, reading each comment, looking for any clue that might point to what happened to her.

'Morning, Pen.' Barnes appears behind her. 'How are you?'

'I'm fine.' She puts her phone down. 'You?'

'Oh, you know—I could complain, but there's no point,' he says with false cheer. 'I just spoke to Sanders. Sounds like a bunch more information has come through on your Hampton Beach woman.'

Barnes turns to his screen, and Pen studies the back of his head for a few moments, trying to understand his mood, before she turns to her own. She logs in to Erica Pawley's case file and scans the recently uploaded autopsy report along with the latest notes.

Her time of death is estimated to be sometime on Monday evening. She was stabbed five times in the chest and torso with a run-of-the-mill kitchen knife. Due to the bleaching of her body they've been unable to retrieve any DNA, and there are no prints on the Polaroid. Since moving to Melbourne three years ago, she has had casual roles in hospitality and retail, and more recently she has done sex work.

Pen considers this. It's no secret that people engaging in sex work are often subjected to violence, but she's finding it jarring that The Photographer has targeted someone like Erica Pawley.

Pen pushes back her chair and heads off to find Sanders. The door to his office is ajar, but she knocks anyway.

'Yep!' His voice is clipped like he's already in a hurry.

Pen enters his office. He's at his desk and wearing reading glasses, which makes him look a lot older. 'Sir,' she begins, 'I was just reviewing Erica Pawley's autopsy report and the latest notes. Is there anything to suggest that her sex work had something to do with her murder?'

Sanders removes his glasses and drops them in a drawer. He folds his hands together and sets his gaze on Pen. 'In what way?'

She swallows. 'I just think it makes her very different to the other victims. And she was a mother.'

Sanders takes a loud slurp of coffee from a metal thermos. 'I'm not sure this guy is too worried about the demographics of his victims, Kibbs. He's an opportunist, and sex workers provide opportunities.' He puts the thermos down, his expression softening. 'It sounds like Erica Pawley regularly did shifts at a brothel in Footscray as well as walking the streets. She had no fixed address but had been staying on and off with a friend in Windsor for several weeks. Then she failed to return home on Tuesday night when she said she would. The friend didn't become worried until Wednesday evening when she still hadn't heard from Pawley, but she didn't contact the police because she was worried she might get Pawley in trouble. I think our guy deduced that murdering someone like Pawley meant he had a couple of days up his sleeve before anyone would come looking.'

Pen bristles. What Sanders is saying makes sense, but something still nags at her. 'Is there any suggestion that Makris or Holm was engaged in sex work?'

'No, and I'd be reluctant to suggest we're following that line of inquiry.' Sanders's tone is stern. 'Their families are upset enough as it is.'

'And nothing to link Mackenzie Jackson to sex work?'

'Nothing.' He stands, and his chair makes a comical creak. 'Kibbs, like I said yesterday, all the evidence points to these being discrete cases. If you can find a link between the Jackson case and the others, I'm all ears. Until then, I'm sure you have plenty to be getting on with, as do I.'

Dejected, Pen heads back to her desk, considering the threads of evidence. She checks her email. Phone records are filtering in, and she scans the information in the reports. James Delway doesn't appear to have been in the vicinity of Ned Higgins's party on Saturday night, or at least his phone wasn't. Pen continues to review bank details and notes on CCTV footage, but it's all amounting to nothing.

She looks across at Barnes's empty desk and wonders where he is. Then she wonders if Frost and Sanders have split them up—and if so, why.

She reviews the Pawley autopsy report again. The woman suffered, that much is clear. Pen opens Marta Holm's autopsy report, noting the differences. Holm was strangled, Pawley was stabbed. Does it mean anything? Maybe Sanders is right, and they're looking for an opportunistic killer. The evidence suggests crimes of passion, frenzied kills, yet the contact with the media and police implies a high level of forethought and rational thinking.

She feels a bit faint and realises she's starving, so she heads to the kitchen, hoping to find something to ward off the clawing emptiness in her stomach.

A detective constable she knows only slightly, Serge Zappa, and a female officer who was at the Jackson scene yesterday are in the kitchen talking about Erica Pawley.

Zappa is theorising that she was probably killed by a client. 'It's too easy,' he says, snapping his gum. 'You cruise the known haunts, you zero in on your type, then she willingly gets in your car, for fuck's sake. It's like, cool, I've found my target and now I'll just drive off to a dark, secluded location without raising a red flag. I mean, why do these women risk it? It's madness.'

Pen exchanges a glance with the woman, but neither of them speak.

'Anyway, hopefully the piece of shit is on tape somewhere, and we can nail his arse. He's obviously an arrogant prick, leaving those photos like a bad guy in a movie.'

'I just feel so sad for those poor women,' says Pen quietly. 'They must have been so scared.'

The female cop nods grimly, grabbing an apple from the pitiful offering in the communal fruit bowl and leaves.

Zappa reaches across Pen, yanks open the cupboard above her and plucks a glass from the shelf. He fills it with water and downs the lot in one go, his Adam's apple bobbing furiously. Pen wonders how he manages not to swallow his gum. He levels his head and wipes his sleeve across his lips. 'Ah,' he exclaims, sated. Then, 'I dunno, I reckon this type of thing is actually quite good for us.'

Pen folds her arms across her chest. 'Sorry?'

He smacks his lips together and rinses out the glass, leaving it in the sink. 'Makes the public appreciate us.'

She stares at him.

He holds up his hands. 'Don't look at me like that. I'm not saying it's good that it *happened*, I just mean that there's an unintended benefit. Everyone's so blasé these days—posting their location online, shouting to the whole world who they are and what they're doing all the time—and I get it, I've got sisters and a girlfriend who love all that oversharing shit. But honestly, it's dangerous.' He saunters to the fridge and pulls out a Tupperware container filled with something brown, then opens the microwave and places it inside. 'Cases like this remind people that they need to be careful, that there's danger out there. And then inevitably people start to understand the role we play in keeping everyone safe.' The microwave beeps, and he opens the door, stirring the gunk with a spoon before closing the door and resetting it to heat for thirty seconds. 'It's a super soup, full of protein. I only heat it a bit in summer, just to take the edge off. I have it two, sometimes three, times a day.'

'Right.' Pen opens the biscuit jar and pushes her hand through the layers of Monte Carlos to get to the lone Kingston at the bottom.

He spins around. 'You don't like to hear it, but I'm not wrong. Have you seen that survey about the most trusted professions? Trust in cops is declining. But I'd bet anything that after something like this, we'll be ranked far more favourably. Especially if we can deliver a good result. It's just basic psychology.'

Pen is struggling to stop herself from slapping him. She wills the microwave to overheat and blast him and his stupid views into smithereens.

It beeps again, and Zappa retrieves his revolting-looking bowl of soup. 'See ya.' He glides out of the kitchen.

Fuming, Pen makes a bowl of cereal from the communal supplies and takes a seat at a table in the tearoom. She pulls out her phone and resumes her trawl through Lyra Makris's cooking videos. As Pen scrapes the last spoonful of cereal into her mouth, she watches a video uploaded in September of Makris explaining how to impress someone with a foolproof chocolate biscuit recipe.

Pen narrows her eyes. The third comment from the top was left by Mackenzie Jackson.

CHAPTER NINETEEN

THURSDAY, 23 JANUARY, 10.46 AM

Oli meets Yvonne Gilchrist at a cafe near the woman's house. Her red-rimmed eyes are like saucers as she nervously transfers her phone from one hand to the other.

'I'm so sorry about your friend,' Oli says, once they're seated at a table in the far corner.

Yvonne's gaze flits to the door. She is fine-boned, but Oli gets the feeling she doesn't normally look so slight. Her petite frame is swimming in an oversized shirt, and her short blonde pixie crop is limp around her face. Empty holes line her earlobes, and she appears to be make-up free. She is stripped of all colour and joy. 'Thank you,' she says. She puts her phone down, and her right fingers robotically pinch and release a silver chain bracelet on her left wrist.

They order drinks. As soon as the waiter leaves their table, Oli leans forward, forcing Yvonne to meet her gaze. 'Tell me about James Delway.'

A scowl mars her grief-stricken face. 'He's an arsehole.' Her words come out like a sword being drawn.

At the adjacent table, a woman wearing sweats and a baseball cap glances at them before continuing to scroll on her phone, but Oli can tell she's tuned in to their conversation.

She keeps her voice low and presses. 'Why?'

Yvonne falters, looking defeated after her brief surge of anger. 'She really liked him—Lyra, I mean. But she knew he was bad news. You know how that's a thing sometimes? Like, I think she knew for months before they split that he was going to break her heart, but I don't know . . .' Yvonne seems annoyed at herself for not being able to articulate what she means.

'I get it,' Oli assures her.

'She told me that he'd gone off her at my birthday last year, so in June. She was so upset, and she was worried he was seeing someone behind her back, someone he worked with. But then when she went overseas in August, he totally flipped and texted her flat out the entire time, saying how much he missed her. He completely ruined her holiday.'

Oli's stomach clenches in recognition. Dean used to do that—reel her in and then spit her out. 'But then they broke up officially in December, right?'

Their drinks arrive, and Yvonne sips her orange juice, her face expressionless. 'November, actually. Turns out he *was* seeing someone else, or he must have been because he had a girlfriend about two minutes after they split. He's still with her.'

'What makes you think he's lying about where he was on Saturday night?' Oli asks, trying to push the conversation away from speculation.

Yvonne slams the glass of juice onto the table. 'Do you know what he did to her?' she growls. She doesn't wait for Oli to reply. 'He told her that he would post photos she'd sent him when they were together if she didn't leave him alone. He threatened her. I told you, the guy is a psycho.'

Oli's heart starts to pound, a drumbeat in her chest. 'And did he go through with posting those photos?'

'Not that I know of, but Lyra was beside herself worrying that he would. She'd just got a sponsorship deal, nothing major, just a small content partnership for her cooking website. She was terrified that if someone from the brand saw the photos, they would pull the money. And, of course, she was paranoid her family would find out too. Her mum would have killed her.' Yvonne falls into a solemn silence.

The lady in sweats has been replaced by two young men who seem captivated by some video playing on one of their phones.

Oli says gently, 'Do you have proof he was blackmailing her?'

'Proof?' Yvonne shakes her head. 'No. She just told me about it.'

'Did you talk about it over email? Or text?'

Tears well in Yvonne's eyes, and she looks very young. 'Not sure. Text, I think. But it might have been over the phone. Lyra was calling him a lot, you know, trying to reason with him. He'd done a real number on her—all the back and forth had made her kind of obsessive.' Yvonne clutches her juice glass. 'She was convinced she wanted him back.'

Oli smiles sadly. 'And the photos he was threatening to post, they were . . . ?'

Yvonne throws her hands up. 'Like, naked selfies, I guess. Whatever. Just private stuff she didn't want him sharing. They were together for months, and she thought she could trust him.'

'I have no judgement about your friend. I just want to find out what happened to her.'

Yvonne nods. 'I told the cops that I saw her. Lyra. On Saturday. I didn't say anything much about James because, I don't know, I guess I don't have evidence or whatever. Then the more I kept thinking about it, I just . . . And then I saw what he's saying about her to the media, and I . . .' She looks at Oli, her expression pleading as she exhales shakily.

Oli breathes out too. She knows Yvonne is hurting, but she needs to thread the needle. 'Okay, so tell me why you think James is lying about Saturday night.'

'I can't prove that he's lying. His alibi is weak. Ned told me that James was home all night with Diana, which doesn't seem right. He would never miss one of Ned's parties. He's big into that scene. Diana's his new girlfriend—she's very young, and he's her boss.' Yvonne lifts her chin defiantly. 'As if she's going to speak out against him.' A sob escapes Yvonne's lips, and she steadies herself. 'James made Lyra lie when they first started going out. He was seeing this other girl—she had a beer business and sold her label through James's bar. She was really into him. But he was bored with her and started to hit on Lyra.'

'How did James meet Lyra?'

'She worked at the bar too, just on the weekends. She stopped when she got the full-time job at the media agency in July. But back then, James used to get Lyra to make up stuff about where he was when the other woman came in.'

Oli pictures the smug face of James Delway on the *60 Minutes* promo and wishes she could slap it. 'Have you told the cops about this?'

'Sort of,' replies Yvonne. 'But I don't want them to think she's a bad person. The lead detective, he already grilled me about what Lyra was into, and I don't want them to go digging up her private photos. It's so unfair that it's her reputation being dragged through the mud.'

'It's not fair,' Oli agrees, 'but there's not much anyone can do about it.'

'I was hoping you can investigate him,' Yvonne says desperately. 'His friends are more likely to talk to you than the cops.'

'Yvonne, listen. The cops will be all over James, and if they find anything that links him to what happened to Lyra, they will arrest him. I understand everything you're saying, but it's not proof of Delway's involvement in what happened.' Glancing down, Oli sees her phone lighting up with text message and email alerts. She focuses on Yvonne again, forcing herself to ignore it.

Yvonne's dark eyes glaze over and fix somewhere near the cafe door. Her lips barely move as she says, 'He didn't care about her. He treated her like garbage, and she was amazing.'

Oli senses the immense weight of the woman's sadness, and she closes her eyes for a few moments. 'It sounds like Lyra was a very special person.'

Yvonne buries her face in her palms. 'She was the best. I was supposed to go to the party with her, you know. I said I would. She wanted me to be there—she was nervous James might turn up, and she told me she was excited about some other guy.'

'Another guy? Who was that?'

But Yvonne's not listening. Her face collapses, and her mouth twists as she tries to talk through her tears. 'But I didn't go. This guy I know invited me over to his place, and so I went. I didn't even text her back.'

Oli reaches across the table. 'This is not your fault, you know that.'

'He's an arsehole just like James. And I ran over to his house like a moronic puppy, even though I know he's not into me.' She grabs her head and lets out a strangled wail.

Oli moves her chair around the table and gathers the young woman in her arms.

'I should have gone with her,' Yvonne whispers after a few moments. 'I'd do anything to go back in time and not be a selfish bitch.'

Oli doesn't argue with her, knowing that her reassurances aren't going to help Yvonne. If the woman is lucky, time might soften the sharpness of her guilt.

'Who was the guy she was excited about seeing?' Oli presses gently.

'Initially I thought it was James.' Yvonne gulps back a sob. 'Like maybe he'd been messaging her again or maybe she wanted to look good in front of him to try to get him back. The more I think about it, the more I'm convinced it must have been someone else. I doubt James would go there again, and she was glued to her phone the entire time she was at my place, so she was definitely in contact with someone.'

CHAPTER TWENTY

THURSDAY, 23 JANUARY, 4.01 PM

'I'm looking at it now,' Frost says. 'Is this the only comment she left?'

'It's the only one I've found so far,' Pen says. She clicks on another of Makris's videos and scrolls through the comments. 'But I'll keep looking.'

'Right. Thanks, Kibbs. Leave it with us. We'll look into it.' He hangs up.

She places her phone on her desk, her exhilaration fading. Frost didn't seem particularly interested in the link she'd discovered between the two women.

Goldie Silverman approaches Pen's desk, looking a lot more put together than she has the right to after the forty-eight hours they've had. 'There's a call for you,' she announces.

Pen swivels her chair around to face her. 'Who is it?'

Silverman looks down at her notebook. 'Olive Groves. She reckons James Delway might have been blackmailing Makris. Threatening to post nudes of her.'

'And she wants to talk to me?'

With a nod, Silverman tears out a page of her notebook with a flourish. 'Says she knows you. Here's her number.' Commandeering Barnes's desk, Silverman scrolls on her phone, one ankle resting on top of her knee as she leans back against his chair. After a moment she looks at Pen expectantly.

Pen punches Groves's number into her mobile.

'Oli speaking.'

Her voice is so familiar from the *Newsday* podcast that Pen is momentarily disorientated. But then she tenses, recalling that barrage of questions at the crime scene. 'This is Detective Kibbs,' she says curtly.

'Hi, Detective Kibbs, we met the other day—you helped me when I fainted. I know Superintendent Frost.'

Pen grunts softly in acknowledgement.

'Thanks for calling me back. I appreciate it.'

'You have information on James Delway?'

'Possibly. I met with one of Lyra Makris's friends for a piece I'm working on, and she told me some things that I thought it was worth passing on to you.'

Pen wonders which of Makris's friends has confided in the journalist. 'I'm listening.'

Groves explains that Delway allegedly threatened to post private photos of Makris online.

'But you don't have any evidence?'

'No,' admits Groves. 'I just think it isn't the kind of thing Makris would have shared with her friend if it wasn't true. James Delway sounds extremely manipulative.'

Pen doesn't reply, but she wonders if it's possible that Makris and Delway did interact on the night of the party despite there being no suggestion of contact from their phone records. Perhaps Makris confronted him about his threats, and things got out of control . . . ? But his new girlfriend, Diana, is adamant they were together the entire night, so unless he's blackmailing her too, it doesn't seem that Delway had the opportunity to abduct Makris. She thinks about the message that was sent to *Melbourne Today.* In many ways it's a form of blackmail, and Delway is clearly an attention-seeker.

'Her friend is convinced that Makris planned to meet with someone she was interested in romantically on Saturday night,' Groves continues. 'Do you know if she was seeing anyone?'

'Thank you for passing on the information,' says Pen.

'Is there a chance she left the party to meet with someone? Are Delway's movements accounted for yet?'

'No comment.' Pen's tone is blunt now.

'Do you think there's a chance Delway was involved?' Groves presses. 'I figure you'd have arrested him if you had enough evidence—'

'Thanks again,' says Pen, cutting her off and ending the call.

She finds the woman's entitlement to information maddening. How did Frost deal with her when they were a couple? She remembers the tension she witnessed between them at the end of last year and again yesterday. Are they secretly together? She feels a ripple of intrigue at the thought.

Silverman doesn't adjust her casual position but waves a hand to get her attention. 'Our party boy is posting some interesting content online.'

'Higgins?'

Nodding, Silverman holds out her phone. 'He's doing a tour of his house, walking everyone through Makris's final hours while providing anecdotes of their friendship.'

'You're kidding.'

'Unfortunately, I'm not,' Silverman says drily. 'Honestly, my mum is right about my generation—we really do suck. Anyway, did the journo have anything useful to say?'

'Potentially.' Pen explains what Groves told her. 'It might be worth trying to get a search warrant for Delway's computer and phone to see if he made any threats to Makris or other women. If there was anything in Makris's emails or texts, though, we'd know already.'

'He might have contacted her on another platform—WhatsApp or something we don't know she was using.'

'True,' says Pen. 'I can ask Yvonne and see if she knows, but my gut says he's not our guy. And there's nothing to tie him to the other murders.'

'Makes sense,' replies Silverman agreeably. 'He's probably just a garden-variety arsehole.'

'Has anything else come through from the dating app companies?' Pen asks.

Several of Makris's friends shared that she'd used Tinder before she met Delway, but they didn't think she'd used it since. None of the other app companies had accounts registered to her personal or work emails, but there's a chance she has multiple Tinder accounts.

'Not that I've seen.' Silverman pops a lolly in her mouth. 'Last I heard, they were dragging their heels.' She propels herself off Barnes's chair. 'Catch you later.' She bounds away.

Feeling exhausted, Pen admires the woman's energy.

She returns to her screen, still thinking about James Delway. Surely if he were involved in his ex's disappearance, he'd be keeping a low profile. Same with Ned Higgins.

Pen sighs, wishing these cases had a clearer path. Everyone is tripping over each other trying to find weak spots, but she gets the distinct feeling they're collectively making very little progress. She wonders if Frost really is following up on that link between Mackenzie Jackson and Lyra Makris.

CHAPTER TWENTY-ONE

SATURDAY, 25 JANUARY, 11.49 AM

Oli pulls into the driveway of her mother's house and sighs. She gathers her things, including the bouquet of flowers and chilled bottle of wine she purchased after her appointment with her breast surgeon, Dr Brooks, earlier this morning. Then she struggles out of the car, pushing the door closed with her hip and glancing warily at the modest townhouse.

Oli never lived here. Her mother and her stepfather, Max, moved out of Max's family home and into the brick townhouse a decade ago, ostensibly to downsize, although Oli suspects Max needed to free up some cash. She's always believed he has a low-level gambling addiction—whether to the pokies, the horses or the share market, she's never been sure, but Max avoids answering questions about how he passes the time. And he hovers in doorways whenever Oli visits, as if he's worried she's going to search his drawers or demand access to his ancient PC that intermittently whirrs like it's about to take off. Whatever it is that Max gets up to, he always seems to return in time for dinner, and mercifully he seems happy to look after Sally and navigate her various ailments, both real and imagined, something for which Oli is willing to overlook a multitude of sins.

Stepping onto the porch, she repositions her sunglasses from the bridge of her nose to the top of her head. She notices that the plants crowding the small space are wilting. She wedges the flowers she brought under the crook of her left arm and knocks gently on the door. Closing her eyes, she steels herself.

The past twenty-four hours have been a blur of writing, recording and editing. She's tired deep in her bones, but she can already tell being here is going to make her feel restless and impatient. She's itching to keep working, especially on the cybercrime investigation. So far, she's found five people willing to be interviewed, including three victims, a psychologist and a teacher. The smallest amount of digging has revealed a considerable amount of material. Dean is thrilled she's planning to pursue the story, and he's insisting she meet with the mother from Amy's school who has been championing the cause with him.

The door swings open.

'Lily?' Oli says, surprised.

'You seem thrilled to see me,' her sister replies drily.

'Of course I'm happy to see you. I just thought you were coming later.'

Lily chews on a nail as she waves Oli inside. 'I was, but Shaun is in the middle of a deal, so we had to come earlier otherwise we would have been stuck at home all afternoon.'

Oli follows her sister down the short dark hallway, wondering for the millionth time why her mother insists on blocking out natural light.

As they enter the kitchen, Sally Groves makes a beeline toward her from the other side of the room. Oli marvels at her diminishing size: she seems substantially smaller than she did on Oli's last visit.

Oli pats her back, feels the sharp ridge of her spine. 'How are you, Mum?'

'It's good to see you, Olive,' comes Sally's muffled reply. 'I don't see nearly enough of you these days.'

'I'm here now, Mum.' Oli forces a smile.

'Are you feeling well?' asks her mother sharply. 'Your face looks a little puffy.'

Last time she visited, she's pretty sure her mother said she looked gaunt. 'I'm feeling okay, Mum.'

'Sally.' A soft rebuke from the kitchen doorway. 'Oli's fine.'

'Hi, Max,' says Oli.

'Oli, it's good to see you. Can I get you a drink?'

'A tea would be lovely, thanks. And I brought this.' She places the wine on the bench.

Lily snatches it up and examines the label. 'Oh, this is lovely. I'll have a glass. Shaun, you'll have a glass of wine, won't you?'

'Sure,' he mumbles from his spot on the couch. 'Hey, Oli,' he says, without taking his eyes off his screen.

The faint popping of tennis balls being lobbed back and forth tells her the TV is on in the lounge, even though no one is watching it.

'Hey, Shaun.' She watches him type for a moment, considering how unacceptable it would be if she were glued to her laptop the way he is. Her family might be low-level obsessed with the content of her news stories and desperate for gossip about high-profile media personalities, but they don't take her work seriously enough to excuse her from family time.

Max fixes her a tea, and they settle at the small kitchen table while Shaun continues to tap away on his laptop from the couch. As a journalist, Oli has learned to type quickly, but Shaun has unlocked another level of speed. It's so fast that it sounds fake, and she wonders if he's just randomly bashing keys to avoid engaging in conversation with his in-laws.

Her mother takes a dramatic slurp of tea and looks worriedly at each of her daughters in turn. 'Olive, this serial-killer story is just dreadful. Tell us what's happening. Honestly, it's just the most awful thing, isn't it?'

'Yes,' says Oli. 'It is.'

She thinks about her conversation with Detective Kibbs on Thursday. The young woman was very brusque, and Oli got the feeling the police are grasping at straws. It's normally something she would speak to Rusty about, but after their interaction the other day and his blunt text message, she thought it best to leave him alone.

'Those poor women,' adds her mother. 'Bless their souls.'

Lily sips her wine and eyes off a mini yo-yo biscuit before snaking out her hand to secure it and shoving the entire thing in her mouth. 'I don't know,' she says, her voice muted by the crumbs. 'That woman they found at the beach the other night was a sex worker, wasn't she?'

Oli closes her eyes briefly, trying to ignore the crawling feeling across her arms and legs.

'She had children,' says Sally, 'so I don't think she was a sex worker—although she might have been one of those dancers.'

Lily shrugs and raises her eyebrows at Oli. 'What? I'm not saying she deserved it, just that it's not *totally* surprising.'

Sally looks unsure; she's waiting, as she often does, for someone to tell her what to think.

'It's certainly been challenging to report on,' says Oli, after a long pause. 'No one knows quite how to cover this story, especially as the killer seems to be courting media coverage.'

'Seems a bold fella,' chimes in Max.

'Seems like a piece of shit,' adds Shaun, now typing madly on his phone.

Oli doesn't say anything, hoping that the subject will change if she stops talking.

'You do have to wonder if they had a feeling about what was going to happen,' says Sally tentatively. 'You know, like a premonition.'

'No one walks around thinking they're going to get murdered, Mum,' says Lily. 'Not even sex workers.'

'I worry about it sometimes,' sniffs Sally.

Lily rolls her eyes. 'You'll be fine, Mum. Seeing as you barely leave the house.'

'Anyway, hopefully this will prompt some real progress at a policy level,' Oli says. 'Dunkley seems to be taking it very seriously at least.'

'I hate her,' says Lily. 'She's so smug.'

'I'm not much of a fan either,' admits Sally. 'I don't like the outfits she wears.'

'Her husband is a creep,' declares Lily.

Sally clutches her tea. 'Is he? How do you know?'

'It's so obvious. Plus, he used to be a swimming coach.'

Oli sighs. 'How is your work going, Shaun?'

'Good,' he replies from the couch. 'Busy. Lots of opportunity.'

'Shaun is bringing this advanced new technology to Australia,' adds Lily. 'Like a virus-protector thing. Aren't you, babe?'

'I am.' He still isn't looking up from either of his screens.

'I'm doing a story on cybercrime at the moment—sex-based cybercrime,' Oli says.

'Oh, how awful,' whispers her mother. Oli wonders if she's thinking about what her ex-husband did to Oli. They never talk about it; instead it sits like an invisible elephant between them, suffocating any chance of a healthy relationship.

'Is cybercrime really technical?' asks Lily, wrinkling her nose. 'Like only super-smart creeps can do it?'

Growing more annoyed by the second, Oli ignores her question. 'It's becoming a real issue. People are sharing fake nudes and creating avatars of their exes. Kids are being coerced into sharing photos of themselves. There's a lot of blackmail too. It's really serious.'

Shaun chimes in. 'Yeah, and AI is getting increasingly believable. Very realistic. I've seen and heard some stuff where you can't tell what's fake and what's real.'

'Are you looking at naked photos online, babe?' Lily's tone is teasing, but Oli knows she would kill Shaun if she discovered he was looking at porn.

'I'm not just talking about porn,' Shaun replies, evading the question. 'I mean, look at all the deep fakes. There's been a lot of them ever since the US election, and they're getting really sophisticated. The software isn't expensive. I've seen deep fakes popping up in scams a lot more over the past few months. It's good for my business, but some of it is pretty distasteful.'

Oli nods slowly. She hadn't considered professional scams and blackmail, and they might be worth exploring as well. 'I might chat to you more about some of the tech stuff, if that's cool,' she says to Shaun.

'Sure,' he says good-naturedly. 'You can plug my business if you like.'

'You two and your work,' groans Lily, despite the fact that she's a huge fan of Shaun's work when it means he earns loads of money.

Her mother stands and starts wringing her hands. 'Shall we eat lunch?'

'Great idea,' says Max. 'We've got a buffet situation, so everyone can please themselves. I hope that's okay.'

Lily refills her wine while Oli helps Max and Sally arrange dishes on the extended table. They all sit—except for Shaun, who's had to join an important call.

Oli avoids talking about work, instead peppering them all with questions about everyday things. She asks Max about his children and grandchildren, then asks Lily about her house renovations.

'You'll have to come and see it, Ol. You won't like it because it's so modern, but I'm sure you will still be impressed.'

'No doubt,' says Oli.

Sally pushes food around her plate like a child. 'When will you come visit again?'

'Jesus, Mum. I'm here right now.'

'You're always so busy.'

Oli closes her eyes and then opens them again. She hates this house with its small dark rooms, the stale air and the relentless drone of the TV. A wild feeling comes over her—and for a split second, she thinks she might up-end the table.

Before she loses her nerve, she says, 'I actually have something to tell you all.'

Lily knocks back the last of her wine and reaches for the half-empty bottle, looking at Oli expectantly.

'I guess you should all know that I'm sick.' She tries to place the fork on the side of her plate; it clatters noisily onto the table. 'Well, not sick exactly. I feel fine, but I do have cancer.'

Everyone stares at her. Even Shaun looks up from his laptop.

Regret and relief come in equal measure as her mother's hands twirl in a manic dance and Lily spills wine all over the table.

CHAPTER TWENTY-TWO

SATURDAY, 25 JANUARY, 2.34 PM

A strong northerly wind snakes over the asphalt, nudging empty plastic bottles along the gutter in the alley that runs past the north side of the police station. Pen's eyes are still adjusting to the natural light after the morning she and Silverman spent with the Cybercrimes Unit, reviewing the progress on their online hunt for The Photographer that's been playing out in parallel to the real-world search. The team have been analysing the goings-on in various dark-web chat rooms, looking for something, anything, that might prove to be a lead. Many of the people in these forums have a problem they are looking to solve—and in most instances, someone is willing to solve it, for a price.

Over the course of the morning, Pen became aware that a seed has nestled in her mind and is putting down roots. Douglas Jackson is someone used to paying for his problems to go away. This thought kept springing to mind while, on the dark web, she consumed descriptions of unfathomable violence and acknowledgements of criminal activity.

She returned to her desk just as Frost headed outside. On a whim, she grabbed her phone and followed him, hoping to share her theories about the Jackson case.

Frost is standing about twenty metres away along the narrow space on the other side of an overflowing skip bin, talking on his phone. Pen is surprised to see him light a cigarette and suck on it eagerly; she didn't know he smoked. He seems deep in conversation. She studies his expression as best she can from this distance and wonders if he's talking to Olive Groves.

After a few moments she returns a call to her mother, figuring she may as well make use of the time while she waits. 'I'm not sure I can get there, Mum,' Pen says, after Marnie reminds her about the Friday night opening of her aunt's one-woman play on the power of meditation.

'You need to have a break, Penny. It's not like every time there's a murder your rights go out the window. Have you spoken to someone about your hours?'

'I already told you that I wasn't sure I could make it. It's not just about work.'

'Well, I don't know what else it could be.' Her mother snorts haughtily. 'It would do you good to see some art, Penny. As far as I can tell, you don't really *do* anything.'

Pen's teeth grind together. She doesn't consider her aunt's play art, but she knows better than to get into an argument with her mother when she's like this. 'I just wouldn't want you to buy me a ticket and then have it go to waste. If I end up being able to come, I'll get a ticket at the door.'

'That won't work,' her mother says. 'Sephira says it's almost sold out.'

Pen doesn't respond, stepping back as the wind shifts a plume of smoke in her direction. She peers past the skip bin to see Frost extinguishing the cigarette with the toe of his boot as he extracts a fresh one from a packet. He looks like he's finished his call.

She interrupts her mother, who is describing the outfit she plans to wear to the play. 'Sorry, Mum. Got to go. I'll text you later this week.'

'Surely if no one else dies, you can make it on Friday.'

Pen hangs up and fishes a tissue from her pocket, pressing it into her underarms to mop up her perspiration. She glances at Frost again—he's just scrolling his phone and smoking—then she walks over to him.

'Kibbs,' he says, surprised. He holds out the cigarette. 'Now you know my dirty secret.'

She pretends to notice the cigarette for the first time. 'Oh, I don't mind.'

'It's only when I'm stressed,' he adds, throwing the butt to the ground and executing the same movement with his boot as before.

She holds his gaze for several seconds. 'It is a pretty stressful time,' she says finally.

'What's up?'

Pen appreciates him cutting to the chase, even though her insides suddenly knit together with nerves. 'Well, it's just that I guess I'm worried that Mackenzie Jackson's case is going to fade away.'

Frost's forehead wrinkles. 'Have you been talking to Barnes?'

Puzzled, she shakes her head. 'Not really? I mean, we talk all the time, but I haven't spoken to him about this specifically.'

'Okay.' Frost offers no further explanation. 'Explain what you mean then.'

'The Photographer case needs to take precedence for obvious reasons, but we have to keep pushing on the Jackson case. I really think we'll find something on Douglas Jackson if we stay the course.'

Frost looks past her, down the length of the alley. 'There's a lot of evidence that he was controlling and coercive. But, Kibbs, he didn't leave the house that night. And he was with our people for the majority of the days after she disappeared. We've reviewed phone records, and there's nothing to suggest he went anywhere near where her body was found.'

'He could have left his phone at home.'

'True,' says Frost, and she can't tell if he's trying to placate her.

She knows this is her opportunity to tell him her theory. 'What if he had an accomplice?' she stammers.

'Like who?'

'I don't know, but he's a powerful man. What if he had her killed?'

Frost frowns. 'Like an organised hit?'

'Yes. He could have paid someone else to kill her. There's precedent—several cases in the US and other places. I'm following up a bunch of leads on the dark web with Farina's team. We don't have anything concrete yet but there are profiles claiming to be hitmen for hire.'

'But he didn't have contact with anyone after she left the house, and you know the CCTV backs up his version of events. She left the house willingly, and he couldn't have predicted she was going to do that.'

'He might have planned the argument. He might have known he could manipulate her to leave. I was there at the house the morning after she went missing. Jackson was so sure of himself—it's feasible he could manipulate her to storm outside. Plus, he might have had a burner phone that he used and got rid of.'

'Maybe,' says Frost.

'And what about the incoming call? Maybe that had something to do with it.'

'I don't know.' He sounds sceptical. 'We've traced it to the landline of a telemarketing firm.'

'I just think it's worth considering that her husband might be involved, even if he didn't kill her himself.'

Frost's phone rings, and he glances at it, his mouth turning down in a grimace. 'I've got to get that. But I appreciate you coming to me with this, Kibbs. It's an interesting idea, and I know you want to see it through. I'll look into it, I promise.' He takes his call.

Pen walks back along the alleyway, trying to avoid breathing in the rancid smell from the skip bin, as she trudges back to her desk.

CHAPTER TWENTY-THREE

SUNDAY, 26 JANUARY, 4.47 AM

Oli sips tea from her favourite mug as she listens to the BBC World News. The scenes from her dream are fading, but she's still rattled by the visions of her father. She closes her eyes and inhales deeply, then pushes her lips into an open pout, expelling the air from her lungs until there's nothing left. She rarely thinks about the man who disappeared from her life when she was a teenager, leaving catastrophic trauma and financial debt in his wake. On the rare occasions he enters her mind, an internal alarm goes off inside her body, and every trace of him is swiftly and comprehensively rejected.

Her erasure of him had seemed so effective that she'd begun to suspect she no longer remembered what he looked like—but in her dream just now, he was eerily vivid. She smelled him. Felt his hands on her skin. He spoke to her, explaining the medical procedure he was about to perform. Then his gloved hands came toward her as she cowered on a hospital bed, alone in a dark room full of beeping machines.

Oli reaches her arm above her head and gently prods her underarm, tracing her fingers along her ribcage to the lump. It's as if the cancer is happening to another person. A parallel Oli. The envelope containing the scan is on the bench where she left it days ago. *Evidence*, she thinks. *Proof that this is really happening to me.* She adjusts her pillow and watches as the headlights from the occasional passing car cast yolk-coloured arcs across the shadowy kitchen. She thinks how strange it is that she had no idea she was harbouring a deadly disease. But now she knows, she swears she can feel decay radiating from her core.

Oli sighs. The nightmare about her father was clearly triggered by the disastrous family lunch, and she knows the dream about her father was really about her mother. Her parents are fused together in her mind as a messy tangle of guilt and anger.

Sally sobbed into a tissue for the best part of an hour after Oli had announced her cancer diagnosis, while Lily alternated between yelling at their mother to get it together and barking questions at Oli so she could Google medical information that she read aloud to the room. Oli knows she needs to talk to Sally and Lily properly about her illness and treatment at some point, but the mere thought of it makes her insides roil.

She grabs her phone and shoves her AirPods into her ears, then strips off her pyjamas and pulls on a shower cap. While she waits for the water to warm, she listens to the international news headlines. There's talk passengers from China will be screened for the Wuhan virus at all major airports. Oli makes a mental note to speak to TJ about finding someone to interview about the disease, although there's probably not going to be too much interest unless it makes its way to Australia, not with everything else going on. She listens to updates on Trump's impeachment trial, breaking news about another phone-hacking scandal involving Jeff Bezos, the estimated financial toll from the summer's bushfires, and speculation about the Australian Open final. There's no mention of The Photographer.

Wrapped in a towel, she combs out her hair and puts on some make-up, one eye on the *Melbourne Today* website as the BBC presenter continues to talk in her ear. Since she and TJ started the business, she can't recall a day that hasn't revolved around news: consuming it, making it, planning it. But her surgeon wants her to have a procedure within the next month, which means she's going to have to take some time off. To pause.

She'd hoped that confiding in her family would make the prospect of telling TJ and Chelsea easier, but she feels more anxious about it than she did before. There's a story on *Melbourne Today* speculating about whether a presenter from a children's show is pregnant, and Oli shudders at the thought of everyone finding out about her diagnosis and wanting to talk to her about it.

In the bedroom she opens her wardrobe, tugs a shirt off its hanger and plucks some underwear from the built-in drawer. She discards the towel and avoids looking in the mirror as she dresses. Her body feels like that of a stranger—or, worse, a former friend who has let her down. Over the years she hasn't always been kind to herself, has criticised her full figure and her above-average height. She's often felt conspicuous and awkward, disliking the amount of space she occupies and the way her size has prevented her from slipping under the radar. Insecurity about her physical appearance is one of the reasons she chose print journalism over TV, but in the past few years she finally grew into her own skin. Podcasting led her to embrace her husky voice, and while she still finds the attention uncomfortable, she no longer feels like an impostor. But the cancer has allowed the old doubts to creep back in.

The roads are quiet as she drives to the nearest McDonald's. The ABC newsreader details the rallies planned to take place across the country to protest the increasingly controversial Australia Day public holiday, before cutting to a grab from the prime minister honouring the thirty people who died during this summer's bushfire emergency.

As she enters the restaurant, she smiles at the assistant manager, who hums to herself as she mops the tiled floor. The staff here are all used to Oli turning up before sunrise and setting up in the corner with her computer. 'It's the only place that's open early!' she used to declare to TJ when he found the wrappers in her car and teased her about it, but really, she just likes it. Not once have the staff asked her a personal question, and she doubts they even know her name. It's the opposite of the warm, non-negotiable intimacy of Tomato Tomato. While she adores that, sometimes the impersonality of McDonald's is what she craves.

A few minutes later, cappuccino and Bacon and Egg McMuffin—sans bacon—in front of her, she types up a few notes for their morning news drop and sends them to Chelsea, asking that the Mackenzie Jackson funeral headline runs directly after the latest story on the other murders. Trying to avoid making someone's death feel like a footnote is the least they can do.

Swallowing the last of her muffin, Oli makes some edits to the site, updating stories with the latest verified information. The little squirrel icon appears in the top left corner of the screen, letting her know that TJ is online. He'll be updating the sports, science and politics verticals from the comfort of his home office, probably consuming a spinach and kale concoction that Carol has made him drink following their early-morning run.

Fuelled by the food, Oli puts the finishing touches on her feature story about Lyra Makris and publishes it alongside the photo of Yvonne and Lyra at a wedding last year. It's going to be their lead story in their newsletter today too. She emails a link to Yvonne, but she knows the grieving woman will be happy with the article: she approved the draft yesterday.

Checking her emails, Oli skims through several new responses to the shout-out she put on the site, inviting anyone with experience of personal content being made public to share their story with her. All the stories are awful, but one is especially tragic: a woman claims her daughter committed suicide after the boy she was seeing shared a video of them having sex with his friends. Oli flags the email to follow up later and sets a reminder to call Dean. She wants to check that Amy is okay and not feeling hopeless about what happened.

She listens to the edit of the fifth episode of her DV podcast again and reviews her plans for the structure of the final episode, despite not having heard back from Dunkley's office about the interview request.

Just before 7 am, she checks Twitter again. A high-profile blogger has posted a link to an article that has just gone live: *The problem with Lyra Makris's ex-boyfriend that should worry all of us*. It's a strong piece, and Oli finds herself agreeing with most of her points while also feeling relieved that she published her own feature about Lyra today. She would hate to look like she was jumping on a bandwagon. *Delway might not be responsible for her death,* the writer argues, *but he seems determined to punish her slowly postmortem, humiliating her when she can't defend herself.*

Oli scrolls through photos of Lyra at the end of the piece. The young woman smiles easily at the camera, often with an arm looped around a friend. There are several photos of her laughing with Delway, which now come across as chilling.

A Google Alert pings on Oli's phone, and she clicks on the Facebook link. A girl called Felicity has tagged herself in several photos with Lyra, commenting, *Miss you so much Lyra!! Glad I got to spend this special night with you.* There are several shots from Ned Higgins's party Oli hasn't seen previously, but she recognises the backdrop from others: the lush grass, large pool and faux-Mediterranean outdoor area.

She always finds photos taken right before someone dies particularly sad, and these are no exception. Lyra clearly went to a lot of effort with her appearance. Her hair was bouncy from a blow wave, her make-up flawless. The black dress she'd borrowed from Yvonne was low-cut but elegant, and it accentuated her slim waist.

'Where are you?' Oli murmurs, imagining the pain of her loved ones as they lurch through each day, desperate for some form of closure.

Oli clicks back through the shots, pausing on the second-last one. She squints and leans forward, her pulse rate increasing. She takes a screenshot of the image and enlarges it, waiting as the pixels blur and then focus.

Beyond Lyra's right shoulder is Ned Higgins. In the photo his image is only a few millimetres from hers, although he would have been standing several metres away, next to the pool fence. His face is partly obscured by the stem of a champagne glass, but it's clear he's glaring at the missing woman.

CHAPTER TWENTY-FOUR

SUNDAY, 26 JANUARY, 1.31 PM

Pen clicks on another of Mackenzie Jackson's social media contacts, examining every photo and comment, looking for anything that hints at an extramarital relationship. Sanders had told her not to come in today, insisting that she get some rest, but after a futile attempt to read a book first thing this morning, she gave up and has been deep-diving into Jackson's digital footprint ever since.

She's made pages of notes but she's pretty sure there's nothing worth following up. Mackenzie Jackson was an extrovert and appeared mildly flirty with everyone from her siblings to her in-laws, her former colleagues and her friends. With that context in mind, there is nothing that seems particularly suspicious. Pen zooms in on a few of the photos from her Instagram page. Dead woman tropes aside, the woman really did have a smile that lit up a room. She seemed so happy, despite her friends' claims that she lived in constant fear of Douglas's wrath and strange rules. Pen stares at photos of Mackenzie with Douglas's lookalike brother,

her sister-in-law, their kids and his mother. Pen doesn't linger on the photos of Mackenzie with her children—god knows what will become of them now.

After exhausting Mackenzie's Facebook friend pool, Pen has a shower and washes her hair twice. She shaves her legs and scrubs her face with the expensive skin mask Walter bought her for Christmas. As she steps out of the shower she receives a text from Olive Groves with a photo of Ned Higgins. *I debated whether to send this to you, but on balance I think you should see it if you haven't already.*

Pen studies the photo for a long time. It certainly looks sinister, but it isn't enough to take any action. Since she and Silverman went to his house, Ned Higgins has been extremely forthcoming with information, and while the interviews they've conducted have generated mixed reports on the integrity of the party boy, there hasn't been anything concrete.

Still wrapped in a towel, she has a brief nap and wakes to find Elliot asleep on his chair in the corner. Out of distractions, she fetches her laptop from the end of the bed and logs into Chatroulette. In the first room she enters, there is a man wearing a hoodie, his face barely visible. After a few monosyllabic replies to her questions, he leaves. Trying not to feel stung, she clicks into another room.

A young man, clean-cut and wearing a black T-shirt, sits on a couch in a dim room. Pen thinks he is in his mid-twenties, maybe slightly older. He has an English accent and is very chatty. They talk about TV shows and movies, and then he manoeuvres the conversation to what she is wearing and what she likes. And then out of nowhere, he starts yelling at her, his face contorting with rage. He calls her a stupid bitch and demands that she take her clothes off, and she starts crying, a hand over her mouth, as she slams the laptop shut.

She needs to get out of the house.

She pulls on underwear, shorts and a T-shirt, and wakes Elliot. Grabbing his leash, she hustles him out the door. It takes ages for the adrenaline to leave her body and before she knows it, they've walked all the way to the edge of the city.

She turns to head back just as rain starts to come down in hazy grey sheets. The storm comes from the south and brings with it cool air.

They return to the apartment block soaking wet and Elliot comes to an abrupt halt at their front door. She tugs at his lead. 'C'mon, big guy.' She nudges him with her foot until he finally crosses the threshold of her apartment. She pulls the door closed and leans her body against it, closing her eyes dramatically like people do in movies and TV shows, trying to quiet her monkey mind.

So much for clearing her head. *What a waste of a day*, she thinks as she opens all the windows to take advantage of the cool change before having another shower. Once she's dry, she pours a wine and arranges some grapes on a plate. She peels an orange and eats one of the wedges, trying not to think about how the man's eyeballs had bulged as he spat out, 'Bitch.'

After the fruit is gone, she pours another wine and calls Barnes.

'Pen?' he sounds distracted and disorientated, like he's just woken from a nap himself.

'Sorry to call. I wasn't sure if you were working today. I should have texted you.'

'No, it's fine. Totally fine. I'm working—and even if I wasn't, you're always welcome to call.'

'Frost didn't send you home . . . ?'

'He wouldn't dare,' quips Barnes. 'What's up?'

She wants to tell him her theory about Douglas Jackson paying to have his wife killed, but for some reason she holds back. 'What have you been doing?' she says instead.

'Trying to trace Erica Pawley's movements in the days before she was found. I tell you what, Pen, the poor woman had a rough time of it. I'd bet any money in the world she had an undiagnosed mental health disorder. She just couldn't get a break. And that was before what happened last week.'

'Why aren't you working on the Jackson case?'

'I am. Frost asked me to step in on this while the pressure is on.'

Pen feels annoyed about being told to have a day off all over again, but she's mindful not to take her frustration out on Barnes. 'Did you come across anything relevant?'

'Bits and pieces. It turns out she did work at the brothel in Footscray on Monday but only until around eight that night. Her friend doesn't think she went home after that. I've been speaking to the other woman at the brothel, but none of them seem to know where she might have gone.'

'Maybe she was seeing someone.'

'Maybe. One of the women said she was in a relationship around Cup Day last year, but she was pretty sure it fizzled out when the guy found out what she did for work. No one I spoke to seems to think she was seeing anyone, not seriously anyway.'

'She might have been working the streets and got picked up?'

'That's what I'm starting to think . . . But then you have to wonder, does that mean this guy is randomly selecting his victims?'

'Didn't Sanders say she often worked the streets? Maybe the killer had been watching her.'

Barnes makes a dismissive sound. 'I don't know. I'm getting mixed reports about that. I don't think it was *often*. The women she works with said she'd been doing it less and less, but I think she was using again, so maybe she was desperate for money.'

Pen considers this. 'Maybe he cruises the streets at night and just finds women to follow. It's possible all three of them were abducted—we don't know where Marta Holm was before she was attacked. Lyra Makris's phone records indicate she left the party and was close to home when she was abducted, and it's possible that Erica Pawley was on the street too. And we know Mackenzie Jackson was on foot.'

'That's different, Pen. Douglas Jackson is still in the hot seat for that one.'

'Not if we can't pin anything on him,' she retorts.

There's silence for a few moments.

'What about Makris's ex, James Delway?' Barnes says. 'Isn't he caught up in an alibi lie for last Saturday night?'

'Sort of,' Pen says. 'Silverman and I finally spoke to him last night. He's still denying being there, and we can't prove he was. A couple of drunk girls claim they saw him out the front of the house, but a bunch of his friends say they didn't see him there.'

'Convenient.'

'Very.' She sighs. 'Anything new on Mackenzie Jackson?'

'Nothing. That case will get rolled back even further shortly—too much else going on.'

'I hate the way the Jackson case has been downgraded just because no one believes she was killed by the serial killer of the moment. It's bullshit.'

'I'm not going to argue with you on that one.' Barnes's voice is kind.

'Anything else? I've been going crazy trying to relax,' she admits.

Her comment is met with an extended silence and she wonders what he's thinking.

'You need to try to switch off,' he says eventually. 'It's not good for you to be churning over this stuff without a break.'

'Says you.' Pen laughs, trying to diffuse the tension that seemed to arise out of nowhere. 'But humour me. I swear I've watched every show on Netflix, and I'm bored.'

'Well, I know we've received seventeen emails since this morning from people claiming to be The Photographer, but as far as the tech people can tell, they're all bogus. Don't worry, though. We'll waste more resources looking into each and every one.'

'God, it's unbelievable. Like everyone has gone a little bit mad.'

'It seems so,' says Barnes calmly.

'It's been five days and nothing.'

'Yeah.' He breathes into the phone. 'Waiting for something awful to happen is a particular kind of torture.'

Pen looks at her laptop, which she hasn't touched since the nice man with the British accent started screaming at her. A breeze comes through the open window and ruffles the pages of her notebook. It's still light outside, the summer day stretching into the evening without any trace of the earlier storm.

They hang up. Pen closes the windows and makes herself dinner. She turns on the TV for company but soon zones out and finds herself thinking about a stalking case she was assigned to when she first joined the force.

A young university student, Jessa Brown, was being hassled by a stranger. It began with wrong numbers, a cryptic note on her car, and an email from a secret admirer. After a few months, the messages turned threatening, prompting Jessa to report them to the police.

'It'll be a bitter ex-boyfriend,' was the assessment from Pen's boss at the time, a man whose default mode was ironically best described as bitter. 'He'll get bored and move on. She just needs to ignore it until he finds someone else to bother.'

Angry at his dismissiveness, especially as he hadn't seen the fear in Jessa's eyes when she came in begging for help, Pen had staunchly rejected this theory and vowed to protect Jessa as best as the system allowed her to. But even her resolve waned when four months later, nothing further had happened. She thought perhaps her boss had been right.

Then suddenly, Jessa was bombarded. Notes in the mail, emails, phone calls. It was as if her stalker had died and come back to life with a vengeance. Nothing was ever traced to anyone, although Pen isn't sure confirming the identity of the person was ever prioritised by their tech team. Jessa was convinced she was being watched, not least because the stalker was telling her he was watching her.

Three days before Jessa was almost beaten to death outside her apartment by a man who worked at the real estate office next door to the cafe she frequented, Pen met with her to review the latest missive of emails and texts. Jessa had lost weight, and her blue eyes looked huge in her thin face. She wore a woollen cardigan even though it was over thirty degrees, and her hands shook as she sipped her tea.

'I'm going to move back home,' she told Pen, folding her body in on itself as she talked. 'Live with Mum for a while. I just can't handle it.' She chewed her nails, dislodging an old scab. A bead of blood formed on her finger as she looked up, her expression pleading. 'Like, I know he might never do anything, but it doesn't matter. The fear is driving me insane. The not knowing how this ends. I wake up out of breath. I feel like he's behind me everywhere I go. It's going to kill me, Pen, even if he doesn't. It's unbearable.'

Pen lost touch with Jessa a few years ago. Last Pen heard, the woman had moved back home to Perth and was living in a high-care facility near her mother's house.

Turning off the hotplate, Pen transfers the stir-fried vegetables to a bowl. She serves Elliot's dinner, sits down at the kitchen table to eat, and stares at the footage of the news—the same shots of the crime scenes they have been showing for days.

'And now we wait,' she murmurs.

CHAPTER TWENTY-FIVE

MONDAY, 27 JANUARY, 7.32 AM

Oli's fingers fly across her keyboard. She edits as she types, correcting clunky words and muttering the updated sentences to ensure they read well. Erica Pawley's former neighbour in Sydney provided some great quotes, with anecdotes that paint a picture of a loving young mother who despite her struggles wanted a good life, a simple life. Oli's had no luck tracking down the victim's ex-husband, who seems to have gone to ground since her identity was confirmed. But the neighbour's comments, along with some words from the women who worked with her at the brothel, are more than adequate.

Oli finishes the piece, proofreads it and sends it to Chelsea to review.

She's at her desk dressed in what looks like a child's pinafore, her hair in braids woven with silver ribbons, as she talks on her headset while still managing to type at breakneck speed. 'I'll wait,' she says, sass dripping from her voice. 'Like I said, I've got all day and a big media platform at my fingertips, so it's in his best interests to find the time to speak with me.'

Oli smiles. She knows Chelsea is trying to interview the owner of the gym where Douglas Jackson allegedly lost his temper and verbally abused a staff member in October. They received a tip-off from one of their subscribers who frequented the gym, and Oli and TJ are keen to keep Mackenzie Jackson's story alive, seeing as how it's been overshadowed by the endless Photographer coverage.

'I can make myself available then, no problem.' Chelsea's tone becomes abruptly helpful. 'Yes, this is the best number to get me on.' She thanks the receptionist and ends the call. Still typing, she says to Oli, 'I've reviewed that piece and tweaked a sentence and fixed a typo. Want me to push it live?'

Oli nods. 'Go for it.'

'And what about my *It's Time to Rethink Australia Day* piece? TJ proofed it—are you happy for it to go too?'

'Yep, that's fine.'

Oli watches Chelsea for a moment. She has more front than a department store in the eighties. Setbacks will be the making of her, and inevitably they will come. Oli hopes she'll see them for the gifts they are. She's heard a lot of stories from her ex-colleagues about young journos throwing in the towel and jumping ship to other industries when the going gets mildly challenging, and she likes to think that Chelsea is made of tougher stuff—and that she and TJ have prepared her for tougher stuff.

It's just the two of them in the office this morning. Yael doesn't tend to come in until after-school drop-off, and TJ is out having a breakfast meeting with Spencer, the potential freelancer from the ABC.

Letting the sounds of typing and the soft babble from the TV screens fade away, Oli reviews some social posts and pushes them live, checks the home page, stops herself from checking the subscriber data and gets out her notebook. Sliding her AirPods into her ears, she starts following up contacts from her cyber-abuse shout-out. The emails that she has received so far read like horror-movie scripts. People whose trust was betrayed in the cruellest way. Private people who had their entire world turned on its head when real or fake images of themselves were broadcast online and only removed when they agreed to pay gobsmacking amounts of money. Women blackmailed to perform sexual acts in exchange for explicit videos, filmed without their consent, not being sent to their employers. She's started to refer to her new investigative series as Project Shark.

Along with her three experts to interview—a cybercrime contact, a psychologist specialising in online behaviour of teens, and a high-school teacher—she now has thirteen new leads to follow up. Most promisingly, she has received two responses from teens, both girls who claim to be victims of online abuse. She can feel the investigation starting to take shape, sense its cadence. As with all good ideas, it is taking on a life of its own.

She's aware the timing is less than ideal, with her surgery looming and the job offer unresolved, but she feels compelled to forge on. She's confident she can work around her treatment, especially if she can get the bulk of the prep done before she has surgery. TJ and Chelsea can move into preproduction while she's on leave, and she can record when she's back. And if Air 24/7 really want her, they will wait. It strikes her that this series might be her legacy in more ways than one.

She pushes the thought from her mind and continues planning.

The scenarios need to feel realistic and accessible, to convey that cyber abuse can happen to anyone, but she doesn't want to be a fearmonger. Most importantly, she needs to pull everything into a compelling narrative. Maybe she should consider having one story that runs through the series to keep people coming back. But even if she can pull this off, each episode needs to hook listeners and conclude with them wanting more. She makes a note to brief the sound engineer they hire on a casual basis to develop music and sound design for the series.

Then Oli spends the next few minutes on the phone listening as a forty-five-year-old woman called Natasha tells the story of how her teenage daughter was embroiled in an online sex scandal two years ago. It ended up costing her both her private school scholarship and her part-time job. It's a harrowing story, and the once vibrant young woman still hasn't recovered.

'He robbed her of joy,' Natasha says shakily. 'Of course, she should never have let him take the photos, she knows that, but she was young, and she loved him. And he promised he wouldn't share them with anyone.' Natasha takes a gulp of air, which leads to a sob. 'The next thing she knows she's in the principal's office, and they are threatening to go to the cops! They were going to charge her with child pornography, even though the photos were of *her*. The whole thing would have been laughable if it wasn't so horrible. The shame almost killed her, the gossip was overwhelming. The teachers were no better than the students—they were all talking about it. Same with the other parents. I was so worried she was going to kill herself I barely slept for a year. I still can't bring myself to tell my parents. I've told them so many lies about why she changed schools. I'm lucky they live overseas, but one day they will find out.'

The woman starts to cry, and Oli feels sympathy well up. Again, she pictures Amy.

She spoke to Dean last night, and he assured her Amy seems to be going okay. But now she wonders if this is true. He really should take his daughter to see a professional. Oli isn't sure how he'll react if she suggests it. Maybe she can mention it to the mother of Amy's friend she's meeting with on Wednesday.

'Would you consider telling your daughter's story on our investigative podcast series?' Oli asks Natasha gently. 'Like I said in the shout-out, you can remain anonymous, but it might help other people understand how quickly things can escalate.'

'That bastard never got punished, you know,' Natasha growls. 'No consequences for him.'

'I'm not looking to prosecute anyone.' Oli needs to ensure Natasha understands she can't offer justice or revenge. 'Shining a light on the issue will open up a positive dialogue and potentially lead to serious conversations about the need for protection of minors in this space. People aren't aware of how prevalent it is or how complex the laws are.'

'Laws, my arse,' Natasha retorts.

Oli falters as Chelsea springs up from her seat and moves toward the TV screens, her hand over her mouth. She turns to Oli and gestures for her to look.

'What?' Oli mouths at her, following her gaze to the bottom left screen.

The popular co-anchor of *Wake Up, Australia*, Vanessa Blackmore, is holding something in her hands, her made-up face bereft.

Chelsea scrambles to locate the remote controls for the TVs, madly pressing buttons until six Vanessa Blackmores move in unison across the screens. Tears run down her airbrushed face, and her hands shake as she holds a photo of a lifeless woman in front of her chest, the top of it butting up against her chin.

'Please, don't stop filming,' Vanessa begs to someone off camera.

'Are you seeing this, Oli?' Chelsea cries. 'Holy, holy shit.'

'Who is the woman in the photo?' Oli says. 'Do we know?'

'Are you there?' Natasha asks.

Eyes glued to the screen, Oli glides across the room. 'I'm very sorry, but I'm going to need to call you back, Natasha. We're dealing with something here. Speak soon, okay.' She plucks her AirPods from her ears.

Still crying, Vanessa Blackmore chokes out, 'I'm sorry, I had no choice.'

Chelsea is murmuring through her fingers, her eyes bulging in disbelief. The office phone is ringing, but neither of them move to answer it. Chelsea's Apple Watch flashes with an incoming call, and Oli's phone comes to life in her hand: TJ.

'I'm watching it,' she says to him, as he breathes her name. She's surprised to find herself on the brink of tears. 'We're all watching it. Jesus Christ.'

CHAPTER TWENTY-SIX

MONDAY, 27 JANUARY, 9.01 AM

Pen stands next to Barnes at his desk as they rewatch the clip of Vanessa Blackmore for the fifth time. Now Pen knows what's coming, she can see that the popular morning-show presenter was upset before she went off script. In the clip, her eyes are red, and she keeps glancing down at her notes and fidgeting with her watch. After the 8 am news bulletin wraps, Blackmore abruptly stands and holds a sheet of A4 paper up to the main camera, ensuring the image of the woman is clearly visible. With tears running down her face, she explains that the photo was sent to her anonymously and that she has no choice but to do this. She repeatedly says she is sorry, then splutters, 'You all know who this woman is. Who will be next?' before the live feed is cut.

'Zoom in on the picture again,' Pen urges Barnes.

He rewinds the video and presses pause, enlarging the image to the maximum size.

Pen squints and leans forward. The woman is lying in what appears to be a bare concrete cell, her hands secured behind her back. She has been beaten so badly it's difficult to tell her age, but her wavy dark blonde hair is long and tinted by the sun, implying she's young and carefree. She's wearing jeans and a white T-shirt covered with blood and grime, and a piece of grey material covers her eyes. Blood stains most of her bare skin, but it looks like she has a light tan. It's impossible to tell if she is alive.

Speculation is rife within the force that the woman in the photo is Addison Bower-Fry, a promising young musician who went missing on her way home from a gig in Adelaide eighteen months ago.

'Do you think it's her?' Pen murmurs.

Barnes's shoulders rise and fall with his sigh. 'It could be, but I reckon we let our tech people take the maybe out of the equation. No doubt they'll have some fancy program that can match this image to other photos of her.'

Pen nods.

If the victim is Bower-Fry, then this will open a can of worms—not least whether the killer has been active for years and has victims beyond the state of Victoria.

Barnes adjusts his chair and tunes his computer to the live news. They watch a Channel Nine reporter conduct informal interviews with members of a crowd that has gathered outside the *Wake Up, Australia* studios in Melbourne. Several young women are crying and pleading for the authorities to do something about the increased violence across the city.

'I'm so scared,' a woman sobs, her arms around her friend, who nods tearfully.

From behind them, someone yells, 'Do something, Dunkley!'

Pen thinks about Jessa, the stalking victim she tried to help years ago. This feeling is like the fear Jessa described before her attack, the sense of being held hostage.

Across the office, everyone is speaking over each other, and the result is a deafening buzz. Even the most seasoned detectives seem spooked.

Nearby, two officers are watching the YouTube clip of Vanessa Blackmore on their phones, speculating about what led the breakfast TV journalist to do what she did.

'Fuck,' Zappa says, 'it's the front-page story on *The New York Times*.' He walks past looking elated, holding out his phone for everyone to see.

Barnes closes the computer window and clears his throat, pushing up from his chair. 'I'll see you later, Pen. Got some interviews to do for the Jackson case.'

'Okay,' she murmurs.

She checks her watch. It's been just over an hour since the broadcast. Barnes told her that Cloak and Lew went to the television studio to speak to Blackmore, and there's a sense that everyone is waiting for Mum and Dad to return and tell them what to do next. She wonders where Sanders is as she makes her way around the edges of the office, overhearing conversations about tox reports, CCTV, hotline tip-offs, emails and text messages.

In the case room, away from the hubbub, she sees that someone has attached a grainy printout of Vanessa Blackmore holding the photo next to Erica Pawley's photo. Pen sits down and scans her email. There's still no response from Mackenzie Jackson's neighbour, whom she reached out to yesterday.

Her back pocket vibrates, a notification landing on her personal phone. It's a Bumble message from the nice-looking guy whom she messaged a few days ago. *How's your day? Busy? I'm just back from holidays, so slowly trying to get my head into work.*

Pen fights the urge to laugh. Yeah, it's a busy one.

Her phone pings again. *I know you said you're slammed at work but I'd love to squeeze in a drink before the madness of the year kicks in. Doable?*

She shoves the phone back into her pocket. How dare this guy hassle her. She said she was busy, but he obviously thinks she's playing hard to get.

Then, retrieving her phone, she replies, *Might be able to grab a late drink on Thursday or Friday but can't commit until the day.*

Why did she do that? She doesn't really want to meet this man, and work will likely make it impossible anyway. It's as if her fingers have a mind of their own.

She's just about to leave when Frost walks in. 'Kibbs. How are you holding up?'

'I'm fine. I mean, this morning has been—'

'Absolutely wild,' he finishes.

'It's a bit hard to know what to focus on. It feels like the goal-posts keep shifting.'

Frost rubs his chin, and Pen notices he needs a shave. Dark auburn hairs pepper the lower half of his face. 'That's the point. This guy knows exactly what this is doing to us.'

'I expect there will be a full briefing at some stage,' Pen ventures, 'but do you know what happened?'

'Vanessa Blackmore was sent a WhatsApp message yesterday evening. The sender welcomed her home minutes after she'd returned to her Southbank apartment. She'd been at the television studio with her co-host, Barry Goldberg, filming an exclusive interview with Premier Dunkley.'

Pen exhales. 'She was being watched?'

Frost shrugs. 'Possibly. Or someone knew her movements and guessed. Anyway, she has a young son who is looked after by a nanny, so once the nanny left, Blackmore replied saying they must have the wrong person. Then she got another message almost immediately, from a different number.' Frost's mouth twitches, and Pen realises that he's trying to contain his anger. 'The message described what he wanted her to do on air the following day and made it clear that if she didn't comply or if she contacted the police, her three-year-old son would be killed. She received the photo and the script from another number a few minutes later.'

As Pen swallows, the sound of saliva passing down her throat is like the slice of an axe.

'Blackmore took the threat seriously.' Frost's nostrils flare. 'She told no one about the messages and spent the night lying awake in her son's bed. When the nanny arrived at four-thirty this morning, Blackmore instructed her to keep her son in the apartment all day, and then she went to work and tried to pretend everything was fine. You know the rest.'

'Is this your case now? Or Sanders's?' Pen wants to ask what this all means for Mackenzie Jackson's case but thinks better of it.

Frost gives a hollow laugh. 'We're all on this case now. The millions of witnesses have seen to that.' He looks around the case room, his gaze pausing on the photo of each victim. 'This guy is running rings around us. We cannot afford another incident like this.'

Pen holds her breath. No one as senior as Frost has ever admitted this level of vulnerability to her before. 'How do we stop something like this happening again?' she asks quietly.

'We get him.' Frost checks his phone. 'Dunkley's called a presser for midday. I need to do about a million things before then.'

Pen follows him out of the room. 'What was the interview Blackmore and Goldberg did with the premier about?'

'Ah, I'm not sure.' Frost is scanning the office, distracted. 'A pre-election puff piece, I assume. It was scheduled to run on the show today, but obviously they canned it. I'm not sure if the show will be on air this week.' He doesn't say goodbye; he just walks off.

After heading back to her desk, Pen calls Farina.

'Pen . . . hi.' He sounds frantic.

'Hey. I assume your team are about to be slammed with this Blackmore stuff, but before you have no time for me, I wanted to see if you've found any other links between Mackenzie Jackson and Lyra Makris?'

'Didn't you get my email this morning?'

Her body shivers in anticipation. 'No, why?'

'Beyond that one post, we haven't come across anything to link the women.'

Her hope deflates. 'But?'

'It looks like Douglas Jackson and his brother are members of multiple extreme men's rights activist groups.'

CHAPTER TWENTY-SEVEN

MONDAY, 27 JANUARY, 11.46 AM

Oli and TJ try to send Chelsea home, but she refuses: she doesn't want to be alone. In the end they all catch a taxi into the city. They find a cafe on Collins Street, and TJ presses his credit card into Chelsea's hand and tells her to order some food. 'We'll come and get you soon, okay? Just wait here.'

'Should I upload new content onto the site?' Chelsea asks. 'There are bound to be more developments, and I can text you to proof copy.' She clearly wants to remain professional despite her anxiousness.

TJ and Oli exchange glances. 'Just report the basics and text us if you need to.'

Everyone they pass as they walk to Parliament House is talking about what Vanessa Blackmore did. Oli hears her name and Addison Bowen-Fry's in hushed tones, with heads shaking in disbelief. The blustery wind is back, writhing between the buildings, lifting debris into the air and into Oli's bare shins.

As she and TJ reach the Town Hall steps, she detects genuine fear in the eyes of her fellow journalists.

'Let's go in,' TJ says, squeezing her arm, and she is so grateful for him in that moment it's almost unbearable.

He came straight to the office after the broadcast, cool and calm with a clear plan. They managed to get a basic story onto the home page with a grab of Blackmore holding up the pixelated photo. After that they stood there, watching the rolling coverage, reliving the moment when the world turned into a movie.

Oli is still trying to understand why this event feels so egregious—why this is the thing that seems to have pushed everyone over the edge, and why it suddenly feels like all bets are off.

'Press ID,' snaps a security guard.

She fishes it out of her handbag. There are four male guards checking bags at the entrance, and eight others conducting manual weapons searches with a metal rod.

'I've never seen anything like this before,' says TJ.

Oli shakes her head. The whole scene is surreal.

They shuffle forward with the group until they reach the main room and are directed to the east side by another guard. Uniformed cops are positioned around the perimeter, and the vibe is menacing and unsettling.

The premier enters flanked by her husband and Commissioner Maurice Lew. Dunkley and Lew approach the stage together and stand side by side as they wait for the room to quieten.

Dunkley begins, 'What happened this morning is extremely distressing. First and foremost, I want to assure everyone that my office is working hand in glove with the police to find those responsible and ensure the safety of all Victorians. I'm going to have Commissioner Lew take everyone through the events as they occurred to ensure we minimise any misinformation.'

Lew details the morning's events to a chorus of coughs and camera clicks, finishing with a summary of the resources the state has allocated to the police.

'Arse-covering!' someone yells from the back.

The comment is met with several murmurs of agreement.

Dunkley returns to the microphone. 'I want to be clear. What this person is doing is abuse on a mass scale. It's no different to the type of violence that we know is happening in homes across the state. I will not tolerate it, and I can assure you they will be stopped.'

Quiet settles over the room. Oli feels her heart rate accelerate.

'We will take a few questions,' says Dunkley. 'Use them wisely.'

Oli thrusts her hand into the air, but Dunkley points to another journalist, who asks a question about suspects. Lew provides a vague, unsatisfying response.

Before Dunkley asks for the next question, Oli raises her hand.

The premier doesn't meet her eyes but says, 'Yes. Ms Groves.'

She tries to keep her voice steady. 'We all know that violence against women has never had the attention and funding it deserves. You talk about it a lot, but many people feel it's just talk. Are you finally willing to officially declare domestic violence a State of Emergency?'

Dunkley's eyes narrow for the slightest of moments. 'I'm not willing to get into a war of words. It doesn't matter how it's categorised—I'm committed to putting a stop to it.'

'But it does matter,' Oli says. 'Declaring it a State of Emergency would unlock additional funding and resources, and it would ensure the issue remains prominent on the agenda.'

'I can assure you that this issue will remain high on my agenda regardless.' Dunkley turns her attention to a journalist on the other side of the room. 'Yes—'

'Sorry,' Oli interrupts, 'I have another question. I'm working on an investigative podcast series focused on domestic violence. Are you willing to be interviewed for it and to discuss in detail the things you'll do to address this issue? Make some commitments?'

'I'm happy to come on your podcast, Ms Groves,' says Dunkley without missing a beat. 'All you had to do was ask.'

CHAPTER TWENTY-EIGHT

MONDAY, 27 JANUARY, 8.58 PM

Pen braces as the car careens around the corner, blue and red lights flashing. Silverman brings it to an abrupt halt behind the half a dozen police cars in the quiet Flemington street, and they wait as the Special Operations Group break down the front door and swarm the property.

'Go.' Sanders's voice comes through the speakers from one of the other vehicles.

Pen moves quickly, exiting the car and making her way up the steps and into the house, her gun at shoulder height in front of her. The bullet-proof vest is uncomfortable, but she's grateful for it as she scans each of the rooms along the narrow hallway, cleared by the SOG.

In one room there are dozens of boxes that appear to contain gaming consoles, and in another there's a dirty coffee table littered with beer coasters. A third room holds a worn-looking mattress and a pair of stained pillows.

'Out here!' one of the team members yells from a distance, and Pen hears a flurry of heavy footsteps and banging sounds.

She enters the kitchen and takes in the drug paraphernalia littering the benches.

There's an altercation in the yard. Pen and Silverman run outside to see a man being pulled down from a tree. Despite the dim light and his blotchy red face, Pen can tell that it's Ryan Grant, also known as the Real G. As he's led back to the house, he yells swear words and threats of legal action.

Farina and his team have been monitoring several Facebook groups and websites. While it appears Douglas Jackson and his brother are members of groups that champion the rights of men, they haven't been able to detect any activity from either of them. Their investigation did, however, lead them to forums on the dark web where a user called the Real G boasted about strangling a young female colleague, saying he'd taken her on a date and assaulted her when she rejected him. This confession had received enthusiastic support from several forum members.

When an undercover police officer communicated with the Real G, he said he could provide real-life pornography of women who didn't know he was taping them. The police mole continued the exchange overnight and into this morning. Late this afternoon, officers traced the Real G to a residential address using a bitcoin profile he'd linked to a traditional bank account. By this time, he had offered to sell the mole firearms, drugs and fake passports, in addition to claiming he had an associate who could help with fake online profiles and anonymous threats.

Pen appraises the weedy man standing under the fluorescent light in the neglected backyard. His arrogant online persona is gone, and he looks stricken.

Twenty-nine-year-old Ryan Grant is refusing to talk about anything he may or may not have said online, but a basic search of the house produces five firearms and more drugs. Pen questions him about his workplace, but he maintains he's unemployed, and from what they can tell it's true.

'So much for him killing a colleague,' says Silverman.

'I think we should push him more,' says Pen. 'Although I agree it's likely he's a fantasist.'

Sanders walks into the kitchen on the phone. He ends the call then indicates that Pen and Silverman should join him in the adjacent lounge room. Pen is careful not to disrupt the two technicians, who are on their knees pulling apart a couch and combing through the lining with their gloved hands.

'We're going to bring in Ryan Grant,' Sanders says. 'We've got plenty to charge him with. But in the meantime, I want you to make sure he didn't know any of our victims, especially Lyra Makris.' The date of his online claims was what had concerned them initially: the day after Lyra disappeared but before the story hit the press.

Uniformed officers handcuff Grant and lead him out to the van. As they're leaving, Pen notices a stack of beer coasters on the coffee table in the front room. She recognises the logo as being of the bar that James Delway runs in Flemington.

CHAPTER TWENTY-NINE

TUESDAY, 28 JANUARY, 9.30 AM

True to her word, correspondence comes from Dunkley's office confirming the interview.

Oli reads the email. 'She wants us to go to her house tomorrow.'

TJ looks up from his screen. 'That's interesting.' He snaps his fingers. 'You know why? She's listened to your podcast about her. She's trying to disprove your hypothesis that she likes to portray herself as an open book, even though in reality she's standoffish and private.'

'Maybe,' says Oli. She's nervous about the interview. The pages of notes she's made feel redundant, and she wishes they could just get it over and done with.

She glances at the wall of TVs, sees the same news headlines. *Wake Up, Australia* didn't run this morning, and some of the journalists on the other networks are wearing black ribbons in solidarity with Vanessa Blackmore, who has allegedly flown interstate with her son to stay with family.

Oli can feel the collective stress of her peers trying to navigate how to cover the news when it centres on one of their own. Talkback radio is picking apart Blackmore's decision to broadcast the image, and hot takes are being offered on TV panel segments as people express their sympathy for Blackmore before detailing how they would have responded in the same circumstances.

Addison Bower-Fry's family is being hounded as well, their return to the spotlight clearly unwelcome. There's uncomfortable footage of her father filmed the previous evening, his arm around his distraught wife, as he tells someone from *A Current Affair* to fuck off and die.

The police haven't confirmed if they believe it's Bower-Fry in the photo, and Oli assumes they probably don't know, but this hasn't stopped the avalanche of hashtags and true-crime forums from embracing the story. Last night, over five hundred people gathered at the park she went missing from last year to march for justice.

Oli stares at the tweets from scared women that the news reports are using to pad out their coverage and shakes her head.

'What time does Dunkley want to do the interview tomorrow?' TJ asks.

'In the afternoon—I assume she'll go to Mackenzie Jackson's funeral tomorrow morning as well. But I might not go.'

TJ raises his eyebrows. 'How come?'

'I want to prep for the interview and follow up some people for the cybercrime podcast. Plus, I don't think we both need to go . . .'

'Probably not. And let's be honest, it's going to be awful.'

Oli doesn't reply, but inwardly she agrees. It's partly why she doesn't want to go. Attending the funeral of a woman in her early forties doesn't seem like something she needs to put herself through right now.

She loads copy onto the site, quoting a terrorism expert from the University of Melbourne whom she interviewed earlier about The Photographer.

'Strictly speaking, this person is not a terrorist as he doesn't have an ideology,' the expert told her. 'But the effect is similar. It's reasonable to assume he is motivated by causing widespread fear.'

'Isn't it possible we just don't know what the ideology is yet?' Oli asked.

'Yes, that's possible—however, my guess is that this person has been hurt in some way and therefore believes they are justified to hurt back.'

CHAPTER THIRTY

WEDNESDAY, 29 JANUARY, 10.48 AM

Pen stands in the shade of a huge oak tree on the opposite side of the street from St Peter's Church in Toorak, sipping a takeaway iced coffee. She's keen to avoid Frost but wants to be close enough to intercept Annie Soto, Mackenzie Jackson's neighbour, after the funeral. Pen wonders if Barnes is here. She assumes he is, but he hasn't replied to her text.

There are so many people here that they have left the doors open, and familiar melodies reach across the road to Pen. Earlier, she saw Douglas Jackson and his children, flanked by his brother and mother, all dressed in black, being swept into the church shortly after they arrived. Pen considers the possibility that he had nothing to do with his wife's death. If that's the case, the man must be hurting, even if he wasn't a particularly nice husband. She pulls the last of the iced coffee through the soggy paper straw and walks fifty metres up the road to deposit it in the bin.

Pen spots Dunkley arrive with her family and a security guard, who swiftly escorts them into the church. It's no surprise she's here: she has made a habit of showing up at the funerals or memorials of slain women and has attended numerous vigils, even giving impromptu speeches when asked. Wendy Willoughby waves to a young girl as she follows her siblings up the stairs. Her sleek black dress highlights her model figure, and her long hair glints in the sun. Pen doesn't know much about the premier's children. They seem to be part of a new celebrity cohort that has emerged since Trump was elected—or maybe it's always been around, but social media has given it a more relentless platform. Glossy, smart and charming, they are more attractive than they have the right to be, seeing as their parents aren't models or famous actors, but they carry the same privilege and appear to move around the world in the same presumptuous way. Pen assumes Dunkley knows that Delway and her daughter have history, but she wonders if the staunch feminist knows how much of an arsehole he is.

Pen makes calls and taps out emails on her phone, listening to the intermittent songs playing in the church. After an hour, a little kid runs outside, squealing loudly, and his father rushes down the stairs after him, yelling his name and telling him to stop. The strains of a hymn follow them outside, and the media throng lift their cameras in anticipation. Pen notices Groves's business partner, TJ, among them, looking handsome in a tailored suit and dark sunglasses. Well-dressed people soon stream from the church. Several women are wearing pale blue, which Pen assumes held some significance for their dead friend.

Annie Soto emerges and slides large dark glasses on before embracing several other women, while her husband and sons stand a short distance away, looking at their hands.

Pen waits for a break in traffic and cuts across the road to stand next to the bluestone wall. They must have parked in a street on this side of the church, because she saw them walking from this direction earlier.

Sure enough, Annie gives the women one final hug and then gestures to her family, and they walk toward Pen. She lets them pass, then follows them until they're a safe distance from the church. 'Annie!' she calls out.

All four spin around. Annie tilts her head slightly. 'Yes?' The woman is holding two copies of the funeral service, Mackenzie's face visible on the cover. Her glasses hide her eyes but her grief is obvious.

'Annie, hi. Sorry to accost you like this. Detective Constable Penelope Kibbs. We spoke a few weeks ago.'

'I remember.' Annie's tone is guarded, and she adjusts her handbag, swinging the bulk of it to the front of her body like a shield.

The man inches closer, his arms protective around his sons.

Pen says, 'I would love to talk to you now, if that's okay. It will only take five minutes.'

'We're on our way to the cemetery,' she says stiffly.

'Five minutes,' Pen repeats.

She can see her reflection in Annie's huge black frames. Funeral-goers and traffic pass by for a few moments, until Annie says softly, 'Okay, five minutes. Jeff, will you take the boys to the car, please?'

'Are you sure, An?' Jeff asks.

'I just want to ask her a few quick questions,' Pen reassures him. 'It won't take long.'

Looking doubtful, Jeff herds the kids toward the car, while Pen guides Annie away from the path and down a side street.

'Thank you.' Pen falters then decides to be honest. 'This isn't my case anymore, but I can't stop thinking about your friend, about Mackenzie . . . And something you said the other day has been bothering me.'

Annie's mouth contorts, and she sucks in a shaky breath. 'I can't stop thinking about her either.'

'Was Mackenzie involved with someone else, Annie?'

'I don't know.' Her stance is cross-armed, defensive.

She doesn't trust me, Pen thinks.

'But I think you do,' she says gently. 'And I think she was. And it's important that you tell me, because everyone is convinced that Douglas hurt her—and maybe he did, but if there's a chance he didn't, I need to know so we can find the person who did.'

Neither speak while two elderly women walk past, arm in arm, their eyes red and swollen.

'I don't want to get involved,' Annie says stiffly. 'I wanted to come today and honour her, but now I just want to stay away from the whole thing and move on.'

'Because you're scared?' asks Pen.

'Of course I'm scared!' Annie glances around and hisses, 'My neighbour was murdered, maybe by a man who is *still* my neighbour. I do not want to be sticking my neck out.'

Pen doesn't say anything; she senses she doesn't need to.

Annie sobs, just once, and then her nostrils flare. She gulps air in quick huffs before she manages to pull herself together. 'Look, she only told me because I bumped into her in St Kilda. It must have been late November because my youngest son had just had his birthday on the twenty-third. I was returning a costume and got out of the car, and she was standing there. Straight away I could tell something was up. She was acting strangely, and so of course I asked her what she was doing there and if everything was okay.' Annie pauses, and Pen can tell she is remembering, wanting to get the details right for her friend. 'She said she was fine, but she was quite dressed up, and so I asked her where she was going. She said she was on her way home. I asked her where she parked, then she sort of laughed and said she didn't drive. Then I realised she was tipsy, so I told her if she waited for a few minutes, I could give her a lift home.'

'And did you?'

Annie nods. 'I told her to wait in the car, and I quickly dropped off the costume. When I came back, we headed home, and I asked her again what was going on. I told her she could tell me anything and that I wouldn't say a word if she didn't want me to. I knew she had a time of it with Doug—we all knew.'

A time of it, Pen thinks. And she imagines this phrase being used all over the world to describe the coercive control and violence she has spent the past few days consuming.

Annie continues, more quietly than before. 'After a few minutes, Z—that's what I called her—said, "Annie, oh my goodness, I've done something stupid, but it's making me so happy."'

'Did she tell you who he was?'

'She didn't really tell me anything, just that she'd been seeing someone for a few months and that she was happy. All I know is that he lived in St Kilda, not far from where I saw her on Fitzroy Street.'

Pen's heart is hammering so fast she thinks she might faint. 'Did she tell you anything about him? Even the tiniest detail might help.'

'Nothing. And I didn't ask.' Annie squares her shoulders as tears spill down her cheeks. 'But you know what? Usually I don't approve of that kind of thing, but all I could think was, *Screw right and wrong and screw Doug. If anyone deserves a bit of bloody happiness, it's her.*'

CHAPTER THIRTY-ONE

WEDNESDAY, 29 JANUARY, 3.47 PM

Oli and TJ are in the car together on the way to Clarissa Dunkley's, when Chelsea calls. 'There's something wrong with the aircon in the office,' she says. 'It's over forty degrees in here. I've turned it off and on a few times and tried to reset it, but it's cooked.'

Oli puts her on speaker, so TJ can hear. 'Can you call the landlord?'

'I did.' Chelsea sounds out of breath. 'He said he can't get an electrician to look at it until tomorrow afternoon at the earliest. Apparently this is happening all over the city.'

'Okay,' says Oli. 'You can't be in there without aircon on a day like this. Just shut everything down and go home, and we'll be in touch after we're done with Dunkley.'

'Do you think the heat will damage any of the equipment?' asks Chelsea.

TJ is distracted, following the sat nav to Dunkley's place.

'As long as it's off, it will be fine,' says Oli, even though she has no idea.

TJ curses as he turns into Dunkley's driveway. 'There's always bloody something, isn't there? Hopefully the whole place doesn't need rewiring.'

Oli nods. Marion Disney's name flashes up on her mobile, and she flips it over so that TJ can't see. She makes a mental note to call the woman back, although she's still not sure what to tell her.

'I think this is it.' TJ leans out of the car to press the buzzer, but the gate is released before he has the chance.

Oli looks around for a security camera and sees three, with beady black eyes trained in their direction. She shifts uncomfortably and fixes her gaze straight ahead, watching as the heavy-looking gates slide open to reveal Premier Dunkley's house. Oli's eyes are drawn to the bright green circle of lawn in the middle of the driveway. She wonders if it's fake before figuring it's more likely that Dunkley has an army of eco-gardeners and an elaborate recycled water system. The woman rarely misses an opportunity to practise what she preaches.

'Nice place,' TJ murmurs, guiding his BMW along the agapanthus-lined driveway and coming to a stop just shy of the front door. There's a hybrid Toyota parked in the open garage, and two sleek mountain bikes hanging from custom hooks on the outer wall are protected by an awning. Past the bikes and under the shade of an impressive oak, Oli is surprised to see a motorbike propped against the garage, a P plate visible on its rear.

'It is nice.' She admires the large planter boxes on either side of the front door that are full of native flowers and grasses. But as TJ flicks off the engine, she surveys the double-storey residence and notices several imperfections: a large crack in one of the front windows, broken bricks, peeling paint, and an exposed plastic pipe in the front garden bed, looped with bright blue tape.

The large navy front door swings open as they are getting out of the car, and a smiling Dunkley emerges, one manicured hand shielding her face from the sun. 'Hello, welcome! Gosh, it's warm out here. Come in, I've got the cooling on.'

They exchange greetings and handshakes as the premier ushers them inside the house.

Dunkley is wearing a white shirt with tailored dark green trousers that have a faint geometric pattern running through them. Her make-up is as impeccable as always, and her dark bob is caught in a clip at the nape of her neck with wispy tendrils pulled out to frame her face. She is barefoot, and Oli notices the ruby polish on her large toenail is chipped. Oli feels like an oaf standing next to her, and she hunches the way she always does when her height makes her self-conscious.

Dunkley takes a deep breath that doesn't dislodge the smile from her face. The fingers on her right hand twitch in a strange repetitive movement, and Oli wonders if she is nervous. 'Please excuse the mess. I've barely been home these last few weeks.'

Oli and TJ murmur politely that the house is fine, which is true. It looks homely but clean.

'Through here,' Dunkley trills, turning to make sure they are following. 'It's just me today. I figured we didn't need any of my PR people hovering around, and you're doing me a favour coming here. I've been out this morning and buried in reports since, and I need to head straight to a fundraiser this evening, so I'll have to be a strict timekeeper, I'm afraid.'

As promised, the house is cool, and the contrast to the humidity gives Oli goosebumps. She catches glimpses of a large lounge, an old-fashioned kitchen and a tiled powder room. The hallway is adorned with photos, but Dunkley is moving too quickly for Oli to dwell on them; she recognises Willoughby and Dunkley's children, as well as the occasional celebrity.

In the sitting room, the high ceilings make the space look bigger than it is. A glittering chandelier hangs directly over a smooth wooden coffee table, its glass dagger pieces pointing at a vase of peonies. There's a baby grand piano in the corner, and the bay window along the right of the room showcases an overgrown fern garden. An antique serving table on wheels has been positioned between a couch and two armchairs; it sports a marbled tray with a jug of water and three glasses, as well as a plate of savoury biscuits, an assortment of dips, and six mini-cupcakes with more icing than cake.

Dunkley positions herself in the middle of the plush grey sofa, forcing Oli and TJ to take a seat on the leather armchairs opposite. 'Can I start with an apology?' She looks at them each in turn but doesn't wait for an answer. 'I was unaware you had reached out to me to do this interview before the press conference. My well-meaning staff have a hard time managing my schedule and understandably make decisions on my behalf, but I want you to know my answer would always have been yes to this.'

Oli is certain this is a lie but thanks her and gets out her notes.

Dunkley indicates the tray. 'I thought a cool drink was best with the weather.' She takes a pointed sip of water, shutting down any possibility of a tea or coffee.

Oli is impressed at Dunkley's stage-managed efficiency, but she's feeling increasingly on edge. She's used to interviews with high-profile personalities being controlled—this feels different. Dunkley is simultaneously effusive and guarded, and it's making Oli second-guess the best approach.

'Beautiful place. I love the mix of traditional and modern. It gives such a sense of character,' TJ enthuses. Oli feels a pulse of gratitude. He's so good at small talk and has such a knack for putting people at ease.

'This was my husband's parents' place.' Dunkley dips her head as if embarrassed by this admission. 'They wanted a sea change when they retired, and the thought of this place leaving the family, well'—she leans forward conspiratorially—'let me just say that was not a popular idea within Shane's family.' She flicks her hair away from her face and gestures with her hands as if to move her own story along. 'So, we did our sums, sold our kidneys and our souls to the bank, and bought out his siblings.'

'Worth it,' TJ replies, still looking around appreciatively. He gets out his phone and places it on the table. 'I'll just get this ready to go.' They've agreed he will play the role of producer so that Oli can focus on the interview.

Dunkley looks at the phone and executes a curt nod. 'Of course.' She places her own phone on the couch next to her, and it lights up with a message. She glances at it before focusing her gaze on Oli expectantly.

'Is it just your youngest child who lives here?' Oli always likes to begin with a personal question.

'All my children still live at home! I know it's fashionable to complain about it, but honestly, we love it. I don't want them to ever leave.' She laughs, and Oli has the pleasant feeling of being let in on a secret. 'And, of course, we're lucky. We have the space, so we're not tripping over each other, and they do spend a lot of time at our beach house. We're all mad about the beach, and we all love to swim.' Dunkley leans forward, looking at them each in turn. 'Anyway, that's enough small talk. You should ask your questions.'

'Of course,' says Oli, impressed at her directness. 'Thank you again for agreeing to this interview and for being a part of our investigative report into domestic violence.'

Dunkley laces her fingers and arranges them on her lap. 'I'm happy to help. This issue, it, well, it—' She pauses. 'It makes me very mad. And sad.' She reaches across the couch and tugs a tissue from a pearly box.

Oli watches with fascination as Dunkley dabs at her eye then clutches the tissue in her left fist. Being in proximity to someone so high profile is always slightly disorientating, and for the woman to be so vulnerable is only heightening the surrealness of the situation.

Dunkley twists the tissue between her fingers until white crumbs fall onto her trousers. 'The stories, god, they break me in half, they really do.' She drops the remaining tissue on the empty plate in front of her. 'Anyway, this isn't about me, but I'll tell you something for free—there is a lot I'd like to see changed from a policy and reforms perspective on my watch.'

'I'd like to dive into that,' says Oli enthusiastically. 'But first I'd like to ask you again whether or not you will declare the recent spate of violence against women a State of Emergency. A lot of experts say it's the only way to get the issue to be taken seriously.'

Dunkley's phone flashes on the couch as she purses her lips. 'I'm not going to get caught up in a war of words. But what I do know is that it is a very serious issue that deserves attention and resources and money.'

Oli reels off a slew of grim statistics, then she quotes the prime minister, the chief commissioner and the state opposition leader. Dunkley ducks and weaves, agreeing with some points, challenging others, and adding her own perspective at times. Oli's adrenaline kicks in as she finds Dunkley a worthy sparring partner. The woman is sharp, something Oli knew from her research and the numerous press conferences she's attended over the past few years, but up close her ability to think on her feet is even more impressive.

Oli presses her on the lack of domestic violence training available for police and highlights several instances where officers allegedly ignored victims' claims of threats and stalking until it was too late. Dunkley rebuts this firmly but politely, acknowledging where things could be better but managing to do it in a way that absolves her of any blame.

'Many victims' families believe the sentencing in DV cases needs to be harsher and that parole needs to be overhauled,' says Oli, aware they're running out of time. 'Where do you stand on this?'

Dunkley closes her eyes, presumably gathering her thoughts. 'When I think about how close some of the monsters were to being locked up for years before they went on to commit murder, it's hard to argue that there shouldn't be stricter sentencing. Can you imagine a loved one being killed by someone already convicted of a crime? The anger on top of the grief must be crippling. I—' Her mobile lights up again, and she says, 'Sorry, but I need to get this.' She stands and walks out of the room. 'Yes, I can, but I only have a few minutes.'

Her footsteps fade as she heads down the hallway, and Oli lets out a breath she hadn't realised she was holding and looks at TJ. He hits pause on the recording. Oli can tell he thinks what they have so far is good. She knows it too. Dunkley's no-nonsense passion when it comes to this topic is compelling, and her perspective is exactly what the last episode needs.

Oli doesn't want to lose momentum, but it's inevitable now that Dunkley has left the room. She takes the opportunity to eat a biscuit and sip some water.

'You've handled her perfectly,' TJ says. 'This is going to be great.'

'I hope so.' Oli so badly wants this DV series to be the thing that confirms them as a serious news platform once and for all. 'We should give some of the organisations I dealt with the heads-up. They said they would promote it through their channels when it launches.'

'For sure.' TJ flips open his laptop and enters his password. 'And we should talk to Yael too. She might want to change the advertising plan with Dunkley on the hook.'

Oli nods. She's already made mental notes of the quotes that will work well in promotional grabs.

'With the office out of action, do you want to work from my place tomorrow?' TJ asks. 'It would be good to do the edit on this together and plan our content for next few days. And we can plot out your cybercrime investigation as well.'

'Sounds great.' Oli loves TJ's house, and it will be nice to have a change of scenery.

'Cool. Carol is flying to Sydney for a conference tonight, so just come over anytime in the morning. I'll be up.'

'I'll come after my breakfast with Georgia, the mother of Amy's schoolfriend. I—' Oli stops short as a floorboard in the hallway groans softly. She turns, expecting to see Dunkley coming back into the room, but there's no one there. Brow knitted, she goes to the door, only to find the hallway empty. She shrugs as she returns to sit with TJ, trying to dismiss the slightly unsettling feeling that they were being spied on.

A few moments later, they can hear people talking somewhere else in the house.

Oli and TJ lock eyes as they listen to the indecipherable but clearly heated conversation rising and falling. One of the voices sounds male, but it's hard to tell with the distance and soft furnishings muting the sound.

'Is that you, Shane?' Dunkley trills as she re-enters the room via a door on the opposite side of the room from where she exited. 'Did he come and say hello to you?' Before they have a chance to answer, she waves a hand dismissively and returns to the sofa. 'I'll get him to come and say hi before you leave. He loves journalists. He wanted to be one back in the day.' Her face is flushed, and she seems jittery.

'Is everything okay?' Oli asks.

Dunkley blinks and tosses her hair. 'Yes, yes. Everything is fine. I just had to take that call. Now, where were we? Almost wrapping up, I believe.'

'We were talking about offenders committing violent crimes while they are on parole.'

Dunkley's answer is articulate and heartfelt. She lays out her desire for better reforms and the challenges in her way.

'Hi, Mum.' Wendy Willoughby appears in the doorway and flashes an easy smile at Oli and TJ.

Dunkley beams. 'Hi, honey. This is my daughter, Wendy. Wens, this is—'

'I recognise you,' she says, striding over to TJ and holding out her hand for him to shake, her gaze intense. 'The news guy. You used to do crime reporting.'

'Correct,' TJ replies, briefly standing as he shakes her hand. Oli can tell he's slightly taken aback by Wendy's boldness. 'I recognise you as well.'

The young woman laughs good-naturedly, unfazed. 'Hi,' she offers to Oli, brazenly assessing her. She turns her attention back to TJ, flicking her long hair behind her shoulder.

'Hi, Wendy. I'm Oli.'

Wendy whips her head around, eyes flashing. 'You're the podcast woman. *Love* your voice.'

'Thank you,' Oli says awkwardly.

'So, what are you grilling Mum about? Broken promises? Who really hates who behind closed doors?'

'Wendy!' Dunkley's tone is a clear warning.

'Oli is about to launch an investigative series on domestic violence,' TJ offers, 'and your mum has agreed to be part of the final episode.'

'Right up Mum's alley. Hey, I've thinking about journalism as a potential career for me. Maybe I could do some work with you guys. I'd be happy to work for free.'

Oli pounces while she has the chance. 'You were at the party last week with Lyra Makris.'

Wendy crosses her arms and says, 'Yeah,' at the same time Dunkley says, 'We should probably leave it there.'

'Yeah,' Wendy continues, 'I've known Ned for years. He's hot, but you wouldn't go there, or at least *I* wouldn't.'

'And you knew Lyra Makris,' Oli says, ignoring Dunkley's cool glare.

'Yes,' says Wendy, suddenly less assertive. 'But I hadn't spoken to her for a while. There wasn't an issue or anything, we just fell out of touch. My sister and I used to see Lyra all the time, but then she moved across town, and we moved here . . . and I don't know, we all got busy. I didn't see her at the party, but I wasn't there for very long.'

Oli wants to ask Wendy about James Delway, but Dunkley stands, brushes invisible lint from her pants, creating a barrier between her daughter and her visitors. 'Thanks for coming to me,' she says stiffly. 'It made my day much easier.'

'I didn't realise you and Lyra were so close,' Oli says to Wendy as she stands.

Wendy shrugs. 'Yeah, she used to do swim school with Dad, so we've known her since we were kids. She was closer to Bronte, but I liked her—genuinely, not just because of what's happened.'

'Did you notice anything off last Saturday night?' Oli presses.

'I'm sure the police have asked all the required questions.' Dunkley ushers them toward the doorway that leads to the hallway. 'Is Dad home?' she asks Wendy, in an obvious attempt to change the subject.

Her daughter peels the paper patty from a mini cupcake and turns to her mother, placing the entire thing in her mouth. 'I think so,' she mumbles as she chews. 'And Bronte and Cole too. They're in the lounge, arguing.'

'About what?'

Wendy swallows the last of the cake and plucks a grape from the platter. 'Don't know and definitely don't care.'

'My youngest children tend to clash,' says Dunkley breezily. 'They are like chalk and cheese, despite being so close in age.'

'More like champagne and caviar,' says Wendy. 'Both of them are pretty up themselves.'

'Wendy!'

'Time for me to say goodbye!' she trills, grabbing another cupcake and gliding from the room.

'Sorry about that,' Dunkley says. 'She loves pressing my buttons.'

'She's certainly confident,' says TJ, exchanging looks with Oli.

They follow Dunkley back down the hall, and this time Oli pauses to look at the dozens of framed photos that line both walls. She recognises a young Wendy, before she discovered blonde foils and fake tan, screaming with delight as her dad dipped her into the ocean. Shane Willoughby is still an attractive man, but in his twenties he was movie-star handsome.

'Oli.'

Realising that TJ and Dunkley are waiting at the end of the corridor, she rushes to catch up. Glancing into the lounge, she can see a young woman and a young man stretched out on opposite ends of an oversized couch.

'These are my other children,' Dunkley says loudly. 'They are part-zombie. Bronte, Cole, say hello!'

Bronte looks up from her phone, a bored expression on her face. She's not as attractive as her sister, but they're similar. Cole eats from a bowl of popcorn on the floor next to the couch, a pressure bandage wrapped around his left knee.

'Hi,' they say obediently.

Dunkley smiles. 'I really must get ready. The fundraising event is black tie, so I've got a bit of work to do.' She waves her hands toward her face and hair and laughs self-deprecatingly.

'I'm sure you'll scrub up great,' says TJ.

'I'm not sure where Shane is—he might be in the yard. Anyway, hopefully you got what you needed. As you know, domestic violence is an issue that I am very determined to address however I can, and I appreciate your publication shining a light on it.'

'We really value your time,' says Oli sincerely. 'Thank you. We'll let you know when the series goes live.'

They step back into the heat and get in the car.

TJ puts on his sunglasses and waves to Dunkley, who lifts her hand before disappearing into the house. 'She's smooth,' he says. 'I'll give her that.'

'You sound suspicious.'

'I can't shake the feeling she was playing us, but that comes with the territory of someone with so much media training.'

'We've had media training too,' says Oli, laughing as she scans the headlines.

'You know what I mean. She walks that line between being forthcoming and secretive so well that it's impossible to tell what she's really like.'

Oli clicks on an *Age* article. 'Bryson's just accused her of budget mismanagement on the roads project. Reckons it's millions of dollars in the hole, and one of the major contractors is on the brink of collapse. That's probably what her phone call was about.'

'Don't get me started on Vic Bryson. He's even more disingenuous than Dunkley.'

Oli loads Twitter, scrolling past the hundreds of updates. 'She does seem genuinely passionate about tackling domestic violence.'

'Let's see what the polls tell her to think about it pre-election.'

As Oli watches Dunkley's house grow smaller in the side mirror, she thinks about the way the premier had twisted that tissue between her hands when she spoke about the women she was trying to protect.

CHAPTER THIRTY-TWO

THURSDAY, 30 JANUARY, 7.33 AM

Sanders is in a foul mood. He stands in front of Lyra Makris's case board and taps the back of his fist against her photo as he eyeballs everyone in the room. 'Nothing,' he barks. He moves to Erica Pawley's and Marta Holm's case boards and does the same thing. 'Nothing.' He takes slow, exaggerated steps toward the case board with the photo of Vanessa Blackmore and the photo she held up to the TV cameras. 'Broadcast on national TV and still nothing. We don't even know who this woman is, not that it's stopped everyone else from deciding.' He clasps his hands together at the base of his spine and spins around, showing off his toned physique. 'In case you haven't been paying attention, we've got absolutely fucking nothing on this guy, and we're starting to look very stupid. I don't know about you, but I don't want to look stupid. Now get out of here, and don't come back until you have something.'

Pen wants to talk to Farina about the online case his team are building on Douglas Jackson, but he rushes out before she can get to him. Initially Farina suggested that Jackson might have been using an alias on the dark web, as there had been similarities with the comments in one of the men's rights forums and an anonymous profile, but they traced the account to a New Zealand user. Pen wants to push Farina on what's next; she's certain if they keep looking they will find something on Jackson.

'Where were you yesterday?' asks Silverman, as they file out of the room with the others.

'I spoke to Ned Higgins's former uni tutor,' Pen says, evading her question. 'She doesn't believe his IT skills are particularly sophisticated, but she also said he missed a lot of classes, so she wasn't prepared to be definitive. He didn't do well on his most recent assessment.'

'I hated IT in high school,' says Silverman. 'If all the criminals end up online, I'm out of here.'

'I hear you,' murmurs Pen. She has half an eye on Sanders, who is deep in conversation with Frost on the other side of the office. She's desperate to talk to him but also mindful not to agitate Sanders further.

'Do you think we need to interview Higgins again?' Silverman asks.

Pen sighs. 'I'm not sure we're going to get anything else out of him. We know he'll lawyer up, and there's nothing to suggest he was anywhere near Hampton Beach on the day Erica Pawley was found.'

Silverman bites her lip. 'I know, we're parking suspects because we don't think they could have been responsible for all the murders, but I still like Higgins for Makris. We know he was interested in her. Maybe he propositioned her at the party, and she rejected him. There's nothing to say he didn't kill her the night of the party and then move her the next day. No one was looking for her until Monday.'

'I know,' says Pen. 'And the industrial cleaning he arranged at the house the day after is wildly convenient.'

'And we know he was living in Adelaide when Bower-Fry went missing,' Silverman says.

'But he was overseas when Marta Holm was killed,' Pen counters. 'And we know Makris's phone was at least somewhere near her apartment early Sunday morning, which doesn't track neatly with him being involved. On the other hand, he is a narcissist with a history of misogyny, so it's not impossible to imagine him courting the media.'

'And we're back to square one,' Silverman drawls. 'No wonder Sanders is pissed.' She twists her compact body to each side until her back produces an alarming crunching sound. 'Oooof. I needed that.'

'We need something else to bring Higgins in again,' says Pen.

Silverman clasps her hands together. 'Right, well, while we wait for a lead to drop out of the sky, I'm going to tie up the paperwork we need to submit for Ryan Grant. Then let's stay close on doing more digging on Higgins and Delway so we can divide and conquer.'

'Sure,' says Pen absently. She's aware she's fobbing Silverman off, but she's distracted by the fact that Sanders and Frost have disappeared from view. She glances at Frost's office but can't tell if he's in there.

Reluctantly, Pen takes a seat at her desk, thinking about what Silverman said. Are they looking for more than one person? The notion of a copycat killer has been bandied around ever since the communication about Makris was received, but they have nothing to prove it either way.

Pen allows herself to acknowledge another suspicion that has bubbled up in her mind over the past few days: they could be looking for a cop. Someone with inside information about the cases and how a case is run; someone who can manipulate information to ensure they remain close while never being within reach.

Pen makes some calls regarding Higgins's time in Adelaide, trying to build a picture of what he was like then. She speaks to a roommate who says he was a great guy and who confirms he had a girlfriend for a few months. Pen gets her name but has no luck tracking her down.

The door to Sanders's office eventually swings open, and he stalks across the room toward the lift, talking on his mobile.

Pen waits until the lift doors close before quickly making her way to Frost's office. She knocks and waits, relieved to hear his deep voice. 'Come in.'

'Hi.' She enters and closes the door.

Frost's left eyebrow lifts slightly. 'What can I do for you, Kibbs?'

Pen explains what Annie Soto told her about Mackenzie Jackson being in a relationship when she died. She implies Annie contacted her, and fortunately Frost doesn't press her on it.

He stays seated at his desk and leans back in his chair slightly once she's done. 'What do you think this means?'

'What do *I* think it means?'

He laces his fingers together and nods. 'Yes.'

'I think it means that Douglas Jackson might have found out about his wife's affair and wanted revenge. We know they argued the night she disappeared.'

'You don't think it means this alleged romantic interest might be the killer?' asks Frost.

'Of course that's possible.'

'But you don't think so. You still think that Douglas Jackson arranged to have his wife killed.'

'Have you seen the stuff Farina's team found online that they've traced back to Douglas Jackson?'

'It's vile, but it doesn't mean he's a killer. Plus, he's saying he can't remember signing up to the groups, which is supported by his lack of activity.'

Pen tries to calm the panicky feeling that is forming in her gut. 'Okay, so say this other person Mackenzie was seeing is a suspect. Where is he?'

'You tell me. We've gone through everything—emails, phone and bank records, diaries. There's nothing to suggest Mackenzie Jackson was seeing someone else.'

'There must be some sort of paper trail,' Pen says, after a short stretch of silence.

'If there is, we haven't found it.' Frost gets up and tucks his shirt into his pants. He straightens his collar and runs his fingers through his hair, glancing toward the mirror on the back of his door.

'Maybe he and Douglas know each other, and this person seduced Mackenzie under his instruction so that he could manipulate her.'

'That's a lot of maybes,' says Frost, tossing chewing gum into his mouth.

Pen doesn't reply, just holds her head high and keeps her eyes on his.

Frost looks back at her for a long pause before saying, 'It's good intel, Kibbs. We'll keep pushing to verify it.' He picks up his phone, and she understands the conversation is over.

Leaving his office, she's annoyed with herself. She should have framed the conversation differently and been more prepared with theories. Now he thinks she's hot-headed and sloppy.

She returns to her desk to find Barnes at his, looking fresh and focused. 'There you are—I've got something,' he says eagerly.

'What?'

'Douglas Jackson used to beat the shit out of his ex-girlfriend.'

Pen's pulse quickens. 'Tell me everything.'

Barnes explains that he tracked down the ex after an anonymous tip-off suggested she was worth speaking to, but she refused to talk to him. He then located her mother, who eventually revealed that Douglas had abused her daughter so badly on one occasion that she was admitted to hospital overnight and subsequently had to undergo dental surgery. Her daughter is happily married now and won't make a statement because she doesn't want her husband to know what happened.

'The mum also says her daughter is terrified of Jackson and doesn't want to do anything to provoke him.' Barnes takes a swig of water. 'Pen, we're closing in on him, I can feel it.'

Pen nods. 'How will this help prove the Mackenzie case, though? We can't use this to charge him now.'

This seems to annoy Barnes. 'It proves he's violent, and there are people out there who know what he's capable of. He'll slip—and we'll be right there to scrape him up into prison when he does.'

It had been on the tip of her tongue to tell him about Mackenzie's affair, but his reaction makes her reconsider. Frost obviously hasn't told Barnes about it, which seems odd, but she senses it's best he doesn't hear it from her.

Barnes seems to realise how worked up he is and checks himself, clearing his throat. 'How are you going with the Makris case? Any progress?'

She explains the half-links and circumstantial evidence on Delway and Higgins. 'There's nothing that neatly ties either of them to all the victims.'

Barnes's eyes are on his phone. 'Sounds like you've got a lot, but it adds up to not much.'

'Thanks. That's really helpful.' Pen walks off, hoping he doesn't follow.

She locks herself in a cubicle in the level three bathroom and allows herself a quick cry. A few minutes later she feels better, although she looks so awful that she stays in the bathroom for another fifteen minutes, waiting for the puffiness to subside from her face. She's angry at Barnes and his negativity, but she is also feeling displaced, caught between the two cases.

Lyra Makris's mother is desperate to hold a funeral for her daughter but refuses to do it without a body, and their inability to grant her this one thing weighs heavily on them all. Similarly, the trauma Vanessa Blackmore's TV stunt caused the family of Addison Bower-Fry is unfathomable; they have been catapulted back to the intensity they experienced in the aftermath of her disappearance.

Once the blotchiness has subsided, Pen exits the bathroom and takes the lift to level six to see Farina. She wants to avoid Barnes and the potential awkwardness of an apology, and she figures she can make some calls from the meeting rooms upstairs. Farina isn't at his desk, but she recognises one of the other techs. 'Hey,' she says, 'is Farina around?'

'In the main room.'

Pen thanks him and walks through to the next section of the building, where she finds Farina bent over, peering into a screen, while one of the young guys in his technical team zooms in on an image.

'Your back is going to be cooked, you know.'

Farina straightens and flashes her a tight smile. 'I was just about to call you. We think there's an issue with the photo of Lyra Makris.'

CHAPTER THIRTY-THREE

THURSDAY, 30 JANUARY, 8.17 AM

Oli is running late, and her stomach growls as she leans her head against the window, trying to see what's holding up the traffic. She's meeting Georgia in Canterbury, a suburb she isn't particularly familiar with, and she missed a turn-off earlier and now seems to be stuck in an endless stream of back-to-school traffic. She releases the brake, and the car edges forward. Of course Lily chooses this moment to call—she's called every day since the ill-fated lunch, mainly to relay how distraught their mother is.

Oli lets the call go through to voicemail. 'Hey, Siri,' she says. 'Text Lily.'

'Texting Lily,' replies the robotic voice.

'Hi, Lil. I'm working, I'll call you later.'

'Message sent.'

After more stop-start, she approaches a strip of shops and sees the sign for Pearl Cafe. She finds a park and pays for a ticket, shaking her head at the six-dollar fee for the hour and a half she estimates she'll need.

'Olive!' A friendly voice calls her name when she steps inside. 'Over here.'

Oli makes her way to the table where the glamorous woman who greeted her is seated.

'Georgia,' the woman says, sticking out her hand. 'It's so great to meet you. I absolutely love your podcast.'

'Thanks. Great to meet you too.'

'Even if the circumstances aren't the nicest.' Georgia frowns—or at least, Oli thinks she does. The skin on her face is so tight that it's hard to tell.

They order coffees, and Oli orders some buttered toast. Then she asks Georgia about her family. As well as thirteen-year-old Priscila, she also has a nine-year-old son.

'Thank god school has gone back this week. Honestly, I love the little monsters, but Jesus Christ, they grind my gears.' She huffs a laugh. 'Cila is in the same homeroom as Amy. Year Eight. But truly, I worry just as much for my son as I do my daughter,' she says, her manicured hand splayed across her heart. 'It's a minefield for them to navigate this kind of thing just as they are trying to figure out who they are. And the hormones—lord, remember the hormones!' She cackles and sips her coffee, smiling at some decades-old memory. 'It's like being invaded by the devil himself.'

Oli smiles but can't relate. Her teenage years were clearly very different from Georgia's.

'I'm very keen to hear your perspective,' says Oli. 'Dean obviously has his, but he tells me you've been more involved in talking to the school about it, is that right?'

Georgia chews her plump bottom lip, looking troubled. 'I've spoken to all the senior staff, including the principal, several times.' She takes a dainty sip of her tea. 'On the whole I'd have to say that their response has been very disappointing.'

'I understand their position is that it's not their responsibility . . . ?' Oli ventures. 'What is their stance, exactly?'

'Inconvenience. They would prefer it all to go away. But sadly for St Mary's of the bloody Sea, that isn't going to happen.'

Oli knows in that moment that Georgia is often underestimated, and that she uses this to her advantage.

'They don't want to know about it?'

'No, they don't. But they need to. This is so prolific, and no one is teaching our kids how to deal with it. Honestly, Oli— Can I call you Oli? It's like giving our kids loaded guns and then being surprised when they shoot someone.'

Oli is starting to like Georgia. 'I'd love you to take me through what happened from the beginning, if you're comfortable to talk about it. Before you do, I should say that I would also love to interview you for the podcast series I'm working on. It's unpaid, but you can be anonymous if you like.'

Georgia flicks her hand dismissively. 'I don't need money. And I'm very happy to be interviewed—I want everyone talking about this. But I should check with my hubby whether he would prefer I'm incognito.' She laughs. 'John worries about his reputation, he's a CEO.' She accentuates each letter slowly, then giggles. 'He takes himself very seriously, god love him. He's horrified by this whole thing, his "baby girl" etcetera, etcetera, but he's very supportive of my advocacy in this space.'

'Thanks, Georgia.' Oli leans forward, a sure-fire way to create intimacy. 'Tell me about your daughter. Tell me what happened.'

'Well, my girl, Cila—she's a Priscila, but she hates it, so Cila is a compromise for now—she started hanging out with this boy, George.' She pauses and rolls her eyes. 'Yes, George. She called him G so it sounded less like my name . . . but anyway, I'm rambling. Sorry. So, at the same time Cila met G, Amy met Roland, and they became a little foursome. I thought it was sweet, you know, young love—or not even that, really, just little people figuring out how different relationships work. I told Cila they were welcome to spend time at our place, and they did. As far as I knew there were no issues.'

'What happened?'

'Well, unbeknown to me, the boys were encouraging the girls to pose for them. Sometimes together, sometimes individually. Often in their bathers or gymnastics outfits. We have a pool, so it wasn't uncommon for them to be swimming, and I admit I wasn't always monitoring them—they were all strong swimmers. But it was happening at school too. In the locker room and even at recess.'

'Some of the photos were taken on the school grounds?' Oli confirms.

'Yes.' Georgia nods emphatically. 'I've seen them.'

Oli takes several notes. 'I appreciate this is a sensitive question, but do you know if the girls were willing to pose for the photos or were coerced into it?'

'No, it's fine.' Georgia leans her elbow on the table and rests her head against her palm. 'I've talked to Cila about it at length. I think they felt special and grown-up. They liked the attention. But they had no idea what they were agreeing to.'

'No understanding of consequences,' suggests Oli.

'Zero. Cila liked G, liked being able to make him happy.' She laughs. 'I mean, it's hardly something that only young girls are susceptible to. If someone indicated they wanted sexy photos of me, I'm sure I'd be tempted.'

Oli doesn't agree or disagree. 'And it escalated,' she presses.

'It did.' Georgia's made-up eyes drop to gaze at the table. 'At some point the girls posed nude. Or topless, I should say.'

'How did you find out?' asks Oli, her hands curled around her coffee, despite its heat.

'I only found out when Cila came home in tears on the second-last day of school and told me everything. Otherwise, I would have remained blissfully ignorant of the entire saga, which just goes to show how insidious the whole thing is. I mean, we had no idea. Dean had no idea. The school apparently had no idea, so who knows how much of this type of thing is happening under our noses?'

'And you spoke to the school about it straight away?'

'Of course. I mean, it's a pretty big deal. I thought they would appreciate me trying to work with them to address it, but they were extremely unhelpful. They don't want to consider any education or proactive steps to prevent it from happening again. When I really kicked up a fuss, they said they think discussing it risks putting ideas in the students' heads. Long story short, they said it was my responsibility to make sure my daughter respects herself enough to keep her clothes on.'

Oli blinks. 'Wow, that's—'

'It's bullshit, is what it is,' says Georgia cheerfully. 'I pay a freaking fortune in school fees, and they don't want to know about it, which is wild considering some of the photos were taken at the school! And certainly, the text messaging is happening during school hours.'

Oli nods as she takes more notes. This tension over responsibility is awful, but it will make for a good narrative.

'I knew things had cooled between Cila and G. He stopped coming round, and when I asked her about him, she was evasive. But she still talked about him sometimes, so I didn't think much of it. Of course, now I know that little turd was blackmailing her. Getting her to do stuff with him—nothing too revolting, thank goodness, but who knows how far it might have gone.'

'And he was threatening to send the photos to their friends?' Oli prompts.

'To me and John! He was threatening to send the photos to us anonymously. Can you believe it? We welcomed that kid into our house and treated him like a little prince.'

'I'm sorry,' says Oli.

'Thank you. It was awful to realise that he used her shame against her.' Georgia scowls. 'And I hate that he dragged us into it and used the good relationship we have with Cila against her like that.'

'It's the ultimate power play, isn't it,' Oli muses, thinking of James Delway and Yvonne's accusation. 'A grenade of shame ready to be unleashed. A young girl is going to do almost anything to keep photos like that under wraps.'

'Totally. It's the reason I'm so passionate about this. It might be just a photo, but it can ruin your life.'

'Do you know how he planned to send the photos to you? From someone else's phone?'

'Oh, apparently there's some computer program that generates text messages so you can send things anonymously.'

'And kids use it?'

'Yeah, they have different accounts and fake profiles so parents can't check them. Mostly they just send silly jokes and mess around with each other. But I know it's been used as a cover for bullying, and now they can send explicit photos. Honestly, Oli, I don't know what parents are supposed to do. This stuff is everywhere, and they need devices for school.'

Oli is jotting down more notes. She knows kids live in a tech-orientated world, but she's still shocked at tweens being so entrenched in it that they have multiple identities and use fake phone numbers to send pornography.

'It's admirable what you're doing,' Oli says. 'A lot of parents would just want this buried and never spoken about again.'

'I'm a cancer survivor,' Georgia says. 'This kind of shit barely scratches the surface.'

Oli pauses mid-scrawl. 'Oh, I'm sorry.'

Georgia makes a face. 'Don't apologise, hun. It's all good. I'm in remission. I gave the big C the big FU about three years ago. She's too scared to come back.' Her face becomes serious. 'Jokes aside, I was lucky—but seriously, no stress, I talk about it all the time.'

'Back to the girls,' says Oli, feeling overwhelmed and impressed by Georgia's bolshy attitude to her illness. 'Do you know which of the boys actually sent the images?'

'George shared some images of Cila with his mates. He's essentially admitted to that.'

'And then what did they do with them? Did they send them to other people?'

'I don't think so, although Cila was telling me she thinks they sent them via Snapchat to a few people, so they might have been screenshot and saved—we don't know.'

'And who shared the pictures of Amy? Was it Roland?'

'Now we come to the part of the story that I'm scared to tell you.' Georgia ducks, as if trying to avoid Oli hitting her.

Oli cocks her head. 'What do you mean?'

Georgia's expression is pained. 'This is quite sensitive, and I swear to god I only became aware of this very recently, like a few days ago, after I'd agreed to meet with you.'

Oli's insides twist. It must be about Dean. Surely he hasn't done something to the twins. All the shame from her father's abuse bears down on her, and she feels dizzy. 'What did he do?' she says, then holds her breath.

'*She*. I'm talking about Kate.'

'Kate . . . ?' Oli exhales, trying to understand. Kate is the quieter, more reserved twin. 'Are there photos of Kate too?'

Georgia shakes her head. 'No, no. Oli, love. What I'm saying is that it was Kate who sent the photos of Amy to the other schoolkids.'

CHAPTER THIRTY-FOUR

THURSDAY, 30 JANUARY, 9.39 AM

Sanders flicks through various images of Lyra Makris's bloodied face, pausing to examine the annotations Farina and his team have made.

'What exactly does this mean?' he says, handing the prints back to Farina.

They're in one of the small rooms on the fifth floor, and as Pen looks at the wall behind Sanders's head, she swears that it moves closer to her. Below them, an ambulance wails along Spencer Street, and the air-conditioning unit heaves with the effort of cooling the stuffy building. Pen feels sweat trickle down her back and wishes she'd remembered to bring her bottle of water.

'We think the image may have been doctored.'

'It's fake?' Spittle flies from Sanders's mouth and lands on the corner of the printout. 'I was told it was legitimate. We've based our entire investigation around it.'

'We don't necessarily think it's fake. Based on our recent analysis, we believe it has been manipulated in some way. There are some minor inconsistences that indicate interference.'

Sanders pinches the skin between his eyebrows. 'But you don't think the other photos were manipulated?'

'We're not sure,' Farina admits. 'The specialist UK cyber expert our team have been working with has doubts about the image Blackmore was sent.'

'That might be fake too?'

'"Fake" is a problematic word,' says Farina. 'We think the Blackmore image is a photo of a photo.'

Sanders looks close to erupting. 'So, what the hell does this mean? Are they real or not?'

Farina hesitates, clearly unsure of how to react to Sanders's frustration. 'We believe they are real photos but like I said we now believe there has been some manipulation.'

'What about who sent them? Have you made *any* progress on that front?'

'Well,' Farina says, 'seeing as we can't trace the origin of the communication, we're unable to confirm the images were sent by the same person. We think it's likely, though, that there is one perpetrator, and he's mixing things up, making it harder for us to track him down. The way he is operating suggests someone highly skilled, possibly a professional hacker.'

'Didn't we already know that?' Sanders's face flushes a deep red. 'This motherfucker has been sending us personalised love notes, and we haven't been able to track him for over a week now, so I'm pretty bloody aware that he knows his way around a computer.'

His outburst is met with a few moments of silence.

'What is this bugger playing at?' Sanders exclaims, bringing his fist into his open palm.

Farina doesn't reply.

'He's angry,' Pen offers quietly. 'He's angry, and he likes being in control. He's enjoying tormenting us.'

Sanders looks at her for what feels like a long time. 'What else?' he barks, turning back to Farina.

'We're investigating several dark-web chat rooms, trying to locate anything that might be relevant.'

'Chat rooms?'

'Yes, sir. Forums on the dark web. We've found several instances where people have offered to doctor images or generate fake identification, so we're making sure we can't find anything that is linked to this case.'

'But you haven't found anything yet?' says Sanders.

Farina shakes his head. 'Not yet.'

Sanders sniffs derisively. 'Right. Well, inform me immediately of anything, even the vaguest potential lead.'

Pen's nostrils flare. 'We might have found something. There are a few exchanges that suggest people also engage strangers to conduct illegal activity—drug-trafficking, mainly, but other things too, including murder.'

'You've got messages showing someone commissioning a murder?'

'Not explicitly, but we should explore the possibility that Douglas Jackson commissioned someone to murder his wife.'

'Douglas Jackson is hardly an underworld figure.'

'It's not unheard of for an individual with money to hire a hitman on the dark web,' she insists.

Sanders looks annoyed. 'I have you assigned to the Makris case, Kibbs.'

'Yes, sir. But I worked the Jackson case for over a week, and I interviewed Douglas Jackson at the house. It's worth exploring. We know he didn't leave his house the night Mackenzie went missing, but there's an unexplained incoming phone call. I'm thinking they could indicate correspondence with a hitman. And we all know the Jacksons' relationship was turbulent.'

'It sounds pretty convoluted.' Sanders turns to Farina. 'What do you think?'

'We have been monitoring online exchanges that suggest people are available to carry out targeted hits in exchange for large sums of money. Most of them predate the Jackson case, and we can't link any activity to Douglas Jackson at this stage, but we know he has used the dark web in the past—and he is a wealthy man, so it's not implausible.'

Pen summons up the courage to look Sanders in the eye.

He widens his stance and folds his arms across his muscular chest. 'Has Douglas Jackson got any unexplained money transfers?' Again, he directs the question to Farina.

'Not as far as I'm aware, sir.'

'Any indication that he is active in any of these specific chat rooms?'

Farina fumbles and drops several sheets of paper on the floor. 'Not at this stage, no. But that's the challenge in these spaces. They all use a network called Tor or other browsers designed to enable anonymity, so it's incredibly difficult to trace their users.'

Sanders's phone vibrates, and he clicks his tongue as he scans a text message.

Pen can feel his interest waning. Desperation ripples through her, and she is mortified to feel tears stinging her eyes. 'Sir, I really think—'

'Do you know what I think?' Sanders interrupts. 'I think we need to focus all our efforts on catching the psychopath that is making us look like fucking idiots. The killer that is picking women off like they are clay pigeons, not some suburban father with anger issues.'

'Douglas Jackson has full custody of his two young children now,' Pen says quietly.

'There is no history of abuse toward the children—we've canvassed that extensively.' Sanders exhales slowly, his gaze back on Farina. 'If you find anything that suggests Douglas Jackson arranged a hit on his wife, let Frost know. Until then, please have your team spend every waking hour on trying to hunt down that Photographer bastard.'

Farina straightens the printouts and nods, pushing his glasses back up the bridge of his nose. Pen stares at one of the computer screens to his left and tries to keep her emotions in check. Sanders's disdain for her is painful.

'Absolutely, sir,' he says. 'We're doing everything we can.' He clears his throat and opens his mouth to say something before closing it again.

'Spit it out,' says Sanders, clearly losing patience.

Farina takes a deep breath. 'I appreciate that you want to deal in absolutes, sir—but I do think it's worth tabling that if the image of Makris has been manipulated, then this changes things significantly.'

'What does that mean?'

Pen interjects. 'He's saying there's a possibility Lyra Makris is still alive.'

CHAPTER THIRTY-FIVE

THURSDAY, 30 JANUARY, 9.48 AM

Anxiety gnaws at Oli as she drives to TJ's. The thought of having a conversation with Dean about what Kate did is unpleasant, like a physical task she wants to avoid, but as much as that is weighing on her mind, she senses it's a distraction from the real dread she feels. There's been no significant updates to report on the murdered women for days now. As far as she and TJ can tell, the cops have no idea where Lyra Makris's body is. While they're supposedly following up several leads to trace the origin of the killer's messages, they are no closer to finding the person who has wreaked havoc on the city. The silence is becoming more terrifying than the receipt of a new message or the discovery of a body, as everyone wonders and waits.

Marion Disney calls as Oli approaches TJ's house. She answers, and the industry stalwart's voice comes through the speaker. 'Olive. You've been busy.'

'Yes, sorry I missed you yesterday.'

'Have you been too busy to think about our conversation? I'm starting to plan for the second half of this year, so I'm keen to know if we should progress our discussion.'

'I really haven't had much time to properly think about it.'

'I understand,' says Marion. 'It's been a wild couple of weeks. Why don't we work to a deadline? If you're anything like me, you need a deadline after so many years in this crazy industry. Let's talk again in two weeks. We can do it over an expensive dinner. My shout.'

Oli finds herself telling Marion that dinner sounds great.

'I'll text you the details.'

TJ's ornate front gate is open, and Oli is so flustered that she takes the turn too quickly and almost knocks over an abstract bronze sculpture as she pulls into the driveway. She disconnects her phone from her charger and drops it noisily into the centre console.

A few moments later, the heavy wooden door swings open, and TJ steps onto the black and white Tudor tiles. He's dressed in casual attire reminiscent of the royal family on a hunting expedition, although he's succumbed to the heat and opted for tailored shorts. He's smiling and holds a ceramic mug in each hand.

She gets out of the car and smiles back at him. 'Morning.'

He holds out one of the mugs. 'I made you an iced coffee.'

'Thank you,' Oli says. 'Let me just get inside and offload all this.'

He waits as she collects the last of her things, centres her weight and shuts the door with her hip. 'All good?' he asks.

She feels weighed down by secrets. Her cancer and her conversations with Marion. Her feelings for Rusty. 'Yep!'

'How did you go with the school mum?'

'Really well. She'll make a great interview subject. She has a good perspective on her daughter and what happened.'

'Great. I've had a positive start to the morning too—a potential angle I want to get you across relating to Bower-Fry.'

He gestures for Oli to enter the house, and she steps into the hallway and makes her way toward the kitchen.

'I spoke to the electrician. He's got to pick up some parts from somewhere to fix the aircon, but he thinks he'll be able to do it today, so hopefully we'll be back in the office tomorrow.'

'That's good.' She deposits her things on the glossy marble bench with a grunt. Shaking out her arms, she reaches for the coffee and takes a sip. 'Did you speak to Chelsea and Yael?'

'Yeah. They're going to work from home.'

Oli lets her eyes wander around the huge room. She hasn't been inside TJ's place recently, but she used to be here often, mostly in the weeks leading up to the launch of *Newsday* before they rented their own space. It's at least three times the size of her apartment, and a lot nicer.

'Thanks for this.' She indicates the coffee. 'You said Carol is away for work? Where is she?'

Slight wrinkles crease TJ's forehead. 'Sydney. She's at some conference, a junket it sounds like. She's up there quite a bit these days.'

'Is that new?' Oli indicates an abstract painting hanging on the wall above the large oval dining table.

'Nah. It was in storage from our old place, and we finally swapped it for the antique map that was there. I think the colours work better with the new seats. Carol's not sure.'

'It looks great.' The bold artwork certainly trumps the second-hand posters and fabric wall-hangings she has accumulated over the years.

TJ points to the kitchen table. 'We can set up in here. Or we can use the study, if you prefer?'

'Here is fine.' She finishes the coffee, which is at least as good as what she buys from the cafe near the office, and sets up her laptop on TJ's table. 'I was thinking we should edit Dunkley's interview while it's still fresh. Then we can check in with the team, and then I can take you through the loose outline I've done for the cybercrime series. And then we can chat through your Bower-Fry piece . . . ?'

TJ nods as he scrolls messages on his phone.

'Sounds good. There are some great grabs from the Dunkley interview. I'm sure you clocked them yesterday. They will work well for promos, and—' TJ's voice cuts off, his gesturing arm suspended in midair. His flushed cheeks turn ghost-white.

Oli's stomach drops. 'TJ, what is it?'

He shakes his head and moans softly.

'What? TJ, you're scaring me.'

He shakes his head again and points at her then frantically at the back door.

Fear runs like ice through Oli's veins, but she understands and makes her way through the kitchen to the back door. She watches as TJ types something on his phone, his shoulders hunched up around his ears. After several excruciating seconds he places the phone on the table and heads toward her, his face so drawn he looks like a different person. Oli closes the back door and grabs his arm. 'TJ,' she whispers, 'tell me what's happened.'

His jaw tenses, and he looks at the pool. Oli senses he's avoiding looking at her to keep his emotions in some kind of order. His mouth small, he murmurs, 'Someone sent me a message. Like the one Vanessa Blackmore got.'

Oli's eyes widen in alarm. 'No.'

He nods. 'Holy shit, Oli. What am I going to do?'

A roaring fills her ears. 'What did it say? Was there a threat?'

He holds his fist up to his mouth and breathes against it with increasing intensity. 'He knows I'm home. Here, I mean. The message said I need to stay here and not speak to anyone.'

A dry sob forces itself from Oli's mouth. 'And do what?'

The words come out in a rush. 'Publish a video of a murder victim on the *Newsday* site.'

'What video?' Oli presses.

'I don't know!' TJ grabs the back of his head and clenches his teeth as if he's in pain. 'He hasn't sent it yet.'

'What else did he say?'

TJ exhales through his clenched teeth. 'That he will kill Carol if I tell anyone or contact the police.'

Oli feels the world tilt. 'Did he use her name?'

TJ's head moves in the affirmative, and he buries his face in his hands. 'Oli, what the fuck am I going to do?'

Shaking, she puts her hands on TJ's shoulders, her clear-eyed stare locked on his wild one as she says to him in a calm, authoritative whisper, 'You need to check whether there's another message. You should keep communicating with him. And then we are going to make sure Carol is safe.'

TJ puffs out his cheeks and briefly places his hands on top of hers so they push further into his shoulders. 'Shit, Oli. I can't believe this.'

'No. But it's happening. Vanessa Blackmore and her kid are fine. Remember that.'

'That's because she did what he asked.'

'One step at a time,' she says, sounding surer of herself than she feels.

'Do you think he's watching her? Has he been monitoring us through my phone?'

'I doubt it,' she says. 'But I can wait out here if you like.'

She watches him return inside and pick up his phone, then cry out and step backwards. His hands clutch his skull as he crumples to the floor.

CHAPTER THIRTY-SIX

THURSDAY, 30 JANUARY, 10.34 AM

Pen returns to the case room. When she realises no one else is there, she closes the door and sits facing the wall featuring the case boards. Looking at each victim in turn, she mentally walks herself through the timeline again.

'Sometimes it's good to stand back and just have a good old think about things,' Barnes told her when she first worked with him. 'Just stop for a second and *think*.'

She's been uneasy about this case from the beginning, never feeling like she has a grasp on any aspect of it. Maybe that's to be expected, but there's more at play than the killer's slipperiness. Partly it's the gear shift from the momentum Pen felt working closely on the Jackson case with Barnes to working on one with dozens of people and multiple victims, but she senses it has also been due to her own insecurity. She doesn't know what to do on a case of this scale and continually feels inferior to her peers, something that isn't helped by having to report in to Sanders again.

Pen shakes her head and refocuses on the case boards. She's done everything she can for Mackenzie Jackson, and she knows Frost and Barnes will do their best to get justice for the slain woman.

'Patterns, patterns,' she murmurs, running her eyes across the victim timelines. 'What are we not seeing?'

Addison Bower-Fry disappeared over eighteen months ago. Marta Holm was found on Christmas Eve. Lyra Makris went missing roughly four weeks later. Then, only three days after that, Erica Pawley was killed.

Pen considers these intervals, trying to make sense of them. Are there victims that the police aren't aware of yet? Or did something happen in the killer's life that prompted such a gap and then the recent frenzy? A break-up? A betrayal?

That makes Pen think about James Delway. He certainly seems the vengeful type, but they can't place him in Adelaide to align with Bower-Fry's disappearance, and his girlfriend has provided him with an alibi for the night they believe Erica Pawley was killed.

Pen stares at the photo of Lyra Makris. They might not have definitive proof that she's dead, but it doesn't make sense that she is alive. He killed the others, so surely it's just a matter of time before her body is discovered somewhere. Pen's aware that things should feel hopeless, but the faint digital fingerprints that Farina and his team found in the image feel like a chink in the killer's armour. She's just hoping that it's a weakness they can exploit.

Is there a clue in the women themselves? Holm was a backpacker on the adventure of a lifetime. Makris was a young woman passionate about food, reeling from a difficult break-up. Pawley's life was longer, but it had been a struggle. And Bower-Fry was a talented musician on the brink of success. Why these women? Did he know them, or was the whole point that he'd never laid eyes on them before in his life?

The door to the case room opens, and Barnes enters. 'Hey!' He puts steadying hands on her shoulders. 'Sorry I missed your call. Was right in the thick of something that I couldn't hit pause on.'

Pen's brow furrows. She can't remember calling him. Or does he mean yesterday?

'What are you doing in here?' he asks.

'I'm just trying to piece a few things together.' She doesn't feel much like talking to him. 'What about you?'

'What haven't I been doing?' Barnes drops his voice, even though no one else is in earshot. 'I'm pushing Douglas's ex to speak up about what he did to her, and I'm finally getting through.'

'I thought she didn't want to get involved?'

'She's involved whether she likes it or not.'

Pen shifts in her chair, watching him.

'She needs to report what Douglas did.' Barnes sounds annoyed. 'It's critical.'

'She doesn't need to do anything,' says Pen quietly.

He shrugs. 'Honestly, she looked relieved to be getting it off her chest after all these years.'

'Where was this?' asks Pen.

'At her place in Clifton Hill.'

Pen's phone buzzes in her hand, causing her to startle.

Barnes notices and laughs.

'Kibbs.' She answers Farina's call primly, turning away from Barnes.

'The guys have found some more forums on the dark web that might be worth you taking a look at. There's a member calling himself "click" who has been active over the past few days.'

'I'll be up shortly,' Pen tells him.

Barnes is on his phone, apparently watching a news clip. 'God, I can't stand how Dunkley and her husband think they own this bloody news story. Swanning around at crime scenes.' He leans closer to his screen. 'Would you just fuck off already.'

'Are you okay?' Pen asks.

He looks surprised. 'Me? I'm fine. Burning the midnight oil a bit too hard, maybe, but you know all about that.'

'Okay,' she says.

He slips his phone into his pocket. 'I'd better check in with Frost,' he says, cracking his knuckles. 'He wants a download on Jackson's ex.'

She nods.

'I'll catch you a bit later.' He comes over and claps her on the shoulder, but then his hand is gripping her. 'Don't stay holed up in here all day. Make sure you get out and do some proper detective work. The real stuff doesn't happen through a screen.' He grips a little harder, then releases her.

'Bye,' she manages, as he walks out.

After a few moments she leaves too, wondering what the hell to do about the booze she smelled on his breath.

CHAPTER THIRTY-SEVEN

THURSDAY, 30 JANUARY, 10.39 AM

Oli trips on the doormat as she rushes inside, falling heavily against the doorframe and cutting her finger as she rights herself. TJ barely seems to notice as she hunches next to him on the floor. She doesn't realise her hand's bleeding until she puts her arm around him and smears red streaks on the shoulder of his white shirt.

'TJ?' she says sharply.

His breathing is ragged as he stares in confusion at the blood on his shirt, slowly seeming to become aware of her presence.

Oli jams her finger into her mouth to stem the bleeding coming from her knuckle. 'What's on your phone?' She lowers her voice, aware that he seems to be in shock. 'TJ, tell me.'

'It's a video,' he whispers incredulously.

'Of what?' She fights an urge to shake him. 'What is it, TJ? Is it Carol?'

'It's of Mackenzie Jackson.'

TJ whimpers and reaches for his phone. He brings it to his face to unlock the screen. Presses play on a darkly lit video.

Mackenzie's familiar face takes up most of the screen before it pans back. She's lying in a room with a concrete floor, like the one in the photo sent to Vanessa Blackmore. Her matted blonde hair is loose. The only indication it's a video is the ticking movement of a wall clock's second hand.

'My god,' Oli whispers.

'He's going to kill Carol. I just know it.' TJ's face twists in panic.

Oli experiences a primal urge to sink onto the floor and stay there. Her head, arms and legs feel heavy, and the cut on her hand throbs. She pushes her fist against her forehead, trying to think. Everyone had been so sure that Mackenzie Jackson was killed by her husband. As far as they knew, there was nothing linking her to the other murders.

Oli navigates an unexpected surge of rage toward the mystery killer and the sick delight he's taking in fucking with everyone.

TJ's body jerks sharply as his phone beeps with a message. He cries out, 'God!'

Oli closes her eyes and rallies all her strength, knowing there isn't an alternative. This is happening, and Carol needs them. 'Tell me what it says.' Her voice is firm.

TJ's breaths come out in little huffs. 'That we need to run the video on our home page and promote it on our social media channels by midday today, or Carol will be next.' He turns to her, and tears run down his cheeks. 'This is bullshit, right? He's in Melbourne—he won't be able to get to her, will he?'

Getting to her feet, Oli scans the room for the TV remote, flicks on the giant screen and turns up the volume on ABC News. She fetches her notepad and pen from the table; she doesn't think the person messaging TJ can hear them, but she doesn't want to take any chances. Crouching next to him again, she writes: *Text him back that we're prepping the files. I'm going to call Rusty. We can't upload that video, but we'll make sure Carol is safe.*

Oli watches TJ read what she's written. His eyes widen, and he looks at her, shaking his head, with pure fear in his eyes. Spittle has dried at the corner of his mouth, making him look hungover or dehydrated. The blood from her finger has left dirty rust marks on his shirt. *No police,* he mouths.

We have to. Rusty will know what to do. Text Chels and tell her that we're managing all content today. I'll go outside to make the call.

TJ still looks anguished, but the tension leaks out of his posture. He moves his head in an almost imperceptible nod and takes a deep breath. She can tell he's grateful that she's taking charge.

She flips to a new page in her notebook. *Where is Carol staying?*

He takes the pen from her and writes, *The Hilton.*

She squeezes his shoulder firmly, willing the universe to keep Carol safe. Gripping her phone, she steps outside to call Rusty.

CHAPTER THIRTY-EIGHT

THURSDAY, 30 JANUARY, 11.02 AM

Pen blinks hard a few times to ward off eye strain before returning her attention to the file. Farina and his team have saved down the contents of hundreds of dark-web chat rooms that they have identified as being used primarily by individuals based in Melbourne. *It's like a morbid treasure hunt*, Pen thinks, pausing to read a thread where a guy describes in explicit detail how he tortured and killed his neighbour's dog. She notes down the timestamp and usernames of any interactions she thinks might be worth further investigation. Letters blur as she scrolls, the same words jumping out over and over. The hate and misogyny is so vibrant, it's like she can feel it. Can taste it. If only they could discount it all as meaningless, the ramblings of people who will never act on these desires or impulses. But they can't because often enough these comments are an indication of real-world violence. And the worst part is that these online monsters aren't monsters at all: they're just people going about their lives. She thinks about the man who stared at her on the tram the other day and wonders if he's ever posted in one of these chat rooms. She thinks about her charming, affable brother. What is he like when he's with his mates? Is he still the kind, silly Walter she knows, or does he morph into someone dangerous?

Pen takes notes of several comments where men offer access to their young siblings, cousins and stepsiblings in exchange for money. Then a comment where a man seems to be soliciting sexual acts with his disabled sister. *Bitcoin is fine if cash is a problem,* he writes.

Pulling her eyes away from the screen, Pen slugs back some water and tries to think about something else. There's a movie she is keen to see, some spy caper, like a James Bond type of thing without James Bond. But she can't seem to pull her brain away from the darkness.

Her friends know her job can be tough, but how could she ever explain this? How can she explain the visceral feeling of disgust, the doubt and fear? The notion that no one is who they appear to be, and how she's become accustomed to expect the worst of everyone. How even though she's been trained to read situations and people, she still often gets it wrong. And how really, she isn't very good at this job at all—but seeing as she's not good at anything else either, she's hopelessly stuck. Stuck navigating the cesspit of humanity, stuck keeping the community safe. *What a joke*, she thinks.

She scrolls a few more pages. Her gaze snags on a series of messages in a popular men's rights chat room. Then she reads: *She needed to be shown her place, but things got a bit out of control.*

Pen finds the start of the exchange, her heart thumping.

Her phone vibrates with a text message from Billy, the guy from Bumble. On a whim she'd given him her mobile number, and she has to admit it's nice to get texts that aren't from her mother or a friend making her feel bad about her non-existent social life. She surreptitiously checks the message.

I've got a few options for our drink. Do you have any allergies?

She fights back a laugh. No allergies, just an aversion to any kind of healthy relationship.

I'm still not sure I can make it, she replies. *But I have no allergies so happy with whatever you pick and then I'll let you know if I get caught up with work.*

She sends the message and instantly regrets it. He's going to keep thinking she's being coy and pretending to be busy.

As she reads more of the dialogue on the screen, she thinks he would probably cancel their date if she told him what she's doing right now. Surely she would be categorised as 'not worth the drama'.

Mr Incredible replies to F_101: *How did you show her who's boss?*

F_101 answers: *Stupid bitch tried to trick me. I told her $50 for whatever I wanted and she agreed then said it was $100.*

There's a flurry of replies, with the consensus being that this woman was a scheming bitch.

Definitely not worth $100, agrees F_101. *But she was being a real bitch and things got out of control and now I have a bit of a problem on my hands.*

Pen feels her phone vibrate again as she reads quickly, her brain struggling to process the horrible words.

I hope you fucking killed her.

Stupid bitch deserved it, don't feel bad.

Make her earn the $100 now. I've always wanted to do one that can't get away.

Pen squeezes her eyes shut for a long moment and swallows away the taste of bile.

An account called click_click03 writes: *Are you based in M? I can help you out with your problem. Complete discretion guaranteed.*

F_101 writes: *I'd appreciate that man I'm kind of freaking out.*

Her mouth falls open as she realises the message was sent early on Tuesday, 21 January. Electricity crackles through her, and she pushes herself away from the desk to find Sanders.

CHAPTER THIRTY-NINE

THURSDAY, 30 JANUARY, 11.07 AM

Rusty doesn't answer. Through the window, Oli can see TJ in the lounge, slumped on the couch where she left him, clutching his phone like a lifeline.

She tries Rusty again, and this time he cuts the call off after only two rings.

'Shit!' She feels paralysed with panic. She types out a text to Rusty, her fingers making clumsy errors before she deletes it and calls another number.

'Kibbs.' The detective's voice is clipped, and she sounds like she's in motion.

'Thank god,' Oli breathes. She tells Kibbs what has happened, trying to stay calm.

There's a pause, and Oli can tell Kibbs has stopped walking.

'Mackenzie Jackson,' Kibbs says sharply. 'Are you sure?'

'I know,' says Oli. 'I can't believe it, I can't believe any of it, but I've seen the video. It's her.'

Oli hears Kibbs take a deep breath. When she speaks, her voice is clear and strong. 'Okay, Olive, I want you to listen to me. You've done the right thing. Finding Carol Jack is now our priority. I am going to alert my superiors to this situation, and we will work with the authorities in New South Wales to locate her.'

'Can you tell Rusty? I can't get on to him.'

'I'll speak to him,' Kibbs says.

'What should I do?' Oli hears the desperation in her voice.

'You stay with Mr Jack.'

'Do you think Carol is in danger?'

'We'll find her.'

'Do you think this person can tell I've contacted you?'

Kibbs hesitates. 'I doubt it. But you're right to be careful. This person is good with technology, and there's a chance he's hacking into other systems.'

Oli glances up at TJ's outdoor security camera. The lens is pointed in her direction. She scans the exterior of the house and counts two more. She has an impulse to duck for cover. The sun lashes at her exposed skin, and the water from a fountain tinkles cheerily behind her. A pair of butterflies appear over the fence and execute a synchronised dance above the pool before moving in tandem to a flowerbed.

Her insides twist with sickening dread. Yet again the world seems to have tilted on its axis, and everything feels untethered and uncertain.

'I—' The dam that has held firm inside Oli over the past few days threatens to crack, and she chokes back a sob.

'Keep your phone on you, Olive. We'll be in touch shortly.'

Oli finds comfort in the young woman's efficiency. 'Okay,' she whispers. 'Thank you.'

'Oli,' TJ whispers, as she returns inside. His face is even paler than before, and his left foot is tapping manically against the floorboards. His phone is next to him on the couch.

'What is it? What's happened?'

'I called Carol's hotel.' He holds up his hands in defence. 'I blocked my number, but I just needed to know she was okay. Ol, she's not there. She never checked in last night.'

CHAPTER FORTY

THURSDAY, 30 JANUARY, 11.14 PM

Pen bursts into Frost's office without knocking. 'Sorry, sir, but I've just spoken to Olive Groves. Her business partner has been sent a message like the one Vanessa Blackmore received.'

Frost springs from his chair. 'Where is she?'

'At Timothy Jack's house in Toorak.' Pen explains what Oli told her about the threat made to Carol and the video file sent to TJ.

'Is Jackson deceased in the video?'

'That's what Groves said. Also, I think I found something relevant to Erica Pawley's murder. In one of the forums Farina's team found, there's—'

'We need to locate Carol Jack immediately.' Frost's hand grips the back of his neck as his eyes roam the room. 'Kibbs, brief Silverman and track her down.'

Pen nods. Her phone buzzes with a text. She scans it. 'Groves says that Carol didn't check into the hotel she was supposed to be staying at last night. I'm not sure how Groves knows that, because I told her not to make any calls except to me.'

'Fuck.' He kicks the ground. 'Okay, I'm going to call Ol— Groves, and then I'll brief Sanders and everyone else who needs to know about this.' He grabs his phone. 'Do whatever you need to do to find Carol Jack,' he orders, then storms out of his office.

CHAPTER FORTY-ONE

THURSDAY, 30 JANUARY, 11.26 AM

Oli and TJ sit in the lounge holding hands, listening to the radio and watching the news on multiple devices for what seems like hours. Outside, the wind blusters, railing against the house and carrying the promise of deadly fires. The ABC Radio announcer is warning people in the Gippsland area that it's too late to leave their homes and that they should activate their fire plans. Oli feels like the message is relevant to them too. They are at the mercy of a killer, trapped in their home, and forced to bunker down and wait to find out what the damage is.

TJ's phone is in the kitchen next to his laptop, and Oli checks it intermittently, but there haven't been any more messages from the killer. There's nothing from Carol either.

The ABC sting signals the eleven-thirty news bulletin, which agitates TJ. 'Should we call Rusty again?' His grip on Oli's hand tightens. 'We can't just sit here doing nothing.'

'We need to wait. Rusty will contact us when he has new information.'

'What if this guy decides it's been too long and does something to Carol? Oli, where the fuck is she?' TJ pulls his hand from hers and drops his head into his palms. 'Why didn't she check in to the hotel? It doesn't make any sense.'

'When did you last speak with her?'

'I saw her after I got home from Dunkley's yesterday. We had dinner, then she headed to the airport just after seven. And then I texted her goodnight at about 11 pm, just before I went to bed. She wrote back saying she'd just arrived at the hotel. We haven't been in touch today, but I knew she was busy at her conference.'

Oli rubs his back but doesn't say anything. She knows there's no point telling TJ everything will be fine.

The radio news bulletin ends, and the anchor begins an interview with a former firefighter.

On the TV, the Channel Nine news ends with a display of emergency numbers and the empathetic face of the newsreader telling everyone to stay safe.

TJ is sitting on the edge of the couch, his head still in his hands, moaning softly.

'Hey, hey,' Oli says. 'Hang in there, okay.'

'What if the worst happens, Ol? I won't be able to cope.'

'Let's just—'

Her mobile rings.

TJ sits bolt upright, and she almost drops the phone in her haste to answer.

It's Chelsea. They stare at her name on the phone until it stops ringing.

TJ lets out a whimper and slumps against Oli again. She can feel the wild beat of his heart in sync with her own as she watches the news and prays.

CHAPTER FORTY-TWO

THURSDAY, 30 JANUARY, 11.33 AM

Pen and Silverman work quickly, contacting the required authorities as they try to locate Carol Jack. Within minutes they have determined that Carol never made a booking at the Hilton or any other hotel; she flew to Sydney the previous evening and caught an Uber to a hotel in Darling Harbour. Her workplace in Melbourne knows nothing about a conference in Sydney—they thought Carol was on leave. Her mobile remains off.

Silverman is on the phone to the hotel where Carol caught the Uber, when Frost comes over with Farina, wanting an update. Pen fills him in, while Silverman emails the hotel concierge a copy of Carol's driver's licence.

Silverman hangs up, looking triumphant. 'He thinks he remembers her arriving last night. They are going to do a full search of the hotel now.'

Pen realises her heart is racing.

Frost exerts a huff of approval. 'Olive has loaded the video that was sent to TJ to their preproduction server and given us access.' He hands Farina a piece of paper printed with an email address and password.

Farina nods. 'Smart.'

Frost looks at him. 'I want your team on it straight away.'

'Video should give us more to work with than a photograph.' Farina is already on his feet, ready to head upstairs.

Frost turns to Silverman. 'How big is the hotel?'

'Ah.' Silverman is flustered. 'It's small, I think. Like a boutique place. The guy said they would search all the rooms.'

'Has Sanders been briefed on this?' asks Pen.

Frost nods. 'And Cloak.'

Silverman's phone rings, and she answers. 'Yes.' Her expression does not change for a few moments, then there's a slight softening of her features as she breathes out. 'Well, that is good news.' She mutes the call and turns to them. 'They've found her. She's at the hotel, and she's fine.'

Silverman's relief is visceral, and Pen exhales air from deep in her lungs and throws a thankyou prayer to the ceiling. She's now aware that every cell in her body had been gearing up for another dead body, and she feels almost giddy as cortisol floods her system.

Frost simply nods, his face neutral. 'Speak to Carol,' he says to Silverman. 'Don't tell her anything except we need her to get back to Melbourne. Instruct her not to speak to anyone, including TJ. Arrange to meet her at the airport and bring her straight home.' Frost looks at them in turn. 'Is that all clear?'

'Yes, sir,' they say in unison.

'Good. I'm going to call Oli.'

CHAPTER FORTY-THREE

THURSDAY, 30 JANUARY, 11.54 AM

Oli's phone barely rings before she answers it.

'Please, please,' TJ murmurs, his hands clasped over his mouth.

Rusty's voice is reassuring as always. 'It's obviously me.' This is one of their old sayings, and even in this moment it makes Oli sad to remember how close they once were.

She holds her breath as TJ chokes out an anxious sob.

'We found Carol, Oli.'

'They found her,' Oli exhales, then realises Rusty's voice is strained, and she grips TJ's hand.

'Is she alive? Is she alive? Is she hurt?' TJ manages to choke out.

Rusty hears his questions and says to Oli, 'She's alive. She's in Sydney and she's fine.'

Oli fights back tears. 'She's okay, TJ. She's okay. They have her.'

He buries his face into her shoulder, limp with relief. 'Thank god,' he whispers.

She senses something else in Rusty's voice. 'What?' she asks. 'What is it?'

'Neither of you can share that file with anyone. Do you understand?'

She knows he has to say it but Oli feels stung. 'Of course not. Will you be able to trace the sender?'

'Our people are working on it now, but we'll also need to speak to TJ and get access to all your accounts and files. We'll need to interview you both too, Ol.'

Her thoughts scramble. She's not happy about the police having access to their business information, but she understands it's non-negotiable. 'Of course. We might need to speak to our lawyer, just with having so many confidential documents and sources and things like that.'

'Not a problem,' Rusty replies. 'It will all be above board, Oli, I promise you. But that video might hold the key to cracking this bloody thing, so it's critical this is not made public until we've had more time to work through what it all means.'

Oli senses his stress and considers the pressure he must be under. His job is never easy, but the interest in this case must be taking the scrutiny to another level. 'Neither of us will say a thing, you have our word. Jesus, Rusty.'

'Where is Carol?' TJ sits up and leans toward the phone speaker. 'When can I see her?'

'Tell TJ, Carol is on her way back to Melbourne so he will see her soon. We'll arrange her transportation from the airport direct to home. Ask him not to touch his phone or his laptop until we've had our team examine them, okay?'

'What do we do now?' Oli says.

'You stay where you are,' says Rusty. 'I'll be in touch again soon.'

CHAPTER FORTY-FOUR

THURSDAY, 30 JANUARY, 11.59 AM

Pen listens to Silverman talking to Carol Jack.

'We'll explain everything once you're back in Melbourne,' Silverman says.

The fading adrenaline is like a virus in Pen's body. She feels feverish, her thoughts like bubbles that burst before she can properly examine them. After being so convinced that Douglas Jackson was responsible for his wife's death, she's disorientated at the prospect that her death was linked to the others all along.

Silverman ends the call with Carol and turns to Pen. 'Far out. What a situation.'

'Why didn't Carol check into her hotel?' asks Pen, realising that hasn't been explained.

Silverman presses her lips together and gives Pen a frazzled look. 'Let's just say the Jacks will have quite a bit to discuss once things have settled down.'

'She's having an affair?' Pen asks.

'What a way to be caught, huh?'

Pen shakes her head, trying to imagine it.

Farina calls. 'Come upstairs. Sanders is here, and Frost's on his way. We've been looking at the video.'

Silverman's ponytail brushes the side of Pen's face as they find a place to stand in Farina's small office. A stony-faced Sanders is there, along with Frost, two senior detectives, and Jamie, from Farina's team.

Farina nods at Jamie to proceed and Jamie clicks a button, prompting the video to play on the screen fixed to the wall.

Pen watches as Mackenzie Jackson appears, lifeless on the cold-looking concrete floor, a clock ticking ominously above her.

'It's sixteen seconds in total,' says Jamie, to the room. 'Nothing moves except for the second hand of the clock.'

'She was dead in this video?' says Frost.

Jamie and Farina nod.

'We haven't spent a long time with the file, but there's no sign of life,' adds Jamie.

'Does this video look like it's been doctored like the other shit he's sent?' Sanders's question is like an accusation.

Farina hesitates. 'We think it's different. In the Makris photo it's the colours and grading that is troubling us, but we believe it's a real photo.' He points to the frozen screen of the Mackenzie Jackson video. 'We think this video is real too. But we suspect Ms Jackson's features have been layered over another woman's face.'

'Bloody hell, it looks realistic,' offers one of the older detectives.

'It's sophisticated, for sure,' says Farina. 'But there are indications that the file has been manipulated. It's the same technique that is being used in pornographic and political deep fakes, and it's getting better and better every day.'

'Porn, I get,' says the other detective. 'This is just sick.'

'I bet you'd find it pretty sickening if your face was retouched onto pornographic material,' Farina retorts in his soft-spoken voice.

The detective has the good grace to look at the floor.

Frost adds, 'Farina and his team have contacted an overseas unit, and they'll be reviewing all the correspondence relating to this case. There are elements that are beyond the expertise we have here.'

'As you know, we've had no luck tracking the origin of the email or WhatsApp accounts used by the killer,' says Farina.

'How did the killer communicate with Timothy Jack?' asks Sanders.

'WhatsApp,' says Farina. 'Same as the Blackmore correspondence. The account has already been removed, and we believe we'll hit the same dead end. The phone number was generated in India this morning and has no link to an Australian user. He's using an untraceable server.'

Pen looks at the paused video of the lifeless body on the screen. So much of this job is based on facts. What do they do when they can't even trust their own eyes?

'What about Douglas Jackson?' asks Pen. 'Will you be telling him about this?'

Frost holds her gaze for a moment. 'Not yet,' he says. 'We want to wait a little longer before it leaves this group to see if we can build a better understanding of what we're dealing with. We know there's a risk it will leak, especially now Carol has been located. But we're not confident that video depicts what happened to Mackenzie Jackson, and it may cause unnecessary distress to link her murder to the others.'

Pen isn't sure how she feels about this—it's an impossible situation. 'The video doesn't prove that Mackenzie was murdered by The Photographer.'

'No, it doesn't,' says Frost.

'It doesn't prove anything,' spits Sanders. 'Except this second-rate Zodiac fuckwit thinks he can mess with us.'

Pen closes her eyes. She'd thought this meant Douglas Jackson was off the hook.

'Whether the same person killed Mackenzie Jackson or not, this video might be the key to the whole photograph case, so we just need to remain focused,' says Frost. 'His recent actions feel sloppier, so let's push hard and see what we can find.'

'We'll keep everyone across the analysis,' says Farina, clearly energised by the afternoon's events.

Sanders snorts but gets to his feet.

Frost holds up a hand. 'Before we all go, Kibbs needs to brief us on something she found online earlier that may relate to Erica Pawley's murder.'

Farina gives her a nod of encouragement, as Sanders folds his arms across his chest.

'Yes,' Pen says. 'I've been looking into forums whereby people exchange money or more typically bitcoin for illegal activities. Earlier I came across a discussion where a man detailed a violent assault he'd committed against a sex worker.' She clears her throat, remembering the vile words. 'He might have killed her.'

Sanders leans forward. 'Are you saying you found a murder confession?'

'It's possible. And if so, there's a chance someone helped the murderer get rid of a body on the same day Erica Pawley disappeared.'

CHAPTER FORTY-FIVE

THURSDAY, 30 JANUARY, 12.33 PM

TJ can't seem to stop crying. He wipes tears away impatiently and breathes through a shaky sob. 'I don't understand why I can't speak to Carol.'

'I'm not sure,' Oli says. 'I guess they just need to do everything by the book.'

'I need to speak to her.'

'She's on her way. And Rusty and his team will be here to speak with us soon too.'

TJ frowns, clearly frustrated.

'I need to call Chelsea,' says Oli. 'She'll be worried that both of us aren't answering calls and messages. Why don't you go and get some water?'

TJ does as he's told, and she watches him head to the kitchen, a shadow of his normally bouncy self.

Chelsea answers the phone. 'Is everything okay?'

'Sort of.' Oli explains that they have been tied up doing follow-ups on the Dunkley interview and briefs her to do the edit, knowing that will keep her busy for the rest of the day.

Chelsea is suspicious but accepts the assignment. 'I'll see you guys in the office tomorrow, assuming the aircon is fixed.'

'Sounds great.' Oli ends the call and allows herself to sink into the lounge.

TJ returns, holding a half full glass of water. 'I'm glad you were here, Ol.' His jaw wobbles as he fights back more tears. Understanding passes between them. The morning's events have bonded them anew.

Oli feels hollow, tired beyond reason but strangely clear-headed. 'I'm sick,' she announces.

TJ raises his head, revealing bloodshot eyes. 'What?'

'I'm sick, TJ. I have cancer.'

He blinks. 'What?' he says again.

'I know it's a weird time to tell you, but maybe it's the best time. To be honest I didn't want to tell you at all, but I have to. I'll need to take some time off.'

TJ looks bewildered. 'Oli, no.'

'I'm sorry.' As she says it, she realises that she is sorry. She's sorry that this is happening to her and that it's going to affect the people around her that she cares about. Sorry that it's making her mum even more anxious than normal, and sorry that it's going to be disruptive for their business. Despite everything that's happening in the world, she feels sorry for herself, and this is making her feel even sorrier.

TJ pulls himself up and turns to face her, gripping her hands in his. Some colour returns to his cheeks. 'First things first. What kind of cancer have you got?'

'I have breast cancer. And I'm lucky, I caught it early. They don't think it's spread.'

'What treatment do you need?'

'Surgery. And probably chemo. My surgery isn't confirmed yet, but it will be within the next month.'

He folds his lips into each other, eyes darting from left to right as he considers this.

'I'm sorry,' she says again. 'I know it impacts the business, but—'

He lifts one of her hands to his chest and stares deep into her eyes. 'Oli, listen to me. I don't want you thinking for one moment that you are alone in this. I am here for you every step of the way, big or small. And as for the business, it's probably the kick in the arse we need. It's too dependent on us, and we need to change that. We both know it in our bones, but we don't know how to fix it, and now we'll just have to figure it out.'

She feels overwhelmed by his response. 'I know.'

'You need to be focused on getting better, not worrying about subscriber numbers. I have some ideas.'

'I don't want to stop working,' she says quickly. 'I know things will need to change for a while, but I don't want to lose any momentum. Especially off the back of the domestic violence series. And I want to get the cyber one out as soon as we can this year. I really believe in it.'

He manages a smile. 'I wouldn't let you stop working even if you wanted to, Ol. But you are the priority, not the business. Without you, there is no *Newsday*.' He sighs and then resets his position, gripping her hands with renewed feeling. He chokes out a sob. 'There's no one else I'd rather be in business with, Oli. I admire you so much, but we need help. You being sick means we have no choice but to change the way we do things.'

He hugs her, and she can feel how invested he is. She won't be going to that lunch with Marion Disney.

TJ pulls away and declares he wants to have a shower before Rusty arrives. Oli looks at his rumpled hair, bloodstained shirt and bloodshot eyes, and she agrees a shower is a great idea, waving him upstairs.

Something about what Rusty said has been bothering her. Once TJ is out of earshot, she calls Rusty back. She doesn't even wait for him to say hello before she says, 'Where was Carol? Had the killer contacted her at all?'

There's a brief pause, then Rusty says, 'We don't believe so, no. Until we contacted her, she was unaware of the situation.'

'But she hadn't checked into her hotel? Where was she?'

'Carol and TJ have some talking to do, but the most important thing is that she is safe.'

Oli understands the subtext of Rusty's comment, and her heart breaks for TJ all over again. 'God, Rusty.' Tears spill from her eyes. 'I was so worried.'

'That's the goal,' says Rusty. 'This guy is trying to create widespread fear. I'm surprised he targeted TJ. His issue seems to be with women.'

'I guess Carol was the intended victim and TJ was just the access point . . . ?' Oli offers, but she agrees the choice jars a little.

'Maybe.' Rusty's thoughts are clearly elsewhere.

'I guess Douglas Jackson is off the hook?' she says tentatively.

Rusty seems to snap to attention. 'We should be at TJ's in about thirty minutes. Carol shouldn't be more than another hour after that. Once we're finished with the interviews, we'll make sure there are people you can speak to if you need.'

'Honestly, I'm fine. I'm so relieved Carol is okay. It was just hard being here with TJ. We were trying not to panic, but I wasn't sure what to do.' She presses her fist into her forehead. 'God, I'm glad we didn't publish that video.'

'So are we,' says Rusty. 'You did the right thing, Ol. The most important thing at this stage is to deprive this guy of oxygen.'

'Do you have any idea who he is?'

Rusty's voice carries an aggressive tone she's rarely heard before. 'You know I can't tell you anything, but we're getting closer, Ol. We are going to get this arsehole—I promise you that.'

CHAPTER FORTY-SIX

THURSDAY, 30 JANUARY, 8.12 PM

Pen agreed to meet Billy at 8 pm, but it's almost a quarter past by the time she steps off the tram on Swanston Street and rushes up Little Collins. He suggested they meet at Lila, a wine bar that he's been to before, popular but not too noisy. When Pen spots the sign, she slows her pace and takes a few deep breaths. She can't change the fact that she's late, but there's no need to be flustered. Defensiveness has already set in as she considers her opening lines. *Sorry I'm late, my colleagues and I are trying to catch a serial killer, and we aren't really getting anywhere. You've probably read about it online.*

At least she doesn't feel tired. Interviewing Groves and TJ was oddly exhilarating, and Pen enjoyed watching Frost and Groves carefully avoid each other.

They got word toward the end of the day that Farina's team don't believe the Mackenzie Jackson video is credible—they have concluded that the sender used AI software to merge a photograph with an existing video.

The Photographer's meticulously controlled campaign is starting to slip.

The wine bar is accessible via a narrow flight of dimly lit descending stairs. On the floor below, sleek lines and soft furnishings create warm intimate pockets branching off from a central bar area.

She's on the brink of turning around and heading back upstairs to the safety of her apartment when a man who can't be more than twenty, with round glasses and manicured facial hair, appears at her side. 'Do you have a booking? Please, let me take your coat.'

'Oh, thanks. Sure, thank you.' Pen removes her coat and fluffs out her hair. She looks around and sees a man holding his hand up in recognition on the other side of the bar: Billy. 'I'm just over there,' she adds, and the baby-faced waiter waves her through.

Pen is relieved to note that Billy looks like his photos. He's Eurasian, with a friendly, expectant expression. They hug politely in greeting. He smells like fresh laundry with a hint of aftershave, which is always preferable to the other way around.

She apologies for being late and says nice things about the venue.

'It's great, isn't it.' Billy leans forward conspiratorially. 'I know you're probably wondering if I've been here on another date, and I have—but don't worry, that was ages ago.'

Pen thinks it's an odd thing to say, but she gives him the benefit of the doubt. Maybe he's nervous too. They order and talk easily through some starters and share a salad. Pen admits that it feels good to be out, drinking and talking with someone whose day job involves nice normal things. Billy works at Telstra as a software engineer. He deals with difficult stakeholders and a manager who sounds borderline psychotic, but he doesn't have to deal with serial killers or look at images of murdered women.

'Where do you live?' she asks.

'In Carlton, right near where that girl who was killed lived.'

'Right,' Pen says.

'That stuff is all so full on, huh? Totally bizarre.'

'It really is.' Pen sips her G & T and squints at the sudden assault of lemon. 'How long have you lived there?'

'Only about a year. I split with my wife just before last Christmas, actually.'

'Oh, I'm sorry. That must have been hard.'

'It totally sucked,' Billy says cheerfully. 'I was in a pit of despair for months, but I'm all good again now.'

She eyes him as he chomps on an arancini ball. He does seem happy. He has an easy manner about him and doesn't shy away from difficult topics.

'Well, that's good. My friend split up with her husband a few years ago, and she's definitely happier now too.' She's not sure why she said that. The friend she was thinking of spends half her time bemoaning the quality of men she meets and wondering if she will ever be in a relationship again even though her ex is a lazy misogynist who blamed her for everything from the weather to his inability to hold down a decent job.

'It helps that my ex-wife had a lot of problems.'

Pen blinks, wary. 'What kind?' she asks lightly.

Billy leans forward and says earnestly, 'She was crazy. Honestly, some of the things she did even I find hard to believe. I look back now and think it's wild that we stayed together so long, but you know how sometimes when you're in something, you just can't see a clear path out? It was like that for me.'

Pen makes a neutral sound.

Billy holds up his hands. 'Sorry, I know the word "crazy" is on the nose now, but she put me through the ringer. She lied about where she was, and who she was with, she stole money from our friends. I'm pretty sure she had a gambling problem. And then there was the cheating. I don't know the full extent of it, but even what I do know is brutal.'

Pen considers this. 'That sounds very difficult. Did she cheat on you with people you knew?'

Billy laughs. 'Oh, yeah. It was all very close to home. She ended up leaving me for my brother.'

Pen's eyes widen. 'Really? Are they still together?'

'Yep!' Billy takes a swig of beer. 'I mean, she's probably mucking around on him by now. My mate's wife still sees her and reckons she's the same—but Pete, that's my brother, he doesn't see it.'

'That must be very strange for you and your family. Were you and your brother close?'

Billy smiles, but Pen detects sadness behind his eyes. 'We were very close. All of us. My wife and his wife were friends as well. We saw each other all the time. My parents are still struggling with it, but I'm just glad we didn't have kids. My brother has two, and that's made things messy.' Billy laughs. 'Sorry, this is totally not the convo to be having on a first date. You don't want to hear about this.'

Pen's mind is working overtime to piece some thoughts together. 'No, it's fine. It must have been a massive shock. Did you have any idea?'

'Not really. Our relationship was so volatile at that point that I think I was just focused on holding everything together.' He waves his hands dismissively. 'But that is *definitely* enough about all that—I want to talk about *you*. Are there any skeletons in your wardrobe? Any crazy exes I should know about?'

Pen smiles and ignores the question, bringing up Elliot instead. Luckily Billy loves dogs, and he babbles happily about his childhood pet and the dog he looks after when his neighbour goes away. He's nice, she thinks. He's good-looking, and despite the problematic ex-wife, he seems like a decent person. She tries to ignore the lingering doubt wrestling its way into her thoughts. Her ex had seemed nice to begin with too.

The waiter returns to remove their plates. 'I'll send someone over to sort you out another drink.'

Billy quickly checks his phone and smiles when he catches her looking, locking the screen and returning his attention to her. He has friendly eyes, and she likes the dark green fabric of his shirt. Does she want to stay for another drink? She's not sure. She feels like she should; she can hear her friend Mia's voice in her head. *What's wrong with you? He's fine, nothing not to like. Honestly, Pen, do you want to end up on your own with a bunch of dogs to keep you company?* Pen ignores the imaginary Mia but must admit the pull of home is strong. What is wrong with her that she would rather spend time with strangers on the internet than with a living, breathing person?

A chic female waiter appears at their table, and Billy orders a glass of red. 'I know it's hot, but I'm sick of beer. Plus, I'm trying to be classier this year.'

Pen hesitates then does the same. With no food to eat or drinks in front of them, she feels the momentum of their exchange slipping. She scrambles to think of something to say and asks him where he's travelled to, breathing a sigh of relief as he enthusiastically rattles off international destinations.

The drinks arrive, and Pen reaches for her glass, keen to have something in her hand.

'I've got a trip booked in May to the Philippines, which I'm pumped about,' Billy is saying. 'Have you been?'

'I haven't. But it sounds great.'

'Where do you want to go? Do you like to travel?'

'Work makes it hard, but I do like to travel,' she replies without thinking. The wine is kicking in, and her thoughts reach her mouth more quickly.

'Let's talk about your work. It will give me a chance to think about where I should suggest you go on holiday next.'

She ducks her head. 'My work is so boring, honestly.'

'I reckon it's probably more exciting than mine. Computer coding can get repetitive.'

'So can reviewing contracts,' Pen says, forcing a laugh. 'Tell me more about your work first. What kind of coding do you do?'

He shrugs. 'All kinds. Increasingly what I do these days is security related. All the systems are so fragile, it's like whack-a-mole just trying to keep everything going.'

'Do you get lots of hackers?'

'Constantly. There are so many fake profiles.'

Pen thinks about the accounts they are trying to trace. 'What are people trying to hack?'

'Everything. People are trying to get stuff for free and get out of paying bills. We get sent scams all the time too, doctored invoices, you name it.'

'Really?'

'Yeah. It's the Wild West in the online world, I tell you.'

On the table next to theirs, a woman in a neon-pink jumpsuit waves to get the attention of the waiter and asks him to take a photo of her group with her iPhone. She moves to the other side of the table to stand behind her partner. The other couple arrange themselves in the same way. Pink jumpsuit leans forward and tickles her partner just as the waiter says, 'Cheese.'

The man doubles over, swatting her away, and they all laugh.

'I know I said I didn't want to talk about it,' says Billy, watching them. 'But that's how I knew about my wife and my brother. I took a photo on my birthday, and when I was going through my phone the next day, I saw it . . . And the way she was looking at him, well.' Billy takes a big swig of wine. 'It was suddenly the most obvious thing in the world.'

CHAPTER FORTY-SEVEN

THURSDAY, 30 JANUARY, 8.21 PM

Oli steps into her apartment, locks the door and dumps her bag on the bench before heading straight to the bathroom. She strips off her clothes and has a long shower, trying to scrub off the events of the day. Once she's out, she checks the headlines on her phone. There are now nine Australians confirmed to have the coronavirus disease, with several more waiting to confirm their results. She clicks the link and scans the article. China has over seven thousand infections and hundreds of reported deaths. Oli closes her eyes. With everything else going on, she'd forgotten about the virus; it seems more sinister than everyone presumed. *Breathe*, she instructs herself. *Breathe.*

After a few beats, she continues to work her way through all the major news sites. There's nothing about what happened to her and TJ today, not even a hint. For a moment she lets herself consider the way things might have gone: Carol dead, her image splashed all over the news, and TJ left to pick up the pieces. Oli shudders. Thank god that's not the reality they are dealing with.

She didn't get the chance to speak to Rusty alone until she and TJ had been interviewed. It was a short, unsatisfying conversation in TJ's driveway, and Oli yearned for one of their relaxed dinners. She wanted to tell him everything: about the job offer, about the interview with Dunkley, about the twins and about her illness. But it was clear from the dark circles under his eyes and the manic way he flicked his fingers at his thumb that she needed to wait. He wasn't in the right frame of mind to take on her news, and she owed him that kindness at least.

Carol arrived home from the airport flanked by two detectives, looking bereft. She threw herself at TJ, crying and apologising. He soothed her, whispering in her ear and running his hand along her back. She hugged him, wiping mascara from underneath her eyes. She hugged Oli too, then sat on the couch between them and, in typical Carol fashion, demanded to be told everything. Oli noticed that while she clutched TJ's hand, she didn't meet his eyes, and she wouldn't meet Oli's either.

Oli opens the pantry and then the fridge, trying to decide what to eat. The thought of going out or ordering takeaway feels too hard, and she settles on a carrot and wanders aimlessly from room to room as she chews. She can't believe she told TJ about her cancer, but she's glad she did. At least it's done.

Thinking about this prompts her to remember she missed a call from Dr Brooks, the breast surgeon, this afternoon. She retrieves her phone from the charger and pulls her notebook from her handbag. The carrot finished, she plucks an apple from the fruit bowl and bites into it, playing her voicemail messages through the speaker so she can create a list. Before long, she has a page of notes, people to call back, things to follow up. She places the apple core in her compost bin and tackles her emails, turning the page of her notebook to create a new list. It's helping, working through what needs to be done. She replies to the easy emails straight away and earmarks others for later. She saves the message from the surgeon until last.

Oli sips a glass of water as she listens to Dr Brooks explain that he's scheduled her surgery to take place in just over three weeks, followed by an initial course of chemotherapy for a month. *After that, we'll see,* Brooks says, his tone reassuring. He asks Oli to contact his office to confirm the details. She saves the message then sits in the quiet kitchen, thinking.

TJ will support whatever she wants to do in terms of telling the rest of the team and will be happy for her to take whatever time she needs, but he was right: they will need to get some help. She logs back into her laptop and clicks on to the *Newsday* home page. There's barely any new content since this morning—they instructed Chelsea to do only basic updates today—but it's odd to read yesterday's headlines, considering what's happened since.

She's procrastinating, and she knows it. She checks the time. Just after 9.30 pm. She FaceTimes Dean before she can lose her nerve. He answers, and after some customary small talk she fills him in on her conversation with Georgia.

He makes a face. 'You're telling me Kate was the one who sent the photos of Amy around the school?'

'Yes. That's what Georgia's daughter told her. Apparently, Amy knows. You need to talk to them, Dean.'

'I do talk to them.' His lower lip juts out slightly.

'I'm sure you do, but you're going to need to really dig into this. Get them to tell you what's going on in their heads.'

He drops his face into his palm and shakes his head, revealing flecks of grey hair at his crown. She studies herself in the small window at the top right of the screen. She looks tired.

'God, this is hard.' He looks up at her. 'They've been at each other for months. I don't know what's going on between them, but it's been impossible to navigate. I thought maybe Kate was jealous because Amy finds it easier to talk to boys, but she doesn't seem interested! It's just so hard to figure them out now.'

'You need to ask them, Dean. Spend time with them one on one. Eventually they will open up to you.'

'Obviously I knew the teenage years would be challenging, and it's worse than I expected. Half the time I feel like I don't know the girls anymore.'

'I think that's normal. They probably don't even know themselves half the time.'

He appears to physically pull himself together, straightening and pushing his chest forward. 'It sounds like you're still going to do the series?'

She tilts her head. 'Of course. This news about Kate doesn't change anything. You were right—it's an important topic that needs more attention. My plan is to interview lawyers, psychologists and policymakers, and blend this material into the real stories. It should come together well.'

'You're welcome.' She can tell the heat has gone out of it for Dean. He loves an enemy, he gets energy from conflict, and this situation has become less black-and-white for him.

'You really do need to talk to them, Dean. My podcast series isn't going to fix anything for your girls, nor will getting the school to admit fault.'

'Message received.' He looks at her. 'I hear what you're saying, don't worry.'

'Okay.'

'Hey. I heard you got Dunkley on your next series. That's a good get. Super topical.'

'How did you know that?'

He gives a half-hearted laugh. 'I know people, Oli. And everyone talks. But seriously, my life might be a bit of a shitshow, but it sounds like things are going well in your world.'

'I'm okay.' She might be vulnerable, but no way is she letting herself go there with Dean.

His face disappears, and the screen goes blank. Has he taken another call? 'Dean?'

He returns briefly. 'Sorry, I'm just . . . Give me a sec.'

News alerts and texts ping onto her phone, and she flicks them away, watching as the lines in his brow grow deeper.

'Ol, are you seeing this?'

'Seeing what?'

'Something is happening. It's like the Vanessa Blackmore thing.'

Dread lurches through her.

'Fucking hell,' he murmurs. 'There's a video of that murdered woman, Mackenzie Jackson, all over Twitter.'

CHAPTER FORTY-EIGHT

FRIDAY, 31 JANUARY, 6.32 AM

Pen tugs Elliot's lead, but he refuses to budge. She yawns and drinks more coffee from the mug she brought down from the kitchen. 'C'mon, buddy,' she says, manoeuvring him to the spot on the lawn he seems to prefer when doing his business.

Lights flick on in the surrounding apartments, creating the impression of an uneven chessboard. A few people step out onto their balconies, and a small dog on the first floor greets Elliot with a gruff bark.

The question of what to do about Barnes drinking on the job rolls through her mind unpleasantly. He's put her in an impossible position, and she's angry, no furious, at the inconvenience of his behaviour. It's the last thing she needs, the last thing any of them need. What the hell was he thinking? She's also preoccupied with Billy's story about his wife leaving him for his brother.

Billy. Pen cringes at her awkwardness last night. As they were paying, she was overcome with panic at what might happen after they left the wine bar; when they stepped outside, she just mumbled a thankyou and bolted to a nearby taxi rank.

He texted her almost immediately saying he'd had a great night and would love to see her again, but she's yet to reply. Does she want to see him again? He seems like a nice person, but how the hell can she be sure? She feels anxious at the thought of a second date and the inevitable intimacy she will have to navigate if she keeps seeing him. It might be easier to be thankful the dinner wasn't a disaster and leave it at that.

The Mackenzie Jackson video was uploaded onto YouTube around the time she got into the cab last night, and the link was sent to Melissa Warren, a high-profile tabloid journalist who enthusiastically shared it on her late-night talk show before consulting with the police. She called Sanders straight away to see if he wanted her to come in, but he didn't answer and never called her back. The video was removed sometime overnight—not before it was viewed more than seven thousand times. Now it's being played by all the major networks, with Mackenzie's body pixelated, as breathless newsreaders speculate about what it means.

Pen arrives at the station half an hour later and is glad Barnes doesn't seem to be in yet. She's tempted to think that the issue will resolve itself somehow, or maybe she's overreacting. He's under a lot of pressure, they all are. So maybe he had a drink during the day—is it such a big deal? But she knows it is, and her discomfort persists.

Pen notices the family photos on Barnes's desk, usually obscured by him sitting there, positioned behind the tray of paperwork under the shelf. His ex-wife features prominently in both photos, smiling with her arms around Barnes and their daughters. It's odd that he would want such a stark daily reminder of his former relationship, but maybe their break-up was amicable. Pen can only ever remember him speaking about his kids, so it's hard to know.

Her thoughts drift to Douglas Jackson again. He called his brother the night Mackenzie went missing. This makes sense—the brothers are close. But what if there's more to it? What if he called his brother because that's where he suspected Mackenzie had gone? From the online activity Farina and his team have uncovered, it's clear the brothers have a predilection for vile, misogynist content. Is it so far-fetched that Patrick, not Douglas, could be responsible for Mackenzie's death?

Silverman calls out to her from across the office, waving her hand. She looks rested, her long hair clean and falling in loose waves around her face. 'Get over here, Kibbs!'

Pen obeys.

Sanders is there, sitting on Silverman's chair and looking pleased for once. 'We may have some good news.'

Pen looks between the two of them. 'What is it?'

Sanders says, 'We've just had word that James Delway's girlfriend was arrested last night for drug possession and suspected trafficking. This seems to have prompted a rethink about the alibi she provided for her new boyfriend over the past few weeks.'

'She wasn't with him the night of the party?' says Pen.

'She was, but she claims he went out for a few hours.'

Pen's heart rate picks up. 'What time?'

'She says he left after 10 pm and that he was back when she woke up around 3 am. To top things off, she claims he is her drug dealer and that she thinks he went out to fulfil deliveries.'

'Shit,' says Pen. 'Did she say anything about the night Erica Pawley was killed?'

'Same deal,' says Sanders.

'And it seems that his friendship with Ned Higgins is far more intense than either of them let on,' adds Silverman. 'Delway's girlfriend said that he's with Higgins all the time.'

'I fucking knew it,' says Pen. 'Do you want us to bring him in?'

'It's in play,' says Sanders. 'We're going to get them on the drugs charges first and go from there. I'm going to interview Delway myself, and Higgins, but I suspect we won't be able to speak to them until tomorrow, after they engage lawyers.'

'If they are friends, it's plausible that Delway visited him when he lived in Adelaide,' says Pen. 'They could be working together.'

'Let's not get ahead of ourselves,' says Sanders, but Pen can tell he's thinking along the same lines.

'What do you need us to do?' she asks.

'Nothing. I want the two of you to go home and get some sleep, see your boyfriends, whatever. The next few days are going to be critical, and I need you sharp, not looking like shit.' He looks at Pen when he says the last part, and she averts her gaze.

She opens her mouth to protest, but Silverman speaks first. 'I could use some sleep. And a massage.'

Pen nods and drifts back to her desk. She gets her bag and slips her laptop inside. Barnes is still nowhere to be seen. Taking a deep breath, she heads over to Frost's office and knocks, feeling relieved when there's no answer.

CHAPTER FORTY-NINE

FRIDAY, 31 JANUARY, 7.49 AM

Oli can feel her eyes drooping. She pinches the skin on her thigh and shakes her head. 'C'mon,' she murmurs, giving herself a little pep talk. She's tired from waking up early to get a story about the Mackenzie Jackson video live on their social media accounts. Mercifully the fixed aircon is humming away and the temperature in the office is cool. She makes herself tea and starts pulling together a deep-dive piece on Addison Bower-Fry, conscious that they've dedicated no coverage to her possible link to the case. She hasn't checked in with TJ—the cops still have his devices anyway—and she doesn't want to text Carol, but yesterday he told her he would be in this morning. She hopes Rusty won't be pissed about her running a story on the Mackenzie Jackson video but seeing as everyone else is reporting it, she figures it's fine. Remembering what Rusty said, Oli has been careful not to confirm the legitimacy of the video in the *Newsday* social posts, nor has she speculated on whether this incident is linked to the other murdered or missing women.

She checks the website stats, which are significantly higher than normal. She feels the hunger for this story, and pictures people all over the country waking up and reaching for their phones, clicking from link to link desperate for new details.

She makes another tea and uses the bathroom before settling in to pull together a write-up on Addison Bower-Fry. Even though it isn't a Melbourne story, the age and circumstances of her disappearance meant that the coverage at the time was comprehensive, and Oli is surprised to find that she can draft a skeleton piece from memory. She clicks online to recall more details and to verify the specifics of the young woman's disappearance and the media frenzy that followed.

Oli's scanning old news articles when Chelsea arrives. She's started doing the daily news recording from home, and Oli suspects it's because she doesn't want to be commuting to the office in the dark. Oli greets her, trying to seem as normal as possible. She expects Chelsea to sense something is off, but she's distracted by the Mackenzie Jackson video.

'Can you imagine,' says Chelsea, 'if it was your mum and everyone is watching a video of her lying there like that?' Her voice trails off, then seems to snap back into focus. 'It's fucked.'

'I know. It's awful. And the fact that it's been so widely shared before we can verify its authenticity is concerning.'

Chelsea tilts her head. 'You don't think the video is real?'

'I don't know. But I want us to be extremely careful about how we cover this until we have more information.' Oli explains that she is finalising a feature on Addison Bower-Fry and asks Chelsea to focus on the morning headlines. 'Also, are you okay to cover Erica Pawley's funeral tomorrow? Otherwise, we can get a freelancer to do it.'

'I'm fine to go. Also, I've set up a call with a criminal profiler from the States. Seeing as there isn't much to report on the investigation, I thought it might be interesting to get his take on the kinds of things the cops will be looking at.'

Oli is pleasantly surprised at her initiative. 'Sounds great. Like I said, I'm keen to avoid too much speculation about the video, but that could be an interesting angle regarding the likely mindset of the police. Great thinking.'

Yael comes up the stairs with her distinctive gait just before 9 am, giant sunglasses covering half of her narrow face. The bicep on her left arm strains from the weight of her oversized drink bottle. 'Thank god the aircon is working again,' she declares. 'It's an oven out there.'

'How are you going?' Oli asks her.

Yael places her things on her desk and ruffles her cropped dark hair. 'Turns out a psychotic murderer is great for business. Sales are healthy. I might even have some good news for you on a sponsor for winter by the end of the day.'

'Subs are up too,' chimes in Chelsea. 'There've been over twenty new subscribers since yesterday.'

Oli feels the familiar conflict of emotions at this news. 'Really? That's great.'

'And once we get your series out later this week there will be more,' Yael calls out from her desk. 'It's shaping up to be a good year.'

Oli forces a smile, and they settle into their work. Oli toys around with whether she should record a longer form piece about the Mackenzie Jackson video but decides against it, seeing as they can't recount what happened yesterday.

She continues her research, re-reading old interviews with Bower-Fry's parents and siblings and the bandmate who was briefly a suspect in her disappearance. Oli's heart feels heavy as she reads how the young woman excelled in drama and sport, starring in school plays and making the state swimming squad. She turned down modelling jobs in pursuit of music and eventually made the difficult decision to stop swimming competitively to focus on her music career. Oli clicks on a photo of fifteen-year-old Addison receiving a silver medal after a swim meet in Melbourne. There are photos of her with her teammates and coaches.

Oli's guts lurch. Without saying a word to the others, she grabs her phone and heads to the boardroom to wait for TJ.

CHAPTER FIFTY

FRIDAY, 31 JANUARY, 8.29 AM

Pen sits in the car park facing Patrick Jackson's bustling St Kilda restaurant. At least ten people are waiting for a table, and the staff are run off their feet. She keeps an eye on the handsome middle-aged man as he moves between the main entrance to the kitchen, talking with his staff and chatting to regular customers. He has an open, friendly face and a relaxed demeanour.

She tips her head back against the car seat, attempting to stretch out her legs in the confined space. She probably should have stayed at home and caught up on sleep. Instead, she returned to her apartment and agonised about whether to respond to Billy's text, before searching everything she could find about Patrick Jackson online. Then she drove across town to observe him firsthand.

Pen watches as one of the male waitstaff laughs at a joke Patrick makes—and wonders if she is losing her mind. Her original plan was to catch him off guard and confront him in his restaurant, but she can already tell she's not going to do that.

Her thoughts roll back around to Barnes. She now wishes Frost was in his office earlier; that way, the inevitable awkward conversation would be in the past.

She picks up her phone and finds Frost's number. Hesitates.

Barnes has been good to her, a supportive mentor and friend, but she has a duty of care, a responsibility that goes beyond protecting him just because he's been nice to her. But ratting on a fellow cop is the last resort, and she dials Frost's number knowing she might very well be putting her own career on the line. She thinks she can trust Frost, but what if her peers find out. What if Barnes does?

'Frost speaking.'

Pen coughs.

'Hello, Kibbs?' He's somewhere noisy.

'Yes, sir.'

'I hope you took Sanders's advice and you're getting some rest.'

'Yes. Sorry to call when I know there's so much going on, but I need to speak with you. I couldn't find you when I was in earlier. I can be quick.' She squeezes her eyes shut and berates herself for rambling.

The chatter in the background fades as he moves to a quieter location. 'I'm listening.'

It's her turn to pause. Is she really doing this?

'Kibbs?'

'Have you seen Barnes today?'

'Barnes . . . No, why?'

'Something is wrong. I'm not sure exactly what is going on, but he isn't in a good place.'

'What makes you think that?' Frost's tone is neutral.

'I think he'd been drinking before I saw him in the office yesterday morning. He wasn't acting like himself, and I could smell it. I know this is small fry compared to everything else we're dealing with, but I wanted to say something. I know it could compromise an investigation.'

She presses her fingertips into her forehead as she waits for Frost's reply. *Fuck*, she thinks, *this was a mistake.*

'I don't want him to get in trouble . . . He's a great detective, one of the very best, but I think he's losing perspective on things. From what he told me it sounds like he's hassling Douglas Jackson's ex-partner, and well—'

'You're right to say something,' Frost says quickly, his voice gruff. 'I've already spoken to someone regarding concerns I have about Barnes's recent behaviour, so you raising this is not entirely surprising. You're aware what you've told me will need to be formalised and investigated?'

Pen's breath catches in her throat. 'Yes. I understand.'

'Thanks, Kibbs. I know this wasn't an easy call to make, but it was the right one. We'll talk more later—I have to go.'

He hangs up, and Pen drops her phone into the console and puts her hands on the steering wheel to keep them steady. She watches Patrick for another few minutes, then puts the car into reverse, driving the short distance to the address she looked up earlier.

The street is wide with beautiful leafy trees, and she parks underneath one, just shy of the house with the rambling rose growing over the front gate. She switches off the engine and sits completely still. She can't believe she just reported Barnes. She allows herself to consider that it might lead to the end of his career, and she feels sick.

As if on cue, Barnes calls her.

She answers, knowing that ignoring him will make her feel even more like a traitor.

'Good morning.' He sounds upbeat. 'How are you?'

'I'm okay. Sanders sent me home.'

'I heard.'

'Are you in today?'

'Sure am. I'm just tying up a few things. I'm hoping to speak to Jackson's next-door neighbour. The women mentioned hearing them arguing at Christmas, so I'm going to see if she can remember about what.'

Listening to him now, Pen realises how manic he sounds. When did that happen? Was it just over the past few days? She recalls how swept up in Mackenzie Jackson's case she had been, how good it felt to be working in lock step with Barnes and how certain he'd been that Douglas Jackson was to blame. Was that what made her so fixated on him too?

'I'm actually following up a lead on the Jackson case as well.'

'You are?' Barnes says doubtfully.

'It's got nothing to do with Douglas Jackson.'

'What are you doing then?'

Pen doesn't think it's a good idea to voice her theory about Patrick to Barnes, so she only says, 'I'm going to speak to Mackenzie's sister-in-law. She wasn't interviewed with the rest of the family, but she's known her for a long time, and from what I can tell, they were close.'

Barnes mutters something unintelligible before saying, 'When are you speaking to her?'

In the rear-view mirror, Pen clocks a black BMW turning into the street. 'I've got to go, Barnes.'

'Pen, I really don't think—'

The front gate of the Jacksons' property slides open, and the BMW turns into the driveway and comes to a stop under the carport draped with blooming jasmine. Pen watches a woman get out and collect bags of shopping from the passenger seat. After throwing back the last of her cold coffee, Pen pops a mint in her mouth and gets out of her car. She approaches the house, slipping inside the gate just as it begins to close. She waits until the woman has unlocked the front door before she calls out, 'Eloise? Eloise Jackson?'

The woman startles, her hand drawn to her chest like a magnet. 'Oh! You scared me.' She laughs. 'Silly. Sorry, I've always been a jumpy person.' She is wearing a deep purple T-shirt dress that hugs her slender frame. Her honey-coloured hair reaches just past her shoulders and carries a slight wave. She has dark brown eyes and full round cheeks. Her mouth is artificially plump, and her forehead is smoother than it should be at forty-five, but Pen can tell she's always been very attractive.

Eloise looks at her expectantly.

'I'm Detective Constable Penelope Kibbs.' She shows her ID. 'I'd like to ask you a few questions.'

Eloise tenses. 'What about?'

'I'd rather talk about it inside.'

'I'd rather not,' she replies curtly.

Pen nods. 'Okay. We can talk about it out here then.'

Eloise's jaw flexes. She seems to be working out how to respond. 'Is this about Mackenzie?'

'Partly.'

The woman seems to be weighing up her options. 'Let me just put the shopping away, okay?'

Folding her arms, Pen leans against the stair rail. 'I'll come with you.'

Resigned, Eloise heads inside, leaving the door open behind her. Pen follows and watches as she efficiently puts the shopping items away in the state-of-the-art kitchen.

'This kitchen is amazing,' Pen says.

'Patrick was a chef before he started to run restaurants. A good kitchen is important.'

'Do you cook too?'

'Yes.' Her task complete, Eloise reluctantly says, 'Would you like tea or coffee? Water?'

'No, thanks. I'm fine.'

Pen notices some children's books on the table and a soccer ball and goals on the lawn in the backyard.

Eloise's hands flutter at her side. 'Why don't we sit on the porch. It's nice out there.'

'Sure.'

After Eloise grabs a huge water bottle, they head to the front of the house. She perches on the edge of the bench seat positioned under a beautiful gable window. 'Patrick's spoken to the police already.'

'But you didn't,' says Pen, sitting down next to her.

Eloise doesn't reply, just stares at her hands.

Pen decides to lay her cards on the table. 'Eloise, did Mackenzie come here the night she disappeared?'

Eloise stares straight ahead. Her mouth is clamped shut, and the breaths through her nose become ragged.

'Eloise? Please answer me. I don't want to have to take you down to the station.'

'I don't know,' she says, her tone hostile. 'I went to bed early.'

'Was Patrick at the restaurant that night?'

'Patrick's always at the restaurant,' she says robotically.

'Were you and Mackenzie close?'

Eloise bites her lip, pauses. 'Not really. Like, we got along fine at family events, but we didn't have much in common.'

'You just married into the same family.'

'That's right.'

'What about Patrick? Were he and Mackenzie close?'

'I guess so.'

'Is there anything you want to tell me about what happened to Mackenzie, Eloise?'

'No.'

Pen sighs. 'I don't believe you.'

Eloise shrugs.

'I think Mackenzie came here looking for your husband.'

'Why would she do that?'

'Because they were having an affair.'

Eloise barks out a laugh, followed by a soft snort. She drives a manicured hand into her long hair, pushing it away from her face.

'I'm wrong . . . ?'

The woman doesn't say anything, just nudges at a nail protruding from a wooden slat of the deck with her sandalled foot. Pen notices that the purple of her toenail polish exactly matches the purple of her dress, and she wonders what it must be like to be so put together.

'Eloise, please talk to me. I'm trying to understand what happened to Mackenzie, and you might be able to help me.'

A car rolls down the tree-lined street, and Eloise's gaze follows it. A sprinkler system turns on in the garden, and she jumps again.

'Eloise,' says Pen firmly. She feels jittery from a combination of caffeine and lack of sleep. 'Did you speak to Mackenzie the night she disappeared?'

Eloise lets out a shuddery sob. 'No. I spoke to her the day before.'

Pen leans forward, sensing a breakthrough. She tries not to sound too pushy as she asks, 'Did you speak on the phone or in person?'

'In person,' Eloise whispers.

'And on the night she went missing you were here?'

'Yes.' Eloise brushes a tear from her cheek.

'Was Patrick here?'

'Yes.' It comes out as a whimper. 'He was supposed to be at work, but he came home sick.'

Pen frowns. The sun is burning her arm, and she adjusts her position, trying to understand what Eloise is saying. 'But didn't Mackenzie come here to see Patrick?'

Eloise looks at Pen, her eyes pooling with tears. 'She came here to see me.'

CHAPTER FIFTY-ONE

FRIDAY, 31 JANUARY, 8.38 AM

Oli dials TJ's number and hears his phone ring nearby just as he enters the office from the car park. 'Morning!' He removes his sunglasses and smiles broadly at everyone. He waves at Oli.

'Hey, mate,' says Yael.

'Morning,' says Chelsea as she emerges from the studio.

TJ drops his satchel on his desk and holds up a bulging paper bag. 'It's going to be a big day, so I brought some baked goods for us to share. Does anyone want a coffee from next door before we crack into it?'

Chelsea and Yael attack the baked goods, but Oli heads back to her desk, her pulse racing. Has she finally found a lead? And what are the implications if she has? Horses, not zebras, she reminds herself. It's more likely to be nothing than something out of the ordinary.

Chelsea asks for an oat latte, and Yael says she wouldn't drink the coffee from next door if TJ paid her to.

Oli watches TJ approach her desk. He looks the same as always, like he could step onto a TV set and host a game show. Only his eyes give him away: they are watery, and the whites are tinted pink. She'd bet all the money she has that he used eye drops in the car park before he came upstairs. She wonders if he got any sleep or whether he was up all night talking to Carol.

'Ol?' he asks. 'Do you want a coffee?'

'Hey,' she says quietly. 'Are you okay? I wasn't sure you'd come in today.'

'Of course I'm here. The aircon is working again, and we have this video to deal with.' More quietly he says, 'Thanks for doing the piece this morning. I should have texted you to say I'd be late. Things at home are . . . difficult.' He swallows, and his jaw shakes ominously.

'No worries. I just wanted to get something live about the video while we work out our broader angle.' She squeezes his arm, and he flashes her a quick smile.

'How about *I* go get the coffees,' says Yael, stepping between them and plucking TJ's credit card from his hand. 'I assume you want your horrid little espresso shot?'

'You know me too well,' he booms, smiling. After Yael has left, he asks Oli, 'How are you?'

From his tone she knows he's referring to their conversation about her cancer diagnosis. 'I'm fine.' She waves his concern away. 'We can talk about that later. First, I need to show you something.' She unplugs her laptop and leads him to the boardroom, closing the door.

TJ scans the article then looks at Oli searchingly. 'Addison was a swimmer?'

'She was. She was very good.'

'Okay. And?'

'Look.' She points at the image of the team. 'That's Bower-Fry with Lyra Makris and Bronte Willoughby. She used to come to Melbourne to compete in swim competitions when she was a kid.'

TJ's eyes widen as he peers at the trio of beaming girls.

'And that's their coach.' She points to a photo of a tanned, athletic man with shaggy brown hair.

'Fuck!'

'Yeah. We need to speak to Shane Willoughby.'

CHAPTER FIFTY-TWO

FRIDAY, 31 JANUARY, 9.03 AM

'You and Mackenzie were seeing each other?' says Pen. It's all becoming clear.

Next to her Eloise nods then stiffens. Her eyes double in size.

'What is it?'

'It's Pat,' she hisses, as a silver sportscar stops at the end of the driveway. The automatic gate clicks as it slides open.

Pen's stomach lurches.

Springing to her feet, Eloise frets, 'He won't like you being here.'

'Well, he doesn't have a choice, does he?' Pen says, sounding more confident than she feels.

Patrick Jackson guides a shiny silver car into the driveway and parks, opens the door and gets out without breaking eye contact with his wife. Again, Pen is struck by how similar he looks to his brother.

'Patrick,' Eloise breathes.

'Ellie,' he says, 'what's going on?'

Pen is aware her dark suit means she will struggle to pass for a friend who has called past for a casual drop-in.

Eloise's fingers twist furiously in a mesmerising dance. She reminds Pen of the rescue puppy Walter successfully begged their mother to let him adopt when they were young. The poor thing had spent the best part of three weeks hiding under Walt's bed, only coming out at night to sneak food and water.

'She's the police,' Eloise stammers. 'A detective. She just turned up wanting to talk to me.'

Patrick's mouth works its way into a grimace, and he rocks his weight from the balls of his feet to his heels as he looks Pen up and down. 'About what?'

'I wanted to talk to your wife about Mackenzie Jackson. I'm involved in her case, and I'm following up some inquiries.'

'Is that right?' His affable tone doesn't match the steel in his expression. He steps onto the porch and takes his wife's hand. With the index finger of his other hand he lifts up her chin, then he plants a kiss on her mouth. 'Are you okay, Ellie? This lady's not upsetting you too much?'

Eloise shakes her head aggressively. 'I'm fine.'

'You heard her, we're fine, thanks.' He smiles at Pen, keeping Eloise angled in front of him as he opens the door. 'You can go now.'

Pen follows them inside. 'I'd actually like to ask you some questions too.'

'I don't have time. I only came home because I could see Ellie wasn't looking after things here, but I need to get back to the restaurant.' Into his wife's hair, he says, 'You can come with me. Get your things.'

Pen can't see any security cameras, but Patrick obviously watches his wife when he's at work. Pen wonders if he knew about Eloise and Mackenzie's relationship before the night she disappeared. She wonders if Douglas Jackson knew.

Eloise steps uncertainly toward the kitchen, then lets out a low whimper.

'Come on, Ellie,' spits Patrick. '*Move.*'

'Why don't we take a seat, and you can answer my questions,' says Pen. 'Eloise can have a rest. She's clearly not feeling very well.'

'With all due respect, my wife is none of your business.' Again, the friendly tone of his voice doesn't match the hard edge in his eyes. 'This is a family matter.'

'With all due respect,' Pen replies, 'I'm not sure that's true.'

They lock eyes. He's less than three metres away. If she pulls her gun, she could force him into the corner of the room and call for backup.

'Ellie, come back here, honey.' All the warmth has gone from his voice. '*Now.*' His expression is gloating as she returns to his side; he must know what Pen is about to do.

Using his wife as a shield, he reaches into his satchel.

Pen's phone vibrates against her waist in her pocket as she reaches for her gun.

'Don't even think about it,' says Patrick, pulling out a knife.

'Don't hurt her, please,' says Eloise, her eyes squeezed shut. 'I can't bear it.'

'Shut up, shut *up*!'

Pen holds up her left hand, keeping her right close to her waist near her gun. 'Patrick, I just want to ask you some questions. That's it. Then I'll go.'

'Liar!' he spits. 'You're a fucking liar. You're all liars.' He grabs Eloise by the arm so hard that she yelps, which causes him to grip her even harder. The knife hovers at her neck.

'Let her go.' Pen can tell Patrick has been on edge for weeks and might implode. 'Let her go, and we'll see if we might be able to fix this.'

Patrick's knuckles turn white as he clutches his wife, one arm around her middle, the other holding the knife at her throat. Eloise's body slumps against him, her eyes glazing over, and Pen can tell that they've done this dance many times before.

'I need you to let Eloise go,' repeats Pen, feeling her phone vibrate in her pocket again.

'Get out of my house or I'll fucking kill both of you,' Patrick says, approaching her.

Pen feels a deep sense of calm come over her. This man may kill her. This might be it. Now that she's standing here, in this moment, it does seem strangely inevitable. But she is sure of one thing: he will not kill Eloise.

Pen takes a step backwards.

'No,' Patrick snarls. He inches sideways. 'Go through there.' He gestures over his shoulder to the kitchen.

Pen moves in the direction he's indicated.

'Wait, you can't leave. Fuck!' He smacks a hand against the side of his head.

Eloise moans quietly, and Pen thinks that she too can see the inevitable horror ahead of them.

Patrick's fury becomes palpable as he thinks through his limited options. 'This is all your fault, you stupid slut,' he snarls at Eloise. His transformation into wolf is complete as he pants, teeth bared and eyes wild. 'You and that fucking whore did this.'

Pen reaches for her gun as Patrick moves in slow motion, pulling Eloise with him, his sweat and her tears making her slippery in his arms. Feeling the floor beneath her feet, Pen imagines a piece of string running all the way up to the ceiling above her. She stands as tall and straight as she can. She remembers her training in chunks, remembers Barnes telling her that it's important to learn to shut out all the noise and focus.

The glint of Patrick's eyes matches the glint of the knife as he throws Eloise aside and runs at Pen. She hears Eloise hit the wall and yelp like an animal. Pen fixes her gaze on his fleshy right shoulder and fires, just as he thrusts the blade through the air toward her. The entire world seems to freeze.

Then there's a silent explosion of colour. It's in front of her, it's inside her. She can't see Patrick's face anymore. She can't see Eloise, she can only see red.

He got me.

She's surprised to register the thought just like she would acknowledge any other. Her knees give way. As she falls to the floor, she thinks that Barnes was right about the noise. Her gun clatters down, and she moves her hand to the knife lodged deep in her torso.

The silence gives way to the loudest buzzing she has ever heard.

CHAPTER FIFTY-THREE

FRIDAY, 31 JANUARY, 9.09 AM

Dunkley's executive assistant is polite but guarded. 'I'm sorry, I can't give you Mr Willoughby's number.'

TJ leans forward and talks into Oli's iPhone speaker. 'We were at his house two days ago. The premier was happy to talk to us.'

'I'm aware of the interview you did with the premier, but that's not relevant when it comes to giving out information now.'

'What's Dunkley's schedule today?' Oli asks.

The assistant sighs loudly. 'She has a speaking event and then meetings. And she's dealing with this video, of course. She barely has a second to eat.'

TJ is googling madly on his phone. He holds it up to show Oli what he's found.

She presses mute on her mobile.

'This is an old number I found for Willoughby online. I'll try it.'

She nods, and TJ leaves the room to make the call. She unmutes the phone. 'Is Mr Willoughby accompanying Dunkley today?'

'I don't believe so,' replies the assistant. 'Sorry, Ms Groves. I need to go. Feel free to send me an email outlining your request, and I'll get back to you when I can.'

She hangs up.

TJ comes back into the room. 'It rang out, and there was no voicemail.'

'We should just go to the house, see if Willoughby's there. I doubt he'll be attending a corporate event with her.'

'And what, we just ask him if it's a coincidence that he knows two murder victims?'

Oli lifts her shoulders. 'I guess so. Dunkley was forthcoming about her family knowing Lyra, but I just think it's odd that they also knew Addison and that hasn't been made clear.' She taps her phone against the side of her hand, thinking. 'My sister said something recently about everyone knowing Willoughby is a creep. Have you ever heard any whispers about him? I had a quick look online, and there's a bit of chatter, but it's all speculation. I feel like something would have come up when I did the deep dive on Dunkley if there was anything concrete. Everyone seemed to think he was a great guy.'

'I haven't heard anything,' says TJ. He looks at his watch. 'I'm not sure if the police are going to make a statement about the video, but let's get the team set up and then we'll head to Dunkley's . . .'

Through the glass they see Yael return with the coffees. She holds up TJ's espresso, and he smiles and gives her the 'in a minute' gesture.

'All right, should we go?' He seems unsure, happy to take Oli's lead.

'Yep. How about you drive. I want to do some more digging on Shane Willoughby on the way.'

Oli steps out of the boardroom and tells Chelsea that she and TJ have a lead they need to follow up. She briefs her on finishing the piece she's written on Addison Bower-Fry.

'Is everything all right?' Chelsea asks, perceptive as always.

'Kind of,' says Oli. 'We'll be in touch later, okay? Call us if you need anything.'

In the car, Oli clicks on link after link about Shane Willoughby. 'He's fifty-three, and his birthday is in July. He was born in the United Kingdom, but the family moved here when he was four. An older brother and two younger sisters. He was in a relationship with a promising sprinter before he met Dunkley. He claims it was love at first sight. She doesn't.'

Oli crosses her legs at the ankles, trying to quell the twitchy feeling in her limbs. 'He was into shooting as a kid. Used to go hunting with his dad back in the UK. Says he regrets it now.'

'Not exactly the worst thing in the world,' says TJ. 'A lot of people like shooting.'

'After he retired from being a coach, he went back to university and studied IT but has focused most of his energy on philanthropy and supporting Dunkley's career.'

'He basically sounds perfect,' says TJ. 'I mean, maybe the computer thing is interesting, but an IT degree from over ten years ago isn't going to make him an online expert now.'

'No,' Oli murmurs, her vision blurring as she thinks. 'TJ,' she says slowly, 'what you said to Dunkley's EA about being at the house the other day . . .'

He glances sideways at her. 'Yeah?'

'We were talking about the office aircon being broken and needing to work from your house the following day. You mentioned Carol going away. Do you remember?'

'I think so. When we were in the lounge and Dunkley left to take the call, right?'

'Right,' she says excitedly. 'And remember how Dunkley said Willoughby came home, but then we didn't see him?'

They stop at a red light, and TJ turns to her. 'You're saying you think Willoughby heard us arranging to work from my place and mentioning Carol being in Sydney, and that's why I was targeted. You think he sent the video.'

'I don't . . . No, I'm not sure. It's just that I thought someone was listening to us outside the room the other day. I figured it was Wendy eavesdropping. But now . . . I just have a weird feeling about him.'

'If there's a chance he's a deranged killer, surely we shouldn't be going to see him.'

'Maybe we can do some quick alibi checks.' She googles Dunkley and filters the results by date. She takes a screen grab then does it again, this time entering a different date. 'He was with Dunkley at an event the evening Lyra went missing. And it looks like he was overseas when Addison went missing in Adelaide.'

TJ seems disappointed. 'Do you still reckon he's worth talking to?'

'I don't think my Google search is definitive, and he did know two of the missing women. You never know, talking to him might lead to a new angle.'

'You don't have to tell me twice. I don't believe in coincidences, you know that.'

They drive in silence for a few blocks.

'How are you, really?' she asks.

'How are *you*, really? he replies.

'I—' She stops when he starts to laugh. She looks at him, surprised, then finds herself laughing too.

A minute later, TJ stops laughing and sighs. 'I don't even know how to answer your question. Let's talk about it once I know what the fuck is going on.'

'How is Carol?' Oli ventures.

'She's pretty shaken by the whole thing.'

She looks across at him, and he lets out a bitter laugh.

'I must be the world's worst investigative journalist. I had no idea.'

'It's not your fault,' Oli says, smiling sadly at him.

He pulls up outside Dunkley's house and clears his throat, indicating that the conversation about his personal life is on pause for now. 'Right. Let's see if Mr Swim Coach is home.'

They get out of the car and meet each other on the pavement, exchanging a look before Oli presses the intercom button to the right of the gate.

There's a click, followed by a male voice. 'Hello? Full disclosure, I can see you. There's a camera.'

'Mr Willoughby? We're journalists. Olive Groves and Timothy Jack, from *Newsday*.'

'Sorry. My wife isn't here. You'll have to come back another time or attempt to accost her somewhere else.'

'We know. We'd like to speak with you.'

'Me? Why would you want to do that?'

'It's about The Photographer case. You knew two of the victims.'

There's a long pause. 'Where did you say you were from again?'

'*Newsday*,' says Oli.

'You did the domestic violence podcast with Clarissa the other day,' Willoughby says. 'She thinks you're doing important work. I'll let you in, but let's just keep it between us, okay? No need for her to know. She doesn't trust me when I'm unsupervised.'

The door to the side of the car entrance buzzes open.

Shane Willoughby meets them at the front door, holding a steaming mug. 'Hello, journalists! Welcome back. Please, come in.'

They shake his hand and step inside.

'Tea, coffee?'

They request water and take a seat at the kitchen bench. The appliances are modern, but the décor is worn and homely. On the fridge door, Oli notices several photos of Willoughby and Dunkley on their wedding day.

Willoughby places the water in front of them and brings his hands together expectantly. His dark hair is damp and curls at the ends, and his tanned skin glows with good health. He's charming and curious, asking them questions about the business and offering opinions on the state of their industry. 'Seems to me that the media landscape is changing by the second. It must be very hard to stay abreast of it all. Is it hard adapting to all the digital and social media stuff?'

'We're embracing it as best we can,' says TJ. 'And we work with a lot of young people.'

'Aren't young people wonderful? Long may they live and be smarter than us all.' Willoughby finishes his tea, rinses the mug and puts it in the dishwasher. 'All right, let's have it. You want to talk about the girls? Sorry, I know they are women, but when I knew them, they were girls. Both wonderful.'

Oli asks him a series of questions about his time as a coach and what he can remember about Lyra and Addison from back then. They talk for twenty minutes, but Oli senses that aside from some sweet anecdotes, he doesn't know anything. He only met Addison twice, and he hasn't seen Lyra in over six years.

'I'm obviously keen to help in any way I can,' Willoughby says, when their questions become thin. 'This whole situation is a nightmare. I can't imagine the pain of their parents, the grief—but also the abuse, and it is abuse, this public parading of their loved ones in this way. That video of Lyra, my god. But I don't see how I can help. Both girls were confident and lovely and just so full of life. Opinionated and fiery, exactly what we all want young girls to be like.' He smiles. 'I remember Lyra putting a few of the boys in their place from time to time. She was so competitive and hated the way they mucked around. She made it clear she didn't have time for romance, or not back then, anyway.'

Oli finishes her water and gets to her feet, thanking Willoughby for his time. TJ follows suit.

Willoughby walks them to the front door. 'My wife is deeply upset about all this. I've been worried about her. She's such a crusader, and women's rights are something she has been passionate about from a very young age.' His eyes shine with pride. 'No matter what happens at the next election she will always advocate and agitate, but this . . . *horror* is taking a toll. It's all she talks about.'

They shake his hand and thank him again, heading along the gravel path to the gate.

'What now?' TJ mutters, rubbing his eyes.

Oli feels adrift. 'Back to the office, I guess.'

'Wait!'

They turn to see Wendy Willoughby running out of the house, waving a hand at them.

CHAPTER FIFTY-FOUR

FRIDAY, 31 JANUARY, 9.16 AM

Pen manages to push the pain away. It separates from her body and floats somewhere above her. *No, thank you*, she thinks. *I'm not interested in any of that.* She feels something close to peace, although she is aware of moisture on her cheek and a dull ache somewhere behind her. Perhaps her back? It's hard to tell.

But at least there are no awful images. All she can see is white.

At some stage she becomes aware of a strange humming in her leg. *My phone, that's my phone.* After a while it stops ringing, but a few seconds later it starts again. She tries to work out how to get it, but she can't move, can't even feel her hands.

She tries to call out and manages a muted, 'Help.'

'Look what you made me do, you fucking bitch. She's a *cop*, Eloise, a *cop*. Now we're both completely fucked.' His feet come into her vision as he bends down and picks up her gun.

Eloise shrieks, and the sound ricochets through Pen's frozen body.

'Get up. Get up! You need to help me fix this, you silly cow.' Patrick sounds hysterical. 'I'm bleeding.'

I need to protect her. Pen positions her elbows on either side of her body, but when she tries to push them against the floor to get up, the world spins in a terrifying circle.

'You're hurt, Pat.'

'Don't touch me!'

Pen's left hand feels wet and so does her face. She moans and receives a sharp kick in the ribcage.

'Shut the fuck up!' Patrick's coffee breath is on her face, his spit landing on her nose and cheeks.

Her eyes flutter open. His black loafers are centimetres from her face again, and they move in a repetitive semicircle as he paces.

She can't see Eloise.

There's a thumping sound. 'Hello, is anyone home? This is the police!'

Thank god, the police are here.

Patrick's shoes disappear, and Eloise's whimpering comes in fits and starts as he drags her away, he's going to try to escape. And he's desperate, dangerous. He has Pen's gun. She needs to warn the police.

'I can hear you in there. Open the door now!'

Barnes?

'Watch out,' she whispers.

The banging on the door grows louder, then Pen hears a loud smash followed by the tinkling of glass. The door swings open, the weight of it banging against the adjacent wall.

Oli can hear Patrick's laboured breathing. 'Mate, you need to get out of here. There's been a misunderstanding, and I don't want anyone to get hurt.'

'Sir, you're injured, so why don't you put the gun down, and we can get you looked at.'

'This is between me and her!' Patrick cries. 'I need you to leave.'

'The gun, sir,' says Barnes in his gentle voice. 'Or I will shoot you.'

'Fuck you!'

Pen can't see what's happening, but she can feel footsteps pulse through the floorboards. Men shouting. A woman crying. Pen moves her feet, tries again to shift position, but she has no strength. She feels detached from her limbs.

'I mean it, sir, I—'

A gunshot is drowned out by Eloise's screams, and Pen finds herself praying. *Barnes, please. Don't let her die.*

Something heavy falls to the floor behind her, then Barnes's face is in front of her with a worried expression. 'I'm so sorry, Pen.' He shifts her onto her side, arranges her limbs just like she did with Olive Groves at Mackenzie Jackson's crime scene last week, tilting her neck slightly upward. He takes her pulse, his lips moving as he counts.

'I'm sorry,' Pen whispers.

'Pen, listen to me. You're going to be fine. You just need to hold on a tiny bit longer.'

'Eloise.'

A tear drips from Barnes's eyes and onto her face. 'She's going to be fine. She's outside.'

'Go to her.'

'I can't leave you like this.'

'I don't even know what happened,' she murmurs. 'I'm sure I'll be fine.'

She notices Barnes looking down along her body, and she does the same. Sees the handle of the knife protruding from her stomach and thinks she must be hallucinating.

Pen looks across the room at Patrick Jackson. He has fallen in an awkward angle; his left leg twists away from his body. His expression seems relaxed, his thick brows framing his handsome face. His lifeless dark eyes are almost shut.

He reminds Pen of the image The Photographer sent to the paper of Lyra Makris.

She closes her eyes. And then the pain comes.

CHAPTER FIFTY-FIVE

FRIDAY, 31 JANUARY, 9.48 AM

Wendy's smile is wide, but she glances nervously over her shoulder. 'Hi again.' She places a hand on her chest to catch her breath, her eyes glued to TJ. Her long blonde hair is parted down the middle, and she's wearing a pale blue drop-waist dress and sandals that lace up her calves. She looks like she's time-travelled from Woodstock.

Without speaking, TJ indicates Oli should lead this conversation.

'Hi, Wendy,' says Oli.

'Hey, so, I was listening to the conversation you had with my dad. Sorry, but it's not like I wasn't going to once I realised what you were talking about.'

'Yes.' Oli makes sure her expression doesn't change, but inwardly she's on alert. Is Wendy about to dispute what her father just said? Oli eyes the house nervously and wonders if they should have this conversation somewhere else.

'You're barking up the wrong tree,' Wendy says, flicking her long hair from one side of her forehead to the other. 'Dad is a saint. Honestly, his infinite patience is almost ridiculous, and he is kind to a fault. I mean, can you imagine being with my mum?' She rolls her eyes. 'The man deserves every medal on the planet.'

TJ opens his mouth to reply, but Oli silences him with her eyes. 'We just wanted to speak to your dad, seeing as he knew Lyra and Addison,' she assures Wendy, keeping her voice light. 'Journalists are always looking for connections.' She doesn't want any trouble with Wendy. As friendly as the young woman seems, Oli has no doubt she could make things difficult for them if she wanted to.

'We all knew them. Everyone at the swim school did. Addison less so—we only met a couple of times at interstate meets.' Wendy narrows her eyes. 'But I know what you were thinking. Creepy swim coach preying on teenage girls. It's an obvious, lazy trope.'

'Like I said, we were just exploring connections,' Oli says patiently. 'There hasn't been much to work with.'

'I suppose not,' says Wendy. 'Dad has always been a goofball. He's so far from creepy it's not funny. The boys would always pester the girls after training and on the meets, and Dad was forever telling them to back off. Lyra really liked him—she was always telling me and Bronte that our dad was so nice.'

'Your dad said he hasn't seen her in years, is that right?'

'Pretty much. We bumped into her at the end of last year at a Christmas thing.'

'Who did?'

'We all did. It was some media event Mum dragged us to—Lyra's company was involved.'

TJ and Oli exchange a glance.

'Did you all speak to her?'

'We all said hi, but she was busy with clients, and we were dealing with Mum and the media, so it was just a hi-and-bye situation.'

'Do you ever remember anyone hassling Addison or Lyra back in your swimming days?' TJ asks.

Wendy raises her perfect eyebrows. 'It was a long time ago. I really can't remember.'

'Can you remember anyone making you feel uncomfortable?' TJ presses.

Oli stares at Wendy as she answers, sees her mouth moving but doesn't register the response. She's thinking of the research she did for the Dunkley podcast last year. Intelligent and athletic, the premier's son, Cole, had been a promising athlete with an almost guaranteed future in AFL—until he badly injured his shoulder and needed surgery. If Oli remembers right, he worked on his mother's campaign alongside his sisters, helping with events and social media.

'Wendy,' she says calmly, 'was your brother at the Christmas event too?'

'Yeah. Like I said, Mum made us all go.'

'What about the party when Lyra went missing. Was Cole there with you?'

She shakes her head. 'He's friends with Ned, but he didn't go. He had a date that night.'

'With his girlfriend?' Oli asks.

Wendy drops the volume of her voice. 'They broke up a little while back. It's supposed to be a secret, just because of her profile—but now they're dating again, I guess it's fine that you know.'

'Is Cole here?'

Wendy shakes her head. 'He's gone to Sydney for a couple of days for some job.'

Oli's fingers drift to her pulse, and she counts silently along to the rapid beats. *One, two, three.* Cole was here during their Dunkley interview. He might have heard their conversation about working from TJ's the following day and Carol being away.

'How close are Cole and Ned?' she asks, urgency creeping into her voice.

Wendy edges back slightly. 'They're close. They have a habit of going out with the same girls, but they seem to work it out. Ned loves to surf as much as Cole does, so he's at our beach house all the time.'

'Where is the beach house?'

'Torquay,' says Wendy slowly.

'When were you last there?' Oli asks.

The young woman makes a face. 'I haven't been for ages. At least a year. But Dad and Cole go all the time to surf. Dad was there yesterday—he only got back this morning. I think Cole and Ned were there earlier in the week with a bunch of friends.'

TJ and Oli exchange another glance.

'It's basically a bachelor pad at this point.' Wendy laughs, but it comes out as a hollow trill. She clearly senses something is wrong. 'What's going on? Tell me.'

'We need to get going,' says Oli. 'It's been good to chat.'

'Just call me anytime,' Wendy says. 'I'm always happy to help. Like I said, I'm interested in journalism.'

They leave her standing in the driveway and head to the gate.

'We need to find the address of that beach house,' says Oli, when they reach the car. 'I'll call Rusty on the way.'

CHAPTER FIFTY-SIX

FRIDAY, 31 JANUARY, 9.57 AM

Barnes is with Pen in the ambulance. She hears the words 'blood loss', 'internal bleeding', 'surgery'. At least the pain has gone again. She's not good with pain. She's starting to think she's not good with anything—not following instructions, not managing a covert mission.

'I'll call her family when we get to the hospital,' Barnes tells the ambulance officer. 'Will they be able to see her?'

'Depends on how the surgery goes,' the man says. 'The doctors will be able to tell you once they've assessed her.'

'How bad is it?' Pen asks, but no one replies. Perhaps she didn't say it aloud . . . ? 'Tell me,' she mumbles to Barnes.

He doesn't seem to hear this either. He's still talking to the ambulance officer, but every few seconds he glances down at her worriedly, his face a shocking grey. 'Hang in there, Pen.'

'Is he dead?' she whispers. 'Douglas Jackson.'

Barnes looks at her. 'Patrick, you mean. Yes. I shot him.'

'Eloise?'

'Eloise is fine. She's worried about you.'

'I'm sorry,' she says, or at least she thinks she does.

She can feel the ambulance go up a ramp and then come to a stop.

Barnes's face hovers close to hers. 'You're going to be okay.'

The doors to the ambulance open, and for a few moments all Pen can hear is the efficient sounds of machinery fitting together, enabling her stretcher to be eased out of the vehicle. Bright light hits her face, and she closes her eyes again.

Barnes's voice is thick with emotion, and he squeezes her hand. 'I'll see you soon, Pen.'

Another male voice says, 'Are you still with us, Penelope?' Then, louder: 'I need help over here! Penelope!'

CHAPTER FIFTY-SEVEN

FRIDAY, 31 JANUARY, 10.09 AM

'The beach house feels suspicious, right?' says TJ. 'Like whoever is doing all this needs privacy and a separate computer set-up.'

Oli looks up the address of Dunkley's place in Torquay, remembering there had been a fuss about it when she was elected due to the high value of the property. Next she starts scrolling through Instagram, trying to find something she remembers from her research when the Lyra story first broke. 'Look,' she says, 'Ned Higgins posted a bunch of photos on Instagram in November last year and tagged Torquay as the location. There's a shot of him with Cole, and I think Lyra's ex-boyfriend is in the background.'

TJ glances at it when he pauses at the traffic lights. 'Reckon they were staying at Dunkley's place?'

'Maybe.' Oli tries to call Rusty, but he isn't answering. She tries Detective Kibbs, who doesn't answer either.

'Do you think we can trust Wendy not to say anything to her family?' TJ says, craning his neck to look for oncoming traffic as he guides the car onto the freeway.

'I doubt it. Part of me thinks she's fed us information to send us on a wild goose chase.'

'Why would she do that?'

Oli raises her eyebrows. 'She loves the drama. Can't you tell how much she enjoys being amid a crisis?'

'Surely no one wants to be embroiled in something like this.'

How much does TJ's naivety have to do with the way Wendy Willoughby looks? 'I wouldn't be so sure about that. Wendy welcomes whatever attention she can get. She chased us down just now, remember?'

Oli thinks about Dean's girls. In many ways, Wendy reminds her of Kate. God help Dean in the coming years.

She tries both phone numbers again. 'Rusty still isn't answering, and I can't get on to the other detective from his team. Should I try to call Sanders? Lew?'

'I'm not sure about Lew. He's so close to Dunkley, and this is hardly a refined theory.'

'Sure, but you think we're onto something, right? I mean, for starters, it sounds like Willoughby lied to us about not seeing Lyra Makris for years.'

TJ narrows his eyes but nods. 'Do you think he just figured it wasn't worth mentioning because they barely spoke? Or maybe he forgot. But he could have overheard us at his place the other day.' TJ grimaces. 'Surely his schedule would make it impossible for him to do something like this?'

Oli looks at the window, trying to think. 'I watched a documentary recently on the Zodiac Killer case. Did you know the authorities now believe there were two killers?'

'What do you mean?'

'Well, perhaps not two killers, but two people communicating with the cops and the media. One was the real killer, and the other one was just an opportunistic attention-seeker.'

'And you think that's what is happening now?'

'Rusty said something yesterday that made me think the Jackson video you were sent was fake.' Oli squeezes her eyes shut. 'I don't know. Maybe I'm just grasping at straws.'

'The video looked real.' TJ sounds defensive.

Oli recalls the gruesome scene from the video. 'I know. But some of the people I've been interviewing for this cybercrime piece have had fake videos and photos made of them and posted online. It's near impossible to tell the difference.'

'The future is here, and it's a nightmare,' murmurs TJ.

'I'm calling Sanders. Even if we're not sure what's going on, we can't sit on this.'

'We want the exclusive, though.'

'No shit.'

Oli calls through the switch and is transferred to a detective called Zappa, who puts her through the ringer before eventually transferring her call to Sanders.

He listens to what she has to say, then says, 'This is an incredibly serious accusation, Ms Groves.'

'For the record, I'm not accusing anyone of anything—but there's enough circumstantial evidence that surely you need to speak to Shane Willoughby and possibly his son.'

Sanders mutters something under his breath.

'We're on our way to the Torquay property now,' Oli adds, much to TJ's annoyance.

'I do not want you two cowboys rushing in there,' Sanders hisses. 'Do you understand?'

'Then send a crew. But if he's involved in some way, we want an exclusive.'

'In case you haven't noticed, we're a little busy. I'll follow up your information, and we'll determine the next steps. After that, we can discuss what your newspaper has permission to cover.'

She doesn't bother correcting his newspaper comment. 'So you agree this is a credible line of inquiry?'

'I have no strong view at this stage. But I'm open to following up all relevant information, and a few things you've mentioned might make chatting to Mr Willoughby worthwhile.'

'Do you think he has access to the criminal investigation via Dunkley? We wondered if the killer had inside information.'

'Unlike you, I'm not going to speculate, but I repeat, do not go inside the property and do not share your theories with anyone. I'll send you my direct number now. I want you to call me with any new information. I do not want Victoria Police linked to an unverified fuck-up with the premier's family. Understood?'

'Understood,' says Oli.

'Christ,' Sanders mutters under his breath and hangs up.

'He's pissed,' says Oli.

'He always comes across like that,' says TJ. 'It looks like it's the next street on the left. Dunkley's place is a bit further along around the bend, but maybe we should park near the corner and walk. What do you think?'

'Good idea,' Oli says as Sanders's text comes through.

He parks then goes to the rear of his BMW and opens the boot. He leans around to Oli's side as she's getting out. 'Here,' he says, throwing her a T-shirt and a visor that must be Carol's. 'Put them on.'

She's about to protest, but he's already swapping his shirt and dress pants for running shorts and a Nike T-shirt, so she dutifully removes her shirt, pulls on the T-shirt and dons the visor.

They walk along the street. Oli observes the sprawling homes, all with vibrant green lawns and lush gardens despite the recent heat. Nearby, water splashes and children squeal with laughter. A dog barks excitedly until a woman's voice yells at it to shut up.

TJ points out the property that matches the photos in the article she found online. It's modern but fits snugly into the landscape. Plants and grass sprout artfully from various surfaces, and the pebbled driveway flows attractively into a landscaped picnic lawn with a built-in barbecue and firepit. The carport is empty, and she points it out to TJ.

'Hopefully there's no one here,' he says. 'Makes it easier.'

She points to the surfboard propped against the side of the house. 'Would you leave a surfboard out like that?'

TJ shrugs. 'Maybe around here you would.'

They walk past the house and look at it from the other side.

'What do you think?' she says, shielding her face from the sun.

'I guess we wait. We can head back to the car. Or we can walk down to the beach and check out the house from there . . . ?'

'Let's do that,' says Oli.

They pass the house and make their way to the public walkway that leads to the beach. It's a beautiful day, and they walk in companiable silence. Birds twitter and chase each other around the lower branches of shrubs, and Oli catches a glimpse of the dark blue ocean. She'd love to go for a swim. She breaks away from TJ and walks toward the water, mesmerised by the sparkling waves.

She looks back toward TJ then scans her eyes along the landscape and up to the house. The white façade looks particularly dramatic against the blue sky, and the sun reflects off the floor-to-ceiling windows, making them impossible to look at for more than a moment.

Oli's Apple Watch buzzes with a news alert. 'There's been a shooting in Melbourne,' she tells TJ.

He's still looking at the house. 'Really?' Suddenly his arm shoots up. 'Hey!' He runs toward the house across the sand.

Oli shades her eyes from the glare, trying to see whom he's yelling at. As her eyes readjust, she can see a tall, lean figure in a hoodie standing on the balcony that runs along the side of the house.

'TJ!' Oli cries.

He is halfway across the beach already and shows no sign of slowing down. She runs after him, her sandals spraying sand everywhere.

When she looks back at the balcony, the person is gone. She's sure it was a male. Was it Shane Willoughby following them? Or was it a younger man?

TJ yells something at her over his shoulder, but it's lost in the wind. Did he say to call the cops?

Oli reaches the bottom of the stairs that lead to Dunkley's house from the beach just in time to see the hooded figure disappear around the side of the property. TJ is at the top of the staircase, and she pauses, trying to work out if she can hear one set of footsteps or two.

TJ swears, and she can hear a door opening. 'Fuck, TJ, what are you doing?' she whispers.

She pulls her mobile from her pocket as she sneaks along the side of the house and down a short flight of stairs into the backyard. She edges along the perimeter, her eyes scanning the house for signs of movement. Another news alert about the shooting lands on her watch. It was a police shooting. She thinks of Rusty and prays he wasn't involved.

She ignores the missed calls and messages on her phone and calls the number Sanders gave her, but it goes to voicemail. 'We need backup at Dunkley's Torquay house now!' she whispers. 'There's someone here.'

She reaches a shed and turns sideways to squeeze in between the building and the fence line until she is in the back corner of the yard. She looks up both sides of the shed. Nothing. She can't hear anything except the steady crash of the ocean. After a few moments, she moves along in the other direction, but a soft sound brings her to a sharp stop. She hears it again. A faint whimpering. There's an animal in the yard. Or is it coming from the shed?

Oli presses her ear to the wall but can't hear anything. She peers out past the small structure and across the lawn. *Where are you TJ?* Clutching her phone, she edges around the front of the shed and realises that it's actually a studio. She tries the door, but it's locked. She inches sideways and tries to push the sliding window open, but it's locked too. The glass is tinted, and the blinds make it impossible to see inside.

Feeling exposed, Oli returns to the side of the studio. She comes face to face with a man wearing a black balaclava under his hooded jumper, aiming a gun at her.

CHAPTER FIFTY-EIGHT

Pen is back in the bath. She stretches out her legs; there's so much room, more than usual. She looks at her legs. She remembers her high-school boyfriend told her she has great legs. Two days later he cheated on her with his sister's best friend.

The water is still running, but when she reaches for the tap to turn it off, she finds that it's gone. Maybe it's not supposed to turn off. There's no plug anyway, so the water just flows out while more water flows in.

Pen looks around for some food. And where is her wine? She must have forgotten to get some. She didn't even remember to bring her laptop or her phone, but Elliot is asleep on the floor near the door, she can hear the high notes of his snoring above the drone of the water. And there's music too. She doesn't recognise the track, but she likes the electronic melody. She should listen to new music more often, try more new things. Take some risks.

Energised by this thought, she tries to sit up. Something is pinning her down. Her arms and legs move, but the rest of her body is stuck. Thank god there's no plug or she would drown. A strange sensation seizes her. It feels like she's being cut in half. The pain feels like red, it feels like black. The music becomes louder, and she sinks further down into the bath. Something is blocking the drain, and the water is rising.

She moves her hands along the porcelain, then her feet join her hands in the search for the plughole, but it's not there. Her torso is on fire. Soon her limbs stop their frantic movement, and she breathes in and lets the water carry her away.

CHAPTER FIFTY-NINE

FRIDAY, 31 JANUARY, 12.43 PM

The man grabs Oli by the shoulders and marches her to the front of the studio, the gun pressed into her spine. He unlocks the door with a key, opens it and shoves her inside. He takes her phone and stares at her for a long moment before pulling the door shut. The second the door closes, Oli's nervous system splinters into a million pieces. She thought she was going to die. Maybe she will—he's still there, she can hear him breathing not a metre away. She can *smell* him: sweat and salt and fear. Who is he?

The external lock clicks into place, and Oli collapses in a heap near the door as deep sobs roll through her body. Sniffing, she looks around. The room is almost pitch-black, but it's cool, and she can hear the faint hum of an air-conditioning unit. As her eyes adjust to the dark, she can see there's a double bed in the corner with a mound of rumpled sheets on top. She looks around for a light switch, but when she flicks it nothing happens.

Her Apple Watch vibrates with text messages, and she's weak with relief that the hooded man didn't think to take it from her. Messages from TJ, all photos. She clicks on one and squints at the tiny screen, trying to work out what she's looking at. Several computers lined up on a desk. It must be from inside the house. If TJ is sending her photos, he must think there's some significance. Evidence of something. Oli wonders if the man who grabbed her is The Photographer or if he's just some bit player who is getting paid to send messages and doctor images. She remembers the story about the police shooting and realises Rusty never called her back, maybe—

Oli becomes aware that a woman is watching her from the tangle of sheets on the bed. Oli's hand flies to her mouth as she smothers a scream. In the dim light, she can see that the woman's wrists are attached to the bedhead, and her ankles are tied together. Oli rushes across the room, her heart in her throat.

Lyra Makris looks broken and terrified, but she's alive.

Oli reaches out her hand to Lyra, who flinches violently, cowering against the dark sheets. The young woman is covered in bruises and painfully thin, but there is no obvious damage to her neck.

'It's okay,' Oli whispers. 'We're going to get out of here. I'm going to—'

They startle as a gun goes off nearby.

CHAPTER SIXTY

Pen is awake, but her eyes are closed. Heavy material covers her body, making it impossible for her to move.

She senses someone is nearby. And then Frost says, his voice angry, 'Barnes. What the hell happened?'

'I'm not sure, sir,' replies Barnes, from somewhere to her left. 'She said she had a lead on Jackson's brother and that she wanted to speak with his wife. I had a bad feeling. I tried to call her, but when she didn't answer the phone, I went straight to Patrick Jackson's house.' Barnes's voice sounds far away and muted.

Pen tries to open her eyes. Through a sliver, she sees Frost pinch the skin on the bridge of his nose. 'Thank god you did, but my Christ, this is a mess. She wasn't even supposed to be working today. Sanders sent her home.'

Barnes doesn't reply.

Frost sighs and sits down next to him. His face is flushed. 'How are you holding up?' he asks gruffly. 'It sounds like it was a bad scene.'

'It wasn't good. He'd already stabbed her by the time I got there. I made my initial report before, but I wanted to be here when she came out of surgery. Her family is still on their way.'

'Do you know how she's doing?' Frost asks.

Pen's eyes close, and she can't make them open again.

'They won't tell me much.' Barnes sniffs. 'She's been in and out of it a lot, and it seemed like she lost a lot of blood. That prick put the knife straight through her.'

'Jesus,' mutters Frost.

'She's just a kid,' Barnes says. 'A bloody kid.'

'I'll need to go over the details with you shortly.' Frost's voice is gentler now. 'We'll have to conduct an internal investigation. We're getting Eloise Jackson's statement this evening. She seems to be very keen that everyone knows her husband attacked you and Kibbs and that your actions were in self-defence.'

Pen's torso starts to burn again. It's not pain exactly, but it's hot and uncomfortable.

'Whatever you need.' Barnes sounds weary.

'There are some other things we need to talk about too.'

'I don't doubt it, sir.'

Pen hears soft footsteps, then an unfamiliar voice says, 'Is her family here yet?'

'I couldn't get on to her mother or father, but her brother is on his way,' says Barnes.

He's spoken to Walter?

The doctor draws an audible breath.

'Detective Inspector Rusty Frost.' Pen can tell by the direction of his voice that he is standing now. 'How is she?'

A mobile phone rings.

Through the familiar melody, Pen thinks she hears the doctor say, 'Hopefully her family can get here as soon as possible.'

CHAPTER SIXTY-ONE

FRIDAY, 31 JANUARY, 1.06 PM

Oli chokes back a sob. TJ. God, has he shot TJ? She turns to Lyra, careful not to touch her.

'Lyra. Do you remember being at Ned Higgins's party? Do you remember what happened to you?'

Lyra's eyes focus on her, but she doesn't seem to register the question.

Oli moves from the bed and goes to the window. She peers outside, careful not to shift the curtains. There's no sign of life on the pristine green lawn or in the house. Oli forwards the photos from TJ to Sanders's number from her watch, but the message won't send. The man has obviously disabled her phone. Surely Sanders has received her voicemail message by now. But what if TJ is already injured, or worse? Panic overwhelms her, and she grips her head in her hands and shudders through a silent sob. *Not now. You can't fall apart again now. You need to get out of here.*

She returns to Lyra and attempts to untie her, but her wrists are secured by locked cuffs and the cords binding her feet are impossible to undo. Oli winces as she notices the red-raw skin and dried blood on the woman's ankles. She scans the room, looking for something that she might be able to use to untie her. On the table next to the bed are several bottles of pills and a glass of water. There is also a bottle containing something red and what looks like a make-up kit.

'Do you want some water?' Oli whispers.

Lyra doesn't respond.

Oli holds some water to her mouth anyway, but it just runs down her face. 'I'm going to call for help,' she says to Lyra, but her eyes have closed. Oli prays that she isn't suffering from sepsis.

She goes to the door and rattles it, knowing it's futile. She kicks it then looks around for something to smash a window. Apart from the bed, the room is almost empty. Oli looks under the bed but can't see anything that she can use.

She feels herself slipping back into despair. Lyra's head lolls to one side, and for a horrible moment Oli thinks she is dead before her mouth opens slightly and her face crumples in a wince of pain. *We've got to get out of here. Where the hell are the police?*

The door swings open, and Oli is momentarily blinded by sunlight. Silhouetted in the doorway is the hooded man, still wearing the balaclava. He turns and closes the door, locking it behind him. He's been running, he's out of breath, and Oli can see his eyes darting around the room. 'You need to shut up,' he says, pointing the gun at her. 'We need to get out of here, and you will do as I say, or I'll shoot you.'

She nods, fear freezing her from the inside out. 'Where is TJ?'

'Shut up! And move. I'm going to carry her, and you will walk in front of us. Do you understand?'

Oli nods again. She can tell that he's panicking, and she's terrified he might just shoot them both. Her legs shake as he herds her closer to the bed with his gun.

'Why are you doing this?' Oli whispers as he unlocks the cuffs securing Lyra to the bed. Her arms fall limply around her head. 'She needs to go to hospital.'

'Just shut up!' He thrusts the gun toward Oli, and she stumbles, tripping over her feet.

She places a hand over her mouth to smother a sob.

'Stay there,' he barks. He keeps the gun trained on her as he moves backwards to the end of the bed. 'We need to get out of here,' he mutters.

'She needs to go to the hospital,' Oli repeats.

The man explodes, drawing himself to full height. 'This is all her fault. She fucking lied to me! Treated me like an idiot, then fucking laughed about me with her friends.'

'I'm sorry,' Oli says.

He kicks the bed. 'Fuck! What am I going to do now. Fuck!' He looks at Lyra. 'You stupid bitch. Look what you made me do.'

Oli tries to picture James Delway from the clips she saw on social media. Is it him? Or is it Cole Willoughby? Or Ned Higgins, who kept making all those tasteless videos about Lyra's final hours at his party that Chelsea showed her on social media? Oli doesn't know any of them well enough to tell.

'What happened?' she asks.

'Do you know she told me it was bad timing. That we'd make a great match someday, but we needed to wait until we weren't with other people. And then when she was finally single and I asked her out, suddenly it's not the timing, it's just that she's not into it. She said she didn't want a boyfriend.' He waves the gun around. 'But then I see her online, trying to find a fucking boyfriend. So, I create a fake profile, and then what do you know, suddenly she's interested. Stupid bitch.'

He's not Delway. He can't be.

'You pretended to be someone else?' Oli says.

He laughs. 'She was gagging for it. I offered to take her to see him, and she had no idea it was me she wanted all along.'

The police will surely search the house and make their way to the backyard. Oli is desperate to keep him talking. 'Was this from the party?'

'You should have seen how dressed up she was for the fake guy. I was watching her reading my messages from the car. She was so fucking horny for me, and then I see her getting ready to go, and so I pretended to be leaving and tell her I'll give her a lift and she just gets into my car. It was too easy.'

'And then you brought her here?'

He grips the gun and squeezes his eyes shut. 'I wanted to go back to her place, but she tried to run off. She was screaming at me, calling me a loser, and so I told her I would cut her throat if she didn't shut the fuck up and that shut her up. She's barely spoken since.' His breathing is ragged now.

It must be Willoughby. There's no way Higgins could have left his party for hours without anyone noticing.

'What about the other women?' Oli asks. 'Did you know them too?'

His movements are becoming jerky. 'Everyone was so fucking *scared*. But they loved it as well. A serial killer. *Fuck*. It was too easy.'

Oli's thoughts are splintering in multiple directions. 'Tell me about Addison,' she whispers.

He sneers. 'She was always a stuck-up bitch. Someone else obviously thought so too.'

'Where is she?'

'How the fuck should I know?'

Puzzle pieces click into place. *He didn't kill her*, Oli realises.

'What about Marta Holm and Erica Pawley? Did you know them?'

He growls and retrains the gun on Oli with renewed vigour. 'Enough!'

He pulls a small knife from his pocket and uses his left hand to slice through the ties that bind Lyra's ankles to the bedframe. Lyra moans and whimpers, and the man looks up at her, his mouth twisted in a snarl.

Oli's brain works in tandem with her body, and she propels herself forward, her hand reaching for the glass of water, gripping it and bringing it toward his head with all her strength. Sharp pain shoots up her arm as the glass seems to disintegrate between her fingers.

The man howls and drops the pocketknife as he backs away from the bed, one hand reaching to his bloodied head, the gun still in his other hand. Shards of glass glint in the dim light, and Oli scrambles to pick up the knife. She moves toward his hunched figure and lets out an anguished yelp as she plunges it into his upper back. He roars in pain.

Then there's a loud crash. The whole world spins. They are bathed in white light.

Squinting, Oli sees two cops stepping through the door just as a gunshot rips through the room.

CHAPTER SIXTY-TWO

FRIDAY, 31 JANUARY, 5.03 PM

Pen slowly becomes aware of a beeping sound. After several attempts she manages to peel her eyes open. She sees her mother first, then Walter. Then her father steps into frame. They stare at her worriedly, and she has an overwhelming urge to close her eyes again and pretend to be asleep.

'I'll get the doctor,' says Walter self-importantly.

'Tell him she's waking up,' says her mother, between sobs.

'What did you think I was going to tell him?' Walter snaps, as he rushes from the room.

With some effort, Pen swallows. Her saliva tastes like metal. 'What time is it?' she croaks.

'It's just gone 5 pm, love,' says her dad.

'You've been out of it.' Her mother dabs at her eyes with a tissue. 'We said goodbye to you just in case, but I knew you'd pull through.'

Walter catches this as he re-enters the room. 'That is not how it went, Mum.' He rolls his eyes, but his usual bravado is muted.

'Eloise?' Pen murmurs.

'She looks awful, but she's fine,' says her mother. 'She's covered in bruises from that monster. And he broke her arm. It's all over the news what happened. They are including your name now. I've had a lot of people call me, not that I've been able to speak to them.'

A man in scrubs with a broad smile enters the room. 'Hi, Penelope. I'm Dr Bandara. I'm very glad to see you awake.' He orders everyone out and spends some time reviewing her vitals and explaining the surgery she had and what is likely to happen next.

Pen's head spins. Her stomach is thick with bandages, and she has a blurry memory of seeing a knife wedged in her body. 'I can't really remember anything after I shot him.'

Dr Bandara nods. 'You're likely still in shock, and your recovery will take some time. We'll be monitoring you for infections over the coming days, and we'll make sure you have someone to talk to. That will be an important part of your recovery.'

Pen doesn't reply. Everything seems theoretical right now, with no application to reality.

'And rest,' says Dr Bandara. 'You need to get lots of rest.'

He pats her hand and gives her another little nod. 'Everything is going to be okay.' He pushes the curtain aside, and she can hear him talking to her family and instructing them to go easy on her. 'She needs rest. Visitors need to be kept to a minimum over the next few days.'

Pen stares at the ceiling, questions whirling in her head.

Her mother bustles back in looking nonplussed. 'He's nice that doctor, but a little on the strict side. Pen, honey, did you know that journalist is here too? You know him—Timothy Jack, that divine-looking reporter. I used to swoon over his picture in the paper.'

Pen is confused—she just saw TJ at his house yesterday. 'What happened?'

Her mother launches into a breathless recap of the breaking news, reading from her phone. 'Timothy Jack, apparently everyone calls him TJ, was shot at a beach house in Torquay. *The Age* is saying the house belongs to the premier, but that doesn't seem right, does it? Why would he be there? Anyway, it sounds like he's critical but stable. That's good, isn't it?'

'Jesus, Mum,' mutters Walter. 'Remember what the doctor said about keeping her calm.'

'And they found that dead girl.'

Pen blinks at her, disorientated.

'The one from the awful photo. It turns out she wasn't dead after all.'

'Lyra Makris?'

Her mother nods self-importantly. 'Yes, her. The amateur cook.'

Pen closes her eyes, trying to piece it together.

A nurse pops her head into the room and gives them a ten-minute warning. Marnie gathers their things, complaining about the rules.

'Who is Billy?' she asks Pen.

'What?' Pen's thoughts scramble.

'I popped your phone on the charger before, and you've just got a message from someone called Billy asking after you. I'm not snooping—it came up as a preview.' She swipes her fingers on the screen of Pen's phone. 'There's actually a lot of messages for you to read, Penny.'

'Mum,' says Walter. 'Come on.'

'I'm just asking. Is Billy a boyfriend, Pen? All the other messages look like they're from women.'

'Billy's a girl, Mum. Just a friend.' Pen catches Walter's eye, and he winks at her.

'Oh.' Marnie's disappointment is palpable. 'I can't stand all these silly unisex names. Why can't we just agree there are boy names and girl names?'

'That's enough, Marnie,' says her dad. 'Penny doesn't need a sermon right now.'

'It's okay, Dad,' Pen murmurs, uncharacteristically unbothered by her mother's fussing.

Her mum rattling off her favourite boy names is the last thing Pen remembers before she slides back into sleep.

CHAPTER SIXTY-THREE

FRIDAY, 31 JANUARY, 5.13 PM

The sky is a deep royal blue, and a smattering of faint stars are starting to emerge through the fading clouds. The salty breeze weaves through the yard, and nearby a dog barks. Oli sits on the rear steps of an ambulance, a lightweight blanket around her shoulders, watching the scene unfold in front of her. Almost against her will, she finds herself documenting details, filing them away for future reference.

She shifts position to get a view of the street. The media are being held at bay by a strip of police tape and several officers who refuse to answer their barrage of questions. Oli can sense the journalists' desperation as they are drip-fed information, trying to manage the furious demands of their editors, who want to be first with the truth or something close enough to it. The volume increases as the media mob grows, but Oli finds herself tuning out the sounds of their voices.

She thinks back to the moment in the dark room when Cole Willoughby shot himself. She thought he'd shot her, and for a split second she thought she was dead. It wasn't until the policeman had helped her outside that she realised her hand was bleeding from the broken glass.

Oli looks at it, covered in bandages, and wonders how she is going to type. She had refused treatment until a police officer told her TJ was okay, but the officer had seemed unsure what details to share. An ambulance arrived and began to treat Lyra, then eventually a senior officer arrived and explained that TJ had been shot and had been taken to hospital.

Now another officer is calling her name.

'Ms Groves? I believe this is yours.' He smiles at her and grips her shoulder as he holds out her phone. 'Make sure you look after yourself.'

She turns her phone on and sees that she has over fifty missed calls. Chelsea has called six times. She taps a shaky finger on Chelsea's name and holds the phone to her ear with her uninjured hand.

'Oli!' Chelsea's voice is high pitched. 'Is TJ okay? I'm hearing all kinds of insane things.'

Oli manages to stay calm as she explains what she knows. 'Cole shot him in the leg, but he made it to a neighbour's house and got treatment quickly. From everything I've been told, he's going to be fine.'

Her words are met with a long silence.

'And you?' Chelsea asks in a shaky voice.

'I'm okay.'

'No one would tell me anything. And I was trying to get the Jackson story live. I hope what I've done is okay—I didn't know what to do when you both stopped answering.'

'I'm sure it's fine,' Oli soothes. 'What Jackson story?'

Chelsea tells her that Douglas Jackson's brother, Patrick, was shot by a detective but not before he stabbed another detective. 'Her name is Penelope Kibbs. Spencer told me she's had surgery, but I don't know anything else.'

'Kibbs.' Oli pictures the serious young woman interviewing them at TJ's house yesterday and sends a prayer into the universe for her. Rusty must be beside himself.

'Are you sure you want me to go live with the Cole Willoughby headline?' Chelsea asks. 'I can put up a breaking-story hold and wait for the details.'

'I'm sure,' Oli says. 'I'm at the scene now, and I've told you everything I can currently confirm. You can use the exclusive graphics, and once you've uploaded the story you can send an eDM to the database. We'll add more information once it becomes available.' One last time, she reassures Chelsea she's okay, then ends the call.

Her phone rings: Rusty.

'Oli,' he breathes, 'I've been trying to call. Are you all right? I heard what happened.'

She was strong for Chelsea's sake but the sound of his voice breaks something in her; she starts to cry and can't stop.

'Oli, Oli? What is it? Talk to me.'

'I thought he was going to kill us.'

Rusty doesn't say anything, just listens while she cries.

The press pack erupts when Lyra Makris's mother and sister arrive, their faces drained of colour and their eyes like saucers. They clutch each other as they are guided by a stony-faced Commissioner Lew into Dunkley's beach house.

'Lyra's family is here. Apparently, she's refusing to leave the room he kept her in. God, Rusty, can you imagine what they are feeling right now?'

'Not really.'

'From what he . . . from what Cole said, I don't think he killed the other women,' Oli says. 'Or not Addison Bower-Fry anyway.'

'We're not sure yet, Ol. There's a lot to work through.'

'And what about your detective? Kibbs? Chelsea told me she was stabbed. Is she okay?'

'I'm at the hospital now waiting for an update,' Rusty says grimly. 'She's awake, which is positive.'

'I was so sure Douglas Jackson killed his wife,' Oli murmurs.

'We were pretty sure he didn't,' says Rusty. 'But it was Kibbs who figured out the link to the brother.'

The crowd of journos falls silent, prompting Oli to turn toward the house. The forensic team carry Cole Willoughby's body bag to an ambulance a few metres from where she's sitting. Despite the heat, she shivers.

The ambulance door slams shut, and the trill of cicadas is drowned out by the click of cameras and the desperate chorus of reporters begging for details.

Oli starts to cry again.

'Hey,' says Rusty. 'It's okay. You're okay.'

'I'm sorry,' she says finally. 'I know you need to go.'

'I want to see you.' His voice cracks. 'Get yourself checked out, then go home. I'll come over later. I don't know what time it will be, but I'll be there. I'm so glad you're okay, Ol.'

CHAPTER SIXTY-FOUR

TUESDAY, 4 FEBRUARY, 8.01 AM

Pen writes back to Billy's message. She's impressed by the way he is letting her guide their text conversation, and while he's showing care, he's also being careful. He's funnier than she remembers him being. Since he sent the initial message that her mother intercepted, he's only made one vague reference to seeing her in real life again, which made Pen feel simultaneously apprehensive and pleased. Their text-based relationship feels safe and manageable, but she knows it has a time limit. She winces as she adjusts her position on the hospital chair. Billy has been a nice distraction, but her focus is getting back home to Elliot. Walter is looking after him and sending her lots of cute photos, but it's not the same as the real thing.

There's a knock at the door, and Pen adjusts the blanket covering her shorts. 'Come in.'

Barnes enters holding a huge bunch of native flowers. He lifts his hand in an awkward wave. 'It's good to see you up and about.

How are you doing?' He places the flowers on the bed, facing her. He looks older, and his movements are stilted.

'They're beautiful,' she says. 'I'm okay. I'm hoping I'll be allowed to go home soon.'

'That's great news.' He sits gingerly on the chair next to her. 'And how are you mentally?'

She averts her gaze. 'I slept better last night.'

'It's going to take a while for you to get back to your old self, Pen. That was quite the ordeal you went through.'

'You sound like the counsellor Sanders is making me talk to,' she says wryly.

Barnes laughs. 'Well, I'm spending a fair bit of time with a counsellor myself, so perhaps I'm picking up the lingo.'

They finally lock eyes.

'How are you, really?' asks Pen.

He sighs and rubs an eye. 'Honestly, I don't know. Turns out I've really fucked up.'

'Frost told me about Douglas Jackson pressing charges,' she says softly.

He laughs humourlessly. 'Ironic, huh?'

'What happened?'

'I thought he did it,' Barnes replies. 'From that first night at their house, I was convinced. But we couldn't get anything on him, so I kept pushing.'

'You were stalking him,' Pen says.

Barnes lifts his shoulders. 'Yeah, but that's not what it felt like.'

'And you were drinking,' she adds.

He puffs out his cheeks. 'Yeah. Not always, but a lot of the time. I've always had trouble with it, but over the past few months

I couldn't wait until knock-off. The thought of having a drink was what got me out of bed in the morning.'

Pen doesn't say anything.

'Clearly, I feel guilt over what happened to my sister,' Barnes says eventually, 'but there's some other stuff from way back playing a role too—old cases, my marriage breakdown. I wasn't sleeping well, having nightmares, all sorts of stuff. And then, I don't know, the Jackson case really tipped me over the edge, especially once Mackenzie's body was discovered.'

Pen is struck by the irony of them both struggling and neither saying anything. 'Why didn't you tell me?'

He holds up his hands. 'I dunno. I wasn't in the right headspace to think about saying anything. I'm really sorry, Pen. I let a lot of people down, including you.'

She readjusts her legs. Her hips ache when she sits for more than a few minutes at a time, something the physio said should start to improve soon.

'I'm glad you came to the house that day,' Pen says finally. 'I haven't thanked you properly for that.'

'I'm glad too.'

'I know it's caused you a lot of issues,' she ventures.

He smiles ruefully. 'Just another thing to pile on top of the heap. When are you going back?'

'I'm on sick leave for a least another month, then I guess we'll see. There are a lot of conversations happening about procedure and where I didn't adhere to it.'

He chuckles. 'We make a good pair.'

She smiles. 'I guess so.'

His expression becomes serious. 'I'm kidding, Pen. You're

a wonderful cop and a top person. This isn't the end for you. Our situations are completely different.'

'I'm not sure that they are. I'm—' She falters, not knowing how to articulate how hard she has found the past few months. 'I don't cope with things very well sometimes.'

'Pen, I think the fact that you know you don't cope means you cope a hell of a lot better than me. Don't write yourself off. You're smart and you're thorough and you care. Whether your future is in the force or not, you have an amazing career ahead of you, do you hear me?'

'Yes, sir,' she whispers.

Perhaps sensing she's about to cry, he gets to his feet. 'Where can I find a vase?'

She points him to the bathroom. He returns with the vase full of water.

'Sounds like the Cole Willoughby inquest won't happen until next year,' Pen says as he removes the paper wrapping from the flowers.

'Yeah, I saw that on the news this morning.'

'What a nightmare,' says Pen. 'I feel for Dunkley. Has there been anything more on whether Willoughby was responsible for Holm's death?'

'It doesn't look like it,' Barnes says. 'Frost thinks that Dunkley told her family about the Polaroid found with Holm's body and that Willoughby used this as a springboard for the message he sent after he kidnapped Makris. He was smart, using a mix of digital and analogue. We were always a step behind.'

'I wonder what the original Polaroid meant?' Pen says.

'Who knows. But whatever it meant, Holm's killer is still out there somewhere.'

'Same as Pawley's. And Bower-Fry's. Did you see the video Cole's ex-girlfriend posted?'

Barnes grunts. 'If only she'd told someone weeks ago.'

Yesterday Ms Melbourne posted a tearful video—to her four hundred thousand followers—explaining that she'd broken up with Cole in November because she had felt the relationship wasn't right for her anymore, and that he'd gone crazy and threatened to kill her if she told anyone they'd broken up. The video ended with her sobbing an apology to everyone affected by Cole's evil. An hour after she uploaded the video, it had been viewed over half a million times.

'It's not her fault,' Pen says, although she understands Barnes's frustration. She readjusts her position again. Her legs are cramping and she wriggles her toes. 'It's weird to think that Willoughby caused so much damage, but he didn't kill anyone. It all seems so pointless.'

'He ran rings around everyone,' Barnes says grimly. 'And all he had was a computer. How the hell is law enforcement going to keep up with the technology?'

Pen thinks about the forums and marketplaces Farina and his team showed her on the dark web, and she nods. 'We're going to have to be there, in all of those spaces, and tackle it head on.'

'I suppose it's just the new way to go undercover.' Barnes cracks his knuckles. 'It's another reason why we need people like you on the force.' He sits back in the chair and looks her in the eye. 'I mean it, Pen. You're a great detective. I'm sorry you got swept up in all my bullshit, but you have a great career in front of you.'

Pen swallows around the lump swelling in her throat. 'We'll see.'

'Knock, knock.'

Barnes and Pen look up to see Olive Groves at the door.

'I'll leave you to it,' says Barnes. He hugs Pen awkwardly, nods hello to Olive, and leaves. Pen hopes he is going to be okay. Mackenzie Jackson's murder had derailed them both and while there's no doubt he screwed up, he's a good person and a good friend. She hopes he will be able to get a handle on his demons.

Pen straightens her posture and rearranges her hair. Olive is still standing near the door. 'Do you want a seat?' Pen offers.

'Sure.' Olive perches on the edge of the visitor chair. Her long hair is loose rather than tied back in its normal ponytail. Frost had mentioned her having some health issues, but she looks fine. 'How are you feeling?'

'Better,' says Pen. 'There's less pain every day.'

'That's good.' She adds, 'TJ went home yesterday.'

'I heard.' Pen's mother talked of little else besides trying to catch a glimpse of the handsome reporter. 'Do you know how Lyra Makris is doing?' Pen asks. 'I haven't spoken to Superintendent Frost today.'

'I have,' says Olive. 'She's not doing well. She's still recovering from a serious infection, and she's in a lot of pain, but she has started to talk a little. Rusty said they believe Cole drugged and raped her multiple times.' Olive swallows thickly. 'She screams whenever anyone tries to touch her.'

Pen doesn't trust herself to speak. She can't imagine what Lyra Makris endured in that dark room.

On Cole's laptop the police found several 'how to' videos for stage make-up tutorials. They believe he drugged Makris when he abducted her and kept her sedated the entire time, styling her for the photograph he sent to *Melbourne Today* the following morning.

'Did you hear the news about James Delway?' Olive asks.

Pen shakes her head.

'He's been charged with defamation and interfering with a criminal investigation. Plus lying to the police. And that's on top of the drugs charges.'

'Good,' says Pen, remembering the interviews she and Silverman conducted with him. 'He's a piece of shit.'

Oli laughs. 'Yes, he is.' Her expression quickly turns serious. 'Hey, I think what you did was really brave,' she says abruptly. 'I know there's going to be a review of the incident, and I get it, but thank god you did what you did. Patrick Jackson might have gotten away with Mackenzie's murder otherwise.'

Pen isn't sure what to say, but she likes Oli's praise. 'I was just doing what I thought made sense.'

Olive nods. 'When you're feeling up to it, I'd like to interview you. We can check it off with police media and make sure they're happy with the content, but I think it would be interesting to hear from a young voice in the force. You will have a different perspective from the typical mouthpieces.'

'I'll think about it,' says Pen. She wonders if Frost knows Olive is here.

As if reading her mind, Olive says, 'Perhaps don't mention this to your boss just yet. We'll get all the permissions first.'

Pen looks at her quizzically, and Olive grins.

CHAPTER SIXTY-FIVE

THURSDAY, 13 FEBRUARY, 11.21 AM

Oli keeps the surgical mask on as she walks through the hospital foyer and out onto the street. Her surgeon advised her to avoid crowds and suggested she wear the mask anytime she's in public: 'Just until we know a bit more about this virus.' She receives a few strange looks, but she doesn't care. She texts TJ that she's on her way and crosses the road to order an Uber.

Oli has always been observant, but lately details overwhelm her: rhinestones on dog collars, the bittersweet smell of burnt buttered toast in a cafe, stickers peeling on a windscreen. She worries it's because her brain is desperately trying to catalogue things while it still can. Her psychologist, a fine-boned woman with kind eyes and a stylish undercut, warned her that this type of negative thinking is normal but ultimately unproductive.

Oli closes her eyes and consciously resets, before opening them again. Her fingers drift to the underside of her left wrist, and she breathes in as she counts along to the beat of her pulse. The car icon on the Uber app edges closer, and she scans the street until she sees her vehicle approaching.

She opens the door.

'Olive?' asks the driver.

'Yes.' She climbs into the back seat.

The driver eyes her in the mirror. 'You sick, love?'

'Just being careful,' she replies, adjusting her mask.

He waits for a break in the traffic and pulls out. 'You might be onto something. My cousin lives in the States and reckons that Chinese virus is taking people out like there's no tomorrow.'

Oli nods politely, and the driver gets the message. He discreetly inserts an earbud.

As they drive, Oli scrolls the news websites. Cole Willoughby is still everywhere. His handsome face features in every news bulletin and stares back at her from every newspaper. His name leads every radio news segment, and she can't go anywhere without hearing people talking to each other and trying to make sense of the evil that hid so effectively in plain sight. Oli understands the fascination. What he did reads like a real-time cold-case documentary, and his seemingly swift descent into darkness is strangely compelling. A modern-day Ted Bundy, Melbourne's version of the Zodiac Killer—people can't get enough of the golden boy turned bad, and his mother's profile will ensure his story remains in orbit for a long time.

Patrick Jackson has his share of headlines too, but his evil is more commonplace and therefore less intriguing. Oli heard on the grapevine that Douglas Jackson has agreed to a *60 Minutes* interview and plans to reveal how he is coping in the aftermath of his wife's tragic death at the hands of his brother, and she feels sad for Mackenzie Jackson all over again. Even now, these men won't let the woman have peace.

The driver pulls up outside Oli's office and leans forward to squint up at the warehouse. 'This it, love?'

'Yes.' She thanks him and gets out of the car, feeling apprehensive.

Rusty, TJ and Lily offered to come to the hospital with her today, and she politely declined. She knows she'll need to lean on them in the coming months, but she wanted to get her bearings in the unfamiliar medical world first. Her surgery is scheduled for the following week, something she is trying not to think about.

She glances at her phone. She's also trying not to think about the first episode of her podcast, *No Place Like Home*, that dropped at six this morning. She's already received dozens of messages about it, but she hasn't opened them. She wants to wait at least a few hours before she deals with the inevitable critique, good and bad.

Oli and TJ debated what to do about her interview with Dunkley in the final episode—in the end, they decided to run it without changes and add a new intro.

She makes her way up the stairs. TJ clumsily gets to his feet when she enters, his crutches wedged under his arms. 'How did you go?'

'It was fine,' Oli says brightly. 'Really.'

He nods, but his expression remains worried.

Since Carol moved out, his Peter Pan shine has faded. There's an unfamiliar tentativeness to his movements. Oli is aware he's struggling to reacquaint himself with a world he always took for granted, that his confidence and robust ego have been seriously dented by Carol's betrayal.

'I've just been sent the promo clips of Douglas Jackson's *60 Minutes* interview,' TJ says. 'You have to wonder what was going on in that household to have two brothers turn out like that.'

'Misogyny and entitlement,' Oli suggests.

'Do you think it's really that simple?'

She shrugs. 'Lightning doesn't often strike the same spot twice.'

After a moment, TJ says, 'Dunkley's standing down.'

'It's confirmed?'

'There's going to be a statement from the party today, then a leadership announcement next week. Spencer heard the whole family is flying overseas later today.'

'God, what a mess.' Oli looks around the small room and lets her eyes settle on the photo of Cooper. For what feels like the millionth time, she wishes he were here.

'I've got some good news for you,' TJ says, switching gears. 'The numbers on your podcast.'

'Really?'

'Really. We're talking three times our normal figures.'

Oli feels a flurry of pleasure.

'It makes sense, what you said yesterday. You're so good at the investigations. If I'm being honest, I never had the patience.'

Yesterday, Oli and TJ met with a consultant who helped them create the bones of a business plan for *Newsday*, with clear swim lanes for all staff, including themselves. Oli explained she wants to move away from daily news and focus on investigations; TJ was surprised but supportive.

Now Oli presses her lips together. 'You're much better at breaking news than I ever was. I don't have the right energy for it.'

'Looks like it's going to work out pretty well then.' He winks, but it's followed by a sad smile.

Her mind returns to the moment she saw Lyra on the bed. How she reached for her, and how the woman flinched and pulled away. The glass breaking against Cole's head. The shock of the gunshot.

Oli shudders and asks TJ a question that has been bothering her. 'What made you chase after Cole like that? You didn't even know who it was.'

TJ's expression becomes serious as he considers her question. 'I don't know. I've never felt like that before. I saw him, and I figured he knew who I was because he took off. Then all I could think about was how he'd tried to mess with me, and how he'd ruined everything with Carol, and I just saw red. I've never wanted to hurt someone so badly. I wasn't even thinking about whether he was dangerous or not or what I was going to do if I caught him.'

'Do you think he would have done what he did if we hadn't gone to the house?' Oli asks quietly. She feels undeniably guilty about the role they played in his suicide.

'Oli, don't think like that. He had no plan for what to do with Lyra, and we know he was getting desperate.' TJ tips his head to the side. 'And if we hadn't been there, who knows what would have happened to her.'

Oli wonders how Dunkley and her husband are feeling, how they even begin to piece together their broken lives.

'Tell me about your appointment . . .' TJ says.

'It was fine. My surgery is confirmed for Monday morning, then the chemo will start in about a month.'

He nods, opens his mouth and closes it again. Breathes out through pursed lips. 'Carol and I are going to sell the house. I'm going to get a smaller place in the city. I want to be in the thick of things, and I don't want anything big. Our house was way too big for two people.'

'Jesus, TJ. What about Carol?'

He looks at the floor. 'She's going to move to Sydney and give it a go with the guy she's been seeing. I think I want her to—it will make things easier.'

Oli reaches out to squeeze his shoulder. 'It's going to be quite the year.'

'Yep.' He looks her in the eye and nods. 'But I'm ready for it. The stuff with Carol, it's weird, but in a way, it makes sense. We hadn't been working for a while, I just didn't want to deal with it.'

Oli clears her throat, keen to get the final niggle off her chest. 'Hey, TJ, there is something else I want to talk to you about.'

He pauses and looks up at her, alarm on his face.

'It's not about my health. But I was offered a job, and I thought I should tell you in case you hear it from somewhere else. I'm not going to take it,' she hastens to add. 'But for half a second I considered it.'

'Where?'

'At Air 24/7.'

'Morrie Flint's job,' TJ says quickly.

'Morrie Flint's job,' she confirms.

TJ starts to laugh.

'What?' she says, confused.

'Did Marion tell you it was highly confidential? And that she wants to know if you're interested by mid-Feb?'

Oli nods slowly, understanding. 'She offered you the job too.'

'Should we call her together?' TJ is still laughing.

'She's got even more balls than I thought.' Oli shakes her head incredulously. She starts laughing too. She supposes she should feel a bit silly, angry even, but she can't seem to summon the energy. Marion was doing what she does best and covering all bases.

TJ's laughter peters out. 'It's a lot of money, Ol,' he says tentatively. 'Are you sure you're not interested? It would break my heart if you left, especially now, but that's not a reason you should say no.'

She locks eyes with him. Even with the break-up of his marriage, TJ will never have to worry about money the way she does. It would be easy to begrudge him his privilege, but she knows it doesn't impact the dedication he has toward the business, or toward her.

'No,' she says. 'I feel clearer about that than I have in a while.' She pauses, navigating a surge of emotion. 'I'm all in.'

'Hi.'

Oli spins around.

Rusty is standing in the doorway. He's holding two large takeaway cups, with a paper bag from her favourite cafe around the corner tucked under his arm.

'Oh yeah.' TJ grins. 'I forgot to tell you Rusty was coming to visit.'

'I brought you some lunch.' Rusty looks sheepish.

She wants to be annoyed at him for surprising her like this. But she's not.

'Why don't you guys sit in the front room,' says TJ. 'It's very romantic.' He hobbles off to the boardroom.

They go to the meeting room on the other side of reception.

'How is Pen?' Oli asks, sliding the door shut. She takes a seat opposite him and he passes her a coffee and a tuna melt. The smell of the sandwich makes her mouth start to water.

'She's doing much better. Hopefully she will be able to go home this week.'

'That's good.' Oli has developed a soft spot for the serious young detective.

'How are *you*?' Rusty asks. 'How was your appointment?'

She sips her coffee and tells him what the doctor said.

Rusty eats his toasted sandwich but doesn't take his eyes from her face as she talks. 'I've organised to have a few days off after your surgery next week,' he says.

'You don't have to do that,' says Oli.

He puts down his coffee and takes her hand. 'I *want* to, Ol. Let me be there for you.'

They lock eyes, and she nods. She wants him to be there. It's a nice feeling.

'Maybe we can go on a holiday in April, if you're feeling up to it . . . ?' he says tentatively.

'I do want to go away with you. I think for a little while it will need to be like that consultant said to me and TJ yesterday—make plans but be ready to change them.'

'We can do that.' Rusty smiles at her, and she smiles back.

'Oli!' TJ calls out from the main room. 'Come have a look at this. Not you, Rusty,' he adds. 'This is a journo thing.'

'In a minute!' Oli calls in reply.

She goes to leave, but as she walks to the door Rusty stands and pulls her to him, wrapping his arms around her shoulders. She smells his familiar aftershave and listens to his heartbeat through his shirt.

'Thank you,' she whispers.

Rusty squeezes her tighter. 'We're going to make lots of plans, Ol.'

ACKNOWLEDGEMENTS

The central plot idea of *Click* came to me as I was contemplating how hard it is to write crime these days, what with all the mobile phones, CCTV and social media. I'd been considering writing a book set in the nineties, but once this idea took hold I went from trying to remember life pre-internet, to researching the dark web and investigating how to doctor images. For many reasons, it wasn't the easiest book to write, but I'm thrilled I got there in the end, and I'd like to thank several special people who helped me along the way.

Thanks, as always, to my agent Lyn Tranter, I appreciate your feedback and guidance very much. To my publishing support team who helped me turn my initial jumble of words into a book: publisher Cate Paterson, editor Kate Goldsworthy and editor/timeline-wrangler Christa Munns—thank you. *Click* would have been a second-rate version of itself without your care and skills. Thanks to all the other hardworking people at Allen & Unwin, who spend so much time thinking about how best to connect my books with readers. You are all wonderful. And shout-out to Jane

Palfreyman who backed me writing a sequel to *The Housemate* in the first place.

Thanks to Rachael Brown, journalist extraordinaire, for the helpful chats about Oli's work world. I don't think you know how inspiring you are and how much I borrow from your incredible wealth of knowledge. And thanks to Victoria Police Detective John Cheyne for meeting with me and providing helpful insights into the dark world I was trying to bring to life. Your feedback was invaluable (and the mistakes all mine).

To all the booksellers out there, you are the best and I am very grateful for your enthusiasm and selling skills.

To my family, whom I only occasionally take for granted, thank you for the ongoing support. Especially to Nick, Oxford and Linus, who are so used to seeing me hunched over my laptop writing that by the time a book comes out they are already over it. You do a good job of pretending to be excited. And thanks to Nick especially for the literal and figurative heavy-lifting so I could write this book around full-time work.

This book is dedicated to my youngest child, Ripley, who was with me/sleeping on me while I wrote the first draft of this book. Ripley, it's ironic that I dreamed up such a dark plot while in your company as you are such a joyful little person but perhaps your light was why I could go somewhere so dark. Thank you for the cuddles.

Lastly, I'd like to thank the readers of my previous books. You are the reason I was given the opportunity to write this one and whatever comes next. Thank you. I hope you enjoyed *Click*.

ALSO FROM ALLEN & UNWIN

The Housemate

SARAH BAILEY

'Australian crime at its best.'

J.P. POMARE, author of *17 Years Later*

Three housemates. One dead, one missing and one accused of murder.

Dubbed the Housemate Homicide, it's a mystery that has baffled Australians for almost a decade.

Melbourne-based journalist Olive Groves worked on the story as a junior reporter and became obsessed by the case. Now, nine years later, the missing housemate turns up dead on a remote property. Olive is once again assigned to the story, this time reluctantly paired with precocious millennial podcaster Cooper Ng.

As Oli and Cooper unearth new facts about the three housemates, a dark web of secrets is uncovered. The revelations catapult Oli back to the death of the first housemate, forcing her to confront past traumas and insecurities that have risen to the surface again.

What really happened between the three housemates that night? Will Oli's relentless search for the murderer put her new family in danger? And could her suspicion that the truth lies closer to home threaten her happiness and even her sanity?

A riveting, provocative thriller from the bestselling author of *The Dark Lake*, *Into the Night*, *Where the Dead Go* and *Body of Lies*.

ISBN 978 1 76106 820 1